Gotthard V. Lechler

The Apostolic and Post-Apostolic Times

Their diversity and unity in life and doctrines - Vol. 1

Gotthard V. Lechler

The Apostolic and Post-Apostolic Times
Their diversity and unity in life and doctrines - Vol. 1

ISBN/EAN: 9783337403706

Printed in Europe, USA, Canada, Australia, Japan

Cover: Foto ©Andreas Hilbeck / pixelio.de

More available books at **www.hansebooks.com**

THE APOSTOLIC

AND

POST-APOSTOLIC TIMES;

*THEIR DIVERSITY AND UNITY IN LIFE
AND DOCTRINE.*

BY

GOTTHARD VICTOR LECHLER, D.D.,

ORDINARY PROFESSOR OF THEOLOGY, PRIVY ECCLESIASTICAL COUNSELLOR IN LEIPZIG.

Third Edition, thoroughly Revised and Re-written.

Translated by

A. J. K. DAVIDSON.

VOL. I.

EDINBURGH:

T. & T. CLARK. 38 GEORGE STREET.

1886.

PREFACE.

THE Teyler Theological Association in Haarlem in the year 1848 proposed as a prize question an examination of the following topics with reference to the Tübingen school :—

First, the relation of the gospel preached by Paul to the message which the other apostles delivered.

Secondly, the mutual relation of the ecclesiastical communities gathered by Paul from among the heathen, and by the other apostles from among the Jews.

Thirdly, the influence of the Jewish Christian upon the Gentile Christian Churches till the disappearance of the former.

I undertook to answer the question, because the subject appeared to me both important and reasonable, and because the problem proposed was one with which I had been already occupied to some extent. A profound investigation of early Christianity, at a time when it was full of life and spirit, gave me inexpressible refreshment and internal strength in the feverish excitement and troubles of the year 1848 with its destructive forces, through the calm intercourse which I held with a pious generation which was truly progressive and positively constructive.

If in following my convictions I felt obliged to appear in many ways opposed to a theological school existing in my Swabian home and at the University which was my *alma mater*, it was incumbent upon me on the one hand not to fail in the pious respect due to my revered teacher Dr. Baur, and on the other I hoped that I could in my small way disarm the reproach made against the theologians of my native land by Ewald and Heinrich Thiersch, in showing that they had stepped forth against the false criticism proceeding from Tübingen without sufficient use of a scientific armoury.

In November 1849 I received notice that the prize had been awarded to my treatise. I was glad to consider some remarks of the learned adjudicators while preparing the work for the press, which was completed in the summer of 1850. The first edition appeared in 1851 at Haarlem, as the thirty-first of the treatises belonging to the Teyler Theological Association, in 4to.

In the year 1856 I learned that my publication was out of print, and that there were frequent inquiries about it, many voices testifying to its usefulness. Having asked the permission of the directors of the Teyler Institute, full liberty was granted me with the greatest readiness to publish the work in a German edition, with such alterations as were thought necessary.

Accordingly I set about a new and thorough elaboration of the work, having special regard to a description and comparison of the apostolic doctrines as well as to the post-apostolic period, taking into account both the later investigations of others and the criticisms that had been made upon my book as far as I knew them. The second remodelled edition appeared in 1857 from the publishing house of the worthy Rudolph Besser, now deceased.

When he spoke to me about a new edition several years ago, I was obliged to give a decided refusal, because of the copious literature that had appeared in the department of Biblical science and Christian antiquity since 1856, to examine which seemed indispensable, but involving a labour that made a threefold office quite impossible to my advanced age. But after I got the wished-for rest from the duties of superintendent and pastor in 1883, leaving me in the office of academic professor alone, I resolved to undertake a fresh revision of the book, at the repeated request of the present proprietor of Besser's house.

I entered upon the task gladly. First of all the plan of the whole work was changed. In the first and second editions doctrine was always treated of first, both in the apostolic and the post-apostolic period, followed by a description of the life, an arrangement agreeable to the original prize question.

But now I put the life in the foreground, leaving the doctrine to follow. I do so with the conviction that for individuals as well as mankind, in the divine education of the human race and in sacred history, life and experience are the foundation, while consciousness, thought, and teaching form the super-structure. Godet says on John iii. 3, with truth and beauty,—

"Une nouvelle vue suppose une nouvelle vie."

In this way I touch upon a fundamental view that unconsciously dominated the master of the "critical school," and that still seems to prevail among many of its advocates. I refer to intellec-tualism, to which the world of thought and know-ledge appears as a thing moving round itself and concluded within itself; while the ethical world of action and suffering, especially of life that streams from the fountain of everlasting life, is to all appear-ance non-existent and unintelligible.

In other respects also much of the material has been transformed, in order to do justice to the subject. For example, the Epistle of James has been re-ferred to prepauline teaching, whereas it had been assigned before to the development of doctrine con-ditioned by the intervention of the Apostle Paul. The representation of Paul's doctrinal system itself has been essentially metamorphosed in p. 339, etc., vol. i. Entire parts have been written anew, e.g. the examination of the historical value attaching to the

Acts, particularly the first half of the book, on the basis of occasional statements made by the Apostle Paul in his universally acknowledged Epistles, p. 13, etc., vol. i. And again, the discussion of the conversion of the same apostle, in accordance with his own confessions, p. 312, etc., vol. i. Add to this, the section relating to the doctrinal contents of the Epistle to the Hebrews, pp. 119–135, vol. ii., and the comparison of James with Paul, pp. 237–246, vol. ii. In the post-apostolic period we may only mention the results of study regarding the $\Delta\iota\delta\alpha\chi\grave{\eta}$ $\tau\hat{\omega}\nu$ $\delta\acute{\omega}\delta\epsilon\kappa\alpha$ $\dot{\alpha}\pi o\sigma\tau\acute{o}\lambda\omega\nu$, pp. 292–297, vol. ii., and pp. 332–340, vol. ii.

Apart from such portions as have been worked out afresh and fully, all that I give has been subjected to repeated and honest examination. On all sides the writings and treatises relating to the entire subject published in the last decades, so far as they were accessible, have been thoroughly examined, and many former judgments changed. The most careful attention has been given to the expression, that the book may be made plain, clear, and readable. Hence it is, in fact, a new work.

Whether it was worth the trouble may be doubted for two reasons — first, because such a book is no longer required and is out of season; secondly, because it is simply an apologetic production, and as such without scientific value.

In regard to the former, the opinion is entertained in many quarters that the school of Baur — the master having died twenty-five years ago—is in a state of dissolution, so that it is an anachronism to continue the fight against it. But that is not so. Scholars of the critical school, as they fondly call themselves in the sense of exclusiveness, whether belonging to the German, Dutch, English, or French nations, still carry on the combat along the whole line. It is true that they have drawn back in some points, and dropped some statements much too hazardous; but they continue the strife with concentration and emphasis. Hence it is not yet time to lay down the weapons of science against them; the less so as they feel themselves to be the favoured representatives of criticism and genuine inquiry, and look upon all who have reached other results than theirs as a "*gens apologetarum*," as one has expressed it,—a name which has a somewhat dishonourable sound in their mouths. I candidly confess that I am not ashamed of the gospel of Christ, nor even of the name "Apologist." I have never observed that intelligent people hold the position of defender in a debate to be less honourable than that of accuser. Why then should the case be so entirely different in questions of truth and science? Matters would certainly stand in a position wholly altered, if it were correct that in things of this nature "both views are opposed to each other simply as the critical and the uncritical" (Baur, *Christenthum der drei ersten Jahrhunderte*, 2 Aufl. p. 150, note 2). Then would it be indeed a *res judicata*. But in that case, to speak briefly, the one party sits upon the judgment-seat, and judgment is given offhand. It appears to be demanded in the interest of the subject that one should take up a critical position over against such confident utterances. This is what I have done, showing occasionally that the pretended clique of critics are often divided from one another and mutually antagonistic, that here and there one and the same individual even contradicts himself. I never sought debate for debate's sake. My concern was with truth alone. Very often did I gladly and thankfully appropriate knowledge and the admissions of men whom on other occasions I felt compelled to oppose for the sake of the cause I was engaged in. I hope and trust that among the results now presented of diligent labour and faithful investigation into the subject I may have discovered something at least that will stand the test, and contribute to a more correct view of the history of revelation in the New Testament.

THE AUTHOR.

Leipzig, May 15, 1885.

CONTENTS.

C. Church Arrangements and Social Constitution.

CHAPTER II.

The Gentile Christians and the Mixed Churches.

A. The Direct Religious Life of the Gentile Christian Churches, with their Ecclesiastical Organization.

B. Social and Domestic Relations of the Jewish Christians ; their Intercourse with Non-Christians.

C. Constitution and Ritual of the Gentile Christian Churches.

CHAPTER III.

The Mutual Relation between Jewish Christian and Gentile Christian Circles in its General Aspect.

A. The Judaistic Tendency.

SECOND SECTION.

CHAPTER I.
THE JEWISH CHRISTIANS.

CHAPTER II.
THE GENTILE CHRISTIANS.

SECOND PART.
THE APOSTOLIC DOCTRINES.

FIRST SECTION.
DOCTRINE IN THE EARLY APOSTOLIC TIME.

CHAPTER I.

CHAPTER II.

JAMES.

SECOND SECTION.

THE DOCTRINAL SYSTEM OF THE APOSTLE PAUL.

CHAPTER I.

THE ORIGINAL PREACHING OF THE APOSTLE PAUL.

CHAPTER II.

FIRST DOCTRINAL PART.

FIRST PART.

SIN AND DEATH AS REGARDS INDIVIDUAL MAN.

I. SIN AND ITS ORIGIN.

II. SIN AND DEATH,

SECOND PART.

SIN AND DEATH IN GENERAL, AND THE REVELATION OF GOD IN THE PRE-CHRISTIAN WORLD.

I. SIN AND DEATH IN THE WORLD.

II. THE REVELATION OF GOD IN THE PRE-CHRISTIAN AGE, IN THE GENTILE WORLD AND IN ISRAEL.

INTRODUCTION.

—o—

THE latest researches concerning the apostolic age are the result of a perfectly legitimate endeavour, viz. the desire to gain a satisfactory insight into the true course of events, the real historical development of primitive Christianity. No one having a knowledge of the subject will dispute the fact that such an insight has hitherto not been attained. The perception of *development* has been missed by all: by some, because they were unable to distinguish; by others, because they had no eye for unity. Orthodox theology saw in apostolic Christianity an undivided unity, and failed to appreciate the difference between the apostles individually and between whole groups of early Christian communities. Rationalistic theology, on the other hand, was disposed to find nothing but opposition between the doctrines of the apostles, overlooking the agreement which nevertheless exists between them. Hence the true historical process escaped both, the development which comprehends in itself both unity and difference.

The recent researches put forth by Dr. Baur in Tübingen, and carried on partly by himself, partly by a number of younger scholars following in his steps, attempted to give a positive representation of the actual development of early Christianity.[1] The point to which the lever was applied was the difference between Pauline and Petrine Christianity. The immediate aim of manifold inquiries, starting from this point, has been to make that difference more and more prominent, in order to gain a clear view, not only of the apostolic circle itself, but also of the post-apostolic discussions, altercations, and doctrines, down to the formation of a united Catholic Church.

The view thus reached was this, that in apostolic times there was opposition between Paul on the one hand and the early apostles on the other hand, and that a deep gulf was fixed between the gospel of the Twelve for Israel and the gospel of Paul for the heathen. The opposition centred in the fact that Paul completely separated Christianity from Judaism, while Peter and the other early apostles still adhered to a Jewish standpoint. This circumstance gave rise to a struggle in which at first the Judaizing tendency was victorious. It was not till towards the end of the *second* century that by mutual concession and arrangement between the contending parties an agreement was come to. This view of the early history of Christianity unquestionably leads to the following conclusions :—

[1] The treatise, "Die Christuspartei in der korinthischen Gemeinde, der Gegensatz des petrinischen und paulinischen Christentums," etc., *Tüb. Zeitschrift für Theologie*, 1831, 4. 61, by Dr. Ferdinand Christian Baur, formed the epoch-making beginning of critical research respecting early Christianity. The most important of his works which belong here are, *Paulus, der Apostel Jesu Christi. Sein Leben und Wirken, seine Briefe und seine Lehre. Ein Beitrag zu einer kritischen Geschichte des Urchristenthums*, 1845, 2 Aufl. v. Zeller, 1866. *Das Christenthum und die christliche Kirche der drei ersten Jahrhunderte*, 1853, 2 Aufl. 1860 (the year of the author's death.)

1. Apostolic Christianity appears tainted with a dualism, and internally divided, inasmuch as Peter, James, and others are said to have been separated by "a split such as never afterwards occurred within the Christian Church," [1] on the very question which forms the kernel of Christianity. By this means the unity of primitive Christianity is destroyed; the oneness of spirit between the apostles (τὸ αὐτὸ πνεῦμα, 1 Cor. xii. 4; ἑνότης τοῦ πνεύματος, Eph. iv. 3), accepted on the authority of Scripture, denied; Christ divided (μεμέρισται ὁ Χριστός, 1 Cor. i. 13). The question is no longer of one spirit and many gifts, but several spirits are assumed, so opposed to one another that Luther's saying to Zwingli in Marburg, "You are of another spirit," here finds suitable application.

2. By assuming that the early apostles collectively differed from Paul in the fact that they never got beyond Judaism in their manner of thinking, we place Jesus Himself in a light in which He appears not as the only-begotten Son of God, but merely as a man like others, as a Jewish Rabbi. This view of early Christianity also undermines the foundation of faith, for such a Jesus is certainly not *He* in whom alone is salvation. Hence the question is not one of reform, but of the overthrow of Christianity; for on this assumption Christianity no longer *is* what it originally *was*, nor will remain in the future what it now is.

The more unprejudiced men of the school of Baur itself could not close their eyes to this knowledge. So, for example, Ritschl, even Holsten. [2] They found

---

[1] Albert Schwegler, *Das nachapost. Zeitalter*, 1846, i. 7.

[2] Albrecht Ritschl, *Die Entstehung der altkatholischen Kirche*, 2 Aufl. 1857, S. 21 ff. Carl Holsten, *Zum Evangelium des Paulus und des Petrus*, 1868, S. 5 f.

it necessary to limit the assumed opposition between an early apostolic and the Pauline gospel, and on the other hand to seek for that foundation which the two tendencies of early Christianity had in common.

Modern theology nevertheless gives prominence to a view which does justice neither to the interest of faith nor to historical truth. In order to prove this, however, and not to confine ourselves to assertion, it will be necessary to examine the early historical records, taking care that our examination be thorough and unbiassed. Free critical investigation of and concerning Scripture must in the end be to the advantage of the truth : it will serve partly to confirm old truth, partly to bring new knowledge to light. We are persuaded that a truly free examination will result in a conviction that the gospel of Christ is actually " a power of God unto salvation " (Rom. i. 16).

Our examination falls chronologically into two books, according to the two periods through which we are carried ; an examination—

I. Of the apostolic times.

II. Of the post-apostolic times.

In both periods we have to keep in view the life and the teaching of Jewish as well as Gentile Christians.

Accordingly the first book falls naturally into two sections, the former of which has for its object the elucidation of the *life* of the apostolic communities, while the second aims to set forth the apostolic *doctrine*.

FIRST BOOK.

THE APOSTOLIC PERIOD.

—o—

FIRST PART.

PRIMITIVE CHRISTIANITY IN ITS LIFE.

THE subject-matter of this historical inquiry, so far as it relates to the apostolic age, falls according to time into two sections, which are separated from one another by the epoch of the year 70,—a year which is of decisive importance on account of the destruction of Jerusalem and of the temple.

FIRST SECTION.

THE BEGINNINGS OF CHRISTIANITY AS A COMMUNITY; THE RELIGIOUS, MORAL, AND SOCIAL LIFE OF BELIEVERS DOWN TO THE DESTRUCTION OF JERUSALEM.

The whole history of Christianity rests on the person of Jesus Christ; not on the Christ who was, but on Him who is, and who is to come. Just as the life of Jesus was a self-manifestation of Him who professed to be " the Son of man " and " the Son of God," even so the history of Christianity is " a growing up in all things into *Him* which is the head, even Christ " (Eph. iv. 15), a gradual transformation into the image of Christ. But this transformation is a work of the Spirit (2 Cor. iii. 18). Christianity is a *new creation*. Just as the first creation, however, was not finished at one stroke, but was a gradual process, extending over several periods (according to Genesis, six days; according to natural science, six periods of development), and was not accomplished in a single moment of time; so also the new religious moral creation, proceeding from the second Adam, is the work of a series of development-periods, which we call epochs of the Church of Christ, and which give us an impression now of hasting, now of waiting (comp. 2 Pet. iii. 12). Moreover, just as the development of the child goes forward incomparably faster during the first year than at any subsequent time of life, so the development of Christianity as an association proceeds more rapidly in the first two centuries than in later times; and in the first four decades it made strides of greater relative importance and depth in more directions than one than in the following decades and centuries.[1] It is therefore the more necessary to advance step by step, and to consider one form of life after another.

[1] Dr. Hatch, *Organization of the Early Christian Church*, translated by Harnack, 1833, p. 222, finds that "the development was slower than has sometimes been supposed." It is probable that he had in view only a small section of the whole. But the more we enlarge our circle of vision, the more certainly will be confirmed what we have said above.

CHAPTER I.

THE JEWISH-CHRISTIAN COMMUNITIES.

The history of Christianity as an association, begins at Jerusalem. "Salvation is of the Jews" (John iv. 22); not only because the Saviour was "the son of David, the son of Abraham" (Matt. i. 1; Rom. i. 3), "the lion of the tribe of Juda" (Rev. v. 5); but also because the preaching of the gospel had its beginning in Israel (Luke xxiv. 47; comp. Acts i. 8), because "the law should go forth out of Zion," and "the word of the Lord from Jerusalem" (Isa. ii. 3; Micah iv. 2).

In approaching the facts more closely, the immediate *source* from which we have to draw is *the Acts of the Apostles.* This, doubtless, in substance yields us comparatively abundant material, but its credibility as a historical record has by German theologians, during the last half century, been so frequently and so vehemently called in question, that we cannot avoid entering in some measure into those discussions that have been raised by learned inquirers into the historical credibility of this book. We shall, however, at present confine ourselves in the main to the first and smaller half of the book (chaps. i.–xii.), since in treating of the mission of the Apostle Paul to the heathen, and to the heathen-Christian or mixed communities, we shall have to make a minute examination of many points in which it will be necessary also to direct a searching glance towards the historical value of Luke's writing.

We must premise that inquiries and doubts con-

cerning the credibility of the Acts of the Apostles
originally sprang from a desire to gain a clear understanding as to the aim the author set before him in
his book.   In Christian antiquity, Chrysostom pronounced the aim of the book to be to prove the
resurrection of Christ; while at the time of the
Reformation, Luther declared that its main object
was to set forth justification by faith, without the
deeds of the law.   But when, in 1798, Dr. Paulus,
in his Jena Easter-programme,[1] evolved the idea that
the book was written with a view of defending the
Apostle Paul against the reproaches of the Judaists
with respect to the reception of heathen into the
Christian community; he took a course which forty
years later led to results most disastrous to the Acts
of the Apostles.   On the basis of a casual remark
of Dr. Baur's in the treatise on the origin of the
episcopate in the *Tübingen Zeitschrift für die
Theologie*, 1838, iii. p. 142, Schneckenburger wrote,
in 1841, a work entitled *Ueber den Zweck der
Apostelgeschichte*.   He maintained that in the Acts
of the Apostles Paul is defended from the
reproaches of Judaizing Christians by the circumstance that in the first half of the book Peter
is represented in as Pauline a light as possible,
while in the second half Paul appears with strong
Petrine, *i.e.* Judaistic, tendencies.   Baur acknowledged the correctness of Schneckenburger's theory
of the aim of the Acts of the Apostles, but went a
step farther, and maintained that the author had in

---

[1] *De consilio, quo scriptor in actis apostolorum concinnandis
ductus fuerit.*   This programme is usually ascribed to the renowned
Griesbach, but belongs to Paulus, who was his colleague at that
time.

view, not only the defence of the Apostle Paul against the prejudices of the Judaists, but that he also aimed to bring about an understanding between the Judaists and those who held Pauline views ; that the book is an attempt of a Pauline disciple at reconciliation,—in one word, that the aim of the Acts of the Apostles is not solely apologetic, but conciliatory.[1] This result commended itself to the school of Baur, and was in fact the same which had been loudly enunciated by the master as " incontestably proved." [2] The same view was then adopted by Schwegler ;[3] but Zeller has supplied the most comprehensive and thorough examination of the Acts of the Apostles.[4] Many other scholars have also joined this party, of whose names a complete enumeration would here be out of place. The theory of the book as conciliatory did not, however, satisfy Bruno Bauer, who regards the Acts of the Apostles not as a proposal of peace, but as the termination of peace, and as the result of quiescence. According to Bruno Bauer, this book led to the supremacy and recognition of Judaism within the community.[5] This was the exact contrary of the position of Dr. Paulus fully fifty years before.

[1] Review of Schneckenburger's *Schrift in Berl. Jahrb. f. wiss. Kritik*, 1841, Nr. 46 ff. Paulus, *der Ap. Jesu Christi*, 1845, 2 Aufl. v. Zeller, 1866. *Das Christenthum—der drei ersten Jahrhunderte*, 1860, S. 125 ff.

[2] Baur, *Das Christenthum der drei ersten Jahrhunderte*, 2 Aufl. 1860, S. 125.

[3] *Nachapost. Zeitalter*, 1846, i. 90, ii. 111 ff.

[4] Edward Zeller, *Theol. Jarhbücher v. Baur u. Zeller*, 1849-51, newly elaborated in the book, *Die Apostelgeschichte nach ihrem Inhalt und Ursprung kritisch untersucht*, 1854.

[5] *Die Apostelgeschichte eine Ausgleichung des Paulinismus und des Judenthums u.s.w.* 1850.

Bruno Bauer's little book was, however, an unscientific performance, filled with a ratiocination begotten by the daring spirit of the revolution-year 1848. But even Overbeck, whose mode of treatment is scientific, adopts a modification of the theory of Baur and Zeller regarding a conciliatory aim of the Acts, maintaining that it is an attempt of later heathen-Christendom, already dominated by early Christian Judaism, to reflect on its past, and to regard itself as the legitimate fruit of early apostolic Christianity.[1]

Just in proportion as we attribute to the author a tendency of this kind, do we under-estimate the historical value and credibility of the book. Schneckenburger, indeed, although regarding the practical aim of the defence of the Apostle Paul as the centre of the book, zealously endeavoured to repel every suspicion concerning the credibility of the historical narrative. But Dr. Baur dared to reproach the author of the Acts of the Apostles with sacrificing historical truth to the practical object he had in view, viz. the reconciliation and union of Pauline and Judaizing Christians. He spoke not only of "intentional silence respecting certain things necessary to be mentioned," but also of "premeditated alteration of historical fact in the interest of a certain tendency," of "fictions," and of a want of historical fidelity.[2] Following the precedent thus set, others did not hesitate to speak even more strongly in the same tone. Schwegler is of opinion that "unless all signs are deceptive, the first part

---

[1] Franz Overbeck, *Kurze Erklärung der Apostelgeschichte.* Von de Wette, 4 Aufl. 1870, S. xxv. ff. bis xxxi. f.

[2] Baur, *Paulus*, 1 Aufl. S. 201 f., 206 ff. *Christenthum der drei ersten Jahrhunderte*, 2 Aufl. S. 128.

of the Acts is *uninterrupted fiction*."[1]   Overbeck
declares the book " not generally trustworthy, but
requiring proof of credibility in each separate case;"[2]
in other words, he does not allow the *quilibet præsu-
mitur bonus* of the Acts, although he had previously
made the excellent remark that the question whether
the Acts of the Apostles has a purely historic aim
does not directly coincide with the question as to
the credibility of its contents.[3]

In our inquiry into the true position of the Acts
of the Apostles with respect to credibility and
historical truth, it will therefore first of all be
advisable to take up a somewhat critical position
with reference to the traditional axiom of the so-
called critical school about the unhistorical character of
this book, and not blindly to consent to the discredit
in which this recently most calumniated book of the
Bible has been involved.   In this case there is no
doubt that the book, if without prejudice, *sine ira et
studio*, we allow ourselves to be influenced by it,
makes the impression of a plain, artless narrative of
what really happened, and not of "a calculating crafti-
ness."[4]   Add to this the circumstance that we have on
the part of the author an express declaration respecting the task which as historian he proposed to himself.
Since, therefore, it is allowed on all sides that the
Acts were written by the author of the third Gospel,
and since he himself points to the Acts i. 1 as the
continuation of his πρῶτος λόγος, we are justified

---

[1] *Nachapostol. Zeitalter*, i. 90, ii. 111 ff.

[2] *Ante*, lix. f.   [3] *Ante*, xxvi.

[4] Thus expressed by Fr. Bleek, whom none will charge with a want
of the critical instinct, *Einleitung in das N. T.*, 3 Aufl., edited by
Mangold, 1875, S. 389.

in also referring the *prologue of the Gospel of Luke* to his second book, without necessarily implying that the author when beginning his first book had its continuation in view.[1] The author here refers to already existing memorials of the life of Jesus, διηγήσεις which he characterizes as attempts (ἐπεχεί-ρησαν), and manifestly regards as unsatisfactory, promising his friend Theophilus an authentic statement of events (ἵνα ἐπιγνῷς τὴν ἀσφάλειαν, ver. 3) arranged according to succession of time (καθεξῆς). This he hopes to do, inasmuch as he has accurately followed the events from their origin, investigating them by help of communications and accounts transmitted (παρέδοσαν) from such men as had been eye-witnesses from the beginning, and had personally co-operated as ministers of the word (vv. 2 and 3). It is manifest that Luke places his own narrative as a true and authentic representation of events, *i.e.* as one that has been critically tested, in opposition to certain less credible accounts. What he emphatically asserts of his evangelical history in the prologue, we may by analogy apply in like manner to his second book. Hence we must assume that in this book also Luke intended to give actual history, accredited events, an account that might be relied on. The writer is clearly conscious of the obligation laid upon him honestly to test, to draw from the earliest sources, and only to record that which was capable of proof. If in spite of this we find him credited with mistakes, and even intentional

---

[1] Lekebusch, *die Composition und Entstehung der Apostelgeschichte von Neuem untersucht*, 1854, was the first who, p. 254 et seq., expressly applied the prologue of the Gospel in favour of the Acts of the Apostles.

falsification of history, it is fair to demand that those who make this assertion should bring forward the clearest reasons and most convincing proofs, and not start with a presumption of "general untrustworthiness," thus throwing on the book the burden of proof for every single statement which it contains.[1]

Coming to the proof itself, we set aside, as already stated, the second half of the book, which treats mainly of the history of the Apostle Paul, and confine ourselves to the history of the ante-Pauline time of the early apostolic community.

To this end we consult the *Pauline writings* themselves, because these are unanimously recognised by the disciples of the school of Baur, with the exception of Bruno Bauer, as the undisputed production of the Apostle Paul, especially the Epistles to the Galatians, Corinthians, and Romans. Let us suppose for a moment that the Acts of the Apostles are absent from the canon, and that we are dependent for our knowledge of the early history of the Christian Church solely on the Epistles of the Apostle Paul, the question then arises, What can we deduce from these?[2]

---

[1] We cannot recognise the force of Overbeck's objection to the application of the Gospel-prologue to the Acts (*ante*, p. xxi. Anm.). For it is established beyond a doubt that the author of both Scriptures is the same. As he expresses his view in the preface to the first work with regard to his method and aim, it is unreasonable to suppose that he denies these principles in the second work. When Overbeck appeals to Örtel, *Paulus in der Apostelgeschichte*, 1868, S. 40 f., as a witness on his behalf, he overlooks the fact that Örtel, on the contrary, has put the care, fidelity, and credibility promised by the author, Luke i. 1, in the scale for his second book also ; comp. 165 of same book.

[2] Dr. Paulus, in the dissertation quoted above, maintained that without this little book we should from no other source be able to

In the first place, the fact is established that Jerusalem was the seat of the early community, and the centre of the growing Church of Christ. This follows indubitably from the first chapters of the Epistle to the Galatians. When Paul says that after his conversion he did not at once go up to Jerusalem to those who were apostles before him ; but three years later, after a sojourn in Arabia, went up to Jerusalem to see Peter (i. 17 ff.), it becomes manifest beyond a doubt that the earliest Christian community, the leading community, at whose head the apostles stood, was in Jerusalem. This fact is more fully confirmed by the circumstance that fourteen years later, Paul, together with Barnabas and Titus, travelled to Jerusalem, in order to bring to a decision a question highly important to his life-work (Gal. ii. 1, etc.). His statement that he wished to take to the community at Jerusalem a contribution from the Christians of Macedonia and Arabia, before setting out on his journey to Rome, also shows that the community at Jerusalem was the ancient respected centre and birthplace of Christianity at that time (Rom. xv. 25, etc.).

Besides those at Jerusalem, Paul mentions Christian churches in the country of Judæa (αἱ ἐκκλησίαι τῆς Ἰουδαίας αἱ ἐν Χριστῷ, Gal. i. 22 ff.). Compare the

arrive at a knowledge of the beginnings of early apostolic Christianity. In complete opposition to this, Renan, *Les apôtres*, 1867, *Introduction*, ix., asserts that the Pauline Epistles are full of hints respecting the first years of Christian history. We find occasional isolated statements of this kind in more recent critics, for example, in Sieffert's article "Petrus," *Theol. Real-Encycl.* 2 Aufl. xi. 519. But in this connection, if I mistake not, the attempt has never yet been made to gain from such a source a certain insight into early Christianity before the time of Paul.

account in Acts ix. 31, etc., of the visit made by Peter to the churches in Judæa, *e.g.* in Lydda and Joppa. It is, however, worthy of note that Paul speaks not only of separate churches, but also of a collective Church, " the Church of God," as already existing before the time of his conversion and some years afterwards (Gal. i. 13, ἐδίωκον τὴν ἐκκλησίαν τοῦ θεοῦ; comp. 1 Cor. xv. 9). In agreement with this is the circumstance that Luke applies the collective term, " the community, the Church," to the separate churches in Judæa, Galilee, and Samaria, of the very same period (Acts ix. 31).

At the head of the early community at Jerusalem, of the Church of Christ of that earliest date, according to the Pauline testimony, stood the apostles: Paul mentions " the twelve apostles," " all the apostles " (1 Cor. xv. 7), " the apostles which were before me " (Gal. i. 17), " other apostles " (1 Cor. ix. 5); in conformity with which statements it is plain that we must regard them as a distinct circle, as a body endowed with authority. It requires no elaborate proof to show how fully this harmonizes with the accounts of the Acts. By virtue of several intimations of Paul, Cephas, *i.e.* Peter, stands out from the number of the apostles, so that we are justified in inferring a certain hegemony on his part among the apostles. The circumstance that Paul mentions Peter as the first of the apostles to whom Jesus appeared after His resurrection (1 Cor. xv. 5), is not without weight in this respect. But the prominent position which Peter occupied among the apostles appears far more directly from Paul's acknowledgment that he travelled from Damascus to Jerusalem, three years after his conversion, in order to become personally acquainted with Peter (Gal. i. 18, ἱστορῆσαι, employed only of prominent, remarkable, and noble objects and personages). In the course of the same Epistle he mentions Peter as the recognised apostle of the uncircumcised, *i.e.* as the most prominent missionary to the Jews, with whom he compares himself as the missionary to the heathen (Gal. ii. 7) ; with which the honorary title " pillar-apostle " agrees (οἱ δοκοῦντες στύλοι εἶναι, ver. 9). It is true that these events belong to the Pauline era, but they justify us in a backward conclusion respecting the whole time before the conversion of the Gentile-apostle. Even here it is not necessary to prove that in the first part of the Acts also Peter occupies a prominent position among the apostles, that he is their spokesman, acting for them all.

Besides Peter, John is the only one of the Twelve expressly mentioned by Paul who speaks of him as one of the few who were regarded as pillars of the Church (Gal. ii. 8, 9). It is manifest how this corresponds to the fact that in the Acts John appears as the apostle who stands next to Peter, and who is chiefly prominent beside him in doing and suffering (Acts i. 13, iii. 1, 3, 11, iv. 13).

In addition to the apostles, Paul makes special mention only of the " brethren of the Lord." He refers to them as a group closely connected with the apostles, 1 Cor. ix. 5. Among their number he gives prominence to James, the brother of the Lord, Gal. i. 19 ; to him doubtless reference is made in 1 Cor. xv. 7, and we may identify him as that James who is counted among those who " seemed to be pillars " (in opposition to the view of Wieseler, *Commentary*, p. 78 et seq.). These utterances of Paul are in harmony with the Acts, which place Mary, the mother of God, in close connection with the apostles, and with his brethren (Acts i. 14), but afterwards refer specially to James, manifestly the Lord's brother, (xv. 13, etc., and xxi. 18, etc.), as the centre of the elders of the Church at Jerusalem, and a personality of weight and dignity. The two latter cases justify a backward conclusion respecting the period of the early apostolic Church.

Barnabas also deserves mention. The Apostle Paul speaks of him in the Epistle to the Galatians, ii. 1–10, as a like - minded fellow - worker in his mission to the heathen, and in 1 Cor. ix. 6 lays stress on the fact that in addition to his missionary calling Barnabas, like himself, earned his daily bread by the work of his hands. Paul, however, speaks in Gal. ii. 13 of an occurrence at Antioch where, through blameworthy conduct on the part of Peter, Barnabas also was carried away, *i.e.* out of consideration for narrow-minded Jewish Christians, he refused to eat with Gentile Christians. This circumstance and the tone in which Paul speaks of the conduct of Barnabas, afford a glance into the relation in which Barnabas formerly stood to Peter and the Church at Jerusalem. The observation is quite incidental, and only appears in its true light when taken in connection with events narrated of the same important personage in the Acts, *e.g.* iv. 36, etc., ix. 27, xi. 22, etc., xiii. 1, etc.

With respect to individual believers, we are solely indebted to the Apostle Paul for a knowledge of the circumstance that Jesus appeared to more than five hundred brethren, *i.e.* believers, at once (1 Cor. xv. 6), of whom the greater number were still alive in

the year 58, when Paul wrote this Epistle at
Ephesus.

If by means of isolated remarks of the Apostle
Paul we try to form for ourselves a picture of the *inner
life* of the early Church, we find first of all certain
features which reveal something of the *doctrine* of
the apostles. In this same 15th chapter of the First
Epistle to the Corinthians, to which we have already
made frequent reference, Paul speaks of those things,
among others, which are all-important to salvation,
and had been preached in the communities of
believers and in the mission. He says, in 1 Cor.
xv. 11, " Therefore, whether it were I or they (the
other apostles), so we preach, and so ye believed."
By means of the οὕτω κηρύσσομεν, Paul proves the
identity of the fundamentals of redemption. What
are these ? First of all, " that Christ died for our
sins according to the Scriptures, and that He was
buried," ver. 3, next, " that He rose again on the
third day, according the Scriptures," ver. 4. Apart
from the preaching of the gospel by the Gentile
apostle himself, he certainly speaks of the preaching
of the other apostles in the present tense (κηρύσσομεν, ver. 11; Χριστὸς κηρύσσεται, ver. 12); but it
is clear that he does not intend to draw a distinction
between the present preaching and the preaching of
the gospel in earlier years, especially the very earliest
of the Church of Christ. On the contrary, it is
evident, if we take the connection into account, that
by giving special emphasis to that, *quod ab omnibus*
(to quote from Vincentius of Lerinum) *creditum* (et
predicatum) *est*, he lays stress, indirectly, on the circumstance that the preaching of the gospel was in every
time and from the beginning, " *semper*," the same.

We are therefore justified in drawing from the evidence of this passage the conclusion that the preaching and doctrine of the apostles from the first founding of the Church moved round these two points: 1. Christ died for our sins, and was buried; 2. Christ rose again on the third day. But these two fundamental truths, according to the absolutely authentic assurance of the apostle, are illuminated by the Scriptures (κατὰ τὰς γραφάς), *i.e.* are shown to be the fulfilment of Old Testament prophecies. What this leads us to expect, we find fully confirmed by the account of the early apostolic preaching contained in the Acts. The missionary discourses of Peter before the Jewish people at the feast of Pentecost (Acts ii. 14, etc.), and before a heathen audience (chap. x. 34, etc.), as well as his defence at the High Court of Jerusalem (iv. 8, etc., comp. v. 29, etc.), and his address to the people after the healing of the cripple (iii. 12, etc.), harmonize in substance with that which Paul writes to the Corinthians. We cannot fail to see that in these apostolic discourses the two facts, Christ's saving death and His resurrection, are not regarded as of equal importance, preponderating weight being attached to the resurrection. But this may be easily understood, and is in fact psychologically and pragmatically necessary. If Paul himself, in the 15th chapter of his first Epistle to the Corinthian Church (in the year 58), had a special object in placing the resurrection of Jesus in a central position, the same fact must necessarily have formed the centre of apostolic preaching twenty-five years earlier, and in the time immediately following, when the offence of the cross of Christ and the miracle of His resurrection were of such recent occurrence; and the apostles must have ranked first of all as " witnesses of the resurrection of Christ " (Acts i. 22).   We need but briefly allude to the fact that in the early apostolic preaching, references to the Scriptures, and to the mode in which the prophecies of the old covenant are fulfilled by the death and resurrection of Jesus, are not wanting, but play an important part.

But it was given to the apostles to work, not only by the preaching of the gospel and by the word, but also in deeds.   From what Paul tells us of himself, we may conclude that miracles were performed by other apostles also, since he makes frequent allusion to others.   To the Corinthian Christians, with the courage of humility, he thus writes, " By the grace of God I am what I am; and His grace, which was bestowed upon me, was not in vain; but I laboured more abundantly than they all; yet not I, but the grace of God which was with me " (1 Cor. xv. 10).   He here speaks only of his success in mission work, without positively drawing a comparison between himself and the other apostles with regard to miracles.   Even when the apostle says of himself that his speech and his preaching were not with enticing words of man's wisdom, but in demonstration of the Spirit and of power (1 Cor. ii. 4), he does not refer to the miracles which he had performed, but only to the power of the Divine Spirit persuading and convincing the minds of men.   This is not the case, however, when Paul, in Rom. xv. 18, writes of that which Christ had wrought by him to make the Gentiles obedient, " by word and deed, through mighty signs and wonders, by the power of the Spirit of God."   But in asserting his apostolic authority he does not hesitate to say, " In nothing am I behind the very chiefest apostles, though I be nothing. Truly the signs of an apostle were wrought among you in all patience, in signs, and wonders, and mighty deeds" (2 Cor. xii. 11). At the close of this utterance the apostle testifies that in his work at Corinth miracles were not wanting in proof of his true and genuine apostleship. The words σημεῖα, τέρατα, δυνάμεις denote the same thing, viz. miraculous cases of healing, etc.; their relation to the Invisible and Higher being indicated by the first two expressions, while δυνάμεις points to the supernatural power on which they are based. In the expression, σημεῖα τοῦ ἀποστόλου, the definite article gives emphasis to the conception "apostle," thus characterizing these miracles as the mark of a true apostle, the attestation of such an one. Paul now proceeds to make use of this apostolic legitimation in comparing himself with others who were regarded by his Corinthian opponents as apostles of the first rank, of the highest authority. Among these ὑπερλίαν ἀπόστολοι we must include Peter above all, since the opponents in Corinth were of a Judaizing spirit. When, therefore, Paul bears witness that he is in nothing (belonging to apostolic dignity and activity) behind the very chiefest apostle, we have here an unmistakeable and irrefutable testimony to the fact that Peter and the early apostles likewise performed miracles. This Pauline testimony is manifestly corroborative of those miracles related of the apostles in the early Christian era by the Acts, which are so offensive to the refined notions of many modern theologians.

Moreover, the information which St. Paul gives us in passing, with respect to the collective life of the

Churches founded by him, throws back a partial light on the life of the Church in Jerusalem and other parts of Palestine, before the appearance of the Apostle to the Gentiles. Of *baptism* as the mode of reception into communion with Christ and the faithful, Paul speaks so often (*e.g.* Rom. vi. 3, etc.; 1 Cor. i. 13–17, xii. 13; Gal. iii. 27), that it is plain baptism was a primitive Christian custom. Still more clearly does it appear from the statements of the apostle that the holy supper was instituted by Christ Himself (1 Cor. xi. 23, comp. x. 16 et seq.), and was in consequence an already established custom in the primitive Christian Church. These allusions of Paul are in harmony with what is related in the Acts, of baptism (ii. 38, 41, viii. 12, 16, 37, etc., ix. 18, x. 47, etc.) and of the breaking of bread (ii. 42).

As is well known, a prominent part in the Pauline Epistles is occupied by those collections which the apostle instituted in the Gentile-Christian Churches of Asia Minor and Greece for the benefit of the Churches in Palestine, and especially of the Church at Jerusalem. The apostle's third missionary journey has in fact very much the character of a journey for raising contributions. In his First Epistle to the Corinthians (xvi. 1, etc.), he mentions the arrangement he had made in the Churches of Galatia; and calls upon the Corinthian Church to begin the collection at once, even before his arrival, and to carry it on, so that he might then be able to transmit the sum collected to Jerusalem. According to the Epistle to the Galatians (ii. 10), it had been impressed on the apostle and Barnabas at the time of the meeting at Jerusalem in the year 50 or 51 by Peter, John, and James, that in the work of their mission to the Gentiles they should remember the poor Churches (in Jerusalem and Judæa), *i.e.* that they should interest themselves on behalf of their support ; and Paul testifies that in this matter he was most zealous. He treats most explicitly and fully of the subject in the Second Epistle to the Corinthians. Two whole chapters, viii. and ix., are devoted to this theme : the cheerful liberality of the Macedonian Churches is held up to the Corinthian Christians as an example worthy of imitation : not with the meaning that others should be helped and they themselves suffer want, but only by way of equality, in order that their abundant liberality, coming from a willing heart, might lead to gratitude and pious praise of God. In the Epistle to the Romans also (xii. 13) the apostle not only exhorts to charity in the immediate circle ($\tau a\hat{\imath}\varsigma$ $\chi\rho\epsilon\acute{\imath}a\iota\varsigma$ $\tau\hat{\omega}\nu$ $\dot{a}\gamma\acute{\imath}\omega\nu$ $\kappa o\iota\nu\omega\nu o\hat{v}\nu\tau\epsilon\varsigma$), but bespeaks even the collections coming from Macedonia and Achaia " for the poor saints which are at Jerusalem," by which means the Macedonian and Hellenic Christians would make a return in material goods for spiritual gifts ; and beseeches the Roman Christians by their brotherly prayers to God to aid in securing on the part of the faithful in Jerusalem a favourable reception for the present of which he was to be the bearer (Rom. xv. 23–27, 30, etc.). The fact that the apostle regards the arrangement in favour of the poor in the Church at Jerusalem as so important a portion of his apostolic work, is plainly connected with that pitying love and mutual help which was a characteristic feature of the primitive Church at Jerusalem in its earliest days, and took the form of a voluntary community of goods.

Putting together what we have hitherto found to be fundamental respecting the ante-Pauline period of the Christian Church, and we have purposely drawn only from the four Pauline Epistles universally acknowledged, we must admit that we have gained only fragments, but yet fragments of an importance not to be under-estimated. They afford us, to quote from Dr. Paulus, many valuable *notitias originum apostolico-christianarum ;* [1] and serve, which was here our principal point of view, as a confirmation scarcely to have been expected in this connection, of important utterances of the Acts ; as a justification, answering to the expectations we were led by Luke, in the prologue to his Gospel, to form respecting the credibility of his narrative in the Acts. We certainly admit that those Epistles of which we have made use do not contain authentic utterances of the Apostle Paul respecting all the events, discourses, and descriptions narrated in the Acts (chaps. i.–xii.). For example, the figure of Stephen, his character and his fate, are, strange to say, never mentioned in the Pauline Epistles. But this was not necessary. For the death of Stephen, as the most profound critic of the school of Baur honestly acknowledges, is " incontestably the clearest point in the history of Christianity before Paul ; hence we find ourselves here on undeniably historic ground." [2]

By these inquiries we believe we have established our right to employ the Acts of the Apostles as a generally trustworthy source of historical value in elucidating the history of primitive Christianity before the appearance of Paul. We must, however,

---

[1] *Commentatio de consilio,* etc., 1798, S. 3 ; *vid.* above, p. 8, note.
[2] Ed. Zeller, *die Apostelgeschichte,* S. 146.

examine in detail, as it becomes necessary, the attacks and doubts which are directed against concrete statements of the book.

Jesus had chosen His twelve apostles from the tribes of Israel, as the nucleus of a larger band of disciples also composed exclusively of Israelites. The Twelve were to be witnesses to Jesus (Acts i. 8), but also "fishers of men" (Matt. iv. 19), *i.e.* men who gather souls into the kingdom of God. The Twelve were in fact the foundation of the nascent Church of Christ. This is proved not only by the accounts in the Acts of the appearance of the apostles on the occasion of the feast of Pentecost (ii. 14, 37, 42), of their witness to Christ before the people (iv. 33, etc.) as well as before the high council (iv. 8, v. 29, etc.), and of their behaviour in the midst of the community (vi. 2); but also, as we have seen, by the testimony of Paul (1 Cor. ix. 5, xv. 5, 7, 11 ; Gal. i. 18, ii. 9 ; comp. Eph. ii. 20), and in conclusion especially by the Apocalypse (xxi. 14), according to which the twelve foundations of the eternal city of God are inscribed with the names of the "twelve apostles of the Lamb."

The band of believers is subject to the leadership of the Twelve, after as well as before Pentecost. Before this time it is a quiet association shut up within itself, though no longer with closed doors (John xx. 19), as was the case immediately after the resurrection of Jesus, for all fear disappeared after His ascension ; "great joy" filled their hearts, so that their mouth was full of praising and blessing (Luke xxiv. 52, etc.). But they still keep themselves in a kind of seclusion. They do not yet come forward publicly, or invade the national life with their testimony to Jesus Christ; the apostles do not yet throw out the net in order to gain recruits for the kingdom of God. There is a time for all things. Above all, they persevered with one accord in prayer, sometimes repairing regularly to the temple at the appointed hours of worship (Luke xxiv. 53), sometimes assembling in the upper room of a private house (ὑπερῷον) to pray together (Acts i. 13 et seq.).[1]

The hour struck when the day of Pentecost arrived; the promise of the Father, revealed to them by the Redeemer, was now fulfilled, and the disciples were baptized with the Holy Ghost, so that they received *power* to work with joy (Acts i. 4–8). A double gift was thus bestowed upon them: they received the divine command to go forth *now* and work for the kingdom of God, and were inwardly furnished with the necessary gifts of the Spirit. The Spirit was poured out not only on the apostles, but on all the believers who were at that time assembled (Acts ii. 1, etc., πάντες . . . ἐφ᾽ ἕνα ἕκαστον . . . ἐπλήσθησαν πάντες πνεύματος ἁγίου; compare the testimony of Peter, speaking in the name of the other eleven, " these are not drunken," but the divine prophecy of Joel is fulfilled in them, ver. 14, etc.). The gift of the Spirit was not a magically infused, complete, and fully developed knowledge of divine things, but, as the Saviour had promised, *power*, holy, blessed power, proceeding from the wonderful works of God

---

[1] These two statements are not inconsistent with one another (as Strauss, *Leben Jesu*, 1 Aufl. S. 682, maintains). Even Karl Schrader, though strongly disposed to negative criticism, admits that the meetings of believers were of such a nature as not to prevent their continuing with one accord in the temple (*Ap. Paulus*, v. 1836, S. 515).

($\mu\epsilon\gamma a\lambda\epsilon\hat{\imath}a$, Acts ii. 11), glowing through the inmost heart, lifting and strengthening the soul. It was a creative quickening breath of the Almighty, which passed over mankind, and brought forth a new spiritual spring. The "speaking with tongues" was only one of the effects of the Spirit, one of the many blossoms which sprang up. But according to Acts ii. 4–11, these were not connected discourses (Zeller, *ante*, 106), but only short utterances of praise and adoration from minds that were inspired. Out of the abundance of the heart the mouth spake. There was without doubt something striking and animated in the mode in which the disciples spoke and acted. Otherwise the thought would not have occurred to so many eye- and ear-witnesses that the people were drunk (Acts ii. 13). But the most wonderful thing was that Jews of the dispersion who had come to Jerusalem to celebrate the Old Testament feast of Pentecost, even from districts beyond the Euphrates, and from Asia Minor, from Egypt, Libya, and Cyrene, from Arabia, Crete, and Rome, heard "every man in his own tongue in which he was born," although the speakers were all Galileans. The matter has frequently been explained, even in Christian antiquity, by the assumption that a miracle of hearing instead of one of speaking took place, according to which the disciples spoke in their own Galilean (*i.e.* Aramæan) tongue; but the listening Jews of the dispersion, by virtue of a certain spiritual rapport, each had the consciousness of hearing his own mother-tongue.[1] But this is opposed to the $\mathring{\eta}\rho\xi a\nu\tau o\ \lambda a\lambda\epsilon\hat{\imath}\nu$

---

[1] Gregory Nazianzen mentions this as the view of others, but does not himself assent to it ; he says, *Oratio*, xli. § 15 : ἐκείνων τῶν ἀκουόντων ἂν εἴη μᾶλλον ἢ τῶν λεγόντων τὸ θαῦμα. So also Erasmus,

ἑτέραις γλώσσαις ... ἀποφθέγγεσθαι, ver. 4. As to what is related in the Acts, it does not refer to the sudden imparting of a permanent facility in speaking foreign languages; of this we can discover no trace. It treats only of a passing phenomenon, which consisted in short utterances of inspired praise and gratitude; and, according to the narrative, in strange dialects and tongues. The whole new creation, the regeneration of mankind through Christ, the pouring out of the Holy Spirit, was a great miracle of the living God; the miraculous appearance of strange tongues in the first moment of exaltation is only a cognate manifestation, following that great world-renewing, divine act.

The incident of the strange tongues stirred up the hearers partly to wondering inquiry, partly to scoffing remark. Hence the apostles felt themselves moved to address those who were assembled, in order to give an account of the meaning of the whole thing. Thus came about the first preaching of the gospel, the first missionary discourse to the Israelites. Of the ideas of this discourse we shall treat in another place. But we must here observe that the coming forward of the apostles was not gratuitous on their part, but was imposed on them as a moral obligation by the actual circumstances; it was obedience and fidelity to their calling. They followed the divine intimation involved in the event. Thus their right to such action was established, and success was not wanting. About 3000 souls, according to Acts ii. 41, were added to the Church. So great was the number of those who

and more recently Schneckenburger. Compare the discussion in my *Exposition of the Acts*, in Lange's *Bibelwerk*, vol. iv. 1881, p. 52 et seq.

were converted in consequence of what happened at the
feast of Pentecost and by the address of the Apostle
Peter.   Doubt has indeed been thrown on this estimate: " Judging by analogy, the spread of faith in
Jesus must rather be regarded as gradual " (Zeller, *die
Apostelgeschichte*, S. 116, etc.).   But who gives us the
right to mete all things by the same measure, to
apply one and the same model in every case ?   Even
if life consist always in pulsation, it still remains a
fact that the pulse, apart from sickness, beats sometimes faster, sometimes slower, going faster than ever
in states of great joy and excitement.   In childhood
the pulse is more easily affected, its speed is known
to be far more readily accelerated than even in youth.
In conformity with this law of development we may
assume that in the period which may be called the
childhood of Christianity, growth takes dimensions
differing from those of a later time.   The history of
the Church of Christ offers examples that are quite
analogous: how magical was the effect of Luther's
first appearance, all hearts being drawn towards him !
but a different movement set in afterwards.

Pentecost was the birthday of the Church of
Christ.   A community of believers was in existence
before that time, but was concealed from the world.
The Spirit of God, which came upon it in that hour,
gave it a life in the light which hitherto it had not
known.   The second half of the familiar saying of
Irenæus, *ubi spiritus Dei ibi ecclesia et omnis gratia*,
is after all another way of saying that the existence
of the Church begins with the outpouring of the
Holy Ghost.

Before investigating more closely the inner life
of the primitive Jewish - Christian Church, let us

bestow a glance on its condition and gradual growth.

Before Pentecost an assembly of the believers took place, at which the post vacated in the number of the apostles by the suicide of the traitor Judas of Kerioth, was filled up by the election of Matthias by lot.[1] On this occasion the number of the assembled brethren amounted to about 120 men. The expression ἐν μέσῳ τῶν ἀδελφῶν seems to indicate that this assembly, appointed on behalf of an important choice, was composed only of male members of the community of believers. This estimate of the number forms the starting-point for viewing the state and growth of the primitive Church. Between the smaller number and the larger one which Paul gives in 1 Cor. xv. 6, "above 500 brethren," to whom Jesus appeared at once after His resurrection, we cannot discover any insoluble contradiction. For the statement in the Acts refers to an assembly at Jerusalem, that of Paul to an event whose locality is not specified; the latter appearance of the risen Saviour may possibly have taken place in Galilee, the native place of the greater number of the disciples of Jesus. The history of the life of Jesus is so unequivocally in favour of this view that the

---

[1] We mention only in passing that Zeller, *Die Ap. Gesch.* p. 115, etc., finds it quite natural that the number twelve should have been made up again, and pronounces it credible that this was done by the choosing of Matthias; nor does he say anything against the statement of the employment of lots. But he questions the fact of a meeting of this kind before Pentecost, because the apostles had probably at that time not yet returned to Jerusalem. Baur, however, even so late as 1860, assumes without hesitation that after the death of Jesus the disciples had their permanent centre of union in Jerusalem (*Christentum der drei ersten Jahrhunderte*, 2 Aufl. S. 42).

arguments of Wendt, on the other side (Meyer's
Handb. z. Ap. Gesch., 5 Aufl. S. 42), have the less
weight, especially since Luke nowhere maintains that
what he does not expressly state did not actually
happen.[1]   At the feast of Pentecost, in consequence
of the power from above imparted to the apostles and
disciples, a very considerable accession was made to
the formerly moderate band of believers in Jerusalem
(which included a number of women besides the 120
men); about 3000 souls received the word and
were joined to the Church by baptism (Acts ii. 41).
We must not, however, at once credit the Church in
Jerusalem with this increase.   For among the
listeners to the apostolic discourse there were
Israelitish guests and proselytes from near and
distant countries (ii. 5, 9–11, 14), whence we may
infer that of those newly converted many were not
living in Jerusalem itself, but partly in Judæa and
Galilee, partly in countries beyond Palestine, who
therefore returned home after the feast days were
ended.   Some of these might, under certain circumstances, form the centre of a small Church in the
dispersion, so that gradually Churches may have
arisen to which also James may possibly have
addressed his Epistle.   If we are not mistaken in

---

[1] Zeller, *Ap. Gesch.* 118, holds an unhistorical origin of the above
"120" as possible, for the reason that 120 is equal to 12 decades
(analogous to the twelve apostles); and Overbeck, *ante*, 12, sees in
it the usual number—forty multiplied by three. This is not to the
point, simply because Luke by ὡς makes the number only approximate. But that the Acts exclude Galilean appearances, to which
the number in 1 Cor. xv. 6 referred (Overbeck, S. 11), is an assertion
without proof. On the contrary, when Luke says in iii. 1 that the
risen Saviour showed Himself alive during forty days, ἐν πολλοῖς
τεκμηρίοις, he bears explicit testimony to numerous appearances before
the ascension, but neither affirms nor denies Galilean appearances.

the above supposition, the Christian Church at
Jerusalem must certainly have had the advantage of
a considerable addition from the time of Pentecost,
though probably the number was still much below
3000.

But we soon hear that the Lord added to the
Church daily those who were saved by His grace
(Acts ii. 47). By $\kappa a\theta$' $\dot{\eta}\mu\acute{\epsilon}\rho a\nu$ Luke so expresses
the thing that we are led to think of a quiet but
steady increase; and get the impression that, after
the mighty wonder at the feast of Pentecost, which
was epoch-making not only internally but also as
regarded the external growth of the Church, the
flow of divinely-human work and life retired into the
appointed bed of a continuous stream. After the
miraculous healing of the cripple and the discourse
of the Apostle Peter on that occasion, the historian
goes on to say, "Many of them which heard the
word believed, and the number of the men was
about 5000" (iv. 4). It seems as if in consequence
of this event, which made no little stir, a larger
number joined themselves to the Church. Nor is it
probable that this healing took place until a long
time after the beginning of the Church. The
miracle, with the effect which it had, serves as a
resting-place at which the result of the previous
growth of the Church may be ascertained. And
here the number again incidentally mentioned refers
without doubt to the Church at Jerusalem. A
second time, probably with reference to a former
period of longer duration, we find the comprehensive
remark, "And believers were the more added to the
Lord, multitudes both of men and women" (v. 14);
here even an approximate number is wanting. The

same may be said of two statements which are made partly before, partly after the account of the commission of the seven men, viz. the number of the disciples multiplied in those days, *i.e.* the Church constantly grew (vi. 1); and again, more precisely, " The word of God increased, and the number of disciples multiplied in Jerusalem greatly, and a great company of the priests were obedient to the faith " (vi. 7).

But just at this time a reaction took place which threatened to destroy the Church, and seemed at least to throw it far back. The persecution, which began with the martyrdom of Stephen, had this effect, that all believers except the apostles fled from the capital, and were scattered partly in Judæa, partly in Samaria, and betook themselves even to more distant lands, to Phenicia, Cyprus, and Antioch (viii. 1, 7, 11, 19). But the diminution of the Church at Jerusalem was a gain to all those districts lying within and without the borders of Palestine; for wherever the believers fled they spread the gospel (viii. 4, 40, xi. 19), as a rule, however, only among the Jews. We shall treat afterwards of the beginning which the gospel then made among the Gentiles. Again, we learn that the Churches throughout all Judæa and Galilee and Samaria had rest and were edified; and walking in the fear of the Lord and in the comfort of the Holy Ghost, were multiplied (ix. 31). Only after a long time do we again find a number given, and this, as formerly, in a general and incidental way, viz. in Acts xxi. 20, where the elders at Jerusalem say to Paul, " Thou seest how many thousands of Jews there are which believe."

Looking back, we find that the disciples of Jesus

may be counted by hundreds before the feast of Pentecost (Acts i. 15, comp. 1 Cor. xv. 6). Immediately after Pentecost, the community of believers increased so rapidly that they were numbered by thousands (ii. 41, iv. 4). But towards the end of the time of the Acts, in the year 58, the number of believers among the Jews, in Palestine alone (for according to the connection of xxi. 20, etc., the Jews of the διασπορά are certainly not taken into account), amounted to many tens of thousands. The latter estimate is not in itself improbable, if, on the one hand, we consider the time to which it refers, and do not, on the other hand, arbitrarily narrow the wide circuit over which it extends; not limiting it to Jerusalem, but treating it as having reference to all Judæa, and even to all the districts of Palestine. So abundantly did God bless with success the activity of the early apostles though limited to the nation of Israel and the land of Canaan, and their fidelity within a circumscribed sphere.

Hence there existed at the end of the period of which we treat numerous Christian Churches in Jerusalem and the whole country of Judæa (comp. Gal. i. 22, etc.; Acts xi. 1), also on the coast (Acts ix. 32–35, etc.), in Samaria and Galilee, and finally in Syria, Phenicia, and Cyprus (Acts ix. 2, 10, 25, xi. 19), some of which were directly, some indirectly founded by the Twelve, and were, in any case, governed and guided by them. In the above-named districts outside Palestine, it might not, indeed, have been easy to find a Christian Church consisting exclusively of believing Jews, for as a rule they consisted of believing Jews and individual Gentiles. On the other hand, we shall scarcely be wrong in regarding the Christian

Churches within Palestine itself as composed entirely of believing Israelites. But even among these there were many distinctions, *e.g.* between Palestinians and Hellenists, of which we shall treat afterwards.

So far we have endeavoured to draw up a kind of statistics of the Churches collected by the early apostles. We described the body, so to speak, of this primitive Christianity. But now we have to become acquainted with the spirit which animated it. The object is to give a delineation of its internal character. But before proceeding to this, we must insert one observation relative to the use of language. We call the believers, of whom we here speak, " Jewish-Christians," in accordance with universal usage. But this name has reference only to national descent, and not to view or tendency. It corresponds to the New Testament expression οἱ ἐκ περιτομῆς, or οἱ πεπιστευκότες ἐν τοῖς Ἰουδαίοις (Acts xxi. 20), in opposition to the πεπιστευκότα ἔθνη. It is natural to conclude that birth and education, intercourse and custom, determine even the opinion and tendency of a man; and that the Jewish-Christians must have been influenced by their descent in their entire conception of divine things and in their religious position. Only we must not forget that this influence might be moderate, sound, and true; or exaggerated, sickly, and false. In the former case, we speak simply of a Jewish-Christian tendency. In the latter case, the tendency is characterized as " Judaizing" or " Judaistic." The latter rests on New Testament usage, for Gal. ii. 14 designates the Jewish mode of life and action adopted by the Gentiles as ἰουδαΐζειν. At all events it is difficult here to draw the boundary line between true and false. There are, however, certain Jewish elements of which we must say decidedly that they do not belong to Christianity, but that through them the ἀλήθεια τοῦ εὐαγγελίου was misunderstood and falsified by the Judaists (Gal. ii. 5); while on the other hand, there are certain Jewish elements which are intimately related to Christianity, and are fully entitled to a place in it. Just as a believer of the Gentiles was not suffered unduly to mingle heathen and Christian usages, however easily he might do so, i.e. was not suffered co ipso to " Hellenize," for the very reason that he had formerly been a heathen; so a Jewish-Christian as such was not essentially a ζηλωτὴς τοῦ νόμου (Acts xxi. 20), i.e. a Judaist. Paul himself was a Jewish-Christian ('Εβραῖος ἐξ 'Εβραίων, Phil. iii. 5), his conception of the gospel being, in fact, Jewish-Christian, though his views and tendency are by no means Judaistic, but the very reverse. But just as a man might be a Jewish-Christian without having a Judaistic tendency, so, on the other hand, a Christian might Judaize without being a born Jew, as e.g. the Gentile Christians in Galatia who suffered themselves to be led astray by Judaizing false teachers, to " be removed unto another gospel, to be circumcised, and to be in subjection to the law" (Gal. i. 6, iv. 21, v. 2, 4). The tendency which we call Judaistic, or Judaism, has been recently termed " Ebionitish," a use of language against which in itself there is nothing to be said. But when the term Ebionism is made to include everything Jewish-Christian without distinction, we must pronounce it an inappropriate and misleading use of the word. A cloudy mixture of true and false is thus produced, a given idea is arbitrarily extended in a way that is unhistorical, and everything is depicted in chiaro-oscuro.[1]

In order, therefore, to trace out as true and complete a picture as possible of the spirit and life, of the inner and outer relations of the Churches of the apostolic period composed of believing Jews, we separate three questions: First, How was their directly religious life constituted, in devotion, worship, and usages?   Second, In what way were they arranged with respect to consociation?   Third, What was the constitution of their domestic and social life, and in what relation did they stand to non-Christians, especially to unbelieving Jews?

(A.) *The direct religious life of the Jewish-Christian Churches.*

Our first object here is to gain as clear a conception as possible of the fundamental direction and the inner life of the first believers belonging to Israel. If we adhere mainly to the Acts, we get the impression that a *holy joy* on the part of the faithful was the keynote of their inner life: the joyful consciousness of salvation, of redemption by Christ who had been crucified and was risen again.   The joyous tone of their heart found expression in the prayer of thanksgiving (here belongs first and foremost the λαλεῖν τὰ

---

[1] Further confusion of ideas might be apprehended, if the innovation of Reuss were to find acceptance, which, however, it has not yet done; he distinguishes, namely, between "Ebionism and Ebionitism" (*Hist. de la Théol.* i. pp. 125, etc.), without any linguistic or historical foundation, making the former stand for a purely internal, Jewish and ascetic tendency, out of which Essenism is said to have grown; and the latter, on the other hand, for the Judaistic tendency within Christianity.

μεγαλεῖα τοῦ θεοῦ, Acts ii. 11, with which compare the λαλεῖν τὸν λόγον τοῦ θεοῦ μετὰ παρρησίας, iv. 31, said not of the apostles exclusively, but of all believers). Further, αἰνοῦντες τὸν θεόν (ii. 47, iii. 8) regarding the healed cripple; comp. what is said of the gladness of heart of the believers, ii. 46, immediately before their unceasing praise of God. The feeling of joy sprang from the certainty of being redeemed. Σώθητε, " save yourselves from this untoward generation," was the injunction which Peter (ii. 40) addressed to those who were awakened by his preaching; salvation (ἡ σωτηρία, iv. 12) was the highest good which the apostles had to offer, attesting its validity through Christ alone; those who received the word were converted and added to the Church, and became partakers of the redemption (οἱ σωζόμενοι, ii. 47). Redemption, according to the testimony of the apostles, and the experience of believers themselves, was twofold: firstly, forgiveness of sins, the purging away of guilt, deliverance from divine wrath (ii. 38, εἰς ἄφεσιν τῶν ἁμαρτιῶν, comp. v. 31 and iii. 19, εἰς τὸ ἐξαλειφθῆναι ὑμῶν τὰς ἁμαρτίας); and secondly, the gift of the Holy Ghost (ii. 4, 33, 38, v. 32), which was given to all who received the word of salvation in faith and obedience, πειθαρχοῦντες. These two favours—forgiveness of sins and the gift of the Spirit—form the chief features of the blessing (εὐλογοῦντα ὑμᾶς) imparted by God's hand to those who were converted, in fulfilment of the promise of the covenant which was given to the patriarchs (iii. 25 et seq.), particularly to Abraham. Hence believers are children of the covenant and of the prophets, heirs of the promise which God gave to the patriarchs in olden times (iii. 25). And yet they look for a still more glorious future, when the Anointed of the Lord, Jesus, shall come again from heaven, and the realization of all the promises of God ($\chi\rho\acute{o}\nu o\iota\ \dot{a}\pi o\kappa a\tau a\sigma\tau\acute{a}\sigma\epsilon\omega\varsigma$, etc., iii. 19–21) shall begin. Is it to be wondered at, if believers in the early days of the original outpouring of the Holy Spirit, in the enjoyment of the peace of forgiveness of sins and possessing manifold gifts of the Spirit, were full of holy joy, as the redeemed, the Church of God ($\dot{\eta}\ \dot{\epsilon}\kappa\kappa\lambda\eta\sigma\acute{\iota}a$ $\tau o\hat{v}\ \theta\epsilon o\hat{v}$, Gal. i. 13 ; 1 Cor. xv. 9)? To use the expression of a Scripture which seems to have proceeded from these circles not long after, they felt like the consecrated *first-fruits from among the whole creation*, inasmuch as they were born again through the word of truth ($\dot{a}\pi a\rho\chi\dot{\eta}\ \tau\hat{\omega}\nu\ a\dot{v}\tau o\hat{v}\ \kappa\tau\iota\sigma\mu\acute{a}\tau\omega\nu$, Jas. i. 18). If in the flourishing time of the German Reformation, an Ulrich von Hütten could exclaim, " When spirits awake, life is a pleasure ! " a similar feeling of the joy of a newly-elevated life, only humbler and more deeply rooted, might well penetrate the souls of the first believers. All their highest possessions, their whole inner being, they owed to the grace of God in Christ, they were a " Church in Christ " (Gal. i. 22, referring to the Churches in Judæa at the time of the conversion of Paul). All the happiness that occupied their thoughts, elevated their minds, and sharpened their consciences, rested on the fact of the revelation of God in Jesus Christ the Redeemer ($\sigma\omega\tau\acute{\eta}\rho$, Acts v. 31). This is confirmed not only by all the statements of the Twelve which are recorded in the Acts, and all hints of the narrator which afford a glance into the souls of the first disciples, but we are indirectly led to the same conclusion by the undeniable testimony of the Apostle Paul concerning the early apostolic preaching which is in harmony with his own. The fundamental truths of salvation, according to the harmonious preaching of the apostles and the faith of the Church, are: 1. That Christ died for our sins and was buried; 2. That He rose again on the third day (1 Cor. xv. 3, 11, εἴτε— ἐγὼ εἴτε— ἐκεῖνοι, οὕτω κηρύσσομεν, καὶ οὕτως ἐπιστεύσατε).

The holy joy arising from the revelation in Christ and the grace of God in the Holy Spirit, as it animated the first churches of Israel, is still reflected in the Gentile-Christian churches which Paul founded. And here we may observe in passing, that the epistles of the Apostle Paul are full of sounds of holy joy, not only out of his own pious heart but also from his Churches—sounds whose echo strikes our ear in his epistles. We may mention one passage from the earliest of his epistles, written about A.D. 54, because Paul here bears witness of his Christians in Thessalonica, that they have become followers of the Churches of God in Judæa (1 Thess. ii. 14, where the idea μιμηταί is perhaps not limited exclusively to like results on the part of their countrymen). He tells them at least that they have become followers (μιμηταί) of him and of the Lord, having received the word (of the gospel) in much affliction, yet with joy of the Holy Ghost (i. 6).

The new life, full of peace and joy in the redemption of Christ, begotten by the Holy Ghost, must reveal and exemplify itself chiefly in devotion, worship, and sacred exercises. The first place in which we find believers immediately after the ascension of Jesus, is the upper room (ὑπερῷον) of a private house in Jerusalem, where they met together. We learn that they continued with one accord in prayer, together with some women, among whom was Mary the mother of Jesus, and with His brethren (Acts i. 13 et seq.). Hence, according to this account, common prayer in the stillness of a room where they were alone together, is the first sign of life among the believers.

What is here narrated of the time before the feast of Pentecost, Luke repeats afterwards as a description of the continual life of believers, Acts ii. 42, 46, where the life of the Church at Jerusalem, setting aside those traits referring to the association, is thus depicted: " They continued stedfastly in the apostles' doctrine and fellowship, and in breaking of bread, and in prayers ;—they continued daily with one accord in the temple, and breaking bread from house to house, did eat their meat with gladness and singleness of heart, praising God." This description, judging from its connection, has reference, in the first instance, only to the life of those newly converted. We here see plainly a twofold element in the piety of the early Church, distinguished externally by locality, since believers meet for the purpose of worship sometimes κατ' οἶκον (ii. 46, comp. i. 13), and sometimes in the temple. The place was at one time public, at another time private. But this very circumstance leads us to conclude that devotion in close and intimate communion with a few associates must differ essentially from worship in the temple, especially if we consider that the Church in whose midst the services of the temple were performed was the theocratic national Church of Israel. It is natural that the private devotion at which only such Israelites were present as were agreed in faith in Jesus as the Messiah who had appeared and the Redeemer, keeping themselves apart from other Israelites, should have included that observance by which the believers were distinguished from other Israelites, while the worship of God in the temple contained only such elements as they had in common with all Israelites. In other words, their private devotion was the expression of the peculiar Christian element, and the means of its furtherance in accordance with the word of the Lord : " Where two or three are gathered together in My name, there am I in the midst of them " (Matt. xviii. 20). But the worship of the temple served a general theocratic object. This statement, however, requires a twofold limitation. First, we must not forget that the meetings of the Israelites for prayer in the fore-court of the temple (and these are, doubtless, mainly in question) consisted in this, viz., that each one prayed for himself according to his need (*e.g.* the Pharisee and the publican in the temple, Luke xviii.) ; accordingly the disciples of Jesus, even when in the precincts of the temple, might still in prayer occupy themselves with that which most deeply moved their own souls ; and the very circumstance that they ὁμοθυμαδόν (ii. 46) visited the temple in fellowship one with another, must help to show their union even here, and also to create a Christian atmosphere. In the second place, it may be objected that it is simply an anachronism, an unauthorised and arbitrary transference to the early time of Christianity of manifestations that took place much later, if we assert that the social gatherings of believers in houses were already of a nature specifically Christian and New Testament in opposition to the Old Testament service of the temple.[1] The second limitation here comes in. So much only we assert: in the nature of things a distinction of this kind undoubtedly existed between the domestic worship of the first believers and their service in the national sanctuary. But that this distinction was clearly recognised by the first Christians themselves we do not maintain. On the contrary, we must suppose that they themselves were unconscious of it, at least in the beginning. But, on the other hand, we believe that by degrees they must have felt it more homely and comforting to meet in houses than in the temple to which all Jews resorted, amid large and mixed assemblies of believers and unbelievers, especially when ill-humour, even enmity, on the part of the Jews was stirred up against them,—a feeling which would arise naturally and grow stronger with time. The whole difference was only elementary and relative ; but the germ of the distinction between specifically Christian and Old Testament piety lay, undoubtedly, in the relation between the domestic worship and the temple service of the first Christians.

This view is justified if we look more closely at the summary description given above : ἦσαν δὲ προσκαρτεροῦντες τῇ διδαχῇ τῶν ἀποστόλων, καὶ τῇ κοινωνίᾳ καὶ τῇ κλάσει τοῦ ἄρτου, καὶ ταῖς

---

[1] This is implied in the view of Rothe, that the Christians had originally no cult in the proper sense of the word, but that only after the destruction of Jerusalem a public liturgic cultus was arranged by the apostles ; Bonner Programm 1851, *De primordiis cultus Christianorum.* This view rests on the false presumption that religious exercises which are not matter of public order in the Church do not come into the conception of cultus ; *vid.*, on the other hand, Th. Harnack, *der Christliche Gemeinde-gottesdienst im apostolischen und altkatholischen Zeitalter*, Erlangen 1854, S. 69 ff.

προσευχαῖς (ii. 42). We assume that this description refers · precisely to the social gatherings of the Christians. Luke certainly depicts here the behaviour of the newly-converted, of those first baptized at the feast of Pentecost. It is indeed a general presumption on the part of commentators that ver. 42 has reference to the whole Church. But the connection with ver. 41 shows clearly that ver. 42 continues the description of the new disciples. Ver. 44, however, which speaks of believers as a whole, as distinguished from the lately-won members of the Church, πάντες δὲ οἱ πιστεύοντες continuing the description to ver. 47, is decisive.[1] But although the words of the 42nd verse are limited to those who first joined the Church at Pentecost, the newly-baptized, yet the declaration is so characteristic and so many-sided, that we may justly place it at the foundation. It is clear from the substance itself that reference is made to that which is peculiarly Christian. At farthest, it might be doubted whether the προσευχαί may not also refer to the devotional exercises in the temple. In the description of the common religious life of believers, as it appeared in their domestic social gatherings, four traits may be distinguished :—

Firstly, according to the context, where the question is only of the relation of believers one to another, the διδαχὴ τῶν ἀποστόλων cannot mean discourses before persons who did not yet belong to the Church, but only before those who were of one mind, whose preservation and furtherance in the truth it concerned, *i.e.* it was not properly speaking the

[1] One of the few who recognize this is Weizsäcker, *Jahrbücher f. deutsche Theol.* 1876, S. 485.

κήρυγμα, the mission sermon. It is important and worthy of note that the teaching activity, which was to lead to a deeper knowledge of the truth and to the walking therein (the διδάσκειν in distinction from the μαθητεύειν, Matt. xxviii. 20, comp. 19), is treated as essential, as the very first and highest part of Christian edification and of the worship of God even in early apostolic times, so that the Christian Church shows itself prominently as a communion of word and doctrine. In harmony with this is the fact that the apostles afterwards gave it clearly to be understood how decidedly they looked upon service in the word of God as their principal calling, which could under no condition be subordinated to other work however useful and necessary: οὐκ ἀρεστόν ἐστιν ἡμᾶς καταλείψαντας τὸν λόγον τοῦ θεοῦ διακονεῖν τραπέζαις (Acts vi. 2, comp. 4).

Secondly, the κοινωνία. It will not do to confuse this idea with κλάσις τοῦ ἄρτου, making it, by *hendiadys*, a breaking of bread in common. This is forbidden by the circumstance that in ver. 42 four clauses are grammatically co-ordinate, each pair being united by καί. The κοινωνία, therefore, forms an idea by itself, and denotes one of the four characteristic features. On the other hand, it is arbitrary to understand the word as a keeping together with the *apostles*: in that case the chief thing must first be put in. On the contrary, the use of language in the New Testament leads to the conclusion that κοινωνία denotes brotherly fellowship, internal consociation with believers, enjoyed and cherished as a moral blessing in itself. Brotherly fellowship manifested itself specially in liberality and joyful sacrifice of earthly possessions for the benefit of the brethren.

Herein lies the germ of the offerings of ecclesiastical love and almsgiving.[1] The common life of the first Christians is, by virtue of its first and second features, a life of faith and love.

Thirdly, the κλάσις τοῦ ἄρτου means neither a temperate mode of living, nor does it refer directly and exclusively to the Holy Supper. The former interpretation finds too little meaning in the expression ; the latter puts too much into it. The allusion is to fellowship at table, to actual meals taken in common. Believers felt themselves to be *one* family, and observed regular meals as love-feasts (Agapæ, Ep. Jude 12), which were at the same time δεῖπνα κυρίου, meals of fellowship with the Lord. This double meaning is also shown in the position assigned to the " breaking of bread," between the κοινωνία on the one hand and the προσευχαί on the other. The Lord's Supper was the most important and sacred part of this meal, and, according to the usual assumption, formed the elevating conclusion of the common daily meal.[2]

Fourthly, the προσευχαί, *i.e.* prayers in common, were, as already appears from i. 13, the proper soul of these devotional assemblies. Luke mentions prayers of praise and blessing (xxiv. 53); and from

----

[1] *Vid.* Löhe, *Aphorismen über die neutestamentlichen Ämter*, 1849, S. 80 ff. Th. Harnack, *der christliche Gemeindegottesdienst im apostol. und altkathol. Zeitalter*, S. 78 ff. Comp. also Nitzsch, *Prakt. Theologie*, i. 174 ff., 213 ff.—Meyer's objection, *Comm. zur Apostelgeschichte*, 5 Aufl. 1880, S. 85 f., that a special reference to liberality is not expressly indicated, is obviated by our exposition, which places the disposition or the κοινωνία in the foreground as a moral good.

[2] Th. Harnack, a. a. O. S. 111 ff., places the fundamental character of the primitive Jewish-Christian worship in the "Sacramental celebration of the ever-valid sacrificial death of Christ." This, how-

the Acts we learn that supplications were also made
at this time (i. 24 and iv. 24, comp. Jas. i. 5,
v. 13, etc.).

In surveying this series of statements in which
the inner life of the early Church moved, we get the
impression that the peculiarly Christian element
which distinguished the first believers from the other
Israelites gained in prominence and in strength by
these confidential and domestic assemblies.   Nor
must we here forget baptism as that peculiarly
Christian act by which those who became disciples
were incorporated in the Church : those who believed
the word were baptized (ii. 41, comp. viii. 12, 36,
ix. 18).

It was the enjoyment of brotherly communion
with those who were of the same mind that gave to
these assemblies their peculiar charm.   Moreover,
the matter was more important than it appeared.
In separating themselves from others, in order to
meet confidentially among themselves, they paved
the way for the self-dependence and independence of
the Christian community.   In this conduct, which
was apparently nothing more than domestic and
social, which took outward expression by virtue of a
free impulse from within, and was to a certain
extent formless, there yet lay the germ of an established public ecclesiastical service.   The early Christian worship, working from within, without express

ever, has absolutely no original documentary evidence to support it,
but rather rests entirely on an *à priori* construction, and presupposes
a doctrine already more fully developed ; while, on the other hand,
it does not agree with the utterances and testimonies of the
apostles transmitted to us from earliest times (*vid. infra*, ii. Theil,
1 Abschn., 1 Kap.), for which reason we dismiss this view as unhistorical.

appointment of the Redeemer, without legal precept, without a conscious plan, made itself, so to speak, autonomous; it was the free product of the impulse of the Spirit, as Harnack very justly maintains.

But the other side also deserves closer examination, that side on which the piety of believers was still connected with the Old Testament theocracy, and with the nationality of Israel, viz. *its participation in the national sanctuary and the Jewish service*. What the narrative (Acts ii. 46, comp. Luke xxiv. 53) states as the custom of all, viz. that the believers continued with one accord in the temple, is confirmed by concrete facts. " Peter and John went up together into the temple at the hour of prayer, being the ninth hour " (Acts iii. 1). This statement justifies the conjecture that the apostles as well as other Christians observed the hours of prayer consecrated by Jewish custom, taking part especially in the morning and evening sacrifice, adhering in the main to the ancient times and acts of worship belonging to the old covenant. In the course of the same narrative we read (ver. 11) that on account of the healing of the cripple in the porch of Solomon, at one of the colonnades in the fore-court of the Gentiles at the east side of the temple, the people gathered round the two apostles (comp. ver. 12); an opportunity of which Peter availed himself to address the multitude (iii. 12–26). After this, when the apostles were arrested, but released from prison by the angel of the Lord, they received the command, " Go, stand and speak in the temple to the people all the words of this life." And they entered into the temple at break of day and taught. It was immediately reported to the chief council, " Behold, the men whom ye put in prison are standing in the temple and teaching the people" (v. 20–25). At the close of this chapter we again find a comprehensive description in which temple and house are classed together quite impartially: "And daily in the temple, and in every house, the apostles ceased not to teach and preach Jesus Christ." Paul himself, in his defence at Jerusalem, mentions an appearance of Jesus, which was vouchsafed to him in a state of trance, while he was praying in the temple (Acts xxii. 17). His arrest, when the people were in uproar, took place in the temple, when he was making sacrifice in the name and company of the four Nazarites (xxi. 27, 30, comp. xxiv. 26, xxv. 18).

From these facts it follows that the apostles and the other members of the early Church remained in constant connection with the theocratic sanctuary of the nation. They visited the temple at the usual times for the purpose of prayer, and probably to take part in other sacred ceremonies, not excluding even sacrifice. At the same time, the apostles made use of the opportunity afforded by the space of the temple and by religious usage to preach to their people the gospel of Jesus the Messiah, and so to prosecute their missionary calling. In this respect the first disciples of Jesus trod unhesitatingly and naturally in the footsteps of their Lord and Master Jesus, who Himself made frequent pilgrimages to Jerusalem at the great feasts, in order thus "to fulfil all righteousness"; as long as He dwelt in Jerusalem He was accustomed to assemble the people round Him in the halls and fore-courts of the temple itself and to teach them. It was by virtue of this adherence to the sanctuary and to the public service of Israel that the believing Jews seemed to their unbelieving brethren as genuine Israelites still, and complete associates in religion. It is certain that the believers themselves regarded this phase of their piety as an indispensable duty, an essential requisite of godliness.

Regarded from our later Christian standpoint, it seems strange, at the first glance, that so much prominence and publicity should have been given to that element in early Christian piety and devotion which was still peculiar to the Old Testament, while the element which we recognize as of the New Testament and peculiarly Christian, as essential and permanent, receded into the intimate domestic circle, and, accessible only to the initiated, moved, as it were, in close proximity. But in this very respect the first Christians gave to the Church of all time a bright example,—first, in keeping themselves far removed from sectarianism and separatism, and adhering with all fidelity to the existing form of worship, so long as it was at all possible; secondly, inasmuch as by domestic worship the house was consecrated as a temple and the family as a church of God. Moreover, we are persuaded, on further consideration, that this relation perfectly corresponds to the divine wisdom, and is in harmony with the law of gradual growth, like that of a mustard-seed, which prevails throughout the history of the kingdom of God. In the region of organic life generally, especially in the history of all human and even divine-human life, the new is constantly developed from within. Hidden in the grain of seed lies the germ from which the new plant grows, while the protecting leaves fall apart; in the bosom of the mother grows the child, sheltered in its retirement till the hour arrives when the man is born to the world. To borrow the beautiful words of Hegel (*Phänomenologie Vorr.*, S. 13, 1 Ausg. 1807): "The growing spirit (of a new time) thus ripens slowly and silently towards the new form, putting off one small portion of the fabric of its former world after another ; till at length this gradual crumbling, which has not changed the physiognomy of the whole, is interrupted by the issue which *at once*—like a flash of lightning—presents the structure to the new world." An able critic of the seventeenth century, John Spencer, thus expresses the same sentiment: "Est arcanum naturæ, sensim et occulte res omnes immutare, et dum res novas molitur, eandem externam speciem retinere.—Sapientiæ et pietati consentaneum est existimare, Deum ritus aliquos antiquos tolerasse, et pertinacem populum ad cultum novum, leniter et sub externa veteris specie perducere studuisse" (*de leg. Hebr. ritual. Tub.* 1732, S. 660). By virtue of this divine law of history, we find also the new spirit of Christian piety, shut up in the beginning in the bosom of the old theocracy, in the quiet circle of domestic intimacy and brotherly fellowship, growing and ripening in concealment towards the time when, loosed from the shell of the old covenant, it was to come forth pure and free.

One point of great importance with respect to the piety of the Jewish-Christian churches has not yet been discussed, viz. their attachment to the Jewish synagogue, after the well-known example of Jesus.[1]

---

[1] The Gospels not only narrate definite cases in which Jesus visited a synagogue on the Sabbath, in order to teach there, and sometimes to perform miracles (Mark i. 21, vi. 2 ; Luke iv. 16, xiii. 10), but they mention it more than once, in a general way, as a regular custom

We have hitherto avoided all mention of this circumstance, because our attention so far has been chiefly directed to the church at Jerusalem, with strict adherence to the information given in the Acts ; but so far as the church at Jerusalem is concerned, we find no account of it, for the Acts tell only of the connection of Christians with the synagogues after the appearance of Paul, and in relation to the Pauline history.[1] In the history of the apostle, however, synagogues are mentioned in such a way that we get a clear idea of the procedure of the Jewish Christians in Palestine itself as well as in neighbouring countries. With the object of arresting Christians in Damascus and bringing them to Jerusalem for judgment, Paul requests of the high priest a letter to the synagogue of that place, that, if he found any of the new religion, whether they were men or women, he might bring them bound unto Jerusalem (ix. 2). And since this official letter could have availed him nothing, if the Christians at Damascus had had nothing to do with the synagogue, we are authorized to conclude that the Christians there, who were at that time all Israelites, stood in close connection with the synagogue, and that by virtue of such relationship the chief of the synagogue had power and authority over them. We are further justified in this conclusion by the circumstance that afterwards, in his

and habit of Jesus to teach the people in the synagogues (Matt. iv. 23, ix. 35, xiii. 54 ; Mark i. 39 ; Luke iv. 15) ; and according to John (xviii. 20), Jesus Himself in His justification appeals to the publicity of His teaching "in the synagogue and in the temple, whither the Jews always resort."

[1] At the most, in the history of Stephen it may be conjectured that the controversial conferences took place with him in the synagogue, though that is not expressly stated.

defence, Paul describes Ananias as "a devout man according to the law," appealing to the testimony of all Jews belonging to Damascus (xxii. 12), which he could not have done if Ananias had not been attached to the synagogue of the place; for in those days regular attendance at the synagogue was an indispensable requirement of the correct piety of Israelites. That which has been gathered only by inference from the passages quoted, is directly stated in the words of James, Acts xv. 21. After he had proposed that they should release Gentile Christians from the obligations of the Mosaic law, only enforcing certain acts of abstinence upon them, he concludes with the words, "For Moses of old time hath in every city them that preach him, being read in the synagogues every Sabbath day." This utterance, whether we regard it as applicable chiefly to Gentile or Jewish Christians, refers in any case to Christians; but the circumstance that Moses was known in every city, by means of the regular readings in the synagogue, can have no reasonable weight in this connection, except in so far as the Christians were connected with the synagogue and visited it regularly every Sabbath. If we refer the utterance chiefly to Gentile Christians, of whom James assumes adherence to the synagogue, the same thing may be taken for granted also where Jewish Christians are concerned. Moreover, if we remember how Paul constantly visited the synagogues, and wherever one was to be found, or, in default of a proper building, a $\pi\rho o\sigma\epsilon\nu\chi\acute{\eta}$, *i.e.* an Israelitish place of prayer (as for example in Philippi, Acts xvi. 13), there began his apostolic activity, we are certainly justified in drawing a conclusion respecting Palestinian Jewish Christians, which at the same time corroborates the position that they stood in regular connection with the synagogues. This fact also follows indirectly from the expression of James and of the elders at Jerusalem, viz. that many thousands of believing Jews πάντες ζηλωταὶ τοῦ νόμου ὑπάρχουσι, etc., xxi. 20. If believers among the Jews in Palestine were so zealous for the law, if they felt themselves bound in conscience to adhere to the customs of their fathers, we must look upon it as a necessary consequence of such frame of mind that they should also hold closely to the synagogues, and should attend the service there on the Sabbath.

The organic connection of Jewish Christians with the synagogue, which must, in accordance with the facts before us, be regarded as a rule, is certainly not to be taken as a mere incidental phenomenon, a customary habit or arbitrary accommodation, but as a moral fact resting upon an internal necessity, having its foundation in the love of Jewish Christians to their nation, and in the adhesion of their religious consciousness to the old covenant. To mistake this would be to underrate the wide bearing of the fact. But lest we should over-estimate its importance, we must at once proceed to another consideration. Within Judaism we must distinguish not only the Rabbinical or Pharisaic tradition of the original canonical revelation, but also within the canon itself we have to distinguish the Levitical element from the prophetic (comp. Niedner, *Kirchengesch.*, S. 141), taking the latter not in a close but a wide sense as the living spiritual development of the theocracy. It lies in the nature of the

synagogue that on one side it should be specially
serviceable to the canonical element in distinction
from the Rabbinical, inasmuch as Moses and the
prophets were read. A Pharisee, in interpreting the
sections from the law and the prophets, might indeed
bring forward his traditions and Rabbinical propositions, but this was only a secondary and accom-
panying thing—the canon being the chief thing. On
the other hand, the synagogue, by virtue of the time
of its origin and of its original aim, was already allied
to the prophetic in distinction from the Levitical
element. With respect to this latter, we borrow the
words of Nitzsch, for it would be trouble ill-expended
to try to say differently what has already been said
so well and strikingly : " Those who were carried
away to the Chaboras, the exiles of the people of God,
were without sacrifice, which was eternally bound to
one place now a waste ; they were without the
beautiful services at Zion. Therefore they lifted up
their hands in prayer to the Lord, when the hour of
sacrifice had come ; worshipped with faces turned to
Jerusalem (Dan. vi. 11, ix. 21) ; appointed prayers
for themselves instead of sacrifice ; on the Sabbath
assembled before an Ezekiel (xx. 1, xxxiii. 31) to
hear the word ; and thus the synagogue arose among
them as a *Proseuche*, or as a common sacrifice of
prayer. Having returned to the Holy Land, they were
more and more deprived of the messages of the divine
word. So much the more were they obliged to keep to
the Holy Scriptures, to the reading and interpretation
of them (Neh. viii. 2–6) ; an exercise repeated every
week, which, joined to the sacrifice of prayer, became
from this time an economic yet legal and testamental
form of service for the numberless bodies of Jews

who were obliged to live in dispersion and pilgrimage. The synagogue is a temple service transformed into prayer, taken over into word-service, and in this condition either made manifold, or provisionally dissolved. A prophetic kind of common worship, as it were, it replaces, supersedes, antiquates the priestly office, and becomes the door to the new covenant and nation of God, which is destined, as a spiritual habitation, a spiritual temple, to replace the external and local at Jerusalem." [1] Bearing this in mind, we shall certainly not over-estimate that adherence of Jewish Christians to the synagogue which was the rule before the destruction of Jerusalem, in the sense of supposing that by it they were more closely bound up in Judaism than was consistent with Christianity. Because the synagogue occupies historically a providential intermediate place between the temple at Jerusalem and the Church of Christ, because in place of a worship for the senses, it gives a service resting essentially in word, which led the way to the worship of God in spirit and in truth, therefore the connection of Christians with the synagogue can by no means be regarded as a tacit denial of the Christian confession. On the contrary, the synagogue, as we see in the

---

[1] Karl Imm. Nitzsch, "protest. Beantwortung der Symbolik Dr. Möhler's," Abdruck aus dem *Theol. Stud. und Krit.* 1835, 204 f.—The investigation of Th. Harnack (*ante,* p. 117, etc.), who emphasizes the dependence of the synagogue upon the temple, the ceremonial, legal character of the synagogue worship and its Pharisaic tendency, is justified indeed when compared with the exaggerated estimate of the synagogue, and particularly with the derivation of the Christian service from it exclusively to be found in Vitringa ; but he appears to err in the opposite direction in overlooking the original and older form of the synagogue-institution, and in taking a predominant view of its later degeneracy after the destruction of Jerusalem.

history of the Apostle Paul, frequently served as a common ground on which believers confessing that Jesus was the Christ promised by Moses and the prophets, came forth to fight and to conquer.

We have already stated that the Christians were accustomed to celebrate the *Sabbath* with the Jews, and adhered to the usual hours of prayer in the temple; it is natural to suppose that they also kept the Mosaic festivals; and the supposition is confirmed, moreover, by the assembly at the Jewish feast of Pentecost (Acts ii. 1); and from the legal customs of the Judaists in the churches of Asia Minor, which were certainly false (Gal. iv. 10; Col. ii. 16), we may conclude that the Jewish Christian primitive Church, kept ἡμέρας καὶ μῆνας καὶ καιροὺς καὶ ἐνιαυτούς, *i.e.* Sabbaths and fast days, new moons, Mosaic festivals, and Sabbatical years in common with the whole nation. But concerning this Israelitish celebration of the Old Testament times of worship, we must not overlook what is of the New Testament, free and evangelical in respect of times. Believers held their religious assemblies daily (καθ' ἡμέραν) in the temple and in their houses (Acts ii. 46), the apostles preached every day (πᾶσαν ἡμέραν, v. 42) the gospel of Jesus Christ in the temple and in their houses; hence their life was one continual service (ἀεὶ σαββατίζειν), and the observance of the Sabbath fell into the background as an appanage to the existing custom. Furthermore, we must conclude, although positive testimony to this effect is wanting, that the domestic services of believers in Israel must, from early times, have commemorated also the day of the resurrection of Jesus—the *Sunday*. For the assumption that the keeping of Sunday is to be derived, not

from the Jewish Christian, but only from the Gentile
Christian churches (Neander, *Pflanzung und Leit.*
i. 273), cannot be proved. Mosheim has justly
remarked that the Gentile-Christian observance of
Sunday could not have spread *universally*, unless it
had its foundation in a custom of the primitive
Church; while Eusebius (*Kirchengesch.* iii. 27, p. 5)
testifies to the fact that Jewish Christians, so far as
they did not conform to the most extreme direction,
consecrated the Lord's day by service, *besides* observing
the Sabbath, which justifies a conclusion at least with
respect to very early times (comp. Schaff, *Kirchengesch.* i. 548; Th. Harnack, *ante,* S. 115 ff.).

We now return to the passage quoted above (Acts
xxi. 20 ff.), inasmuch as it is the strongest and most
comprehensive that we find in the book concerning
the Jewish-Christian tendency of the Palestinian
Christians, to one portion of whom we may with
justice attribute a Judaistic tendency. If the thousands of believing Jews were collectively ζηλωταὶ τοῦ
νόμου, and if they laid so great stress on ascertain-
ing whether Paul too did actually walk according to
the law, τὸν νόμον φυλάσσων, we get a deep insight
into the peculiar character which the piety of those
Palestinian Jews presented. With respect to its
form chiefly, but also to its substance, since form and
substance are from the nature of things inseparable in
such cases, it is essentially conditioned and limited by
Jewish modes of thought and transmitted Mosaic
piety. The more fully this was the case, the more
necessarily was the Christian element in them disturbed, distorted, and thrust into the background by
the Jewish element. The ceremonies, the religious
mechanism, and a legal, slavish, narrow-minded piety,

prevented the growth of the evangelical, free spirit. We have many historical indications of the existence of such Judaistic tendency (properly so called), especially in the bosom of the Church at Jerusalem; and it is noteworthy that James, the brother of the Lord, who presided over the Church there during the apostolic period, and died in the year 62—to whom therefore, together with the elders at Jerusalem, the above utterance (xxi. 20, etc.) is attributed—is represented by witnesses of a later time as a special representative, not indeed of a morbidly legal but of a distinctly Jewish-Christian mode of thought and action. We have a remarkable account of him by Hegesippus, a Jewish Christian of about the year 160, which Eusebius has preserved as a fragment in his *Church History* (ii. c. 23). It runs thus:—"James was holy from his mother's womb. He drank neither wine nor any intoxicating drink, and ate no flesh-meat. His head was not touched with a razor, he did not anoint himself with oil, nor did he make any use of the bath. He alone was permitted to enter into the sanctuary, for his garment was not of wool but of linen. He alone entered into the temple, and he was found prostrate on his knees praying for forgiveness for the nation, so that his knees became hard like those of a camel, because his knees were always bent when he was worshipping God and entreating forgiveness for the people. On account of his extraordinary righteousness, he was called the Just."

With regard to this description, the question arises: (1) What is the *meaning* of it, and of its single traits? (2) What are we to think of the historical truth and fidelity of the testimony? Respecting the former, the meaning of the description as a whole is doubtless this—that we must attribute to James a completely legal, particularly an ascetic piety (comp. Neander, *Pflanzung u. Leit.* ii. 560 ff.; Rothe, *Anfänge der Christl. Kirche*, i. 270; Schwegler, i. 140; Weitzel, *Passahfeier*, 159). The single traits may be separated into different groups. The persistent supplication for forgiveness for the people of Israel is manifestly a purely *Christian* feature; for the guilt for which he entreated forgiveness cannot fitly be found except in unbelief and the rejection of Jesus as the Messiah. This prayer had therefore its origin in faith,[1] and at the same time in a feeling of heart-felt pity, and in a genuine Christian character. It is a misapprehension on the part of Schwegler to say, without any limitation, that James appears in this account " as a true Jew throughout, a pattern of old Jewish piety " (i. 140). The *second* feature is the universal Old Testament piety, which may be inferred

[1] That which is related of Rabbi Zadok, a pupil of Schammai, is of a quite different character. He, having a presentiment of the destruction of the temple, is said to have fasted for forty years, by which means his health was irretrievably shattered (Grätz, *Gesch. der Juden von Untergang des jüdischen Staates bis zum Abschluss des Talmud*, 1853, S. 20). There is no word of the αἰτεῖσθαι ἄφεσιν τῷ λαῷ. — Ritschl, *Entstehung der altkatholischen Kirche*, 1857, S. 226, is of opinion that the tenor of the words points rather to the political deliverance of Israel. But in the parallel drawn of him (Luke iv. 18), the word ἄφεσις, by its connection with αἰχμάλωτοι and τεθραυσμένοι, has in itself the meaning of deliverance and exaltation ; while the other passage which he compares tells directly against his conception, since ἄφεσις ἁμαρτιῶν is undoubtedly a moral not a political advantage. But in the fragment from Hegesippus, ἄφεσις appears rather to have the well-known sense peculiar also to classical Greek, viz. remission of guilt, since *nothing* in the context, least of all the other characteristics mentioned by Hegesippus in his portraiture of James, leads to the purely political thought of deliverance from a servile yoke or from captivity.

chiefly from the impression that his mode of life and
action made upon the Israelites by whom he was
surrounded, on account of which he received the
honourable title, "ὁ δίκαιος, צַדִּיק." In the narrative
of Hegesippus he is seven times called δίκαιος, sometimes even ὁ δίκαιος absolutely, not James the just.
At that period of Israelitish history, the name denoted
those who kept the Mosaic commands blamelessly
(see Stanley, *Sermons and Essays*, p. 329). Some
features point, *thirdly*, to a life-long Nazarite vow,
viz. his consecration from his mother's womb, and his
abstinence from strong drink (comp. Luke i. 15), his
refusal to let a razor touch his head, and the fact of
his never having resorted to a bath-house (bathing
probably only in the open air, for βαλανεῖον is constantly employed by Eusebius of bathing establish-
ments). That James was a Nazarite is expressly
stated by Epiphanius, *Haer.* lxxviii. 14. *Fourthly*,
some things, which appear to be Essene, are
distinguished (comp. Gieseler, *Kirchengesch.* i. 1,
4 Aufl., S. 95, Anm. 4), viz. that James abstained from
the enjoyment of flesh-meat, and did not anoint
himself with oil. With respect to the latter, we have
at least the testimony of Josephus (*Bell. Jud.* ii. 8, 3),
that it was *Essene*, while the conclusion that abstinence
from flesh was an Essene custom rests only on
credible conjecture.[1] Finally, there are some traits
which point to priestly rank and prerogatives, viz.
the fact that James alone—that is, perhaps, the only
one of the Christians of that time—might set foot
in the temple; for this is manifestly the meaning of
τὰ ἅγια, which Hegesippus himself interchanges with
ναός, in distinction, on the one hand, from the fore-

[1] Comp. Schürer, *Lehrbuch der N.T. Zeitgeschichte*, 1874, S. 608.

court, which stood open to all Israelites, including also all Jewish Christians, and on the other hand, from the holy of holies, which the high priest alone might enter, and he but *once* in the year. His dress also agrees with access to the temple, since the priestly garments were of linen. We find indication of the priestly prerogatives of James again, but exaggerated and amplified in Epiphanius, who in his *Panarion* (xxix. 28, 4th ed.; Öhler, ii. 1, S. 229) substitutes τὰ ἅγια τῶν ἁγίων for ἅγια, and asserts that it was permitted to James once a year to enter the holy of holies, at which time he also wore the πέταλον, the diadem of the high priest. Schwegler, far from thinking of legendary embellishment here, is uncritical enough to take this statement for granted without examination, and to treat the words of Epiphanius as an authentic explanation of the narrative of Hegesippus, although he lived a century and a half later. Carrying the uncritical faculty to its farthest point, he even outvies an Epiphanius. For while the latter, in two passages copied by Schwegler himself, limits himself to the statement that James was permitted *once* a year to enter the holy of holies, our critic has no hesitation in allowing him to enter the holy of holies as often as he takes the fancy (i. 137, Anm., i. 142). Epiphanius also takes the liberty of making some wild additions to the traits of strict asceticism, viz. χιτώνιον δεύτερον οὐκ ἐνεδύσατο καὶ τελευτᾷ παρθένος γεγονώς (*Haer.* lxxviii. 13). The use of only one garment until it fell completely asunder was a custom of the Essenes, as Josephus testifies (*De bello Judaico*, ii. 8, 4). Epiphanius seems to have borrowed virginity or celibacy from *his own* time, the flourishing period of monachism, and to have transferred it back to the time of the apostles, whereas Hegesippus is completely silent respecting it. But the casual remark of the Apostle Paul (1 Cor. ix. 5) makes it probable that James, the brother of the Lord, was married.

The latter additions have already brought us to the second question, respecting the *historical truth* of the description given. There can be no question among the thoughtful that Epiphanius gives the description of Hegesippus, with the exaggeration and embellishment of tradition.[1] But we shall not, therefore, reject the whole thing bodily, and on account of the legendary character of the later narrative, throw doubt on the entire narration of the earlier writer. We shall confine ourselves to the account of Hegesippus, keeping the separate portions apart, as above. No objection has been raised on any side to the historical fidelity of those traits which we have designated as genuine and Christian, relatively also as true Old Testament or universally Israelitish ones. We may therefore, without further proof, accept them as historically accredited.[2] On the other hand, doubts exist with respect to such features as we have specified as Nazarite, Essene, and priestly. To begin with the last, we certainly should have a right to question the historical truth of that

---

[1] With nice tact, Ritschl, *Entstehung der altkatholischen Kirche*, 1857, S. 226, Anm. 1, sharply discriminated the later colouring of Epiphanius from the original description of Hegesippus.

[2] We leave out of consideration the view refuted on p. 60, viz. that perseverance in supplication for the people of Israel can scarcely be called a peculiarly Christian trait (Ritschl, a. a. O. 226); nor can we believe there is any foundation for the same scholar's assertion, that the account of Hegesippus concerning what took place at the martyrdom of James was not conceived from a definitely Christian standpoint.

account, if the meaning were that James performed sacrifice and similar offices in the temple. The personal offering of propitiatory sacrifice on his part would at least be equivalent to an actual denial of the propitiation accomplished by Christ. But of this no word is to be found in Hegesippus; at most Epiphanius, with his ἱερατεύειν κατὰ τὴν παλαιὰν ἱερωσύνην (*Haer.* xxix. 4), might be so understood. But the original narrator says only this much : James, who was clad not in woollen but in linen (priestly) garments, had permission to enter the sanctuary, evidently, from the connection, to pray there.[1] Even supposing that he was permitted to enter not only into the fore-court, but into the sanctuary itself, we can scarcely maintain that it would be inconsistent with faith in Jesus as the Redeemer, if He actually made use of this privilege in order to pray in the temple, to pray on His knees for His people. The question is only whether it is conceivable that he possessed such a privilege ? It was only possible if he belonged to a Levitical, especially a priestly family, but the genealogy of Jesus in the Gospels makes this circumstance improbable. This trait is therefore to be regarded as legendary and unhistorical. But that James had taken upon himself Nazarite vows to a large extent, cannot rightly be disputed, for the reason that it was James himself who, with the elders of Jerusalem, recommended to the Apostle Paul participation in a Nazarite vow of

---

[1] Already in olden time the matter was thus explained :—A manuscript of the translation of Eusebius by Rufinus (in Rheims) makes to the original, which runs thus : τούτῳ μόνῳ ἐξῆν εἰς τὰ ἅγια εἰσιέναι, the addition, *orandi, non sacrificandi causa* (Routh, *Reliquiæ sacræ,* ii. 214).

some who were without doubt likewise Christians
(Acts xxi. 23 et seq., comp. ver. 18 et seq.).　Consequently the only remaining portion of the above
description is that which, with Gieseler, we have
denominated *Essene.*　We have the less foundation for
upholding the historical truth of these few remarkable traits, since about a century intervenes between
the death of James and the time in which Hegesippus wrote, and since the latter, as Eusebius himself testifies, borrowed much ὡσὰν ἐξ Ἰουδαϊκῆς
ἀγράφου παραδόσεως (*K. Gesch.* iv. 22, § 8).　If
already in apostolic times the reputation of James
was used and greatly exaggerated by the Judaists
for their own ends, there is the more probability in
the supposition that after the martyrdom of the
revered teacher, the Ebionite party embellished his
portrait with legendary material, according to their
own taste, and surrounded him with a halo of
glory.

In any case, we may regard it as an assumed
historical fact that James preserved the most intimate life-relations with Judaism, since, though a
believing Christian, he still remained an Israelite with
his whole soul, and with a decided belief in Jesus
and confession of Him, yet fully represented Jewish
legality in his life, for which reason he was equally
honoured by believing and unbelieving Jews to the
end of his life (Rothe, *Anf.* 270; Lange, *Gesch.
d. K.* ii. 398 f.; Schaff, *ante,* 385 f.).　We go a
step further, and say that not for himself alone did
he remain with his whole heart an Israelite though
truly confessing Jesus Christ, but he likewise bore
his whole nation on his heart, persevering un-
weariedly in intercession, and in work for the salva-

tion of Israel. The judgment of an angry God on the Jewish nation, and the destruction of Jerusalem, do in fact come to pass only after the rejection of *his* testimony and after his martyrdom, but also, as it appears, soon after his death. We must acknowledge that a just feeling of his importance in relation to Israel lay in the surname Ὠβλίας, more correctly Ὠβλίαμ, עֹפֶל עָם, that is, a wall of protection, a fence of protection for the nation,[1] which according to the account of Hegesippus (in Eusebius, *K. G.* ii. 23), and of Epiphanius (*Haer.* 78), he doubtless received from Jewish-Christians. For as James is *unus pro multis*, his personality serves as a confirmation of the fact drawn from other sources, that the Palestinian Jewish-Christians, during the period of which we treat, continued in religious communion with Israel, and that their piety had in many respects an Old Testament form—a Jewish colouring.

The result of our examination concerning what was peculiar to the Jewish-Christian churches of apostolic times with respect to the direct religious

---

[1] The name "Wall of protection" reminds us of the similar title of honour "Pillars" (Gal. ii. 9), στύλοι εἶναι δοκοῦντες. But the "Protecting fence" must not, like the "Pillars," be referred to believers, but to the whole of the Israelitish nation, in favour of whom James, as long as he lived, seemed to avert the threatened ruin. Here let us compare the instructive words of Eusebius (*Kirchengesch.* iii. 7, § 8 f.), where he says of James, as well as of the other apostles and disciples of Jesus that still dwelt in Jerusalem before the outbreak of the war: Ἔτι τῷ βίῳ περιόντες, καὶ ἐπ᾽ αὐτῆς τῆς Ἱεροσολύμων πόλεως τὰς διατριβὰς ποιούμενοι, ἕρκος ὥσπερ ὀχυρώτατον παρέμενον τῷ τόπῳ· τῆς θείας ἐπισκοπῆς εἰσέτι τότε μακροθυμούσης, εἰ ἄρα ποτὲ δυνηθεῖεν ἐφ᾽ οἷς ἔδρασαν μετανοήσαντες, συγγνώμης καὶ σωτηρίας τυχεῖν. That there is ground for the conjecture of Wieseler, who (*Chronol. des Ap. Zeitalters*, S. 273) is disposed to understand James by the κατέχων (2 Thess. ii. 7), we cannot but seriously doubt.

life may be briefly summed up thus: Among them are certainly to be found the germs of the later Christian worship, in community of doctrine, of breaking of bread, and of prayer. But this peculiarly Christian element existed only in concealment, in the quiet retirement of believers among themselves, in the closer circle of domestic worship. At the same time their piety, — as manifested in attachment to the temple and the synagogue, in the observance of hours of prayer, of the Sabbath, and of the Old Testament feasts, and in many cases in zeal for the Mosaic law and in striving after legal righteousness,— was clothed in the forms of Israelite observances. But this fact is a phenomenon not only excusable, easily understood, and very natural, but it has also a moral justification. The very recognition of the truth that the gospel is designed for all nations, obliges us to approve a form of subjective Christianity such as corresponded to the Israelitish nationality. Before the Jews as a nation should reject the gospel with will and consent, *it was necessary* that the Christianity of those Jews who had become believers should express itself definitely respecting the manners and customs of Israel.

(B.) *The relation of Jewish Christians to the Israelite people: their social and domestic life.*

The connection in which the subject stands leads naturally to the relation of the believers of Israel towards their unbelieving fellow-countrymen, as well as to the place which the latter occupied in opposition to them. If we consult the Acts on this point, the information we gain is complete only with respect

to the disposition which animated the nation and its
heads towards believers. We are told more than
once that owing to events connected with the Church
" fear came upon every soul " (ii. 43): ἐγένετο πάσῃ
ψυχῇ φόβος, and v. 11: ἐγένετο φόβος μέγας ἐφ᾽
ὅλην τὴν ἐκκλησίαν καὶ ἐπὶ πάντας τοὺς ἀκούοντας
ταῦτα. In the latter passage the context puts it
beyond doubt that the intention is to describe the
impression made by the divine chastisement of the
hypocritical and deceptive dealing of Ananias and
Sapphira which came about through the instrumentality of Peter, not only on the Church itself, but also
on all those outside the Church to whose ears the
occurrence might be carried; whereas the former
passage treats of the impression which the feast of
Pentecost itself made even upon the unconverted,—a
holy fear overcame them. But the consequence of
this impression is described in various ways. ·

At one time, for example, the people run together
to the apostles, eagerly pressing round them and
greatly wondering; another time the people, out of
reverence, hold themselves at a respectful distance
from them (comp. iii. 10, etc., with v. 11 and
especially 13).[1]   Moreover the two accounts are not

<hr>

[1] With respect to the latter passage, we must reject Baur's
strange explanation, although given out as the only correct one.
According to it, οἱ λοιποί includes, besides the apostles, all Christians,
so that even these, moved with reverential timidity, held themselves
at a certain distance from the apostles (*Paulus*, 2 Aufl. i. 27 f.). This
conception is only possible if we refer πάντες (ver. 12) exclusively to
the apostles, which is neither necessary nor in keeping with the
context. On the contrary, it is far more natural, keeping to the
simple sense of the words, to refer πάντες to all Christians, including
the apostles, and on the other hand, to understand οἱ λοιποί (ver.
13) as well as λαός of the parallel clause, of non-Christians. It does
not consist with the unanimity of believers, with the brotherly

inconsistent one with another. On the contrary, it is easy to conceive that sometimes one and sometimes the other might be the case, according to circumstances. Here it behoves us also to observe that the captain of the guard of the temple, whose duty it was to summon the apostles before the Sanhedrim, brought them out from the fore-court of the temple, not with violence, but gently, because he and his officers feared the people; they feared lest they should be stoned if they were to do the apostles an injury (v. 26). But in all these cases the language concerns the apostles alone, with respect to the impression which their actions made upon the people and the behaviour of the inhabitants of Jerusalem towards them. The apostles, on their side, taught and exhorted the people and conferred benefits, healing many (*vid.* ii. 14–40, iii. 12 et seq., v. 20 f., and ii. 2 et seq., v. 15).

But the remark made in Acts ii. 47, viz. "they had favour with all the people," extends to *all believers.* Baur questions the historical truth of this utterance, because it is inconsistent with the persecution of the Christians which broke out not long after. Hence he infers that this conception of the relation of the Church to the people can only belong to embellishing tradition (*Paulus*, 2 Aufl. i. 35 ff.). But in the first place, this presupposes, a thing which is important to the conclusion, that the persecution followed

<hr>

fellowship of Christians elsewhere depicted in the Acts, that such a gulf should have existed between the apostles on the one hand, and the remaining churches on the other hand, as the explanation of Baur presupposes. For this reason Zeller, as well as Overbeck, has decided against Baur, and in favour of the usual interpretation (Zeller, *Apost-lgesch.* 125, Anm. 1 ; Overbeck, *Kurze Erklärung*, S. 71, etc.).

immediately upon the period which the description had in view; whereas the seven first chapters of the Acts give no exact chronological determination, and probably include several years at least. It is therefore quite conceivable that many years intervened between that time of popular favour and the period of the first hostility. It is well known that the disposition of the people can change very considerably in the course of a few years. But even granting that the former description and the opposition afterwards recorded are closely connected in point of time, a rapid change of popular favour is nothing very improbable. We have therefore no reason to contest the historical truth of that first account, according to which the Christian Church in the beginning was in high favour with the whole population of Jerusalem; a circumstance which is the less improbable in itself, since believers, as we have seen, attached themselves in all love and reverence to the theocratic institutions of the old Covenant, while that which was distinctive and new in their faith, worship, and life had not been yet manifested.

The Christians, who had not yet even a distinctive name among the people, might appear to the other Israelites only as one of the many religio - social parties which existed at that time in the nation of Israel, without prejudice to the national and theocratic unity of the nation. Setting aside the Essenes, who led an ascetic existence separate from the public national life, the Israelitish nation, at least the influential and leading men of it, were divided in the time of Jesus and the apostles into Pharisees and Sadducees. The disciples of Jesus may be regarded as a similar group, closely keeping together, but by no means exclusively sectarian like the Essenes. In their conscientious observance of the Mosaic law and devout adherence to the sacred hope of Israel, we may discern a certain affinity with the Pharisaic party ; we may even look upon them as a modern variety of the Pharisees. They cannot in any case have been regarded as Sadducees.[1] Besides these two great parties, there were always in Israel separate societies distinguished by peculiar religious and social customs and usages; for example, the Rechabites, who even in the apostolic age had not yet died out, since at the martyrdom of James the Just, one of them called to his murderers : " Forbear ! what are you doing ? he is praying for us, the just one! "[2] It is possible that the Christians may have been looked upon as a peculiarly religious family of this nature, whose moral and social attitude made a favourable impression in many respects ; and was even popular for a time ($\check{\epsilon}\chi ov\tau\epsilon\varsigma\ \chi\acute{\alpha}\rho\iota v\ \pi\rho\grave{o}\varsigma\ \check{o}\lambda ov\ \tau\grave{o}v\ \lambda a\acute{o}v$, Acts ii. 47).

In agreement with the above description, is the account that the first hostilities against the apostles proceeded from the Sadducean party (iv. 1, etc., v. 17, etc.). Although, in the first of these passages, the priests are named also, and in the second the high priest; yet it is clear from the tenor of both, and especially from the reason adduced in the former, viz. dislike to the preaching of the resurrection of Jesus, that Luke finds the initial and impelling motive of the whole proceeding among the Sadducees. He gives it to be understood, by his silence, that the

---

[1] Comp. Schürer, *Lehrbuch des N. T. Zeitgeschichte*, p. 423 ff., respecting Pharisees and Sadducees, 599 ff. the Essenes.

[2] Hegesippus, *apud* Eusebius, *K. Geschichte*, ii. c. 23, § 17.

Pharisaic party in the beginning left the Christian Church unmolested, and by his account of the rising up of the Rabbi Gamaliel I. in the Sanhedrim (v. 34, etc.), he draws special attention to the milder disposition of the Pharisees; finally (xv. 5), he even mentions believers among the Pharisees. This contrast between the Sadducean and the Pharisaic party, with respect to the estimation in which they held the disciples of Jesus and the way in which they acted towards them, is said indeed to be unhistorical, but for what reason! Because it is only too natural to suppose that the discourses of the apostles, and their witness to the resurrection of Jesus, should find no more decided opponents than the Sadducees, the well-known deniers of the doctrine of the resurrection; therefore the remark (iv. 2) has quite the appearance of an *à priori* combination (Baur, *Paulus*, 2 Aufl. i. p. 40). Certainly a most convincing kind of criticism, which refuses to recognise a statement as actual and historical, merely because by virtue of circumstances otherwise known, it is not only intrinsically possible, but is even probable.

More plausible is the thought which Zeller puts into the scale, viz., shortly before this event, on occasion of the process against Jesus, it was the Pharisees who specially urged His condemnation; His reformatory campaign being particularly directed against that party. It is therefore not credible that the position of the parties should have been reversed immediately afterwards, the Sadducees and not the Pharisees appearing as the opponents of the Christians (Zeller, *Ap. Gesch.* p. 138). How then does the matter stand? It is an indubitable fact that during the public ministry of Jesus, it is the Pharisees who first raise doubts respecting His conduct (Matt. ix. 11) ; even devising murderous plans against Him (Matt. xii. 14), and tempting Him with questions : for example, Matt. xix. 3. But if we look at the actual treatment of Jesus, the fact stands out that from his last entrance into Jerusalem (Matt. xxi., etc., and the parallel passages in Mark xi., etc. ; Luke xix. 29, etc.) it is the official rulers of the people who take the lead, the high priests and scribes and elders, — that is, the reigning high priest and the Sanhedrim of which he was the president and whose fellow-members were the elders and those versed in the law ($\gamma\rho\alpha\mu\mu\alpha\tau\epsilon\hat{i}\varsigma$), that is, official assessors. It was the high priests and scribes who protested against the praises of the children at the solemn entry of Jesus (Matt. xxi. 15), and called Him to account for the purging of the temple (ver. 23, etc., and parallel passages) ; and these same heads of the people contrive His overthrow (Mark xi. 18, xii. 12 ; Luke xix. 47, xx. 19). Matthew alone, after Jesus has narrated the parable of the wicked vine-dressers, adds to the high priests whom he names in the first passage, the Pharisees. Afterwards, it is certainly Pharisees who take counsel how they may lay snares for Jesus in word and in questions of doctrine, and they carry out their purpose in league with the Herodians (Matt. xxii. 15, with respect to paying tribute to Cæsar). A Pharisee asks him the question concerning the greatest commandment (xxii. 34), but the Sadducees also put an artful question to Jesus respecting the woman who had seven brothers as husbands in succession (Matt. xxii. 23, etc.). Finally, the high priests, scribes, and elders were present at the secret conference which took place in the court of the dwelling of Caiaphas where it was finally determined to take Jesus by subtilty and to kill Him (Matt. xxvi. 3, comp. the parallel passages). Judas covenanted with the high priests to deliver Jesus into their hands (ver. 14, etc.). Luke alone names the captains (the guard of the temple) (xxii. 4). The armed band which takes Jesus prisoner is sent by the official rulers (Mark xiv. 43, high priests, scribes and elders); John alone speaks of Pharisees also (xviii. 3). The first trial takes place before the high priest Caiaphas, the scribes and the elders (Matt. xxvi. 57); these deliver Jesus, after they have condemned Him, to the governor Pontius Pilate (Matt. xxvii. 1, etc.), before whom they bring the accusation against Him (Matt. xxvii. 12, etc.; Mark xv. 3). Among those who mocked the Crucified One, chief priests, scribes, and elders stand out prominently (Matt. xxvii. 41, etc.). After His burial it is the chief priests also, together with the Pharisees, who urge that a military watch should be placed at His grave (Matt. xxvii. 62, etc.). Here the Pharisees appear again, for the first time with the determination to hold Him fast. But elsewhere in all the hostile proceedings against Jesus during His passion, we find only the high priest with the Sanhedrim,—that is, the official, theocratic representatives of Israel, taking an active part. But the high priests, who at that time stood at the head, belonged to the party of the Sadducees,[1] while Sadducees as well as Pharisees sat in

---

[1] Josephus, *Altertümer*, xviii. 1, § 4; πρῶτοι τοῖς ἀξιώμασι (xx. 9, § 1). It is here shown that Ananus (Hannas), the son of Hannas (John xviii. et seq.), living in the time of James, and holding the office of high priest, and who had five sons filling the same office, belonged to the *Sadducees*. This, however, to judge from the context,

the Sanhedrim. Hence we see that in the persecution of Jesus, the high priests with the chief council were active as the legal heads of the people, while the Pharisees stood in the background plotting and goading them on.

When, therefore, in the apostolic time, after the healing of the cripple and somewhat later, the "priests," together with the captain of the temple (Acts iv. 1, etc.), or the "high priest" (v. 17, etc.), proceeded against the apostles, it is only a repetition in the apostle's case of what had already happened to Jesus. The one new feature in the persecution is that now, because the apostles were chiefly "witnesses of the resurrection of Jesus" (Acts i. 22), the Sadducees appear as instigators, zealous for action (iv. 1, v. 17), while in the proceedings against Jesus, the Pharisees, because of their antipathy to Him and to His modes of thought and teaching so opposed to their own, were most zealous in the background. A contradiction tending to make Luke's account of the interference of the high priest in concert with the Sadducees less credible does not therefore exist.[1]

is by no means "something strange" (Zeller, *Ap. Gesch.* 139), or an exception to the rule, but only serves to make his acts of violence psychologically intelligible.

[1] Zeller (*Ap. Gesch.* 140) is the more convinced that this account is unhistorical, since it may be explained by the tendency of the Acts to make the Christians appear as a fraction of orthodox Judaism, who were persecuted only by such as had fallen away from true Judaism: that is, by the Sadducees. He here overlooks two things: 1. The undeniable fact that the apostles (for they alone, not Christians in general, are referred to in the Acts) declared no truth more constantly and emphatically than the resurrection of Jesus the Crucified One; if this had not stirred up the Sadducees to contradiction and opposition, it would have been quite inexplicable. 2. The fact, also quite

On the other hand, it is remarkable that when the Pharisaic party afterwards rose against the Christians, the persecution extended to the whole Church; while the Pharisees, as the national party, were able at the same time to stir up the Israelite nation, which had quietly looked on at the interference of the Sanhedrim, to fanatical hatred against the Christians (Acts vi. 12, comp. 1 Thess. ii. 14, etc.).[1] Notwithstanding this, we still find, even here, a trace of the not quite extinct popular favour and love towards

credible, that the believers of the primitive Christian Church unconsciously and involuntarily attached themselves to Judaism in the closest manner,—a circumstance which must in the nature of things have exercised a softening influence on the mind of the Pharisees, and have seemed to them to be sympathetic. In other places, Zeller frequently lays emphasis on the latter fact, but in the discussion in question he seems to have left it completely out of sight.

[1] That Gamaliel I., the grandson of the renowned Hillel, an illustrious member of the Pharisaic party, exhorted to moderation on occasion of the second persecution against the apostles, and recommended a temporary delay (Acts v. 34–39), is regarded by Baur as unhistorical (*Paulus*, 2 Aufl. i. 41 f.), and after him by Zeller (*Ap. Geschichte*, 134 ff.) and Overbeck (*Erklärung der Ap. Gesch.*, p. 80 f.). This counsel, the last categorically asserts, "can belong only to tradition." The principal ground on which Baur relies is the fact that Saul, the most violent persecutor of the Christian Church, was at that very time trained up in the school of Gamaliel and moulded after his principles. Against this there are two considerations : first, that among pupils there are frequently hotheads to be found, who draw certain conclusions from the ideas of the master more rapidly than he did himself, and turn the received principles into deeds more resolutely than the teacher. The other point is the fact that the appearance of Stephen indicates a certain change which took place in the consciousness of the Church. Even if he did not take part against the law and the temple worship, as he was accused of doing, yet he recognised in the appearance of Christ a new and higher revelation of God ; and by this means might have aroused in zealous scholars of a Pharisaic master a lively apprehension for the authority of the law and the sanctity of the temple, and have kindled a fanatic rage against the Christians—a frame of mind certainly not in accord with the thoughtful spirit of Gamaliel.

the Christians, in the circumstance that "devout men carried Stephen to his burial, and made great lamentation over him" (viii. 2); inasmuch as ἄνδρες εὐλαβεῖς are not to be understood as Christians, whom Luke continually calls πιστεύοντες, μαθηταί, ἀδελφοί, and the like.[1] After what has been said, we think we may assume that, as a rule, peaceful relations, in many cases even friendly intercourse, existed between the believing Israelites and the rest of the people from the beginning and lasted many years, so that the hostilities of the Sadducean priestly party to the apostles were not able to disturb the relation as a whole. Even the persecution, which broke out about the year 37 against the Christian Church, which seems to have originated with the Pharisees, and by which the Church was scattered and for the most part driven out of the

---

[1] Some expositors—for example, Heinrichs (*Acta App. illustr.* 1806), Isaac da Costa (*Die Ap. Geschichte f. Christl. u. Gem.*, explained and translated from the Dutch by Reifert, 1860, S. 190), and Overbeck (*de Wette*, 4 Aufl. S. 117)—understand ἄνδρες εὐλαβεῖς of Christians. This contradicts the established use of language in the book. The passage, xxii. 12, forms the only exception, and this is explained by the circumstance that Paul there speaks before the Jewish nation, and therefore gives to Ananias of Damascus and one of his hearers an inoffensive neutral name, as it were. He uses, however, even in that connection, the abstract term αὕτη ἡ ὁδός (ver. 4) for Christianity, calling Ananias εὐλαβής, but adding in the same breath, κατὰ τὸν νόμον. Overbeck has therefore no reason to appeal to that passage against the constant use of language. Renan thinks that εὐλαβεῖς refers to proselytes (*Les Apôtres*, 1867, p. 118), to whom, indeed, εὐλαβεῖς, εὐσεβεῖς, φοβούμενοι τὸν θεόν are regularly applied. It is possible that Luke had here in his mind proselytes from Judaism. The εὐλαβεῖς always points to the fact of their being men in whom piety and the fear of God outweighed all fear of man and scrupulous considerations, so that they were not afraid to give honourable burial to one who had been stoned as a blasphemer of God.

capital,[1] only seems to have disturbed the peace for a time; for although, after the death of Stephen, the brethren, with the exception of the apostles, fled from Jerusalem, yet we learn (ix. 31) that "the Church had rest throughout all Judea, and Galilee, and Samaria." Indeed, the very fact that Herod Agrippa I., on occasion of the execution of the Apostle James, made the discovery that it pleased the Jews (xii. 3), presupposes that there were still among the people many who were hostile to the Christians. We may therefore suppose that the latter on their side must also have been more reserved in their intercourse with other Israelites. Nevertheless, at a much later period, shortly before the Jewish war, the head of the Christian churches at Jerusalem—James, the brother of the Lord—stood, according to the testimony of Hegesippus, in such undivided esteem and honour with the whole nation, that the surname of "the just" was given to him; and that the Jews, especially the Pharisees and scribes, treated him as one of themselves, and even expected foreign guests at their feasts to put ready faith in his testimony (Eusebius, ii. 23). Add to this the circumstance that Josephus in the genuine text of his works never speaks of the Christians as a society, the only

---

[1] To assume that the account (viii. 1) πάντες δὲ διεσπάρησαν means nothing more than that a gathering of the Church, which took place at the exact hour when Stephen was stoned, had been dispersed (Baumgarten, i. 158), is absolutely inconsistent with the connection of the words, κατὰ τὰς χώρας τῆς Ἰουδαίας, etc. According to Baumgarten, this dispersion is only the indirect consequence; but the text represents it as the direct result of the persecution which had broken out. That πάντες διεσπάρησαν is not meant in the strict sense of the words, but is used hyperbolically, is almost self-evident; for soon after we again meet with disciples (ix. 26, etc.): that is, members of the Church in Jerusalem.

reason for which must be that he regards them positively as Jews; or, looking upon them as an insignificant party in the Jewish nation, and without a future, intentionally avoids making any allusion to them; so that we may with certainty assume that in the course of the apostolic times, at least until the destruction of Jerusalem was at hand, the relation was on the whole, excepting a few occurrences, peaceable and harmonious, and that there was unrestrained intercourse between the Jewish Christians of Palestine and their unbelieving countrymen.

To understand clearly the state of the consciousness of the Christians themselves, and the relation in which they on their side placed themselves with regard to the Jews, we must bear in mind what has already been said. While they believed in Jesus as the Christ, they were far from wishing to separate themselves from the nation of Israel, as the holy and peculiar people of God to whom the promises were given, and from the theocratic national Church. They were doubtless conscious of being saved from this "untoward generation" (Acts ii. 40), that is, of being separated by their conversion from fellowship with sinners, *i.e.* for the salvation of their souls and the happiness of their lives; for this reason they desired still to remain associates of the people of God (ii. 39, iii. 25). It is certainly not without significance that the elders at Jerusalem regarded the thousands of believers as still belonging to the Jews: πόσαι μυριάδες εἰσὶν ἐν τοῖς Ἰουδαίοις τῶν πεπιστευκότων (xxi. 20); while the believing Gentiles, according to an earlier utterance of the same James, who is doubtless the speaker in the passage quoted above, separated themselves by the fact of their conversion from the Gentiles and turned to God : τοῖς ἀπὸ τῶν ἐθνῶν ἐπιστρέφουσιν ἐπὶ τὸν θεόν (xv. 19). The Jewish Christians were determined to remain in the tabernacle of David, which had been raised up again by the grace of God (xv. 16, comp. Amos ix. 11), and only hoped that all Israel, who were already in possession of the knowledge and covenant-relation of the true God, would soon turn and believe in Him whom God had raised up as His servant and anointed, for the salvation of all. Niedner, in his peculiar manner, thus expresses it, " The religious standpoint of the Palestinian apostles included also the aim which had, in fact, never been relinquished, of re-establishing a universal Christian - Messianic Jewish Church " (*Kirchengeschichte*, p. 141).

Believers among the Hebrews naturally, indeed, felt themselves much more closely related and bound to the believers among their fellow-countrymen than to unbelievers in the nation. The former were to them the ἴδιοι, their own people, those immediately belonging to them (Acts iv. 23): believers among themselves were brethren (i. 15, 16, ix. 30, xi. 1, xii. 17). But this close, confidential relation of believers to one another by no means excluded friendly intercourse with such Jews as did not believe in Jesus, but were yet regarded as members of *one* nation, as associates of the same theocracy, and even as future co-heirs of the same Messianic salvation. The relation, indeed, did not always remain the same. By degrees it became essentially different, just as the inner development of Christian consciousness in believers and their external conditions were moulded. Such external conditions were principally

the hardening of the Jews against the gospel, and
the excitement, impatience, and fanatical hostility on
the part of the people connected with it, which
towards the end of that period, when Zealotism was at
its height, was also roused against believers in Palestine, and, to judge from the Epistle to the Hebrews,
was still increasing (respecting the Epistle to the
Hebrews, comp. Bleek, *Comm.* i. 58 ff.). The inner
development of Christian consciousness itself prepared
the severance of companionship between the believing
Israelites and their compatriots, inasmuch as believers
learned to consider themselves the holy people, the
peculiar people (1 Pet. ii. 9), as the true Israel in
opposition to that Israel which rejected its Messiah
(comp. Rothe, p. 283).

If we turn to a consideration of the social
and domestic life of Christians in their relation
to one another, we must begin by saying that
this subject is one of those respecting which it is
easier to ask than to answer. In order to avoid
the doubtful advantage of history that has been
invented and fabricated, viz. fable, we must content
ourselves with the few facts which arise out of
existing sources.

One thing is indeed clear, namely, that believers
in very early times attached themselves to one another
with great warmth and sincerity. This appears
already from the circumstance that the κοινωνία,
brotherly fellowship among themselves, is named as
one of their most valuable blessings, which the newly-
converted cherished with all fidelity (comp. page 45,
etc.). Immediately afterwards, we hear of all that
believed being together (ver. 44), that they ἦσαν ἐπὶ τὸ
αὐτό, that is, that they met as often as possible (some-

times in the temple, sometimes in houses) in order to enjoy intercourse with one another,[1] for they were *one* heart and *one* soul (iv. 32). If the sentiment so beautifully expressed by Löhe is true for all time, namely, that "conversion to the Lord makes the solitary social," it was so in a high degree among the members of the apostolic primitive Church.

One consequence of this loving adherence, by virtue of a common belief in the Redeemer, and of the hope entertained by all of His coming again in glory, was the so-called *community of goods*. There are two questions to be decided if we wish to arrive at a clear understanding of the actual condition of things, on the basis of the account contained in the Acts: *first*, are we to understand an absolutely complete, universal community of goods? *second*, was it a custom that was legally binding, a statutory arrangement; or was it altogether voluntary? We begin with the second question. That the apostolic community of goods was not a binding law of the association, as among the Essenes,—who put their possessions together and recognised only common property, and legally imposed on every new disciple the renunciation of his fortune for the good of the order (Josephus, *Jewish Wars*, ii. 8, § 3),—but a matter of free-will, is now almost universally acknowledged, especially when the words of Peter (v. 4), that Ananias was free to retain his property as well as his house (xii. 12), are taken into account. Even Zeller (*Ap. Geschichte*, 122) and Meyer-Wendt (*Comm.*, 5 Aufl. S. 87 ff.[2])

---

[1] Renan (*Apôtres*, 1867, p. 62) very strangely understands this of dwelling in only one part of Jerusalem.

[2] Overbeck alone (*de Wette*, 4 Aufl. S. 47) denies the voluntariness of the act, but without a convincing reason.

admit it. The more widely do opinions still differ with respect to the first question. As a matter of fact we may conclude with certainty,— from the circumstance that (in Acts xii. 12) Mary, the mother of John Mark, is mentioned as the owner of a house, and because prominence is given to the conduct of Barnabas in presenting to the Church the produce of his land, as something universally praiseworthy (iv. 36, etc.),—that an absolute universal community of goods, in which individuals renounced all personal proprietorship, did not actually exist. It is nevertheless maintained that isolated utterances have so general an aspect (for example, ii. 44, iv. 32, 34) that they *must* be understood of full community of possessions. An express contradiction in the Acts itself is thus assumed between these summary statements on the one hand, representing an actual community of goods, which are declared to be an unhistorical or traditional exaggeration, and between certain concrete facts, on the other hand, which efface that universality (Baur, *Paulus*, i. 39 : Zeller, *Apostelgeschichte*, p. 122 f. ; Overbeck, 47). Others, as Meyer (*Comm.*) and Schneckenburger (*Stud. u. Krit.* 1855, 514 ff., 537), are also in favour of a universal and complete community of goods, but regard it as historically true. It appears to us, however, partly that the words as they there stand have not been accurately enough examined, partly that they have been judged by a standard not quite fair and reasonable. To begin with the latter objection, it is not customary, where authors are concerned, to accuse them at once of contradictions and of being unhistorical in character, if single statements respecting concrete facts do not fully agree with a description

which is of a universal tendency. The more usual
method is to interpret the indefinite by the definite ;
a course which is the more natural in this case,
since two of the universal descriptions stand in
closest connection with a single fact which is said
to contradict the summary account (iv. 32, 34 f.,
comp. 36 f.). It must be conceded that the statements, ii. 44 f., iv. 32, 34, merely taken by themselves
and understood literally, are at variance with other
passages, for example, the laudatory singling out of
Barnabas and his generosity (iv. 36 f.). But since
the apparently contradictory passages proceed from
one and the same historian, we are compelled to
explain the one by the other. And here, in fact, we
need no excuse if we limit the apparent universality
of the statements in question by the individual
accounts that stand in the same connection. The
very words of that description give us a right to do
this. There is a disposition to lay absolute weight
on all expressions of universality which are made use
of in the descriptions in question, such as πάντες,
ἄπαντα, ὅσοι ; while scarcely a glance is vouchsafed
to the remaining words, and the context fails to
receive the consideration which it deserves. The
connection, for instance, in which passages such as
ii. 44 and iv. 32 stand with 34, etc., gives them a
relation showing that the intention is to depict the *disposition* of believers, their union, disinterestedness, and
brotherly love ; in proof of which disposition the
incident is mentioned that οὐδὲ εἷς τι τῶν ὑπαρχόντων
αὐτῷ ἔλεγεν ἴδιον εἶναι ἀλλ᾽ ἦν αὐτοῖς πάντα κοινά
(iv. 32). Here it is quite clear that the persons
referred to not only possessed private property formerly, but that even at that time they still had

some[1] (τῶν ὑπαρχόντων αὐτῷ, part. pres.). What was novel and praiseworthy was only the fact that they declared (ἔλεγον) what they possessed as not their own (in an exclusive, selfish sense), but regarded everything as common. This manifestly refers to the mode of thinking, the disposition, the way of considering and treating what was their own, but not to an actual renunciation of all private property, nor a complete breaking up of all the relations belonging to property. The same holds good of ii. 44, etc. The εἶχον ἄπαντα κοινά may fitly be understood thus: they *had*, that is, considered and treated everything as if it were common property. It is even expressly stated that they divided the produce of the possessions they had sold, as every man had *need* (ii. 45, iv. 35, καθότι ἄν τις χρείαν εἶχεν). We therefore adhere to our opinion that these descriptions do not refer to such an arrangement, even if carried out with full consent, as would take away from individual believers all their private possessions, leaving them only property in common. Rather do words and connection lead us forcibly to the conclusion that in disposition and mode of thought, the spirit of disinterested, brotherly love was strong enough to move many to give up their possessions for the good of the needy. Notwithstanding this, we repeat the admission that in ii. 44, etc., and iv. 34, expressions are used which, if taken separately and pressed, seem to point to a complete community of goods; but these receive their supple-

---

[1] Thus Bengel, who with respect to ἔλεγον makes the observation: hoc ipso praesupponitur, *proprietatem* possessionis non plane fuisse deletam (comp. Baumgarten, *ante*, i. 68 f. ; Lange, *Geschichte der Kirche*, i. 44, 59 ; Schaff, *ante*, 465 ff.).

ment, their authentic interpretation so to speak, from the concrete facts in iv. 36, etc., v. 1, etc., especially ver. 4.

We have already seen that in the retired, quiet life of believers and their brotherly fellowship there lay concealed the germs of a new and peculiar Christian service, which gradually developed, protected by this concealment. From this circumstance it follows, at the same time, that the domestic and social life of believers, because it was one with the pious life of the community from the beginning, must be regarded as an exalted and consecrated thing. The peaceful intercourse of believers one with another, as of those forming one family, and as brothers and sisters belonging to one another (οἱ ἴδιοι, Acts iv. 23, ἀδελφοί), by means of the κοινωνία (ii. 42), that is, by inner community of spirit and faith, became always closer, their mutual attachment more complete; for as Vinet says: "Intimacy of mutual relationship rises and falls with the earnestness of the thoughts, with the depth of the feelings, with the importance of the interests. It is only in the circle of frivolous and purely material dispositions that the soul remains carefully closed, while restraint is dominant. Fervour and resignation are only to be found in the province of the immaterial. The thought of the Infinite is the closest of all bonds, and two souls mutually penetrate and melt into one only in God" (*Über die Darlegung der relig. Überzeugungen*, etc., German edition, 1845, p. 22). We thus see the meal-times of the believers sanctified and consecrated by the fact that the breaking of bread was a feast of brethren and of the Lord at the same time. Hence arose the pure gladness and singleness of heart with which they ate their food (ii. 46).

We next come upon an incident which is apparently of little consequence, but from which, however, we may draw the conclusion that a friendly relation existed between masters and servants within the Church. Thus when Peter, released from prison by the angel, knocked at the door of a friend's house, a slave of the name of Rhoda came to listen and see who was there. When she recognized the voice of Peter, from sheer joy she forgot to open the door, but ran quickly in again and told those present that Peter stood before the door (Acts xii. 13, etc.). The heart-felt joy of this person, in which she forgot the first duty incumbent on her, gives us reason to suppose that servants of this kind, when believers, were treated by their masters and other members of the Church on the same footing with themselves; that by the spirit of true fraternity and equality the external subordination had been nullified, and a mutual sympathy awakened in all ; a circumstance which, owing to the κοινωνία, we might expect beforehand, and to which the voluntary adjustment of the contrast between rich and poor, effected within the Church by sympathizing and ministering love, corresponds (ii. 44, etc., iv. 32, etc.). It certainly follows from some passages, such as Gal. ii. 10, and others of the same kind, that the majority of the believers at Jerusalem, and probably also in other parts of Palestine, were people of slender means. If, notwithstanding, there was none among them that lacked, οὐδὲ ἐνδεής τις ὑπῆρχεν ἐν αὐτοῖς (iv. 34), this fact had all the greater significance.

(C.) *Church arrangements and the social constitution
among Jewish Christians.*

Light has been shed on this subject in recent
times, first by Richard Rothe in his work, *Die Anfänge
der christlichen Kirche und ihrer Verfassung*, 1 Bd.,
1837, p. 141 ff.; after him by Ritschl, *Entstehung
der altkatholischen Kirche*, 1857; and lastly by Hatch,
Organization of the Early Christian Churches, translated
by A. Harnack, 1833. We are here referred back
to the beginning of the apostolic history. When the
apostles with Mary the mother of Jesus, and other
women, as well as the brethren of Jesus, continued
with one accord in prayer (Acts i. 13, etc.), faith
in Jesus and hope in His promises were the bond
of their union. Prayer was the first and simplest
expression of their faith and hope. But we find
already that community of faith was also an external bond; we see how inner communion reveals
itself and comes forth into the actual world as an
external association. We can almost grasp this
transition verbally in the word used in the above
passage, ὁμοθυμαδόν, which is often repeated in a
distinctive way, especially in the beginning of the
Acts. According to its composition, it means " of
one mind, of one spirit;" but it is frequently
used as equivalent to " at the same time," or
" together." The former meaning belongs entirely
to the inner, moral sphere; the latter to space
and external phenomena. The word combines
the two meanings in itself, just in so far as
the former necessitates the latter. In this small
word we have a slight indication of the transition

from internal unity and spiritual communion into an external bond and association.

Even before the feast of the Passover, we meet with a large gathering of more than a hundred believers where Peter is the speaker, and declares that a new apostle must be appointed in the place of Judas Iscariot. Two men are chosen; but the final determination of the future apostle was left to God by the drawing of lots (i. 15, etc.).

At the feast of Pentecost we find all believers together in *one* house. But as soon as the Spirit is poured out, and a crowd has assembled at the sound of a rushing wind, we find the Christians surrounded by many people, whom Peter immediately addresses. This account leads us out from the narrow circle of those bound together by community of faith into the public world, where believers and unbelievers are mixed together. But the word which the apostles preach has a penetrating power (ii. 37). Many follow the final exhortation to save themselves from the untoward generation, and are baptized. About three thousand souls were added unto them the same day (ver. 41), namely, to the believers; for in ver. 44 we read, "All that believed were together." Here again we may see how inner community of faith expresses itself by an external connection (ver. 47). If we might abide by the usual reading, a new element would enter in only so far as in place of the earlier indefinite προσετέθησαν (ver. 41), a more definite expression now appears: ὁ δὲ κύριος προσετίθει τοὺς σωζομένους καθ' ἡμέραν τῇ ἐκκλησίᾳ; but the words τῇ ἐκκλησίᾳ are certainly not genuine or original. In v. 11 Luke first speaks of the *Church*, which, from the expression ὅλη ἡ ἐκκλησία in ver.

11, appears as a united whole, a collective body. This presupposes that the society, formerly consisting only of single persons (*οἱ πιστεύοντες*), had already gained unity and cohesion, and had therefore progressed a step farther. First we saw an *external association* arising out of the purely internal community of faith, and manifesting itself by an external act of union on the part of those who were bound internally. External association in its beginning is, however, an undefined, fluctuating, formless thing. But this stage of development was surmounted by the fact of the association constituting itself into *a Church, ἐκκλησία*.

A nucleus of association from its first beginning to its centre was presented in the apostles, whose vocation it was to found and to guide the Church by their witness to Christ (*μάρτυρές μου*, Acts i. 8).[1] They were the first who bore public testimony to Christ, by the missionary sermon of Peter (ii. 14, etc.); a second preaching of Jesus to the people followed the healing of the cripple (iii. 12, etc.); vindication and testimony before the Sanhedrim were the further consequence. The new converts adhered to the teaching of the apostles (ii. 42), but the miracles of healing performed by the apostles were also powerful witnesses to Jesus as the Saviour. The apostles stood at the head of all believers, not only by their proclamation of Christ in word and deed, but also as guides and directors. At *their* feet individuals laid down the sums obtained from possessions sold, and destined for the support of the needy (iv. 34 and 37, v. 2).

But the conception of the Church as a united body (*ὅλη ἡ ἐκκλησία*, v. 11) appears for the first time in connection with an alarming " act of divine Church

[1] Comp. Ritschl, *Entstehung der altkath. Kirche*, 2 Aufl., p. 372.

chastisement " (Thiersch, *Die Kirche im ap. Zeitalter*) effected by the apostles. It seems as if the judgment of God inflicted by the apostles on two hypocritical members of the brotherhood contributed to bring to clear consciousness the *unity* of the Church, its solidarity.

The apostles appear as guiding members. We find ministering members in the νεώτεροι or νεανίσκοι, who, when Ananias and afterwards his wife are struck down by the divine judgment of sudden death, cover them, carry them out, and bury them (v. 6–10). Too much meaning has been put into the words in assuming that these νεώτεροι were duly-appointed Church servants in opposition to the πρεσβύτεροι, the ruling elders of the Church, whose existence is already presupposed by the very word applied to them.[1] We should rather imagine that the younger members of the Church, without any obligation or place, voluntarily took upon themselves those manual services that arose in Church life (Neander, *ante*, i. 46 ff. ; Rothe, 163, including note).[2] The relation was still an entirely fluctuating one, not yet established by a definite Church arrangement, but in the spirit of freedom, originating of itself. Until this time we find no definite, appointed office in the Church, except that of the apostles; but this, founded by Christ Himself, appears from the very beginning as an established, sacred office, limited to the number twelve (i. 17, 20, 22, 25), as we have already said.

[1] A. Harnack, *Lehre der Zwölf Apostel*, 1884, S. 142, 147.

[2] Overbeck, p. 70, rightly discerns that νεώτεροι cannot be the name of an office, on account of being interchanged with νεανίσκοι in ver. 10. Nevertheless he maintains that the description gives rise to the appearance of an existing office of which no trace has been retained. —So intent is he on placing the historical credibility of the book in the most suspicious light.

It is a step towards the definite disposition and organization of the Church, when the apostles, on account of the complaints of the Hellenists respecting the neglect of their widows in the daily ministration, introduce the choice of seven men (Acts v. 1, etc.). We here purposely avoid the title *deacons:* firstly, because in the passages of the Acts which refer to it, this name *never* appears; those who are chosen are called simply the ἑπτά, the Seven, in opposition to the Twelve (comp. vi. 3, 5–8, viii. 5, 26, xxi. 8); secondly, because the new office did not *in substance* quite correspond to the later diaconate, but seems to have been more comprehensive and important. Neander, indeed, acknowledges this (*ante,* i. 53), but yet insists that the office was the diaconate proper and also bore the name; so also Schaff (531 ff.), who shows that the opinion that Acts vi. 6 gives an account of the establishment of the diaconate dates from the time of Cyprian (Ep. 3, § 3); so Baumgarten (*Acts,* i. 117), Baur (*Christenthum,* 2 Aufl. 260).[1] The opposite view, with which we agree, was of old upheld by careful inquirers, such as Vitringa (*de Synagog. vet.* iii. 2, 9, ed. 1729, p. 926) and the renowned canonist Just Henning Böhmer, the latter of whom assumed that those chosen were true elders. In recent times attention has been given to the subject principally by Ritschl, *Altkath. Kirche,* 2 Aufl. 353 ff.; Stanley, *ante,* p. 62, etc.; Lange, ii. 74 f., 539 f., and others, who have shown the probability that the office of the Seven included the eldership as well as the later diaconate, both of which may have branched off from it at first. Very obvious is the conjecture frequently brought forward, that

1 Renan, *Apôtres,* 1867, p. 98; comp. *St. Paul,* 1869, p. 506.

the apostles, who themselves formerly undertook the
care of the poor and the distribution, for the common
benefit, of the sums given, may, according to circumstances, have made use of volunteer members. The
inequalities and irregularities which resulted from
this informal management of affairs gave rise
to dissatisfaction; and complaints showed the
necessity of a settled management, by means of
officials expressly appointed for the purpose (see
Rothe, S. 163 ff., comp. 146). From this example
we see plainly that a more definite arrangement,
a firmer organization, an internal building up of
the society's constitution, took the place of a more
unsettled; fluctuating state only as circumstances
arose and a want was felt, so that the formation of
the Christian Church was not an artificial product,
but a gradual growth from within, and the result of a
divine necessity. Hence, as Baumgarten truly remarks
(*Ap. Geschichte*, i. 116), the precedency of the apostles
is of practical importance, in so far as they recognised a better organization to be an actual want and a
progressive advance of the Church, and did not from
one-sided subjectivity underestimate its importance.

Moreover this is the only case in which a glance
into the method of the origin of a Christian Church
office appears. Another office, important even in its
original position, and still more so by later development, suddenly appears in the Acts without our
seeing whence it proceeds. When the prophet
Agabus had foretold a great and universal famine,
the believers in Antioch sent contributions collected
for the brethren in Judæa to the elders (τοὺς πρεσβυτέρους, xi. 30, comp. 27, etc.) by Barnabas and
Saul. These elders, as the definite article shows, are

mentioned as filling an already well-known office in
the Church, without *a single word* having previously
been said of their appointment. It is possible, notwithstanding, that in the case of the elders as of
the seven men, some particular motive led to the
institution of the office; but it is certain that to
these men, as to the Seven (chap. vi.), were transferred functions which were originally in the hands
of the apostles. For charitable gifts for the benefit
of needy believers were originally placed at the
disposal of the apostles, and by them (through agents)
distributed according to need (iv. 35, etc., v. 2).
On the other hand, we must not overlook the fact
that the elders here performed a function which,
according to the account in vi. 1, etc., manifestly
belonged to the Seven, namely, the reception, administration, and application of gifts for the benefit of
those suffering want. The circumstance recorded in
xi. 29, etc., is at any rate favourable to the view that
the office of the seven men was identical with the
office of presbyter, or at least included it from the
beginning.[1]

The elders at Jerusalem appear again in chap. xv.,
where the Church at Antioch sends Paul and certain
others to " the apostles and *elders* " at Jerusalem
about the question of the Gentile Christians (ver. 2).

[1] Comp. Ritschl, *Entstehung der altkatholischen Kirche*, p. 375,
with note. The remark on p. 358, that the office of overseer of the
Church was not an offshoot of apostolic authority, appears to us to
be without conclusive foundation. It is not too much to suppose
that Luke in his account of the appointment of the Seven (chap. vi.)
followed other sources than those which he had in the narrative
of the collection at Antioch and the remittance of the sums to
Jerusalem. On this assumption, the mention of "elders" without
reference to the previously related choice of the Seven, is more
intelligible.

Next to the apostles, it is in fact the elders who with
the Church receive the delegates ; who meet for
discussion and finally come to a resolution ; so too,
the writing which conveys the resolution is drawn
up in the name of the apostles, the elders, and the
Church (vers. 4, 6, 22, 23). In short, it is evident
that the elders are to be regarded as representatives
and leaders of the Church. On his last visit to
Jerusalem, Paul went to James, on which occasion
all the elders were present (xxi. 18, etc.).

In order to get a more accurate idea of the
position and proper office of the elders than is
afforded by the Acts alone, the constitution of the
Jewish synagogue has been consulted. Vitringa in
particular (*De Synag. vet.*, Libri iii., 1696) has tried
to prove that this served as a pattern and model for
the constitution of the Christian Church not only as
a whole but also in detail. Now the Jewish
synagogue had also זְקֵנִים at its head, a court of
Church elders who had nothing to do with instruction,
doctrine, or religious exposition, but only with the
arrangement and guidance of the Church. It is
therefore natural to suppose that the elders of the
Christian Churches also, especially at Jerusalem, had
to do only with the arrangement and conduct of
Church matters, but not with worship and doctrine,
especially as the first appearance of the elders at
Jerusalem (Acts xi. 30) relates only to temporal
possessions and matters of property.[1] On the other
hand, in Acts xv. 2, 4, 22, etc., the elders of the
mother Church appear, next to the apostles, as a
determining court also, on a question referring to

---

[1] Comp. Hatch, *Organization of the Early Christian Churches*,
translated by A. Harnack, 1883, 3rd Lecture.

doctrine. Moreover in the Epistle of James, which was undoubtedly addressed to Jewish Christian Churches, arrangements for the sick are ascribed (v. 14) to the elders of the Church, which plainly have the character of a spiritual charge, so to speak, and are obviously connected with worship. That the elders of the Jewish Christian Churches had also to do with doctrine is proved in particular by the Epistle to the Hebrews, which unmistakeably represents the ἡγούμενοι or overseers of the Church, belonging both to that and former times (xiii. 7, 17, 24), as at once pastors and teachers (comp. Bleek, *Comm.* ii. 2).

The *position of James* in the Church at Jerusalem is remarkable. When Peter, released from prison, was desirous of leaving the city, he gave this commission to the disciples whom he found in the house of the mother of John Mark, ἀπαγγείλατε Ἰακώβῳ καὶ τοῖς ἀδελφοῖς ταῦτα (Acts xii. 17). Since James is thus distinguished, we must regard him, if not as the principal person, yet as one of the most prominent men in the Church. We have in the passage only an incidental hint of the great importance of this man. It harmonizes with the subsequent account (chap. xv.), which gives a clear representation of James and the reputation he had. After several utterances of other speakers, James appears last. His speech, which culminates in a definite proposal, is conclusive, and leads to a decision; but it is not therefore necessary with Holtzmann, in Hilgenfeld's *Zeitschrift*, 1880, p. 200, to regard him as president of the council. We see that he was a person of uncommon weight and influence within the Church. Neither this passage nor the former gives direct evidence of a definite *official* position, but a conclusion to this effect does follow from the last passage in which James is mentioned in the Acts (xxi. 18, etc.). The very circumstance that Paul, on the day after his arrival in Jerusalem, repairs to James, with whom all the elders are present to hear Paul's account respecting his mission to the Gentiles, makes it evident that James was the official centre of the Church; in a certain sense, the head of the elders. We have already observed that after what had occurred, there were at that time no longer apostles in Jerusalem; but James, the brother of the Lord, took their place to some extent, and with almost apostolic dignity remained there as head of the Church. The official position which he occupied is not expressly stated, either in these three passages, or in Gal. i. 19, ii. 9, where he is mentioned by Paul: and though the Church-fathers, from the Alexandrian Clement onwards, give him the title of "Bishop" in its proper sense, this position cannot be proved from the New Testament. Yet the way (to which Rothe, *ante*, p. 263, etc., has rightly drawn attention) in which Hegesippus, the oldest narrator after the New Testament, speaks of the position of James, is very cautious and thoughtful. He says: Διαδέχεται δὲ τὴν ἐκκλησίαν μετὰ τῶν ἀποστόλων ὁ ἀδελφὸς τοῦ κυρίου Ἰάκωβος (Eusebius, *Kirchengeschichte*, ii. 23, § 4). Hegesippus has, indeed, carefully avoided calling him expressly a "bishop," but makes him participate with the apostles in the guidance of the Church.[1] Thus a higher office, *above* that of the

---

[1] It is of *this*, and not of a guidance of the collective Church, as Ritschl, *Altkath. Kirche*, p. 416, explains it, that we must understand ἐκκλησία in the words of Hegesippus.

elders (an Episcopal office in the later sense), apart from apostolic authority, cannot be shown by historical testimony in the Church at Jerusalem during the period of which we .are treating, at least not an office systematically arranged, independent of a person. As a matter of fact, James, the brother of the Lord, did exercise a preponderating, decisive influence on the direction of the Church; but so far as we can see, it was not the result of his official position, but depended solely on his personality. In this we agree with *Ritschl*, p. 417, etc. Of the high estimation in which, for many centuries, James was held, we have proof in the fact that so late as the time of Eusebius the "apostolic chair" of James was preserved and shown as a sacred memorial of apostolic times (see Eusebius, *Kirchengeschichte*, vii. 19, comp. chap. 32, § 29).

Hitherto we have confined ourselves to the Church at Jerusalem, because in point of time it was the first, the pattern, and the head among all the Churches, but it is now time to go beyond the precincts of the sacred city. The very first emergence of the apostles from the narrow circle of the brotherly fellowship of believers into a public sphere at the Passover feast, led in all probability to the result that outside Jerusalem, and even outside Palestine, individual believers were to be met with, since among those who were added in that day (ii. 41) were doubtless strangers from the *Διασπορά* (see *ante*, p. 7). But, even before this time, there were not only in Judæa but also in Galilee, and even in Samaria (John v. 41, etc.), some who, from the period of the personal activity of Jesus, believed in Him as the Christ. These, however, if not exactly few, were still but isolated individuals, and it was not until after the inner association of the disciples had begun to consolidate itself in Jerusalem as a Church, that they also formed companies of believers for themselves, beginning at Jerusalem and extending over the country; a result, so far as we learn from the Acts, of the persecution which broke out after the martyrdom of Stephen, in consequence of which believers, with the exception of the apostles, withdrew from Jerusalem and were scattered abroad throughout the regions of Judæa and Samaria, even to Phœnicia, Cyprus, and Antioch (viii. 1, xi. 19). Those who were scattered went from place to place preaching the word of the gospel (xiv. 7). Thus Philip came to Samaria, and an association of believers sprang up in that place, as also in other towns and villages to which the dispersed Christians had come. In certain places the preaching of the gospel of Jesus, the Messiah, reached receptive minds, for we find believers in Damascus for example (ix. 10, 25), (without having previously heard anything of the spread of the gospel to their place), who were called οἱ μαθηταί, apparently designated by that expression as a united body; we find saints dwelling in Lydda too (ix. 32); and in the neighbouring district of Saron, people who " turned to the Lord " (ix. 35). From Joppa, which lies on the borders of that region, the " disciples " who dwelt there sent two delegates to Peter at Lydda, to invite him to pay them a visit (ix. 38). Finally, the Churches in all Judæa, Galilee, and Samaria are spoken of collectively (ix. 31); and Paul also, in his Epistle to the Galatians, mentions Christian Churches in Judæa, using the plural number, with evident reference to a time soon after his conversion (Gal. i.

22: αἱ ἐκκλησίαι τῆς Ἰουδαίας αἱ ἐν Χριστῷ; comp. 1 Thess. ii. 14: αἱ ἐκκλησίαι τοῦ θεοῦ αἱ οὖσαι ἐν τῇ Ἰουδαίᾳ ἐν Χριστῷ Ἰησοῦ).

From these accounts we may venture to consider the fact as proved, that during the apostolic time, in all Palestine as well as in the surrounding countries, small bands of believers arose by degrees among the Jews, who, like the disciples at Jerusalem, by virtue of an inner community of faith, love, and Christian hope, were also joined together outwardly, and from the formless, fluctuating condition of accidental external association progressed all the more easily to the stage of firm Church-constitution and consociation, since they had a model in the Church at Jerusalem which had been a considerable time in existence. We may even assume that in the course of the apostolic time there was in the end not a single believer who did not belong to a definite Christian Church (Rothe, ante, 279). The Christians formed Churches complete in themselves; and from the nature of the case, we have reason to suppose that the Churches could not have existed for long without a definite organization and regular officers, especially not without elders for their administration and guidance, though the Acts themselves give no express confirmation of this. These were, however, only individual Christian Churches, independent associations of believers. We have not yet arrived at the Christian *Church* in the proper sense of the word, as a united whole complete in itself, and embracing all the single communities. The question arises, Did the Jewish Christian Churches of Palestine and the neighbouring countries exist only as separate communities (independently), each for itself? Or were they already at this time

compacted into a union of such a nature as by virtue
of a definite form to be organically knit together?
Rothe (p. 278, etc.) answers this question in the
negative,—proceeding from the universal law of organic
development, according to which it resolves itself
into a series of several stages, which certainly form a
connected whole, but yet assume definite and individual forms with respect to one another.   But these
distinctive stages of development are the growth of
separate Christian Churches and the formation of a
bond uniting them into one.   The two processes, he
maintains, *must* be separate from each other in time.
As long as the union of believers into Churches was
still in progress, and the form of Church-constitution
had yet to be established, so long was it *impossible*
for the activity of Christian impulse in the way of
union, to be directed to the establishment of a wider
consociation embracing all individual communities.
The result of his investigation of this subject is the
twofold position : first, the *necessity* for an external
union of all Christian Churches asserted itself more
and more strongly, while at the same time the
conception of such a union became clearer; there
appeared even some preliminary *surrogates* of an
ecclesiastical bond as preorganisms of future forms ;
second, negatively, a definite organized ecclesiastical
union of individual communities, consequently a
Christian Church as an external unity, did not yet in
reality exist within the apostolic period (Rothe, p.
281, etc., 301, etc., 310).   Rothe therefore looks on
the apostolic guidance and the institution of apostolic
delegates (συνεργοί), such as Timotheus, Titus, etc., as
a mere substitute for the ecclesiastical bond of the
whole, but by no means as itself that bond, especially

as the connecting relation effected by the apostles was quite formless and accidental, being personal and transitory throughout.

The credit of making a sharp distinction between the conceptions, community and Church, constitution of the community and constitution of the Church, belongs to Rothe, who has by that means advanced our insight into Church history. But with regard to his former statement, we must question the accuracy of the law of development there asserted. Laws have frequently been set forth as universal, on the basis of imperfect induction and insufficient observation of details, the application of which must be misleading; and it appears, in fact, that the able scholar has here one-sidedly directed his attention to one of the two aspects of development contained in this law, namely, the diversity which reveals itself in successive distinctions, as opposed to unity. Experience at least shows that in reality the various stages of development are by no means always distinct from one another in time. Rather does it frequently happen that history, while apparently occupied with a subordinate task, works in silence towards a higher aim. But let us leave the region of universal conceptions for the field of actual history, in order to see what appears in the New Testament regarding the actual union of Christian, especially Jewish Christian communities. Scarcely was the first community outside Jerusalem established, that is, in Samaria,—while the little band of new converts could not yet be regarded as an actually organized community,—when already the apostles took steps regarding them: " Now, when the apostles which were at Jerusalem heard that Samaria had received the word of God, they sent

unto them Peter and John : who, when they were
come down, prayed for them, that they might receive
the Holy Ghost. Then laid they their hands on them,
and they received the Holy Ghost; and the apostles,
when they had testified and preached the word of
the Lord, returned to Jerusalem " (Acts viii. 14, etc.,
17, 25). What does this mean ? Was the object
of the sending of the two apostles merely the advancement of the new converts as individuals, or was it,
at the same time, the completion of that which in
Samaria was still wanting to the settlement of a
Christian Church ? The communication of the Spirit
by prayer and the laying on of hands seems to favour
the former view. On the other hand, we find in the
reasons for this journey of the apostles no indication
that they were moved to their decision by the knowledge of a want in the new converts; for they only
hear that Samaria has received the word of God (but
not that the conversion of the Samaritans is still
incomplete), and at once send forth two from their
midst. These latter also hold it to be a principal
object of their mission to " testify and preach the word
of the Lord " (ver. 25) among the believers in Samaria.
We must now recollect, on the one hand, that the
" doctrine " of the apostles (comp. ii. 42) was the
spiritual centre of the community of believers among
themselves ; but, on the other hand, we must consider
that the apostles, by the fact of sending two of their
number, show that they wish to stand in as close
relation to the foreign Christian Churches as to the
Church in Jerusalem, while the result proved that
they were actually " the *representatives* of Christian
life to all Christian Churches, and therefore the final
and absolute authority in all religious matters "

(Rothe, 303; Baumgarten, *Apostelgeschichte*, i. p. 170, etc.).

We hear afterwards, at a time when the Churches had rest in Judæa, Galilee, and Samaria, when they increased outwardly, were edified internally, and advanced in the fear of the Lord, that Peter travelled about among them all ($\delta\iota\epsilon\rho\chi\acute{o}\mu\epsilon\nu o\nu$ $\delta\iota\grave{a}$ $\pi\acute{a}\nu\tau\omega\nu$), on which occasion he came to Lydda and Joppa in particular, and thence to Cæsarea (ix. 31, etc.). Neander makes use of a modern expression when he calls this a tour of inspection (*Pflanz.* i. 117), but it is one which falls little short of the meaning. We must not, however, limit the object of this journey to a mere inspection and examination into the state of things, but must regard it as a mission in which the apostle confirms the disciples in knowledge and in faith, promotes their brotherly fellowship with one another and with all *other* Churches, probably helping them also with his advice and assistance in matters of external association (comp. Hess, *Geschichte und Schriften der Apost.* i. p. 237, etc.). From the facts already mentioned, it follows that the apostles, while they had their fixed residence in Jerusalem, by no means limited their activity to the mother Church, but as soon as *foreign Christian communities* arose, interested themselves in them as much as in believers in Jerusalem. They exercised supervision over all, in order to advance their spiritual life, in different directions. They formed their living centre, not that one Church was entrusted to one, another to another, but that the apostles collectively exercised authority over all. The latter circumstance appears plainly from viii. 14, and accordingly ix. 32 must be understood in the same sense. The very fact that all companies of Christians in Palestine and the neighbouring countries proceeded as Churches from Jerusalem the seat of the first Church, and that therefore the other Churches were daughters, so to speak, colonies of the primitive Church, not only involved a certain dependence of these latter on the mother Church, but also gave rise to a reciprocal union of individual Churches among themselves, which was not indeed established by a fundamental law, nor literally expressed, nor formally instituted, but which yet existed as an actual bond in real life. Finally, let us draw attention to a passage which Rothe has justly emphasized, namely, ix. 31 : Ἡ μὲν οὖν ἐκκλησία καθ᾽ ὅλης τῆς Ἰουδαίας καὶ Γαλιλαίας καὶ Σαμαρείας εἶχεν εἰρήνην. The various Christian communities of the three districts of Palestine are here described as a whole by ἡ ἐκκλησία in the singular, which is undoubtedly the correct reading, and attested by the four oldest uncial manuscripts and most Oriental translations besides the Vulgate, and is undoubtedly to be preferred to the reading which has the plural αἱ . . . ἐκκλησίαι. The passage proves at least this, that the historian regards the many individual Christian communities as belonging together, as an actual unity; but here, with Rothe, we must distinguish between the conception of the author and the reality : "for it does not follow, from our putting together the individual Christian communities in idea as a united Church, that they were already joined *in actuality*, forming a Church." We must in the main adhere to that union of separate communities among themselves which was conditioned by the importance of the mother Church at Jerusalem, and primarily by the leading position of the apostles. Rothe, as we have already said, considers the latter relation as a mere surrogate, but not as an actual bond of union ; and for this reason, that the relation was, in the first place, informal and accidental ; in the second place, purely personal and transitory. The relation, however, cannot be pronounced accidental simply for the reason that it arose spontaneously and without calculation. Rothe himself concedes that it originated purely in the nature of things, and in the needs of the community, and was therefore not accidental or arbitrary, but the result of an inner necessity. The relation was certainly informal in so far as it was not regulated by laws nor fixed by rule, but was in great measure left to the control of the Spirit and of human freedom. When, on the other hand, the union of the communities into a whole, effected by the apostles and attached to their persons, is declared to be precarious and transitory, we must fully concede that the apostles exercised universal jurisdiction, but not by virtue of an office existing independently of their personality, expressly founded for the guidance of the whole body. They acted, on the contrary, by virtue of a personal authority given to them by the Lord, which was older than everything belonging to an external Christian community that goes by the name of constitution. It is something, however, that the apostles called by Christ were appointed and empowered to be the foundation of His Church (Matt. xvi. 18), and that there was a διακονία καὶ ἀποστολή and a κλῆρος τῆς διακονίας ταύτης (Acts i. 17, 25), before communities of believers were in existence. The Church of Christ has grown from above downwards ; it was the Lord who chose the apostles, not they who chose Him,—He ordained them (John xv. 16). All other offices grew

out of the apostolate ; and the primitive Church at
Jerusalem was not only 'a' Church, but 'the' Church ;
that is to say, the community at Jerusalem originally
represented itself as the Church. We have already
seen that in Jerusalem functions were transferred to
the Seven which originally belonged to the apostles
themselves. Afterwards we found the guidance and
management of individual communities entrusted
to elders ; a task which had formerly rested in
the hands of the apostles, but had been separated
from the apostolic calling as a result of necessity.
The general supremacy over the Churches, however,
still belonged to the apostles, but afterwards became
an independent office, partly through the appointment
of συνεργοί (" delegates "), partly after the death of
the apostles, in another way, by the episcopate, etc.
Hence the apostolic college was the organ of Christian
communion established by the Lord Himself, and was
in the beginning the only one. From this *one* organ
were developed in the course of time, by degrees,
according as wants were felt, other comparatively
independent organs ; to which, therefore, functions were transferred which had in the beginning
belonged to the apostles, so that after some time the
whole existed with all its individual parts.[1] As to
the common bond of the Church in particular, we
must guard against the error that " united action is
no substitute for united forms," as Niedner rightly
remarks in opposition to Rothe (*Kirchengesch.* 152,
note 1). So long as the apostles were at the
head of all, there was not, indeed, an actual union—
consisting in certain posts and offices, arrangements

[1] Comp. Löhe, *Aphorismen über die neutestament Ämter*, pp. 47 and
48 ; Schaff, *ante*, 507, 511.

and forms, but yet a living and personal one, not, however, on that account an unreal point of union and cohesion for the individual Churches, to be realised only at a future time. It was not till later that what had hitherto existed in personal authority and procedure was incorporated in offices and institutions, and retained as an actual bond. Here, too, the law holds good that creative power lives within, in spirit and personality, and that the external is produced and built up from within.

If we have hitherto turned our attention only to one, that is, the specifically Christian aspect of the Church constitution, we must not overlook the other aspect. We must abide by the fact that the Churches of believers among the Jews had not as societies a fully independent existence, but rather rested upon the *Jewish* theocratic association (comp. Rothe, p. 142, etc., 280, etc.). Believers lived in the bosom of the latter, and were originally, as a society, nothing but a limited company of like-minded Israelites among the people of God, who saw the Messiah in Jesus of Nazareth, and did homage to Him. Notwithstanding the fact that they were closely united among themselves, they still remained, as before, members of the civil and religious national community of Israel. They were in a certain sense only a party, a sect ($a'i\rho\epsilon\sigma\iota\varsigma$, Acts xxiv. 5, xxviii. 22) within the national community of Israel, which was comprehensive and tolerant towards all varieties and differences, and with which they purposed remaining in external and internal life-association ; for because they were convinced that Israel was the nation of God, and its theocratic constitution a divine appointment, they could not at all entertain the idea of separating themselves from it.   Such a daring attempt they would have regarded as sin and apostasy from God.   To *us*, from the standpoint of a later time, the matter certainly wears a very different aspect than it does from the standpoint of the first believers.   In the closer union of believers among themselves, and the way in which, with one accord, they held together, *we* see the peculiarly Christian sentiment, something which possesses historical significance, which is new and rich in promise,—the proper kernel; recognizing in their connection with the Old Testament theocracy the shell which must sooner or later be broken through and cast aside.   Their mutual connection with the organs, forms, offices, and regulations arising gradually by inner development, according to the measure of need, we recognize as the germ of the future Christian Church.   Thus we see the matter from a distance, or rather from a height, which affords a free survey of the whole course of things.   On the other hand, those Christians themselves, looking at the matter from the immediate present and personal, regarded union with the old theocracy as the chief thing, as that which was most sacred, permanent, and full of germs to fructify in the future ; while their close relation to one another was something transitory, a preparatory intermediate position, a means to this end, viz. that the *whole* nation of Israel should enter into the new theocracy of Jesus the Messiah, and that thus the Church of Jesus should become the kingdom of Israel (comp. Acts i. 6).   The matter was first placed in a different light by the strained feeling, the ever-increasing unity on the part of the old theocracy against the believers.   This led, in fact, to the result that they *learned* to consider the dissolution of their union with the theocratic Church at first as possible, then as desirable, and finally, as necessary. By this means their minds were prepared for the final appearance of the actual breach with Judaism. These steps with respect to the social position of the Christian Church went hand in hand with the development of the peculiarly Christian consciousness, and with its victory over the Jewish element in Christian piety. The Epistle to the Hebrews has special reference to the process of development here described, if it be granted that it is in reality addressed to Palestinian Jewish Christians. It gives us a glance into a crisis. The readers are conscious of belonging to the nation of Israel and to the Old Testament theocracy, but nevertheless wish to be Christians. As a matter of fact, however, they stand in danger of falling away from Christianity, of deserting Christ Himself, and of apostatizing to Judaism. The author warns them against this danger, and puts before them, on that account, the elevated nature of the new covenant in comparison with the old and the infinite pre-eminence of the person of Christ.

CHAPTER II.

THE GENTILE CHRISTIANS AND THE MIXED CHURCHES.

THE heading of this chapter may give rise to objections against the idea apparently suggested, that there were purely Gentile Christian Churches existing as a separate group at this period, in opposition to purely Jewish Christian Churches. We learn rather from the original document that in the countries outside Palestine, as a rule, mixed Churches alone had been formed, so that Christian societies consisting exclusively of converted heathens can only be regarded as exceptional in early times. They were a mixture of various ingredients, mostly, however, with a preponderance of the Gentile Christian element; while in Palestine itself, and in some of the neighbouring districts, we must regard purely Jewish Christian Churches as the rule. Moreover, in order to commence with the first beginnings and smallest germs of Gentile Christianity, we must go back to the Church at Jerusalem, for this was the mother Church, not only of Jewish Christianity, but of all Christendom.

The law of continuity and of gradual development which governs the history of man and in general all being, implies that for everything new, independent, and important which occurs in history, the way must be paved and prepared in the sphere of that which exists. It is always the greatest in history which is prepared in the most silent and least apparent way. This law also governed the growth of the Gentile Church. The more strange and even objectionable as was the incorporation of the Gentiles in the kingdom of God and the Church of the Messiah in the eyes of the Jews, the more gentle and gradual was the course in which by various significant and preparatory steps God paved the way for the appearance and life-work of the apostle of the Gentiles. In the first five chapters of the Acts of the Apostles, as far as circumstances and events themselves are concerned, we see nothing beyond the narrow circle of Jewish Christendom. The Church at Jerusalem appears to have consisted exclusively of converted Jews, perhaps also of a few proselytes who had been baptized; no event leads us a step farther than this. The subsequent chapters (vi.–xii.), on the other hand, after the conclusion of which the proper Pauline portion of the book begins, relate one fact after the other, which we must characterize as preliminary steps,—a preparatory working towards the aim of raising the Church of Christ above and beyond its original limitation to the Hebrews. Then follows the remarkable "period of transition," as Baumgarten calls it. The care with which Luke has preserved and narrated all the small beginnings and preparations for the spread of the gospel among the heathen, shows that he himself was conscious of this pragmatic connection of events (comp. Lekebusch, *Composition der Apostelgeschichte*, p. 215, etc.).

The individual facts to which we refer are, first, the presence of Hellenists in the Church at Jerusalem; second, the preaching of the gospel by scattered members of the Church, and that not merely before Jews, but also (*a*) before Samaritans, (*b*) before proselytes, (*c*) before Gentiles; third, the conversion of Cornelius by the Apostle Peter himself.

First. The Acts relate that at a time when the number of the disciples increased rapidly, " there arose a murmuring of the *Grecians* against the *Hebrews*, because their widows were neglected in the daily ministration " (vi. 1). This is the first difference within the early Church mentioned by the Acts, and it sharpened into antagonism between the Palestinian and foreign members. Both classes were Jews by nationality. The only difference between them was that the native aboriginal Jews who used the Aramæan dialect, preserved the Jewish characteristics more purely and strictly, owing to their education and habits, while the others, either because they had formerly resided in other countries or were descended from foreign Jews, as a result of education and habit and of the use of the Greek language had assumed Hellenic modes of life, and readily mixed the foreign with the Jewish element, and were besides freer from national prejudices and Jewish narrowness. Now it is not an improbable conjecture on the part of Baur that the strained relations between native and Hellenistic Jewish Christians, the γογγυσμὸς τῶν Ἑλληνιστῶν πρὸς τοὺς Ἑβραίους, might have had its origin not solely in the unequal treatment of the Hellenistic poor, but at the same time in a difference of their respective modes of thought (*Paulus*, 2 Aufl. i. p. 48). This, at least, is favoured by the personality of one of the seven men appointed on this occasion, viz. Stephen, who by virtue of his probable Hellenistic descent may be regarded as the representative of the Hellenistic tendency. This man appears, from the accusations made against him (vi. 11), and from his discourse (chap. vii.), to have distinguished himself by rising above the externality of the Levitical service, and by perceiving that it must yield to the worship in spirit which Christianity represents. In so far Baur (*De orationis habitæ a Stephano consilio*, 1829) has with justice characterized Stephen as the forerunner of the Apostle Paul, in which he is followed by Neander. He held this position not merely by virtue of the inner relation between his tendency and that which Paul afterwards assumed, but also because the passionate enmity of the people of Israel against the gospel, exhibited in the matter of Stephen, was the cause of the preaching of the truth being now gradually extended to the

heathen.   Moreover, the martyrdom of Stephen, and
the simultaneous outbreak of the persecution which
was to destroy the Christian Church, must on the
contrary have given an impulse to the further spread
of the gospel, and resulted in turning the course of
Christianity into the new path that had been opened
up.   This thought is already contained in the words
of Augustine, "*Si Sanctus Stephanus sic non orasset,
ecclesia Paulum non haberet*" (Sermo i. et iv. in fest.
St. Stephani).

That the presence of Hellenists, with their peculiarly
free, large-minded tendencies, in the Church at Jerusalem, was favourable to the spread of the faith among
the Gentiles, appears—

Secondly, from subsequent events.   On account of
the persecution of which Stephen was the cause and
the first sacrifice, the believers fled from Jerusalem.
In their dispersion they preached the word; for the
most part, indeed, only to the Jews, but dispersed
Hellenists carried the gospel beyond the limits of
Judaism proper, and preached it with success before
Samaritans, proselytes, and even Gentiles.

(*a*) It was undoubtedly not the Apostle Peter, but
Philip, one of the Seven (probably himself a Hellenist;
comp. Sieffert, *Theol. Real-Encykl.* xi., 2 Aufl. 616),
who came to Samaria and there preached Christ,
so that many believed and were baptized (viii. 5,
etc.).[1]   The Samaritans, indeed, possessed the Mosaic
law and rested in Judaism, were worshippers of

---

[1] Löhe, in the *Aphorisms*, p. 32, rightly remarks with respect to
Acts viii. 5, 25 : "Thus the first believers from among the Jews,
together with the apostles, had no horror of the Samaritans as they
had of the Gentiles, but were entirely distinct from other Jews in
this respect.   He who had related so fondly the story of the merciful
and grateful Samaritan during His sacred life, may have early over-

Jehovah and practised circumcision, but they recognised no book of the Old Testament as sacred except the Pentateuch. The sanctuary of the Samaritans on Mount Gerizim formed the chief offence to the Jews. The temple at that place had indeed already been destroyed by John Hyrcanus 125 years before Christ. But the summit of the mountain was for the Samaritans of that day the sacred place of the worship of God, and is still considered so by their posterity. The Jews felt this to be presumptuous rivalry with their temple at Jerusalem, which, as they alleged, was the only lawful one. In addition to this they were a mixed race, and were regarded by the strict Jews as unclean, and not much better than the heathen, in which respect the Jews were not so far wrong. It is at least a fact that the Samaritans at various times, yielding to the political situation, denied their relationship with the Jews, and gave themselves out as Sidonians and such like (see Art. "Samaritaner" by Kautzsch in Riehm's *Handwörterbuch des biblischen Altertums*, 1884, p. 1347 ff.). It is just when we take into account the well-known disposition of the Jews towards the Samaritans, that the preaching of Philip in Samaria, together with its result, appears as a decisive and important advance in the cause of Christ.

(*b*) The same Philip became by special guidance the instrument for the conversion of the first *proselyte*, in the person of the chamberlain of Ethiopia (viii. 26). An angel of the Lord directs him to the way that goeth down from Jerusalem unto Gaza, and

come in this matter the hearts of His disciples, and made them like His own." On the religious standpoint of the Samaritans, see Lutterbeck, *ante*, i. 255 ff.

when he sees a traveller drive that way in his chariot, the Spirit tells him to go near and join himself to the chariot. One word leads to another. Philip interprets the prophecy of Isaiah liii. to the stranger who has just been reading it, as fulfilled in Jesus Christ; and the end is, that at his own expressed wish he is baptized. It is true the conjecture has been thrown out (recently by Baumgarten, *ante*, i. 180 ff.) that this high official of Queen Candace was a "proselyte of righteousness," that is, that he had been fully incorporated into the national Church of Israel by circumcision. But there is not a single circumstance to make that assumption necessary, least of all the sexual mutilation, in face of the promise contained in Isa. lvi. 3, etc., while all the features of the narrative find their full attestation in the usual view that the man was only a proselyte in the more extended sense, " a proselyte of the gate." If we follow this view as the most probable, the $A\iota\theta\iota o\psi$ $\epsilon\dot{v}vo\hat{v}\chi o\varsigma$ was indeed characterized by religious impulse and a burning desire for knowledge, a man full of reverence for the true God, who had made this journey in order to worship in the temple at Jerusalem. He was acquainted with the sacred books of Israel and read them with zeal, but was nevertheless uncircumcised, a heathen, unclean. Notwithstanding this, Philip, at the instigation of the Spirit, approached him, preached to him Jesus as the " Servant of God," and when he proved himself a receptive hearer, baptized him. Eusebius, too, describes the chamberlain from Meroë as the first Gentile convert to Christianity ($\pi\rho\hat{\omega}\tau o\varsigma$ $\dot{\epsilon}\xi$ $\dot{\epsilon}\theta v\hat{\omega}v$ . . . $\tau\hat{\omega}v$ $\tau\epsilon$ $\dot{a}v\dot{a}$ $\tau\dot{\eta}v$ $o\dot{\iota}\kappa o\upsilon\mu\acute{\epsilon}v\eta v$ $\pi\iota\sigma\tau\hat{\omega}v$ $\dot{a}\pi a\rho\chi\dot{\eta}$ $\gamma\epsilon v\acute{o}\mu\epsilon vo\varsigma$, *K. Gesch.* ii. 1, § 13).

(*c*) The last step was not so very great. While

the majority of the Christians scattered by the persecution, however far they might penetrate into the distant country, preached the word of Christ exclusively to the Jews, there were yet among them certain men out of Cyprus and Cyrene, consequently converted Hellenists, who in Antioch, whither they had come, spoke also with Hellenes (heathen), preaching the gospel of the Lord Jesus (Acts xi. 20). The most important critics, as Usher, Bengel, Griesbach, Lachmann, and Tischendorf, justly agree that we must here read ῞Ελληνας, and not follow the usual reading ῾Ελληνιστάς, which is, notwithstanding, attested by the majority of manuscripts. The reading ῞Ελληνας is undoubtedly correct, as may be seen from decided internal reasons, ῞Ελληνες and not ῾Ελληνισταί forming the proper antithesis to ᾿Ιουδαῖοι in ver. 19. It *can only* refer to uncircumcised heathen. It is possible that many of these were already " proselytes of the gate," but this was a relation which was perfectly free. There may, with equal probability, have been some among them who had never yet entered a synagogue. If the gospel were preached to such as these, the last step had already been taken, and the word of Christ had come to the heathen. In this matter the chronological question has some weight, Did this preaching of Christ before Greeks, *i.e.* uncircumcised persons in Antioch, take place sooner or later than the conversion of Cornelius by the Apostle Peter? The Acts narrate the latter before the former. The history of Cornelius fills the tenth chapter, and the account of the preaching to the heathen at Antioch follows only in xi. 20, after Peter's justification of his conduct with respect to Cornelius had already been narrated.

Following the precedent of the Acts, the older expositors of apostolic history, most recently Lange (*K. Geschichte*, ii. 143), make the preaching to the heathen by Hellenists follow the conversion of Cornelius, as conditioned and facilitated by it. But if we look at the matter with an unprejudiced eye, and examine the inner connection of events, it becomes obvious that the summary account contained in xi. 19, etc., is immediately connected with viii. 4, comp. 1. Both passages treat of the dispersion of believers by the persecution to which Stephen fell a victim; both indeed testifying to missionary activity on the part of the dispersed Christians. Since Gieseler (*Über Nazaräer und Ebioniten*, in Stäudlin's and Tzschirner's *Arch. für Kirchengesch.* iv. 2, 310) first drew attention to this, he has been followed by Baur (*Progr. über Steph.* p. 30), Schneckenburger (*Zweck der Apostelgeschichte*, 17 u. f.), Wieseler (*ante*, 146), and others. We do not hesitate to assume as the true state of the case, that the preaching of the gospel by Hellenists to the uncircumcised in Antioch took place *before* the meeting with Cornelius, and, indeed, not very long after the death of Stephen, although the author of the Acts does not narrate the spread of the gospel in Antioch in immediate connection with that event.

The preaching of Christ in Samaria, both to proselytes of the gate and finally to Gentiles, was carried out in all places by Hellenists. These three facts belong together; they form a continuous ascending series. The *Samaritans* were allied to the Jews in religion by the worship of Jehovah, by their reverence for the books of Moses and of the law, as well as by circumcision, while as a mixed nation they had Jewish national feeling against them. *Proselytes*, such as the Ethiopian courtier, were in close relation to the Jews on account of their leaning to the Israelitish religion, their participation in the Jewish service, their love to the sacred books. All this, however, was entirely a matter of pure inclination and conviction, not fixed by any sense of obligation. Finally, such heathen as could not even be reckoned as belonging to the outer circle of proselytes, which, moreover, was a fluctuating one, were complete strangers to the Jews, unclean,—ἁμαρτωλοὶ ἐξ ἐθνῶν, as Paul himself calls them (Gal. ii. 15). But now, under the divine guidance, one step after another had been taken towards carrying the gospel out of the region of purely orthodox Judaism, through many border lands, as it were, into the country proper of heathenism. The instruments of God were in this case Hellenists, *i.e.* Jews who by place of residence, language, and education, stood nearer to the heathen, and were therefore, as Baur justly says, called to be "mediators between Judaism and heathenism." Schrader, indeed (*Paulus*, v. 536, zu *Ap. Gesch.* xi. 20), finds it scarcely credible that Cyprian and Cyrenian Jewish Christians should have been the first who preached the gospel to the heathen; he thinks this assumption inconsistent with the independence of Paul and the originality of his spirit. But we might contend with equal justice that the originality of the reformers is not compatible with the fact that isolated forerunners of the reformation existed even some centuries before them.

Till that time only Hellenistic members of the Church had preached the gospel to others besides Hebrews. But now, *thirdly*, one of the apostles of

the Hebrews, no less a one, indeed, than Peter himself, was also destined to become the instrument of
the conversion of a heathen, of one who was certainly
already a proselyte. This circumstance is narrated
with great fulness in the Acts, chap. x. The Roman
centurion Cornelius, at Cæsarea, the Roman head-
quarters, and the second city in the land, in a vision
which he had, is commanded by an angel to send to
Peter. While his messengers are on the way to
Joppa, Peter has a vision in that place, in which
clean and unclean animals are put before him, with
the words, "Kill and eat!" and with the final
warning, "What God hath cleansed, call not thou
common." Peter is still lost in thought as to the
meaning and object of this vision, when the Spirit
tells him, "Three men seek thee, go with them!"
The delegates from Cæsarea are actually there. Peter
journeys with them, enters the house of Cornelius,
and after the latter has told him of his vision, speaks
of salvation by Jesus of Nazareth. During the
discourse the Holy Spirit comes upon the hearers,
and as a consequence, Peter commands them
to be baptized. From all this we see that the
apostle, contrary to his personal inclination, was led
by a higher power and impelled to take a step that
was at variance with his former conviction and mood,
viz. to go into the house of a Gentile who, though he
knew and worshipped the true God (x. 2, 35), was
yet uncircumcised and unclean, to preach the gospel
to him, and to initiate him by baptism into the
Church of God. But the unusual occurrences, the
numerous visions and divine words, finally the communication of the Spirit to the heathen listeners, had
the appearance of direct indications of God, of loud

voices saying, "God wills it!" They moved the apostle to the course he took, and served him afterwards as a justification against those Jewish Christians at Jerusalem who were indignant at what had occurred (xi. 2, 18). Thus, by a series of divine revelations, the title of the heathen to the grace of God in Christ was revealed to Peter and the other apostles in the person of Cornelius and his household.[1]

After these preparatory events a new period of the spread of the gospel among the heathen began with the labours of *Paul*, who had in the meantime been converted and called by God to be an apostle to the Gentiles, and by virtue of his origin in Tarsus was likewise a Hellenist. The Church at Antioch was already considerably strengthened when Barnabas, who had been sent there from Jerusalem, sought out Paul, then living in his native city, and accompanied him to Antioch (xi. 25, comp. vv. 21, 24, 26; Wieseler, S. 147 f.). From that time, during the space of twenty-five years, Paul continued in the closest connection with this Church. It was

---

[1] The narrative of the Acts respecting the succession of events relating to the conversion of Cornelius has given rise to much diversity of opinion. Baur (*Paulus*, 2 Aufl. i. 90 ff.) declares it to be "a free composition," *i.e.* fabricated; Zeller, who follows him, holds the essential contents of the narrative to be unhistorical,—he even judges that they are "from beginning to end absolutely improbable and inconceivable" (*Ap. Gesch.* 1854, S. 179–190, 330); Overbeck (*Kurze Erklärung*, S. 150 f.) pronounces the narrative to be "absolutely unworthy of credit;" and Ritschl (*altkath. Kirche*, 1 Aufl. S. 123) doubts the credibility of the narrative, so far as it goes to prove the privilege of heathen conversion in the case of Cornelius. But even the psychological explanations and pragmatic suggestions which would give a character as natural as possible to the narrative for the purpose of saving its historicity (for example, Neander, *Pflanzung*, i. 115 ff.; Koch, *Petri Theologia*, S. 96 ff.), do injury to the account, and fail to attain their object.

chiefly through his instrumentality that Antioch, which was at that time not only the capital of Syria, but also the third largest city of the Roman Empire, became the starting-point of the heathen mission and the mother Church of all Gentile Christians. The epoch-making importance of Antioch for the Church of Christ already appears from the circumstance that the name of Christian was first used in this city (see *infra*, pp. 126, etc.).

The opening out of the Gentile mission from Antioch had a solemn beginning. During a devotional service, accompanied by fasting, the Holy Ghost commanded through one of the prophets, of whom several belonged to the Church, that Barnabas and Saul should be separated for a special work (the mission). This was done. They were dedicated and sent forth to this service with fasting, prayer, and the imposition of hands (xiii. 2, etc.). Humanly considered, they were sent forth by the Church; the Church at Antioch was a mission-church. The two messengers made their first missionary journey to Cyprus, Pamphylia, Pisidia, and Lycaonia, where they regularly spoke in the Jewish synagogues (xiii. 5, 14, xiv. 1), but also expounded the word of God to proselytes and Gentiles (xiii. 7, 43, 48, xiv. 15, etc.).

We here learn for the first time that Paul, in the course of his mission, was accustomed to address himself to the Jews in the first place, and in the second place to the heathen. This was his habit and his principle, as the Acts are careful to record throughout, from the first appearance of Paul in the synagogue at Damascus till he came to Rome (comp. the complete proof furnished by Zeller, *Ap. Gesch.* pp.

308–311). But even this is declared to be unhistorical, because unworthy of the Gentile apostle ; so Baur (*Tübinger Zeitschrift*, 1836, and *Paulus*, 2 Aufl. i. S. 351 ff.), followed by Schwegler (*Nachap. Zeitalter*, ii. 88 ff.), Zeller (*Ap. Gesch.* 308–311 ff.), and Overbeck (S. 207 ff.). Zeller, indeed, is sufficiently unprejudiced to admit, on the basis of the declarations of Paul himself in the Epistle to the Romans (iii. 1 ff., ix. 3 f., xi. 13 f.), that he did not exclude the Jews of the Diaspora from the circle to which he was called as the Gentile apostle ; he even recognises the probability that the apostle gladly availed himself of the connecting link for activity among the heathen which the synagogue directly presented. But it could not possibly be true that Paul made it a *principle* and *rule* always to address himself first to the Jews, and to the heathen only when repulsed by the former, so that the preaching to the heathen was conditional on want of success among the Jews. The matter, however, does not in reality stand as it is here conceived. The Acts give a different representation. In Athens, for example, Paul "disputed in the synagogue with the Jews, and with the devout persons, and in the market daily with them that met with him" (xvii. 17) ; that is, he addressed himself from the beginning not only to Jews, but also to Gentiles at the same time. It is asserted, indeed, that the latter circumstance is scarcely noticeable, and that its connection makes it of no importance (Zeller, 310 ; Overbeck, 375). But only prejudice can lead to this assertion, since, from the clearness of the words, the appearance in the synagogue before Jews together with proselytes, and that in the market-place before heathen whom he there met, appear

perfectly parallel and co-ordinate. Moreover, it is
expressly stated in xviii. 4 that in the synagogue at
Corinth Paul met both Greeks and Jews, and gained
over persons of both nations to the gospel ; certainly,
to judge from the context, these Ἕλληνες were
proselytes of the gate ; but would Paul then set aside
those Hellenes who already possessed a mind and
understanding to comprehend the truths of the old
covenant, in order to preach the gospel to others
who stood at a greater distance from it ? Paul
certainly referred sin and grace in perfectly like
measure and in the same way to Gentiles as well
as Jews ; but as to the economy of salvation and the
execution of the divine plan of redemption in time,
he has undeniably recognized a prior privilege and an
actual nearer claim of the people of Israel, not only
in doctrine (Rom. i. 16, Ἰουδαίῳ . . . πρῶτον ; comp.
ii. 9 ; 1 Cor. i. 22, etc.), but he has also, as a man
of steady consistency, made it practically prominent
in life and conduct. How deeply moved is the heart
of the apostle when he solemnly protests that he has
great heaviness and continual sorrow in his heart
lest his people should fall short of salvation in
Christ ! He desires, if it were possible, to be
banished from the blessed communion of Christ for
the sake of his brethren and kinsmen (Rom. ix. 1,
etc.). Even in his mission to the heathen he never
loses sight of his purpose to provoke his kinsmen
according to the flesh to emulation with the Gentiles,
and to save some of them (Rom. xi. 14). It is not
inconsistent with the consciousness that he is, in
the first place, an apostle to the Gentiles, when in
1 Cor. ix. 20 he testifies, " I became as a Jew, that I
might gain the Jews ; to them that are under the

law, as under the law, that I might gain them that
are under the law." These utterances are the
expression of his inmost heart. If Paul staked his
evangelical freedom in order to gain the Jews ($\tau o\grave{v}\varsigma$
Ἰουδαίους, not only a few incidentally and by the
way), a steady principle must have been his rule of
action. Who will find fault with him because his
heart beat so warmly and faithfully for his own
people, that at all times and places he preached the
fulfilment of the promise in Jesus first to his own
kinsmen, as those to whom the promise had been
given, and would not leave them until they thrust
him out? Who will censure him if, when he was
shut out from the synagogue in one city, he turned
to the Jews in the next, and refused to regard the
severance from Judaism that was forced on him in
one place as a severance of his connection with his
people? He did not on that account neglect the
Gentiles, but met with them as numerous visitors
in all the synagogues. Nor did he make his mission
to the Gentiles absolutely dependent on the reception
which the gospel had among the Jews, by the fact of
turning *exclusively* to the Gentiles only after the
decisive rejection of the gospel and thrusting out of
himself on the part of the Jews (Acts xviii. 18,
xix. 9).[1]

Let us turn back to the progress of the Gentile
mission of Paul. In his second missionary journey
with Silas he revisited the Churches which had been
founded on the first missionary journey, and which,

---

[1] Comp. Kling, *Stud. u. Krit.* 1837, S. 302 ff. ; Lekebusch, *ante*,
322 ff. ; Baumgarten, *ante*, ii. 1, S. 39–62 ; Meyer, *Comm. zur
Ap. Gesch.* 5 Aufl. 280 ff. ; Trip, *Paulus nach der Ap. Gesch.* 1866,
S. 228 ff. ; Örtel, *Paulus in der Ap. Gesch.* 1868, S. 84 ff.

like that in Antioch, must be regarded as a mixture of Jewish and Gentile Christians. They "confirmed the Churches" (xv. 41), and these "were established in the faith, and increased in number daily" (xvi. 5). The second missionary journey extended throughout Phrygia and Galatia, from Troas across to Europe, where Paul and his associates preached the gospel in the synagogues in the Macedonian towns of Philippi, Thessalonica, and Berea, and founded Churches of believers. From Macedonia, where many believed, especially *Jews*, the apostle continued his course to Greece. He preached in Athens on Mars' Hill; but was specially successful in founding in Corinth, that city of the commercial world, a numerous Church. It was not till after a longer stay that the apostle left this city and travelled back to Antioch by Ephesus (xviii. 22). On a third journey, after travelling through Galatia and Phrygia (xviii. 23), he stopped by the way for three years in Ephesus, from which he went through Macedonia to Hellas (xx. 1, etc.). The return journey was also made through Macedonia. From thence he travelled by Troas and Miletus to Jerusalem, where he became a prisoner. It is a difficult problem to establish anything more exact as to the condition of the individual Churches founded by Paul, as we have too few certain data for that purpose. To begin with the neighbourhood of Palestine, we infer unhesitatingly, from the following grounds, that the metropolis of the Gentile Christians, the Church at Antioch, consisted mainly of Gentile Christians:—1. The nucleus of the Church was already composed for the most part of "Hellenes," according to Acts xi. 20, etc.; 2. It was at Antioch itself that the first propagandist attacks of the Judaists were aimed (Acts xv. 1), by which also a powerful reaction was stirred up on behalf of the Christian freedom of the Gentiles (Acts xv. 2, etc.; Gal. ii. 1, etc.); finally, 3. The most significant fact is that the Gentile mission, which had ever-increasing success, proceeded from Antioch. If we pass from Syria into Asia Minor, following the geographical as well as the historical order, our attention is drawn to *Ephesus* above all other cities, in so far as this great commercial city was even in the time of Paul the centre of the mission for Asia Minor (Acts xix. 10), and afterwards remained the mother Church for that country. In Ephesus Paul found it necessary to leave the synagogue, after which he was in the habit of assembling the believers in the school of the rhetorician Tyrannus, who was undoubtedly a converted Hellene (Acts xix. 9). This very circumstance proves that the Gentile Christian element in the Church had decided preponderance; a fact which is also presupposed by the uproar in the matter of Artemis, and which can only be explained pragmatically on the assumption that worshippers of Artemis had been converted by the agency of the apostle (Acts xix. 19, 23, etc.; especially ver. 27). It appears from the Epistle to the Galatians, that in any case most members of the Christian churches in this country had been originally heathen (iv. 8, v. 2, etc., 12). No passage of the Epistle decidedly shows that native Jews were in the Galatian Churches (comp. Hilgenfeld, *Galater-brief*, 24 ff.). With respect to the other provinces of Asia Minor, it is probable, partly from the missionary history of Paul (for example, Acts xiii., xiv.—Pisidia and Lycaonia), partly from the contents of the First

Epistle of Peter (which shows that the Churches of
Pontus, Cappadocia, Asia, and Bithynia, besides those
already mentioned in Galatia, were Gentile Christian),
that the nucleus of their Christian Churches consisted
of Gentiles.

In Europe, Macedonia was the first, Achaia or
Greece the second missionary province of Paul. With
respect to the Macedonian Churches, it is evident
from 1 Thess. i. 9 that that of Thessalonica consisted principally of those that had been heathen
(comp. Neander, *Pflanzung*, i. 306 f.). The circumstance that in Philippi there was no synagogue
within the city, but only a " proseucha " outside it,
makes it probable that there was no considerable
number of Jews settled there, and that consequently
the Christian Churches could not number many
Jewish Christians. So much the more strongly were
the Jewish Christians represented in the church at
Berea (Acts xvii. 11). Of the Churches in Achaia,
Corinth is the most important ; in Athens, indeed, a
few Hellenes were converted, while we have no
similar statement respecting the Jews in that place ;
yet the Christian Church at Athens does not seem to
have experienced any great increase and impulse in
the time of the apostles. But Corinth, the political
capital of the province of Achaia, was also the
metropolis of Christianity in Greece proper ; and it is
a recognised fact that the Church at this place consisted principally of heathen Christians, as is shown
not only by Acts (xviii. 4, 6, etc.), but also by the
two Epistles of Paul to the Corinthians, for example,
1 Cor. xii. 2 (Neander, *ante*, i. 336 ; Baur, *Paulus*,
2 Aufl. i. 287, etc.).

Finally, in Italy, the Church at *Rome* was confessedly composed of heathen and Jewish Christians mixed. A difference of opinion exists only with respect to the numerical relation of the two parties. Until quite recently, it was the prevailing opinion that the heathen Christian element had the preponderance in numbers. Baur has tried to show from the Epistle to the Romans that the contrary was probable (*Über Zweck und Veranlassung des Römerbriefs, Tüb. Zeitschrift*, 1836, iii. 56 ff.; *Paulus*, 2 Aufl. i. 346 ff.), and has been followed in this respect not only by Schwegler (*nachapost. Zeitalter*, i. 285 ff.), but also by Thiersch and van Hengel (*Interpr.* i. 8 ff.). But such result, as Baur himself admits (*Paulus*, 2 Aufl. i. 369), rests originally on a conception of the object and occasion of the Epistle to the Romans completely at variance with the prevalent view; a conception which is by no means raised above all doubt. This is not the place to make a thorough examination of the view in question. We content ourselves with expressing our conviction that at least the Epistle to the Romans does not require for its explanation the assumption that Paul wished to defend his doctrine against a preponderating Jewish Christian element at Rome. But in the present case all necessity for imagining a Jewish Christian party of preponderating numbers in the Church at Rome is obviated. We are the more inclined to regard the Gentile Christians as predominant in the Church, since the sixteenth chapter shows that in Rome there were many friends and fellow-workers of the Apostle Paul who had undoubtedly gained over a considerable number of believers among the heathen. If we accept this view, with Neander, Tholuck, Lange, Schaff, and others, the conclusion follows that whole Churches founded by

Paul, as well as the Roman one that had arisen independently of him, were composed of Gentile and Jewish Christians together, perhaps with the exception of Athens; so that the Gentile Christian element greatly preponderated in all, except in the little one at Berea.

Thus Paul founded Churches in several districts of Asia Minor, in Macedonia and Greece, or, as he himself puts it (Rom. xv. 19), "from Jerusalem and round about unto Illyricum" (comp. Wieseler, p. 334, with note). Among the Churches founded by him, though he himself speaks of $\pi\hat{a}\sigma a\iota$ $a\acute{\iota}$ $\dot{\epsilon}\kappa\kappa\lambda\eta\sigma\acute{\iota}a\iota$ $\tau\hat{\omega}\nu$ $\dot{\epsilon}\theta\nu\hat{\omega}\nu$ (Rom. xvi. 4), there were certainly few consisting exclusively of heathen. Most of them were in fact *mixed* Churches, which we can only call heathen-Christian, *a parte potiori*. In a certain sense we may regard them all as colonies of the Church at Antioch, while the sphere of the Gentile apostle's activity was extended indirectly by his disciples and associates, as well as by letters, to regions and cities that he himself had never visited. In order to examine the peculiar nature and life of these Pauline Churches, we separate the different aspects of their life, as was done before with the Jewish-Christian Churches.

(A.) *The direct religious life of the Gentile Christian Churches, with their ecclesiastical organization.*

In his missionary labours Paul was often compelled by the opposition of the Jews, which he met with in many ways, to leave the synagogue of the place to which he had at first attached himself, and to form a religious society separate from it; so, for example, in

Pisidian Antioch, in Corinth, in Ephesus (Acts xiii. 45 ff., xviii. 5–7, xix. 8 f.). That was a decided step, fraught with important consequences, not merely to the social position of the existing communities, but also to the organization of their services, which is the thing we have in view on this occasion.

Wherever such separation took place, there was no longer any hindrance in the way of arranging the service with all its belongings, such as locality, times, forms, and acts, in correspondence with the spirit of the gospel. Accordingly, the worship of the Church could arrange itself so as to be a λογικὴ λατρεία (Rom. xii. 1), the worship of God in spirit and in truth, in accord with its peculiar nature as distinguished from Jewish cultus.

The way was opened up, and the independent development of the Christian cultus made possible; but the possible is not at once the actual also. Never at any time does a new thing come forth perfect into life at once. Nor was that the case here, because the Christian Churches founded by Paul, though gathered principally out of the heathen, consisted, nevertheless, at least partly, of converted Jews. But the attachment of the latter to their accustomed form of worship remained unbroken, even when they had separated themselves from the synagogue. It followed, in the nature of things, that the new attached itself to the old. But notwithstanding this, the relations existing in the mixed Churches in heathen lands were essentially different from those in the purely Jewish Christian Churches in Palestine especially in Jerusalem itself. These latter had, indeed, their private assemblies, in which they served God with doctrine, prayer, and the breaking of bread.

Yet they were originally only family gatherings as it were, mere accessories; participation in the services of the temple and the synagogue continued for a long time to be regarded by them as the principal thing. On the other hand, the Churches outside Palestine, wherever a breach with the synagogue took place through the fault of the Jews, had no share at all in any religious acts or services, except in those to which believers only, in the character of a Christian Church, repaired. Moreover, the fact that a particular locality had been selected for the purpose of Christian worship, in distinction not merely from the synagogue, but also from a proper dwelling-place, involved much that was new, especially when the owner was a Gentile, as we know to have been the case for example at Corinth (xviii. 7) and at Ephesus (xix. 9), in which latter city Paul, after his separation from the synagogue, taught in the school of a certain Tyrannus (xix. 19). The Acts, however, give us little information on this subject. In order to form an idea of the worship of the Christian Churches in such places, we are referred to the Pauline Epistles, among which the first to the Corinthians in particular gives some intelligence.

In the discourse delivered at Miletus (Acts xx. 20, etc.), Paul reminds the elders of Ephesus that he taught the Christians not only $\delta\eta\mu\sigma\sigma\acute{\iota}\alpha$, but also $\kappa\alpha\tau'$ $o\emph{i}\kappa\sigma\nu\varsigma$, and that he preached conversion to God and faith in Jesus Christ to the Jews and the Hellenes. He thus distinguishes two different kinds of work, namely, missionary exhortation to the Jews and heathen ($\delta\iota\alpha\mu\alpha\rho\tau\nu\rho\acute{\sigma}\mu\epsilon\nu\sigma\varsigma$, ver. 21), and instruction to those already converted, whom he was in the habit of leading to a deeper knowledge of salvation.

With respect to his work among believers ($\dot{v}\mu\hat{a}\varsigma$), the apostle indicates a twofold method by the words $\delta\eta\mu o\sigma\acute{\iota}\alpha$ and $\kappa\alpha\tau$' $o\check{\iota}\kappa ov\varsigma$—on the one hand a certain publicity in his teaching, on the other hand a seeking out of the members of the Church in their houses, with pastoral care of individuals. But the two latter activities had to do exclusively with the Church which he had gathered, with believers alone. This is in harmony with what the apostle tells us respecting the Corinthian Church. In the context in question he speaks solely of believers themselves. But in 1 Cor. xi., etc., he undoubtedly distinguishes two kinds of assemblies, some such as the Agapæ and the Lord's Supper, others for the purpose of instruction and the preaching of the word in general. Only with respect to the latter does he put the case that a non-Christian might enter (xiv. 23, $\epsilon\dot{\iota}\sigma\acute{\epsilon}\lambda\theta\eta$ $\delta\acute{\epsilon}$ $\tau\iota\varsigma$ $\ddot{\alpha}\pi\iota\sigma\tau o\varsigma$ $\mathring{\eta}$ $\dot{\iota}\delta\iota\acute{\omega}\tau\eta\varsigma$), and that they might thus serve as a means of awakening those who were at a distance. Besides the narrower exclusive assemblies of believers, there were also others in the heathen Christian Churches, as formerly at Jerusalem, at which non-Christians might be present (*vid.* Harnack, *ante*, p. 142, etc.).

If we proceed to read the Pauline Epistles with the idea that they were written altogether to mixed Churches with a predominant Gentile element, we are surprised to observe how much the apostle takes from the Old Testament, and, in a manner, even presupposes it. This phenomenon cannot be explained on the assumption of his following, in the matter, nothing but his personal inclination and custom, without regard to the knowledge and degree of culture possessed by his readers. Paul did not act in that way. On the contrary, he considered always and everywhere the standpoint and culture of those with whom he had to do. Accordingly he had reason to assume a considerable degree of acquaintance with the history, the doctrine, and the prophecy of the Old Testament on the part of his hearers, even among the Gentile Christians belonging to them. We recall, for example, quotations from the Old Testament in the Epistle to the Galatians, consequently to Churches which, as we learn from several indications in the Epistle itself, consisted in a predominant degree of converted *Gentiles* (Gal. iii. 6, etc., iv. 21, etc.; passages such as 1 Cor. ix. 9, x. 1, etc.; 2 Cor. iii. 7, etc.; Rom. iv.). Whence had the Gentile Christians of these Churches their acquaintance with the Old Testament? Doubtless from the circumstance that the law and the prophets were not only read and explained in the synagogues which they may have formerly frequented as proselytes, but also after the separation from the synagogue, in the believers' meetings for worship. What we have thus found by the process of deduction is also probable *à priori*. The announcement of the history of salvation and of Christian doctrine could, as a rule, attach itself to nothing but the Old Testament. The fact that Paul in his Athenian discourse quotes the inscription of an altar which he saw, and on the same occasion supports his assertion by the words of a Greek poet, leads us to conclude that he attached his discourses to the Old Testament, and appealed to it as an authority wherever it was possible. We find this confirmed in many ways in the Acts of the Apostles also. But the one point, viz. the use of the Old Testament as a basis of the

Christian services, cannot have been an isolated one. The fact of putting Moses and the prophets, as sacred documents, at the foundation of the building, led to the retaining of much that was peculiar to the ritual of the synagogue (Vitringa, *de Synagoga vet.* iii. 2, chap. 11), with respect to the reading (ἀνάγνωσις, 1 Tim. iv. 13) and interpretation of them, etc. But even the external arrangements of the synagogue were doubtless adhered to in many respects. The times of worship remained, indeed, as before, viz. the Sabbath as a week-day, Easter and Pentecost as yearly festivals. We also find a trace of the Jewish Passover in 1 Cor. iv. 7, where the context plainly shows that a *purely* Christian Passover is not intended. Just as little should we presuppose the existence of a genuine Jewish celebration of the feast in the Corinthian Church. On the contrary, we must assume, since Paul calls Christ the Passover Lamb, and explains the unleavened bread spiritually of justification and sanctification, that the Christians kept the feast at the same time as the Jews, but in an entirely different sense and spirit, viz. with sole reference to Christ (comp. Weitzel, *Christl. Passahfeier*, 1848, esp. pp. 183, etc.).[1]

Hitherto we have characterized the Jewish Christian, or conservative aspect of worship, in the Pauline Churches. But the epistles of the apostle also contain an element of progression, certain signs

---

[1] Hilgenfeld, indeed, maintains (*Galaterbrief*, p. 89 f.) that Paul, with the heathen-Christian Churches, no longer observed the Jewish feasts, not even with a Christian transformation, and that only the Jewish Christians retained the Jewish Sabbaths and principal feasts. But of this we have not any sufficient, much less any certain proof; while, on the other hand, the passage above quoted indicates plainly enough an attachment to the Israelitish arrangement of festivals.

of a new and peculiar development of Christian worship. The very passage last quoted included something new besides the old, inasmuch as the Passover-time was conceived in a Christian spirit, and the propitiatory death of Jesus solemnized in it. But we also find in the Pauline Churches themselves a trace of *a holy week-day among the Christians.* It is true that from the standpoint of the Apostle Paul and the Pauline Christians no one day could be regarded as more holy than another. In particular, certain days were not to be specifically distinguished from others, as legally enjoined, but rather all days were to be alike holy to the Lord; the whole life was to be a worship (Rom. xiv. 5, etc. ; Gal. iv. 9, etc. ; comp. Col. ii. 16). This principle is certainly not to be limited to those feasts and Sabbaths which were peculiarly Jewish, but should be interpreted unconditionally. But to conclude from this that in the Pauline Churches no days of the week and year were actually distinguished above others in respect of worship, would be a misapprehension of Christian freedom ; for a free separation of certain days, in conformity with Christian custom though not established by law, is quite consistent with the former principle. There are, in fact, a few passages from which we may conclude, not indeed with absolute certainty, but yet with great probability, that during this time the custom of observing the first day of the week by holy celebration gradually spread throughout the heathen Christian Churches. Paul, for example (1 Cor. xvi. 2), gives the Corinthians this advice, that every one should lay by him in store κατὰ μίαν σαββάτου, according to his means, something for the poor Christians at Jerusalem. Now the preposition κατά, without doubt to be taken distributively, implies a weekly repetition; but at the same time, Neander is right in his assertion that the meaning is not that they should bring with them to the Church-assemblies that which they had saved, in which case regular collections at service on the first day of the week would certainly be presupposed, but the $\pi\alpha\rho$' $\dot{\epsilon}\alpha\upsilon\tau\hat{\omega}$ $\tau\iota\theta\dot{\epsilon}\tau\omega$ can only be understood of laying by and storing up (*Pflanz und Leitung*, i. 272). Yet the apostle must have had some reason for definitely fixing upon this very day for the Corinthians, just as formerly for the Churches in Galatia (comp. ver. 1). The day must have had a special meaning for him and for believers in general; nothing is more likely than that it should have been set aside for worship as referring to the resurrection of Christ (comp. Weitzel, *ante*, p. 170). Harmonizing with this indication in the Epistle to the Corinthians, we have also Acts xx. 7, according to which a gathering of Christians took place in Troas $\tau\hat{\eta}$ $\mu\iota\hat{\alpha}$ $\tau\hat{\omega}\nu$ $\sigma\alpha\beta\beta\acute{\alpha}\tau\omega\nu$, at which there was breaking of bread, and where Paul, on his departure, discoursed far into the night. It is undoubtedly possible that this day was chosen solely because it was the evening before the departure of the apostle. But why then is special prominence given to the fact that this, the day preceding the departure, was Sunday, if the particular day had not a meaning besides, and if meetings for divine service did not generally take place on it? From these two passages, therefore, it is probable that already at that time it was the custom to meet for divine service on Sunday in particular, a custom which naturally found easier entrance into *Gentile Christian* Churches than into those which were purely Jewish Christian, inasmuch as the latter continued to observe the Sabbath for a longer period.

Among the sacred acts of the Christians, baptism and the Lord's Supper had a prominent place. *Baptism* attained to higher significance in the Gentile Christian Churches in proportion as the Jewish Christians belonging to them allowed circumcision to drop ; and a fact of this kind, which has been falsely estimated only where Paul is concerned, is obviously at the foundation of the passage Acts xxi. 21. With respect to baptism, however, fewer alterations seem to have taken place than in regard to the *Lord's Supper*. The latter was connected with a common meal in the primitive Church. In Corinth these brotherly repasts were joined with evening meetings, or with banquets of the Hellenes, among whom it was the custom for each guest to take his meal with him in a basket to the appointed house, in order to enjoy his own portion in company (comp. Xenoph. *Memor.* iii. 14 ; Athenäus, viii.). By this arrangement one had less, another more ; one might enjoy a simple, the other a more costly meal ; one might even suffer want, while another had a superabundance. This, however, not only injured the character of the meal as a brotherly repast, but the sacred meal of the Lord was sinfully desecrated thereby. Instead of brotherly equality, the difference of rank and fortune became glaringly prominent, and on an occasion when it should rather have been kept out of sight. Hence Paul rejects the custom with anger (1 Cor. xi. 16, etc.) as vicious, he declares that this is not κυριακὸν δεῖπνον φαγεῖν (ver. 20) ; and reminds them, on the other hand, of the original appointment and the meaning of the Holy Supper. This alteration of the custom with respect to the Holy Supper was therefore a distortion, by a ἑλληνίζειν in the bad sense of the word, against which Paul refers back to the original appointment as the permanent rule, just as the Reformers led back the degenerate Church to apostolic and biblical Christianity.[1]

At the religious assemblies in the Corinthian Church, phenomena frequently occurred which may have been rare elsewhere, and which we cannot look upon as universally Gentile-Christian; for example, the speaking with tongues or the gift of tongues, respecting which Paul (1 Cor. xiv.) gives reproof and counsel. The apostle also mentions in the same letter manifold kinds of communication in assemblies for edification, viz. doctrine, revelation, interpretation, psalms (xiv. 26, comp. 3 and 6). His purpose is not to limit Christian freedom in respect to these things; but in the face of Greek seeking after wisdom, talkativeness, and inclination to unlicensed freedom of spirit, he insists with all emphasis upon the fact that everything should proceed in order (ver. 33), that all things should aim at edification (ver. 26), and that none should exalt himself because of his gifts (chap. xii.). The apostle authorizes every competent and gifted member of the Church to come forth teaching and speaking in it; and does this so unmistakeably, that even those who in recent times have insisted most strongly upon office and its privileges, admit that teaching in the meetings of the first Churches was in no wise a thing attached exclusively to office, that is,

[1] Comp. H. Jacoby, "Die constituiren Factoren des apostolischen Gottesdienstes," *Jahrb. f. deutsche Theol.* 1873, S. 561 ff.; Georg Heinrici, *I. Kor.* 1880, S. 341 ff.; Holsten, *Das Ev. des Paulus,* 1880, S. 354 ff.

the office of presbyter, but that even plain members of the Church both had and exercised the gift of teaching (Löhe, *Aphorismen*, p. 60, etc. ; Münchmeyer, *Zeitschr. für luth. Theol. und Kirche*, 1852, p. 57). The contrast between teachers and learners was still a fluctuating one, by no means fast and firm. We must not, however, imagine an unlimited liberty of teaching for all, for the right which was acknowledged in principle was essentially limited in actual practice, first by the existence of the gift and of an inner vocation, and again, as Paul urges in the present section, by the aim of edification and the necessity for order (comp. the correct observations of Th. Harnack, *Christl. Gemeindegottesdienst*, pp. 157, 149, etc.). The words $\psi\alpha\lambda\mu\grave{o}\nu$ $\check{\epsilon}\chi\epsilon\iota$ in 1 Cor. xiv. 26 point to spiritual songs, also referred to in Col. iii. 16, and still more fully mentioned in Eph. v. 19. These were for the most part hymns of praise to God and Christ, by which, however, we are not to imagine anything of a peculiarly Gentile Christian character, but something in the form of a hymn of prayer, such as the apostle mentions in the circle of the primitive Church (iv. 24, etc.).[1]

While the Old Testament, as a sacred document, was read and explained, as above stated, in the Gentile Christian Churches for the purpose of edification, we find already in the Epistles an indication that the letters

---

[1] An attempt has been made (Lange) to attribute the $\psi\alpha\lambda\mu o\acute{\iota}$ to the Jewish Christians, and the $\H{\upsilon}\mu\nu o\iota$ to the Gentile Christians, but without sufficient foundation. We should prefer to say, with Harless and Harnack (*ante*, 160), that $\psi\alpha\lambda\mu\acute{o}\varsigma$ was the more familiar designation of the spiritual song among the Jewish Christians, and $\H{\upsilon}\mu\nu o\varsigma$ among the Gentile-Christians ; but this, too, is without sufficient foundation, especially as $\psi\alpha\lambda\mu\acute{o}\varsigma$ was a word in current use among the Hellenes also (*vid.* Meyer and Stier on Eph. v. 19).

of the apostles also were read aloud in the assemblies. For example, in 1 Thess. v. 27 the apostle charges the Thessalonians by the Lord that his epistle be read unto all the brethren; and in Col. iv. 16 he gives injunctions that this letter, after having been read in Colosse, should also be read in the Church at Laodicea, while the letter sent to Laodicea was to be read in Colosse also. In this reading of the Pauline Epistles lies the source of the reading and exposition of the apostolic epistles in Church worship, and of the writings of the New Testament in general, so that by degrees they took their place by the side of the Scriptures of the Old Testament as holy books, a development which might originate naturally in Gentile Christian as well as in Jewish Christian Churches.

We find accordingly several circumstances, acts, times, places, and means of religious edification, distinguishing the worship of the Gentile Christian Church from that of the Palestinian Jewish Christians. The relation, however, did not by any means imply that the latter adhered absolutely to the Jewish form alone in their worship, and that the Gentile Christians had entirely separated themselves from it and organized themselves under independent and purely Christian forms; for neither was a peculiarly Christian and new element wanting in the devotion and edification of the Jewish Christians, nor did the worship of the Gentile Christians stand completely apart from that of the Old Testament. On the contrary, new and old elements were to be found in both, but mixed in different degrees and prominent in different ways. Our meaning is, that Palestinian Churches stood from the beginning in close connection with the theocracy of the Old Testament with respect to public worship, and it was only in private meetings of an intimate, social, domestic kind that persons were built up, properly speaking, on Christian ground and soil; which state continued till the believers were thrust out by the Jews. In Gentile lands we find in effect the same progress, only that it here assumed a more rapid pace; while in Palestine, on the contrary, it required longer time. For the Christian Churches outside Palestine were forced, in their very beginning, by the opposition and hostility of the synagogues, to depend on themselves, and to hold religious meetings merely for themselves; so that all assemblies for the purpose of divine worship and devotion at which the Christians afterwards assisted took place on Christian ground and exclusively among Christians. By this means the peculiarly Christian form of service found an open field and fruitful soil, and consequently developed more freely, more rapidly, and more fully from within. Here, therefore, earlier than among the Jews, we find the separation of Sunday as a day sacred to believers for the sake of their Lord, on which they loved to hold meetings for divine service, while the Jewish Christians still observed the Sabbath. Here, too, we find the Passover already conceived and kept in a Christian spirit, while peculiar forms of sacred discourse are developed, and isolated writings of apostles soon take their place beside the Old Testament as regular means of edification. It certainly became evident that Hellenic propensities, customs, and mental tendencies, which asserted themselves here and there in Churches of the Gentile Christians, might easily lead to an unauthorized and unhallowed departure from the divine appointment; an eventuality which the apostle had to oppose; whereas the Jewish Christian Churches in these respects kept that which had been transmitted to them more purely and faithfully, but might, on the other hand, easily incline to evangelical legality, and even fall back into actual Judaism.

If we take a survey of the whole matter, though we cannot speak of a contrast between the Churches of the Gentile and Jewish Christians in respect to piety and worship, we may speak of a distinction in their unity. The unity of both consisted partly in communion with God in Christ on the ground of apostolic doctrine, which was the basis and aim of Christian worship on both sides; partly in the brotherly fellowship of believers with one another, actuated and promoted by that worship. Besides, there were among both not only narrower and more exclusive assemblies, but also wider and more public meetings, the latter accessible even to non-Christians. The distinction between the two rested on the deepest foundation, namely, that in the Churches gathered in heathen lands from among converted Gentiles the service was developed and formed in a freer, more independent, and purer way out of the spirit of the gospel into a peculiarly Christian organization, by virtue of their complete separation from the Israelite temple and synagogue characteristics; while in Palestine attachment to the Old Testament cult was more tenacious and lasting, the development of New Testament cultus requiring more time. In short, the freedom, independence, and novelty of Christianity stamped themselves on the Gentile Christian worship, yet in such a way that neither did the independence of the New exclude an attachment to the Old Testament form of cult, nor did the freedom exclude a law of organization that grew up from within.[1]

(B.) *Social and domestic relations of the Jewish Christians: their intercourse with non-Christians.*

The most important relation in the Pauline or mixed Churches under this aspect is unquestionably that which existed between believers from among the Jews and Gentiles in one and the same Church. At Antioch, Ephesus, Corinth, for example, Jews and Gentiles were separated from one another before the Churches were founded, by religion and peculiarity of race, by habits and mode of life. A fundamental distinction, even a moral gulf between them, must be admitted, although we neither overlook nor under-value the position and mental tendency of the Israelites in Diaspora, that is, of the Hellenists. In our former mention (page 112) of the importance of the Hellenistic Jews in spreading Christianity among the Gentiles, we perceived that they were distin-guished from the Palestinian Jews by this, namely, that they adopted the Greek language and culture; and, on the other hand, had laid aside narrow Jewish prejudices against the Gentiles. But they were Jews notwithstanding: they observed the Mosaic law, especially the commands respecting food and purity, retained circumcision, continued in religious and national connection with Palestine and the temple, remaining in the midst of the heathen a separate people, and were by this means internally divided from the heathen, in whose midst they dwelt

---

[1] Comp. the excellent discussion on this subject by Th. Harnack, p. 200, etc.

in the numerous relations of life ; just as is the case with the Jews to-day in the midst of the Christian nations of Europe. Through the preaching of Paul or his companion and helpers, in one city both Jews and Gentiles became believers, that is, they were convinced that Jesus was the Messiah, their Saviour, and strove after the kingdom of God which was at hand, and into which they wished to enter. The one party as well as the other was baptized, and formed henceforth one Church together. By faith in *one* God and in Jesus His Anointed, the *one* Lord, as well as by the reception of baptism, both parties laid aside something of their former religion, the Gentiles naturally much more than the Jews: the former casting away their gods and abandoning idolatry, the Jews worshipping the one true God to whom they had hitherto prayed, as the Father of Jesus Christ also. This negative and positive adjustment was not, however, directly followed by the result that believers from among the Jews and Gentiles actually became *one* henceforward, or that they lived on an equal footing with one another, considering themselves yet as complete brethren, and acting as such. Their common bond of united worship, the religious association and social fellowship of the ἐκκλησία θεοῦ, in which they were mutually joined, did not remove in all respects that separation in life and intercourse by which they had been hitherto kept asunder. Both were henceforward rightful parts of the Christian Church in the place where they lived, though by no means welded one with another. The Church consisted of two elementary materials of different sorts, of the περιτομή and the ἀκροβυστία, to use the words of Paul. The two elements existed in the Church of Christ, united, as it were, in one and the same river-bed, like two streams which, having been different waters in origin and course, and widely separated by a considerable stretch of land, each stream keeping its peculiar colour, at last completely mix and actually form *one whole.* So the internal union and welding of Jewish and Gentile Christians within the same Church always required a length of time; it formed a problem to the solution of which not a little moral force must be applied. Wherever the Jewish synagogue did not repel believers from itself, there the separation of the social community continued longer than where the same thing took place soon. In the former case the Jewish Christians on their side remained longer estranged from the Gentile Christians. On the other hand, it is not improbable in itself, and is indicated by a passage in the First Epistle to the Corinthians, that believers from among the Gentiles did not at once break off all relation to the temples of the gods, or every contact with the sacrificial feasts (x. 21). By this means they on their side helped to alienate the believing Jews. The Gentile Christians might find many reasons for taking part in the customs and usages of their former religious associates, their heathen relations, in a way which was offensive to their Jewish fellow-Christians, and tended to keep them at a certain distance. To this was added the national feeling on both sides, finding expression among the Jewish Christians as theocratic pride, with contempt and scorn of the " sinners from among the Gentiles " (*adversus omnes alios hostile odium,* Tacit. *Hist.* v. 5); among the Gentile Christians as Hellenic pride of culture, with lofty disdain of the barbarians. Taking all this into

account, it is self-evident that many difficulties had
to be overcome and much time must elapse before
inner community of belief could be developed
into a true community of life; or, on the contrary,
the external bond of fellowship could be intensified
and deepened into a true welding of spirits. It may
easily be supposed that the process of welding, the
work of building into one edifice, could not go forward
without interruption; that frequently an event intervened which not only checked the work that had
already progressed to a certain stage, but at once
threw it far back again. Such an event, for example,
was the appearance of the τινες ἀπὸ ᾽Ιακώβου in
Antioch and the consequences that followed. The
reproach of a ὑπόκρισις, which Paul makes against
the Jewish Christians of the Church at Antioch, and
even against Peter himself, presupposes that though
the social amalgamation of the various elements in that
Church had already advanced pretty far, the brotherly
state was now again placed in jeopardy. But the
frank and energetic appearance of Paul seems to have
averted the danger immediately. For further details
of this event under another point of view, *vide infra.*

Traces are everywhere to be seen of a long-
sustained internal schism between former Gentiles
and Jews within the separate Churches, in all places
where Paul in his epistles warns against self-exaltation, exhorts to brotherly, forbearing regard for
one another, where he requires the strong to assist
the weak, and to give them no cause of offence,
for example, Rom. xii. 3, etc., especially xiv. 1–15
and 13. Here the apostle sets out with a distinction which some of the believers made between
certain meats and days; he labours to convince

them that none should judge and condemn the other,
but that every one should only serve the Lord, live
unto Christ, give no offence to a weak brother, but
rather aim at furthering and edifying him. This
copious admonition presupposes the existence at that
time, even within the Roman Church, of much friction
and tension, especially between believers from among
the Jews and from among the Gentiles. So also in
the discussion in 1 Cor. viii., where the participation
of the Gentile Christians in sacrificial, idolatrous
banquets and the use of sacrificial flesh are spoken of.
The exhortation amounts to this, that none should
wound the conscience of a weak brother by an act
which would be offensive to him. The apostle
returns to this subject in x. 23, etc.; and the
admonition in Col. ii. 16, etc., is analogous to the
foregoing passages in the Epistle to the Romans.

To guide and bring to a successful issue this
blending of the various elements within the mixed
Churches was one of the most important and most
difficult life-tasks of the Apostle Paul. He accomplished it in word and deed by his personal conduct
and example (1 Cor. viii. 13, ix. 19–22, x. 33, xi. 1),
as well as by manly blame of a proceeding calculated
to obstruct the work (Gal. ii. 11, etc.). But the
peculiar manner in which he conceived the gospel
of Christ and developed Christian doctrine tended
greatly to the furtherance of the work of union;
while, on the other hand, this practical task which
had devolved upon him exercised a visible influence
on his own personal perception of Christian truth.
To it in great measure is due his pure and full
recognition of Christian *freedom* (ἡ ἐλευθερία ἡμῶν
ἣν ἔχομεν ἐν Χριστῷ Ἰησοῦ, Gal. ii. 4); and, again,

his clear insight into the kingdom of God and the nature of Christianity, according to which it is *spirit* (Rom. xiv. 17: "For the kingdom of God is not meat and drink; but righteousness, and peace, and joy in the Holy Ghost;" comp. Gal. iii. 3: "Having begun in the spirit, are ye now made perfect by the flesh?"); his emphatic insistence on what was essentially *new*, the new creation in Christ (Col. iii. 9–11); besides, the great prominence which he gives to the truth that there is *one God, one Lord, one Spirit*, whom we serve (1 Cor. xii. 4–6; Eph. iv. 5, etc.), as well as to the corresponding duty to do all to the glory of God, to do everything to the Lord, to live to Him alone (1 Cor. x. 31; Rom. xiv. 6–9, 18; Col. iii. 17), since it is the Lord alone who judgeth His own, while no believer is competent to judge another (Rom. xiv. 10); finally, the development of the idea of the Church as a living unity of the body of Christ embracing different members (Rom. xii. 4, etc.; 1 Cor. xii. 12, etc.; Col. iii. 11; Eph. i. 22, etc., ii. 11, etc., comp. iv. 1, etc.). In the latter passages the significance of the death of Jesus is made specially prominent, as that by which the wall of separation is torn down,—out of two *one* whole being made, of Gentile and Jew only *one* new man, *both* having access to the Father through Jesus in *one* Spirit. All these truths, of the highest importance in the Pauline system of doctrine, have also in the main (which has not always been recognized) a practical side, a reference to the work of fraternization and inner union of believers from among the Jews and Gentiles, first in individual mixed Churches, then in the great body of the Church. Not without a purpose does the apostle, in the very connection where he recommends to the Corinthians a brotherly disposition, and exhorts them to edify one another, and to do all for the glory of God, remind them to be without offence not only to the Jews but also to the Gentiles, and to the Church of God (1 Cor. x. 32).[1]

---

[1] According to the problem of his life which has been discussed above, the Apostle Paul has inestimable importance, both for the Church of Christ and for humanity in general. Not only was he the first to bring out the unity of the human race inherent in the person of the God-man into clear perception, but also to establish it practically and in fact. In pre-Christian times, divided and disunited humanity longed after the union and interpenetration of the different races and nationalities. But nothing good came of it (comp. Bunsen, *Hippolytus*, i. pp. 131, 257 ; Schaff, *Kirchengesch.* i. 471, etc.). Conquering Rome was just then occupied with uniting all the known world into its empire. But all its conquests and its wonderful gift of ruling produced only a formless mass of peoples, a gigantic body without a uniting spirit, naturally so, because itself had not this spirit, but was of the old man which is fleshly, being of the earth and itself earthy. When the second man came,—the Lord from heaven, who is Spirit,—it became possible to bring mankind into actual unity, beginning from within, by virtue of the one life-giving Spirit (1 Cor. xv. 45, 47), under the one head which is Christ. The instrument of God who was called to establish this unity in thought and deed was Paul. As a true Israelite without falsehood, and, at the same time, by the grace of Christ as the apostle of the Gentiles, with deep spiritual doctrinal development, but, at the same time, with that stupendous missionary activity which he had from the grace of God, with his marvellous spiritual gift of rule and original power of organizing, he united Jews and Hellenes in *one* Church, in *one* family, under *one* Head and Lord, in *one* faith and in brotherly love, and brought together the different Churches of the East and West into *one* body, so as to become *one* Church of Christ. The walls of partition thrown down by the divine-human personality and propitiatory death of Jesus, were completely destroyed by the Apostle Paul. Though he did not, it is true, complete and carry through the work of uniting the human race, yet there is still a hope at this day of reaching that goal, and we in faith expect it ; but Paul put the first hand to the united structure, building on the foundation which was laid, viz. Jesus Christ ; which is his world-historical, immortal work.

All these truths were clear and living to the soul
of Paul, but they were not on that account immediately taken into the consciousness of believers
themselves. Besides, much lies between the appropriation of a conviction, and faithful, persevering
action corresponding to it. For this reason the work
of uniting and welding proceeded but slowly, especially
as Paul himself, in conformity with his own principles,
did not endeavour to hasten the accomplishment by
impatient urgency, and moreover would have nothing
factitious, but was clearly of opinion that the thing
could only be developed from within. Yet we have
no ground for doubting that even in the lifetime of
the Apostle Paul important steps in this direction at
least had taken place in many Churches, that a good
foundation had been laid for the work before he was
obliged to leave the scene. It may be seen from the
passage which has been often quoted already, Acts
xxi. 21, that the Jewish Christians in particular
made concessions in the matter. The presupposition
that Paul led the foreign Jews into apostasy was
false. But we must always look upon this as a fact,
that the believing Jews in the Diaspora gradually fell
away from the Mosaic law and Jewish customs; a
result to which communion with their brethren from
among the Gentiles undoubtedly contributed. It is
natural to suppose that the different members
approached nearer and more closely to one another
by mutual services and assistance performed in love
from a principle of faith; that " unity in Spirit " was
also maintained and promoted by " the bond of
peace," insomuch that in the course of time Christians
from among Jews and Gentiles learned to look upon
one another without distinction as brethren and

sisters, the one party forgetting by degrees that they had formerly been Jews, the other party that they had been Gentiles. The point in question was not of an " absorptive union," to make use of a common expression, requiring the Jewish Christians to go over to the Gentile Christians, or *vice versa*, and be completely absorbed in them, but of a union in a higher third, in faith in *one Lord*, and in a communion higher than the Jewish theocracy and the religious national Church of the Gentiles. It was necessary for both parties to renounce something: the Jewish Christians their legal righteousness, their Levitical characteristics, their Jewish exclusiveness ; the Gentile Christians their Hellenic pride of culture, their heathen propensities and customs.

With regard to the question how far this union was realized in the apostolic era, especially in the case of individual mixed Churches, we must not overlook a small notice which at the first glance seems to have little importance, but is yet in many respects full of significance ; we refer to the fact transmitted to us in Acts xi. 26, that " the disciples " were called "Christians (Χριστιανοί) first in Antioch." We take up this remark here in the aspect under which it is a testimony to the progress of amalgamation between Jewish and Gentile Christians. The name should plainly include *all* members of the Church at Antioch, without regard to their descent, whether Jewish or Gentile; for Luke employs the definite article τοὺς μαθητάς. But the name " Christians " presupposes that the believers were already separable from the Jews; otherwise it would not have occurred to any one to give them a peculiar designation. The name was certainly not an invention of the Jews, for they would have been the last to allow the Christians to be called by a name so sacred and so revered by them, viz. "people of the Messiah;" it was their habit rather to give them contemptuous names, such as " Nazarenes, Galilæans," and the like. And assuredly the name did not originate with the Christians; the name of Christ was for them too sacred and special; among themselves they were called only disciples, believers, brethren.[1] The form and nature of the name show that it proceeded from the Gentiles in Antioch.

The very circumstance, however, that the name of Christian was so early, and that it began in Antioch, has been doubted by Lipsius (*Über den Ursprung und den ältesten Gebrauch des Christennamens*, 1873), who has put forth the conjecture that the name originated in Asia Minor where Christianity had become a historical power at an early period, though by no means so early as the Acts represent. His lead has been followed by several, for example, even the cautious and independent Mangold (*Bleek's Einl. in das N. T.*, 3 Aufl. p. 414, note). On examining the reasons adduced by Lipsius, we cannot find them by any means convincing. He asserts that the name came into use pretty late as a self-designation of the believers, that it first appears as a standing appellation in the apologists, as it perhaps began to be employed among the Christians owing to judicial

[1] Yet in the whole period embraced by the New Testament writings, the Christians never appropriated this name, even after it was current ; so little was it in harmony with their faith in the Redeemer. In the two cases in which, apart from this passage, the name occurs, it is mentioned as coming from the mouth of a stranger,—in Acts xxvi. 28 from the mouth of a Jew, King Agrippa, and in 1 Pet. iv. 16 from the mouth of the Gentiles.

trials, after it had been applied to them by opponents; consequently (?) the Acts transferred the view of a later time back to the days of the Apostle Paul (p. 10, etc.). Yet both Tacitus (*Annal.* xv. 44) and Suetonius (*Nero*, 16) mention the name as in use among the Roman people at the time of the Neronian persecution (*Quos . . . vulgus Christianos appellabat*). Lipsius endeavours to weaken the force of these witnesses by the supposition that both may have dated the name back into the time of Nero, while their testimony is valid only for their own time (chap. 116, resp. 120 A.D.). But Leopold von Ranke, that competent judge of an historian, recognises the virtuosity of Tacitus among other things in the "objectivity of his representation and the choice of his words" (*Weltgeschichte*, iii., 2 Abth. 1883, p. 317, etc.). The treatise in question has the merit of having destroyed the fable according to which the name is Roman, and its origin to be sought in Rome itself (Baur, *Paulus*, 2 Aufl. i. 103 f.). Lipsius concedes that the derivation may possibly be from the Latin; but he shows that the form $-\alpha\nu o\varsigma$, $-\eta\nu o\varsigma$, was frequently employed in later Greek for names adopted from unclassical lands, for example, from Persia, Asia Minor, etc.: hence the ancient grammarians designated this form of word as an "Asiatic type." Lipsius points out in particular that Syrian names of this form appear, but he does not thence infer that the statement of Luke in the passage just mentioned is authenticated thereby, but merely that the Antiochian origin of the Christian name is in itself "quite conceivable," only that it is not certain because the account coincides with the pragmatic point of view which the author takes (!)—page 19. The result of our examination is that the doubt raised against this communication of Luke's can only tend to the confirmation of its credibility. The fact itself that the Christian name came first into use in Antioch at the time of the Apostle Paul must be looked upon as assured (comp. Keim, *Aus dem Urchristentum*, 1878, p. 175, etc.; Hilgenfeld, *Zeitschrift*, 1881, 304, etc.; Wendt, *Meyer's Comm. zur Ap. Geschichte*, 5 Aufl. p. 253, etc.). It is a certain fact that the Gentiles then, and a considerable time after, regularly looked upon the Christians as Jews, that is, as one of the inner Jewish sects. If, then, the name Christian came first into use in the great city of Antioch, which was prominent by its culture and intelligence, in the midst of heathen populations, we are justified in concluding that the distinction between Christians and Jews in this case was evident not merely with respect to the Gentile Christians (for all without distinction were called Χριστιανούς), but also with respect to the believing Jews. Touching the Jewish Christians at Antioch, we have fortunately adequate testimony in the words of Paul, from which we learn, indirectly indeed but yet with certainty, that the Jewish Christians at Antioch were accustomed to live on the same footing in every way with the Gentile Christians of the Church, without allowing themselves to be withheld from brotherly intercourse with them by Levitical laws. The reproach of a ὑπόκρισις made against them by Paul (Gal. ii. 13), clearly shows that the contrary was the rule. These passages of the Acts and of Paul therefore throw light upon one another in an unlooked-for way. Taking both together, it becomes certain that the work of amalgamation had already made considerable progress, at least in this powerful metropolis of mixed and purely Gentile Churches, at a very early date, that is, subsequently to the year A.D. 40. The origin of the name of Christian in Antioch is a proof that the Christians of this city had made themselves distinguishable as a society of a kind which could be classed neither with the Jews nor with the Gentiles, but constituted a *genus tertium*.

The brotherly feasts, or agapæ, formed one of the means to this amalgamation. It was greatly in its favour that the Hellenic custom of similar meetings with a social object, common to the country, met the existing Christian custom half-way, so to speak.[1] In the meantime, in order that the aim of a brotherly union on a footing of equality should be attained, it was indispensably necessary to be on the watch lest the Christian custom of brotherly feasts should be deteriorated and profaned by heathen immorality (*vid. ante*, p. 117, etc.).

Besides the most important contrast existing between the Pauline Churches, viz. that between believers from among the Jews and from among the Gentiles, there were still found many social differences which awaited their adjustment, for example, the distinction between slaves and freedmen. But even this the Apostle Paul (1 Cor. vii. 21, etc.) endeavours to adjust in the Church, not indeed by desiring that the slaves belonging to believing masters should be immediately set free, but by urging that

---

[1] The numerous companies and societies flourishing in the first century of the Roman Empire arranged so regular a series of common meals as even to prove injurious to domestic economy (comp. Hatch, *Organization of the Early Churches*, 1883, translation, p. 22, etc., note 13).

slaves who had been called in the Lord should consider themselves as the Redeemer's freedmen, and should be looked upon as such by the free in the Church; whilst the free man, so far as he was a believer, was to be the servant of Christ. These principles were practically followed by the apostle when he sent back to Colosse, to his rightful master, Onesimus, a slave that had fled to Rome, and had been converted by Paul during his captivity,—sent him back now as a beloved brother whom his master might receive as the apostle himself (Philem. 16, etc.). Paul allows the relation between slaves and masters to stand without disturbing it, but he changes it by the Christian spirit from within to a relation of mutual esteem and love, though by this means the external proprietary relation was sure in the end to be metamorphosed and destroyed (comp. my treatise, *Sklaverei und Christentum*, 1878). Only in one respect, as it appears, was the social equality of believers not favoured by Paul, viz. *with regard to sex*, inasmuch as he declares himself against the custom of women speaking in the services of the Church and desiring to teach (1 Cor. xiv. 34, etc.). We must not, however, take this in any other sense than that the apostle was the more desirous of securing to women their natural sphere of activity in the house, the more firmly he set limits to morbid desires of self-assertion, a false insistence on equality, and an unwomanly desire to achieve great deeds. In agreement with this are the utterances respecting married and unmarried life in the First Epistle to the Corinthians (vii. 25–40), which treats fully of such questions. It seems that in Corinth, among certain parties of the Church (not indeed, as Neander conjectures, so much among the Judaists as the followers of St. Paul (*Pflanzung*, i. 405, etc., 424, etc.)), a tendency asserted itself to give unconditional pre-eminence to an unmarried life as an incomparable help to virtue. The apostle opposes this unhealthy ascetic disposition, giving his opinion on the question in a manner equally thoughtful and truly Christian. He does, indeed, concede a certain priority to an unmarried life, but does not put Christian perfection in the unmarried state, nor generally in an external absence and deprivation of earthly goods, but in the disposition through which all, married as well as unmarried, rich and poor, should be ready to deny themselves and to offer every sacrifice which the Lord may require, according to their circumstances.

Thus in the midst of the mixed or Gentile Christian Churches there appeared many social differences, even contrasts, the reconciliation and adjustment of which was an ethical problem for the Church. We have seen in what spirit the apostle of the Gentiles strives to attain this end in the circle of communities where he laboured; but, at the same time, we get the impression that there existed in these Churches a manifold and active life, which had also to contend against stronger and more numerous antagonisms than in the Churches which consisted entirely of Jewish Christians.

The question remains to be answered, How did the Gentile Christian Churches act in the matter of intercourse with non-Christians?

In the first place, if we consult the Acts, we learn that at the very founding of these Churches, heathen inhabitants of the cities in which they were established attacked the Apostle Paul and his companions, perhaps even the believers that had been won over from among themselves. But if we look more closely, we find that these hostilities began in most cases at the instigation of Jews—for example, in Pisidian Antioch (xiii. 50), in Iconium (ii. 2, 4, etc.), in Lystra (xiv. 19), in Thessalonica and Berea (xvii. 5, etc.). It was only in Philippi (xvi. 16, etc.) and in Ephesus (xix. 23, etc.) that the attacks proceeded immediately and directly from the heathen population —in one case under a religious pretext and with an outburst of fanaticism, in the other case under a political cover, but both times in reality from mere motives of selfishness and material interest. If we take all together, the result is that the Christians were attacked by heathen only in isolated cases, and always from a special agitation stirred up by interested persons. We must therefore assume that as a rule they were left unmolested. On the other hand, we may presuppose, in accordance with this fact, that the Christians enjoyed peaceable intercourse with the heathen.

If we compare the epistles of the apostle, we find the above statements respecting occasional hostilities towards the Christians on the part of the heathen, confirmed by what Paul testifies to the Thessalonians (in the First Epistle, ii. 14), namely, that they had suffered many things of their own countrymen and compatriots, even as the Palestinian Churches had suffered of the Jews. Other passages, however, presuppose a frequent friendly intercourse between Christians and Gentiles, for example, 1 Cor. x. 27, etc.: εἰ δέ τις καλεῖ ὑμᾶς τῶν ἀπίστων, καὶ θέλετε πορεύεσθαι, πᾶν τὸ παρατιθέμενον ὑμῖν ἐσθίετε. The apostle could only have spoken thus if he knew that Christians were frequently invited by Gentiles to their feasts. With regard, therefore, to the admonition of the apostle in this case, so much is clear, viz. that he by no means forbids Christians to accept such an invitation, but rather leaves it to the discretion of each one, whether he will respond to the invitation of an unbeliever or not. Further, in the case of mixed marriages between Christians and non-Christians, which must naturally have been very frequent at that time, the apostle does not advise a separation. The believer should rather help to convert the other (1 Cor. vii. 12–16). With respect to *heathen rulers*, the apostle enjoins the Christians to pay them reverence for the fear of God and for conscience sake, for they are appointed by God, that is, they are an institution of the world-controlling and ordering wisdom of God (Rom. xiii. 1, etc.; comp. Tholuck, *Comm.*, 5 Aufl. p. 680, etc.). This, however, is quite consistent with the other exhortation, which deserves attention in a social respect, that Christians should not bring matters of dispute with one another before heathen judges, but should arrange their affairs peaceably among themselves and come to an agreement (1 Cor. vi. 1, etc.). A frequent exhortation of Paul is this, that believers should endeavour so to live as by their conduct to give no offence to those that are without, non-Christians (1 Thess. iv. 12): ἵνα περιπατῆτε εὐσχημόνως πρὸς τοὺς ἔξω, and more definitely (1 Cor. x. 32), ἀπρόσκοποι γίνεσθε καὶ Ἰουδαίοις καὶ Ἕλλησι καὶ τῇ ἐκκλησίᾳ τοῦ θεοῦ. That which is here negatively expressed appears in its positive form in Phil. ii. 15 : ἵνα ἦτε ἄμεμπτοι . . . τέκνα θεοῦ ἄμωμα μέσον γενεᾶς σκολιᾶς καὶ διεστραμμένης, ἐν οἷς φαίνεσθε ὡς φωστῆρες ἐν κόσμῳ.

(C.) *The constitution and ritual of the Gentile Christian Churches.*

According to the account of the Acts, Paul and Barnabas, on their way back from their first missionary journey, had already appointed elders in the cities of Lystra, Iconium, and Antioch, where they had founded Christian Churches shortly before (Acts xiv. 21–23). The expression κατ' ἐκκλησίαν plainly shows that in each of these three cities of Asia Minor, the new converts were already at this time united and incorporated in one Church. Moreover, we cannot well understand the statement that πρεσβύτεροι were appointed κατ' ἐκκλησίαν, as implying that every Church had one elder; but only that several had been introduced into every Church. But the sense of χειροτονήσαντες αὐτοῖς πρεσβυτέρους is doubtful. Does it mean that Paul and Barnabas introduced these elders themselves, and invested with office men who were in their judgment fitted for it by virtue of a peculiar plenitude of authority (Löhe, *Aphor.* 58) ?, or does it mean, they arranged that the Churches themselves should choose men in whom they had confidence. As χειροτονεῖν originally signifies to vote, to choose by the lifting up of hands, by " a majority of hands " (to use a Swiss expression), we may possibly attribute to the word the meaning of an arrangement of the Church's choice.[1] It is philologically safer to allow that

---

[1] This view seems to be favoured by the circumstance that in the recently discovered Διδαχὴ τῶν ἀποστόλων (chap. xv.), the same word is used for the Church's choice, which looks like a reminiscence of the passage in question : χειροτονήσατε . . . ἑαυτοῖς ἐπισκόπους καὶ

the word should be taken here in the signification
of choosing which is attested elsewhere, so that
it denotes neither the appointment of the elders
according to personal judgment and by full official
power, nor does it expressly include active participation of the Church.   In any case, it must be self-
evident that the confidence and judgment of the
Church-members were taken into account (comp.
Rothe, *Anfänge*, p. 150 ; Baumgarten, *ante*, ii. 1,
99, etc.).   But the question whether the Churches
themselves chose, or whether the apostles, by virtue
of their peculiar authority, appointed elders, is a
subordinate one in comparison with the question
whether this account of the appointment of elders
can be considered as historically certain or not.
Schrader has asserted (*Der Ap. Paulus*, v. 543) that
a later arrangement has been here thrown back into
an earlier time, and has been incorrectly and immediately referred to the apostles.   In opposition to this
we remark, *first*, that elders are already mentioned in
Jerusalem *before* the first missionary journey of Paul
(Acts xi. 30), and are supposed to be already in
existence, without a word being said as to the way
in which the office originated.   They are mentioned
quite incidentally ; we have therefore the less reason
for disputing the former assertion.   But if elders

διακόνους.   In the διδαχή, however, the grammatical construction is
decisive, while in the present passage the expression, apart from the
etymological meaning of the verb, is in favour of a choice made by
the apostles.   Yet in the discourse of Peter (Acts x. 41), προκεχειρο-
τονημένοι ὑπὸ τοῦ θεοῦ is used of the immediate divine choice and
calling to be witnesses of Christ.   In the sense thus authorized, the
words are understood by de Wette-Overbeck ; D. Plumptre, *Comm.
in Bishop Ellicott's N. T. Comm. for Schools*, 1879, p. 230 ; Wendt
in *Meyer's Comm.*, 5 Aufl. 1880, S. 310.

already existed as officials in the Jewish Christian Churches, it becomes the less improbable that Paul and Barnabas should have introduced this already-existing arrangement into other Churches also. If elders had not yet been mentioned throughout the Acts, and we learned all at once that Paul appointed elders in those cities, there would be something surprising in the circumstance, which, however, is not the case as matters stand. *Secondly*, we must also consider the condition of these Churches. The local distance of the newly-founded communities in the districts of Pisidia and Lycaonia from their mother-Church, viz. Antioch in Syria, their position with regard to a hostile Jewish population (xiv. 22), their separation from the synagogue, which took place at the very first—all these circumstances necessitated an independent, firm, social constitution; and this might be supposed to exist without overseers. If then the chosen overseers were called πρεσβύτεροι, the circumstance certainly reminds us of the elders in the Palestinian Churches; and their office itself was moulded after the arrangements of the Jewish synagogue. An attachment of this nature to the Jewish and Jewish Christian constitution is probable enough in the very beginning of Paul's activity as the apostle of the Gentiles. Finally, the Acts expressly state that the elders were first chosen on the return-journey; therefore after the Churches had already existed for a period whose duration we cannot accurately measure, and had made experiences, and, in the absence of their founder from that district, must have felt the necessity for an organism of independent guidance. Hence there are reasons enough to make the appointment of the elders not only possible, but even probable (comp. Schneckenburger, *Zweck der Apostelgesch.* p. 235, etc.; Hatch, *ante*, 3rd Lecture, esp. p. 58, etc.).

Only once again does the author of the Acts mention the elders of a Gentile Christian Church, viz. the elders of Ephesus, whom Paul, on his last journey to Jerusalem, requested to come to him at Miletus, that he might confer with and take leave of them (xx. 17). These elders of the Ephesian Church appear quite unexpectedly; it is silently taken for granted that they were already in existence, just as in xi. 30. But what is most remarkable here is, that Paul in the course of his speech calls them ἐπίσκοποι (ver. 28): "Take heed therefore unto yourselves, and to all the flock over the which the Holy Ghost hath made you *overseers*, to feed the Church of God." If ἐπίσκοποι be here taken at once as an official title, it is clear that in this passage πρεσβύτεροι and ἐπίσκοποι are identical. Yet it appears as if ἐπίσκοποι (ver. 28) were not an appellation of office as such, but rather denotes the work to which they were called (oversight of the flock in whose midst they were), and the responsibility which was laid upon their conscience. It was not, however, from accident that this very expression was chosen. Without doubt it was employed with reference to the official name ἐπίσκοπος. 1 Pet. v. 1, etc.: πρεσβυτέρους τοὺς ἐν ὑμῖν παρακαλῶ ὁ συμπρεσβύτερος . . . ποιμάνατε τὸ ἐν ὑμῖν ποίμνιον τοῦ θεοῦ, ἐπισκοποῦντες μὴ ἀναγκαστῶς, has a great similarity to the present passage. Πρεσβύτεροι appears to be an official name, whilst the business of the calling is designated in a free way by ἐπισκοπεῖν, but even here doubtless with an allusion to the official name ἐπίσκοποι.

If we pass to the epistles of the Apostle Paul, we find in the oldest of them, viz. the first to the Church at Thessalonica, written about the year 54 from Corinth, an exhortation in v. 12, etc., concerning the overseers of the Church. The apostle, however, does not distinguish them by a definite express official name (whether πρεσβύτεροι or ἐπίσκοποι), but only notes their position in a general way (προιστάμενοι), and the duties which devolved upon them, so far as they laboured (κοπιῶντες) in the midst of the members of the Church, whose directors they were in Christ's name and power, giving them (νουθετοῦντες ὑμᾶς) moral admonitions and reproofs. Their task is the moral guidance of believers. In *one* Church they even form a majority. Doubtless they were appointed at the time when the Church was founded, and we may conjecture that the same thing took place at the founding of other Churches, an opinion confirmed by προιστάμενος (Rom. xii. 8).[1] The apostle requests the believers at Thessalonica to show great esteem for their overseers, to conduct themselves towards them in love and peace. On the other hand, in one of the latest epistles of the captivity to the Church at Philippi, likewise a Macedonian Church, the apostle even in the introductory salutation (i. 1) addresses the " saints in Christ Jesus who are in Philippi " with the " bishops and deacons." Here it is clear that the officers of the Church, with the other members of it, are included in these two names (σύν). As no πρεσβύτεροι are named, we must assume that they

---

[1] Comp. C. Weizsäcker, "Die Kirchenverfassung des ap. Zeit-alters," *Jahrb. f. deutsche Theologie*, 1873, S. 631 ff.

did not exist along with the ἐπίσκοποι and διάκονοι.
The subject is most naturally illustrated by the fact,
attested also by the pastoral epistles (viz. Titus i. 5,
etc., comp. 1 Tim. iii. 1–7), that in the New Testament elders and ἐπίσκοποι are not distinct offices, but
only different names of *one* and the same office (comp.
Rothe, 173, etc.).

Yet we must not believe that these names of offices
were arbitrarily exchanged.　Such is not the case.
In Palestinian Churches, and among Jewish Christians
outside the Holy Land, we find the overseers always
called πρεσβύτεροι, but never ἐπίσκοποι. ἡγούμενοι,
Heb. xiii. 7, 17, 24, does not appear to be taken for
a proper official title, but only to designate functions,
as in 1 Thess. v. 12.　On the other hand, the overseers of Gentile Christian or mixed Churches are
sometimes denominated πρεσβύτεροι, sometimes ἐπίσκοποι, for example, those of Philippi only ἐπίσκοποι;
those of Ephesus, in the account of the historian
(Acts xx. 17), πρεσβύτεροι; in the discourse of Paul
himself, ἐπίσκοποι.[1]　In his First Epistle (v. 1, etc.)
Peter calls the overseers of Christian Churches in the
districts of Asia Minor, to whom he writes, πρεσβύτεροι—but he designates (ver. 2) their official duties
by ποιμαίνειν, along with ἐπισκοπεῖν, which may be
an allusion to the official name, ἐπίσκοπος.　Now
it is without doubt that the name and office of the
πρεσβύτεροι in Jewish - Christian Churches were
derived from the זְקֵנִים of the Jews.　Hence this

---

[1] This trait, apparently insignificant, if rightly estimated, is in
favour of the genuineness and truth of the Pauline discourse (Acts
xx. 18, etc.).　How different would it have been if the narrator had
used the expression ἐπίσκοποι (ver. 17), and put πρεσβύτεροι (ver. 28)
in the words of the apostle himself!

name was the original one, and afterwards continued to prevail in the Palestinian Churches; for not only do the Acts call the overseers of the Church at Jerusalem, without exception, πρεσβύτεροι, but James also, in his epistle to the Jewish Christians in the Diaspora, speaks of the οἱ πρεσβύτεροι τῆς ἐκκλησίας (v. 14). The case is different in mixed Churches. It is true that the Acts call the overseers in the first Churches of Asia Minor πρεσβύτεροι, but such Hebraizing name was less common among people of Grecian customs and culture in this sense.[1] Among them a name had to be borrowed from known relations, but not from a religious institution of the heathen, lest they should fall into the κοινωνία τῶν δαιμονίων (comp. 1 Cor. x. 20). If the Christian organization nevertheless attached itself to something existing in heathen lands, it could only be to forms of the *civil* community, or of free union. But the Hellenes had several kinds of functionaries for guidance and oversight in communal affairs, who were entitled ἐπίσκοποι. In Athens, for example, this name was given to those officials who were appointed in the cities dependent on the Athenian state, for the purpose of oversight; while in the fragment of an old Roman jurist, a certain grade of police-officers, in charge of provisions, are called *episcopi*.[2] Even Hooker suspected that the college of decurions, that is, the municipal government of provincial towns in the Roman empire, may have served as a model in the

---

[1] The discussion of Hatch, 2nd and 3rd Lectures, pp. 30, 61, etc., proves that the name πρεσβύτερος was used for the Greek γερουσίαι of Asia Minor; but his quotations from inscriptions leave the impression that this was rather the exception than the rule.

[2] For evidence of this use of language, see Hatch, p. 30, notes; comp. Rothe, *Anfänge*, S. 219 f., note 69.

appointment of officers of the Christian Church as the decurions of a Christian commune. He is followed by Rothe (S. 148, 218, comp. 154 f.). Hence we see in the names πρεσβύτεροι and ἐπίσκοποι, as in so many of the New Testament words, a conflux, as it were, of two trains of thought —an Eastern and a Western. The word ἐπίσκοπος in the Churches of the Gentile Christians gradually lost its general meaning, as may be proved, and became the designation of a particular office (comp. Stanley, *Sermons*, p. 68).

In the introduction of the Epistle to the Philippians, as already stated, διάκονοι are mentioned together with ἐπίσκοποι. These, then, are the deacons proper, in the sense of later Church history, whom we accordingly find first in a Gentile Christian Church; for the seven men of the Acts are neither in name nor in reality the later deacons. As in the Macedonian Church of Philippi, so there were also without doubt deacons in the Churches of Achaia. The mention at least of a female deaconess, Phœbe, in the Church of Cenchrea, near Corinth (Rom. xvi. 1, etc.), presupposes the existence of male deacons. It is also worthy of note that the first trace of female church-officers appears in a Grecian Church. The Hellenic national customs themselves made the imposition upon *women* of such duties as belonged to the office of deaconess a necessity, such not being the case in Palestine, for as Grotius has already remarked in the passage quoted : " In Judæa diaconi viri etiam mulieribus ministrare poterant : erat enim ibi liberior ad feminas aditus, quam in Græcia, ubi viris clausa γυναικωνῖτις." In conformity with Greek custom, the sustenance and care of the poor and sick in particular required the womanly help of the sex. Besides, the services of women might also be useful in spreading the gospel among women; and these services could not well be supplied in Greece by men (Rothe, p. 246, etc.). The office of διακονία, whether filled by men or women, consisted in helpful services, partly to individuals (poor and sick in particular), partly to the Church, in employments referring to public worship and to other relations.

With respect to the constitution and order within the individual Churches, the Gentile Christian or mixed Churches developed a peculiarity distinguishing them from those composed of Jewish Christians, mainly in this respect, that in their own free unions they were more self-reliant and independent than the Jewish Christian Churches, which were still regarded as members of the theocratic, national Church of Israel. From the Pauline Epistles it is clear beyond a doubt that the Pauline Churches managed their affairs themselves (comp. Weizsäcker, *Jahrb. f. deutsche Theol.* 1873, p. 641, etc.).[1] In the Churches founded by Paul, we find an office for guidance and administration, as in the Palestinian Churches, only that these officers are here called by the Hebraizing name of "elders"; the office itself having been modelled after

---

[1] A. Harnack, *Analecten zu Hatch*, S. 229 ff., takes quite a different view of the matter: bishops and deacons were originally administrative officers for economy in its wider sense, while, on the other hand, presbyters were officers of disciplinary and judicial affairs. These organisms, having originally a fundamental difference, were only combined in one at a later period. Hatch himself, however (2nd and 3rd Lectures), proceeds more cautiously and not quite so categorically. If we wish to inquire into the beginnings of Christian Church order, it is advisable not to employ, as sources for the primitive Christian constitution, writings which are almost a century later, such as the "Shepherd" of Hermas.

a Jewish pattern, while the same office in Hellenic Churches, in addition to that name, received also the Hellenic one, ἐπίσκοπος, and was formed after the pattern of Western civil appointments and offices. Deacons proper also appear in Gentile Christian Churches for the first time; and out of regard for Hellenic customs, deaconesses also.

In conclusion, the question arises, What was the position of the Gentile Christian Churches with respect to their *connection with one another?* The Palestinian Churches felt the less need of a peculiar alliance among themselves in proportion as they stood within the theocratic communion of Israel, and had in it a common ground. It was different with the Pauline Churches in Syria and Asia Minor, in Macedonia and Greece. The farther these were removed from Jerusalem in space, the greater the progress of their inner development, the more they required a common bond of union among themselves. Such bond they had from the beginning, but it was entirely individual and personal, consisting in the person of Paul himself, as the Gentile apostle. He had founded these Churches, and that mostly without the basis of a Church having been laid. In him they saw their founder, to him they owed their instruction and guidance. In his parting address at Miletus, Paul refers the Ephesian elders not to Peter or the other apostles, but directly to God and the word of His grace (Acts xx. 32, comp. Lange, *ante*, ii. 196, etc.). After they were first founded, Paul visited the Churches again, and kept up even in his absence a living intercourse with them by letter. Hence the single epistles are a bond, as it were, by which the apostle was attached to his Churches, and they to him, and by him to other Churches. If we compare 1 Cor. xvi. 1, for example, we find that Paul here gives a direction to the Corinthians respecting a collection for the Church at Jerusalem. He asks them to act just as he had prescribed for the Churches of Galatia. If the Corinthians, as we have a right to assume, followed this advice of the apostle, the same custom and institution was formed among them by the instrumentality of Paul as that which the Churches of Galatia in Asia Minor already possessed; in a similar way Paul refers to the " Churches of God " and to " all Churches " (1 Cor. vii. 17, xi. 16, xiv. 33). Consider, moreover, the salutations in the Pauline letters. When Paul, for example, in 1 Cor. xvi. 19, writes from Ephesus, " The Churches of Asia salute you. Aquila and Priscilla salute you much in the Lord, with the Church that is in their house," it may certainly be said that such epistolary greetings were just like others. And yet they point to a community of spirit. Individual believers in Ephesus, together with the Churches of Asia Minor on the one side, and the Churches in Achaia on the other, reach out their hands to one another as an allied brotherhood; and it is Paul who brought about this community of spirit between them. Further, when Paul praises the Macedonian Churches to the believers in Achaia, because they were joyful in great affliction, liberal in great poverty, and had contributed almost beyond their power to collections; when this zeal stirs up the Corinthians, and Paul sends brethren in advance that all things may be ready, while the Corinthians have no cause to be ashamed when he comes to them in the company of Macedonian

Christians (2 Cor. viii. 1, etc., ix. 1, etc.), we get an insight into a community of life, a mutual coherence by virtue of which the separate Churches must have become more and more clearly conscious of their relation to one another, and of their union as a whole. Add to this the fact that one Church supported the apostle while he laboured in another (2 Cor. xi. 8, etc.), and we must confess that an intimate bond of union existed between the separate Pauline Churches, which was attached indeed to the person and work of Paul, but, for this very reason, was of a powerful and living nature.

CHAPTER III.

THE MUTUAL RELATION BETWEEN JEWISH CHRISTIAN AND GENTILE CHRISTIAN CIRCLES IN ITS GENERAL ASPECT.

IF we place ourselves first of all on the standpoint of the *Jewish Christians* of Palestine, and inquire what impression must have been made upon them by the news of the formation of Gentile Christian Churches, and what attitude they would naturally assume towards them, the Acts supply us with some material for an answer to the question. The impression made upon the brethren in Judæa by the tidings that Gentiles had received the word of God is thus described in xi. 2, etc.: "When Peter was come up to Jerusalem, they that were of the circumcision contended with him, saying, Thou wentest in to men uncircumcised, and didst eat with them!" The chief stumbling-block is here indicated; it is easy to perceive that these Jewish Christians could not be satisfied with the conversion of Gentiles, unless they had first been incorporated into the Jewish theocracy by circumcision.

Luke calls those who had taken offence and reproached Peter, οἱ ἐκ περιτομῆς—an expression which, since all the Christians in Jerusalem were Israelites, must have referred to disposition and way of thinking, inasmuch as the former laid special value on circumcision, and were in general disposed to strict legality.[1] Consequently the historian himself draws our attention to a difference which existed among the Jewish-Christian believers and Churches in Judæa (xi. 1 ; οἱ ἀδελφοὶ οἱ ὄντες κατὰ τὴν Ἰουδαίαν), according as they were ἐκ περιτομῆς, attaching special value to circumcision, and having a paramount tendency to legality or not. But when Peter, in his account of what had occurred, showed that in this matter he had implicitly followed a higher guidance, when he reminded his hearers that after God Himself had bestowed on those Gentiles the gift of the Holy Spirit, as well as on others, he could no longer resist : " They held their peace and glorified God, saying, Then hath God also to the Gentiles granted repentance unto life " (ver. 18). Thus the knowledge that it was God Himself who

---

[1] Overbeck (S. 168) contests this interpretation of the words οἱ ἐκ περιτομῆς as grammatically unauthorised and impossible on account of the passage x. 45. In the latter passage the immediate context, especially the οἱ συνῆλθον τῷ Πέτρῳ, makes the meaning of the expression clear beyond a doubt. In direct opposition to this, it is plain from xi. 1 that οἱ ἐκ περιτ. cannot be in agreement with οἱ ἀδελφοὶ οἱ ὄντες κατὰ τὴν Ἰουδαίαν. But the language of the Apostle Paul—in Rom. iii. 26 : ὁ ἐκ πίστεως Ἰησοῦ ; iv. 14, οἱ ἐκ τοῦ νόμου, comp. ver. 16 ; Gal. iii. 10 : ὅσοι ἐξ ἔργων νόμου εἰσίν ; Phil. i. 17 : οἱ ἐξ ἐριθείας—proves that οἱ ἐκ περιτομῆς may denote a certain group as to its fundamental nature and tendency.

had granted repentance to the Gentile peoples that they might be saved, and that the finger of God was present in the matter, put an end to all doubt, and overcame the first adverse impression to such an extent that not only were they at rest in their minds, but were able also to praise God. It would be too hasty, however, and would be expecting too much, to imagine that by this knowledge all objections against the conversion of the heathen without their acceptance of circumcision, and against unreserved intercourse with them, could once for all be overcome. The question here did not concern this single case alone, nor merely these particular persons, but the universal principle and general right of receiving a Gentile into the Church of Christ; in this sense it was understood by the companions of Peter (x. 45): ὅτι καὶ ἐπὶ τὰ ἔθνη ἡ δωρεὰ τοῦ πνεύματος τοῦ ἁγίου ἐκκέχυται; those in Jerusalem who heard of it understood its meaning in this way (xi. 1): ὅτι καὶ τὰ ἔθνη ἐδέξαντο τὸν λόγον τοῦ θεοῦ; the impression after hearing the discourse of Peter was of this nature (xi. 18): ἄρα καὶ τοῖς ἔθνεσιν ὁ θεὸς τὴν μετάνοιαν εἰς ζωὴν ἔδωκεν; and afterwards, at the council of the apostles (xv. 7), Peter himself emphasized it as an event of fundamental significance. Notwithstanding this, and in spite of the manifest direction of God in the matter, the prejudice which had been conquered and silenced for the moment, afterwards broke out afresh, and again called in question the Church's conviction, which had been already established by divine agency; a course of events which is so deeply rooted in human nature, and repeats itself so often in similar cases in past and present time, that to declare it to be inconceivable requires great courage. Thus the first step of an apostle beyond the boundaries of Israel called forth a counter activity on the part of the men of circumcision, that is, of the legal, narrow Jewish way of thinking; and this tendency, though repressed for the moment, always raised its head again, making great exertions to obtain the victory and the sole supremacy. We must, in the first place, examine this tendency more closely, and proceed, secondly, to ask what position the apostles themselves and the nucleus of the Church occupied with respect to Jewish Christianity.

(A.) *The Judaistic tendency.*

This tendency first gained prominence owing to the conversion of individual Gentiles. When the first Gentile Christian Churches increased in strength, it made more strenuous exertions. It was in every case the founding, growth, and increase of the Gentile Christian circle that incited the Judaistic tendency to counter activity. For a long time all its manifestations of life had reference to the Christian Church of the large city of Antioch, which, by the missionary activity of the Apostle Paul, became the mother of numerous flourishing Churches of Gentile Christians. The party now set to work with such energy that some of its members travelled in person from Jerusalem to Antioch, in order to procure an introduction for their principles in that place (Acts xv. 1). They set before the Gentile Christians there this principle as a formal doctrine ($\dot{\epsilon}\delta\iota\delta\alpha\sigma\kappa\upsilon\nu$): " Except ye be circumcised after the manner of Moses, ye cannot be saved." Thus the Judaists appeared in the Church at Antioch directly as teachers, and required of its

members circumcision and subjection to the law of
Moses, as an indispensable condition of participation
in the Messianic salvation. The root of this view
was doubtless twofold : in a national respect, adherence
to *the privilege of the people of Israel* to be and continue the dominant and all-determining basis of the
Messianic kingdom ; in a religious respect, *the legal
essence*, or the emphasizing of the Mosaic legislation
as an unconditional rule of conduct to be followed on
all occasions. The tendency of the former would be
to make the Church of Jesus Christ essentially
Israelitish for all time ; the latter would lead to a
misapprehension of the all-sufficiency of the grace of
God in Christ, the thrusting back of the gospel to the
law, and the destruction of evangelical freedom.[1] The
Apostle Paul was not only right in asserting the
importance of preserving the *truth* of the gospel in its
purity in opposition to these people (Gal. ii. 5), but
also in representing them as spying out evangelical
liberty ($\tau\dot{\eta}\nu$ $\dot{\epsilon}\lambda\epsilon\upsilon\theta\epsilon\rho\dot{\iota}\alpha\nu$ . . . $\dot{\epsilon}\nu$ $X\rho\iota\sigma\tau\hat{\omega}$ $'I\eta\sigma o\hat{\upsilon}$, ver. 4)
with a view to bringing the converts into bondage ;
and he was fully justified in characterizing them
as false brethren ($\pi\alpha\rho\epsilon\dot{\iota}\sigma\alpha\kappa\tau o\iota$ $\psi\epsilon\upsilon\delta\dot{\alpha}\delta\epsilon\lambda\phi o\iota$, ver. 4),
who had crept in unawares, by which he implies that
when seen in the light they were not true Christians,
but unbelieving Jews under cover of faith in Jesus.
But however strong the judgments of the Apostle
Paul may be, they contain nothing to justify us in
assuming that these people appeared as *personal*
opponents of the Gentile apostle ; the whole narrative

---

[1] Baumgarten's opinion, that these Judaists had in view from the
beginning the exclusive prerogative of the twelve apostles, the position of the "patriarchal apostolate" (*Acts*, ii. 1, 105 ff.), finds no
support in the original documents themselves.

of the Acts, and the utterances of Paul himself, lead rather to the conclusion that the question here was one solely of essence and of principle. At the Council of Jerusalem in the year 50 or 51, the decree respecting this matter was that circumcision and Mosaic legality were not the universal and indispensable conditions of reception into the Church of Christ, and that the heathen, though not allowing themselves to be incorporated into the nation of Israel, might nevertheless be full citizens of the kingdom of God.

Notwithstanding the decisive failure of this first great attempt on the part of the Judaists to force their principles directly on the Gentile Christians (especially in Antioch), yet they did not give up either their view or their efforts. On the contrary, they prosecuted their cause amid the most varied circumstances and in manifold ways, with extraordinary tenacity and unwearied zeal. The first step had been their attempt to induce the Gentile Christians of Antioch spontaneously to receive circumcision and Mosaic legality, that is, to effect a union between Gentile and Jewish Christians through the incorporation of the former with the latter.

In the time succeeding the apostolic council this method had to be abandoned. The Judaists now entered upon a path apparently contrary, but which appeared to lead to the same goal. They opposed the union of the two parties in the mixed Church at Antioch with the natural object of exerting thereby an indirect moral pressure on the Gentile Christian party, and inducing them to give up their freedom. This was the essence of that occurrence which occasioned the Apostle Paul to come forth with a public rebuke of Peter (Gal. ii. 11); for the cause of Peter's discontinuance of that brotherly intercourse with the Gentile Christians to which he had been accustomed, and of his ceasing to eat with them at table, was the arrival of " certain from James " (ver. 12). The expression ἐλθεῖν τινὰς ἀπὸ Ἰακώβου unmistakeably puts those that came in some sort of connection with the president of the Church at Jerusalem, that is James, the brother of the Lord; whether the connection is to be found in the circumstance that they were people from that circle, or of that view, or persons sent directly by James. Ἀπὸ Ἰακώβου cannot properly be connected with τινές but only with ἐλθεῖν. In this connection it denotes, as in Matt. xxvi. 47, and in other passages, sending by some one. Hence it follows that those people were sent by James. Ritschl (*Entstehung der altkath. Kirche*, 2 Aufl. p. 145) and Holsten (*Zum Evangelium des Paulus und des Petrus*, 1868, p. 357) are of a different opinion: the delegates of James were to counteract the falling away of the Jewish Christians in Antioch from the Mosaic law, and to restore between Jewish and Gentile Christians the intercourse at table and in common life that had been broken off. So much at least is established fact, that Peter, out of solicitous regard for the Jewish Christians, with all their harshness and rigidity, withdrew from the Gentile Christians and from intercourse with them at table. It is therefore easy to suppose that this separation between Levitically pure Jewish Christians on the one hand, and Gentile Christians on the other, was in the mind of the delegates, who wished by that means to make an indirect demonstration against the free Gentile Christians. But Paul with manly candour put such powerful obstacles in their path, that in Antioch their efforts had no further result. The more opposition it encountered, the more tenacious and exasperated did the party become; in fact the *party*, as such, owed its first existence to the opposition it met with. It assumed the form of an independent corporate body which placed their own view above the gospel, and finally, their own persons above the Church of Christ itself. Irritated by the powerful and open opposition of the Gentile apostle, it began to attack the *person* of Paul and his work in particular. This happened first, so far as we can ascertain, in *Galatia*. It seems that Paul, on his second visit to that place, already found occasion to warn the Churches that he had formerly founded against Judaistic errors, and to take measures against them (Gal. i. 9, v. 3 ; comp. Rückert, *Comm.* 309, etc. ; Wieseler, *Comm.* 1859, p. 536, etc.). But it was only *after* this visit that the opponents entered with power into these Churches and brought about an inner revolution in the minds of many. It is clear from the Epistle to the Galatians that they insisted that the Christians should be circumcised (θέλουσιν ὑμᾶς περιτέμνεσθαι, vi. 13), and, moreover, under the pretext that circumcision was absolutely necessary to salvation (ἀναγκάζουσιν ὑμᾶς περιτέμνεσθαι, ver. 12), that only by the law and its observance could righteousness be attained (οἵτινες ἐν νόμῳ δικαιοῦσθε, v. 4). In fact, they not only prevailed on the Galatian Christians to allow themselves to be circumcised (v. 2, etc.), but also led them to resolve to put themselves in complete subjection to the Mosaic law (οἱ ὑπὸ νόμον θέλοντες εἶναι, iv. 21). The Galatians had already begun to observe all the holy times of

Mosaism (ἡμέρας παρατηρεῖσθε καὶ μῆνας καὶ καιροὺς καὶ ἐνιαυτούς, iv. 10).   How great was the success of the Judaistic revolutionary movement, and how threatening the moral danger had become, is best proved by the lively mental excitement under which the apostle wrote his letter. The thing that was peculiar and new in this case was that the errorists attacked Paul *personally*, and endeavoured to shake his apostolic authority in the Galatian Churches. They did this (1) by asserting that Paul had not been called and instructed directly by Christ Himself as an apostle, but owed all his knowledge of Christ and his position as a preacher of the gospel solely to the elder and proper apostles. This appears from the fact that Paul at the very commencement makes it expressly prominent that he did not receive his apostolic office *from* man nor *by* men, but immediately from Christ Himself and from God the Father (i. 1), and that he had the gospel which he preached, not from men but from Jesus Christ Himself by immediate revelation (i. 11, etc.).   (2) The errorists pretended that Paul had departed in his doctrine from the true and genuine apostles. This objection is unmistakeably before the mind of the apostle when he proves his apostolic independence (ii. 1, etc.), and mentions that his gospel had been fully recognized and approved by the other apostles at the time of the meeting in question. (3) It was a further objection that Paul himself was not consistent in his mode of teaching, but that in another place he made circumcision a fundamental and doctrinal requirement (εἰ περιτομὴν ἔτι κηρύσσω, τί ἔτι διώκομαι; v. 11), and that his utterances against Mosaism and circumcision were in the main a mere accommodation to the heathen, and had their origin in a desire to please men (ἄρτι γὰρ ἀνθρώπους πείθω; ... ἢ ζητῶ ἀνθρώποις ἀρέσκειν; i. 10). But who were the people that were able thus to embarrass the Galatian Churches? The conjecture that they were not Christians but unbelieving Jews (Michaelis, *Einleitung*) has no probability whatever;[1] and even the view defended by Neander (*Pflanz. u. Leit.* i. 366 f.), viz., that the seducers were Gentiles by birth, and proceeded from among the Gentile Christians, is untenable, for the reading περιτεμνόμενοι, instead of the perfect participle (vi. 13) on which the opinion is based, has too little probability in its favour; if such had been the case, Paul would certainly have spoken much more strongly. The men of this party were without doubt Christians who had originally been Jews; and it is not unlikely that the first authors of this reactionary movement came from Palestine itself. From motives of self-interest, from ambition and love of spiritual power (vi. 12, etc., iv. 17), they sought, as Paul indicates, to make a propaganda on behalf of Judaism among the Gentile Christians of Galatia that had been converted by Paul; turning in a true sectarian way to those Gentiles who had already accepted Christ, in order to bring them over to Mosaic legality, instead of undertaking the heavier task of carrying on the Gentile mission themselves. What success the incisive, powerful, and spirited Epistle to the Galatians had, there are no positive traces to show. We can only draw the conclusion indirectly from the non-existence of a crass Judaistic party among the Churches of Asia Minor,—as the later

---

[1] Comp. the ample refutation in C. E. Scharling, *de Paulo ap. ejusque adversariis*, Copenhagen, 1836, S. 114 ff.

Epistles of Paul to the Colossians and Ephesians show,—that the confident hope which the apostle expressed in Gal. v. 10 did not disappoint him.

On the other hand, the revolutionary movement of the Judaistic party turned from Asia to Europe itself, and gained a footing on Greek soil, especially at Corinth. This phenomenon points to a new stage of development, not only in so far as the founders of the Judaizing party at Corinth had come from without, as has been shown, probably from Palestine (for they brought letters of recommendation, 2 Cor. iii. 1), but particularly by the fact that the opposition took a very definite personal form. The Galatian errorists had already appealed to the person and doctrine of the chief Palestinian apostles (οἱ δοκοῦντες), and had thrown discredit not only on the teaching, but also on the personal apostolic authority of Paul; a further step in the same direction was now taken; the banner of Peter was straightway set up in a more resolute and open manner (ἐγὼ δὲ Κηφᾶ, 1 Cor. i. 12, comp. iii. 21, etc.), while the person and the apostolic authority of Paul were attacked in a more reckless and hostile spirit than before (εἰ ἄλλοις οὐκ εἰμὶ ἀπόστολος, 1 Cor. ix. 1, etc.), amid suspicion and misrepresentation, partly of the self-renunciation and considerate humility, partly of the confidence and power with which the Gentile apostle had appeared. Their own appearance, on the other hand, seems to have been characterized by great presumption and self-exaltation (οἱ ὑπερλίαν ἀπόστολοι, 2 Cor. xi. 5, xii. 11), even by fanatical and tyrannical obtrusiveness (2 Cor. xi. 20); on which account Paul is not afraid to speak out: οἱ τοιοῦτοι ψευδαπόστολοι ἐργάται δόλιοι, μετασχηματιζόμενοι εἰς ἀποστόλους

$X\rho\iota\sigma\tau o\hat{\upsilon} \ldots \delta\iota\acute{a}\kappa o\nu o\iota \ \sigma a\tau a\nu\hat{a}$ (ver. 14, etc.). The leaders of the party at Corinth asserted their Hebrew origin, their descent from Abraham, and, in short, the alleged privileges of Israel, with the greatest confidence (ver. 22, etc.), at the same time arrogating to themselves a superior and exclusive claim to Christ Himself ($\acute{e}\gamma\grave{\omega}$ $\delta\grave{e}$ $X\rho\iota\sigma\tau o\hat{\upsilon}$, 1 Cor. i. 12; 2 Cor. x. 7: $\epsilon\ddot{\iota}$ $\tau\iota\varsigma$ $\pi\acute{e}\pi o\iota\theta\epsilon\nu$ $\acute{e}a\upsilon\tau\hat{\omega}$ $X\rho\iota\sigma\tau o\hat{\upsilon}$ $\epsilon\hat{\iota}\nu a\iota$), on the ground of their former personal acquaintance with Jesus.[1] As to the doctrine itself that they sought to introduce, there is no doubt that they openly announced the legal views with which we are already acquainted,— brought from Antioch and Galatia,—although, out of regard to the Hellenic national culture, they may have gone to work in the first instance softly and cautiously. They took the way of first trying to undermine the influence and credit of Paul, that they might then take the field at once with their main theme. But what else could cause the apostle to utter the express warning: $\acute{e}\nu$ $\acute{a}\kappa\rho o\beta\upsilon\sigma\tau\acute{\iota}a$ $\tau\iota\varsigma$ $\acute{e}\kappa\lambda\acute{\eta}\theta\eta$, $\mu\grave{\eta}$ $\pi\epsilon\rho\iota\tau\epsilon\mu\nu\acute{e}\sigma\theta\omega$ (1 Cor. vii. 18), than the fact that an inclination tending in that direction had been already developed in many Gentile Christians at Corinth?

---

[1] The passage (2 Cor. x. 7) quoted in the text, shows plainly enough that there was no distinct *Christian* party in Corinth, but that the Petrine or Judaizing party boasted of belonging to Christ in an exclusive sense; for it is unmistakeable that the title of belonging to Christ was here made by the Judaistic leaders who are opposed in the context. The reasons brought forward against this view by Neander (*Pflanzung*, i. 386) and Osiander (*Comm. zu I. Kor.* S. 12) are not conclusive; the passage 1 Cor. i. 12 by no means proves the existence of a " Christ " party co-ordinate with the Paulines, Apollonians, and Petrines. Comp. Baur, *Paulus*, 2 Aufl. 291 ff., 326 ff.; *Christentum der drei ersten Jahrhunderte*, 2 Aufl. S. 58; Räbiger, *Kritische Untersuchungen über die beiden Kor. Briefe mit Rücksicht auf die Streitigkeiten*, 1847, 192, 193 ff.; Scharling, *ante*, 127 f.

On the contrary, what Paul says about flesh offered to idols in 1 Cor. viii. is not to be referred to the Judaizing party; the apostle has here in view not opponents, but the weak (ver. 9, etc.); neither does he fight for gospel-freedom against Mosaic legality, but rather requires from the more enlightened members a loving, conscientious regard for the weaker ones. The First Epistle of the Roman Clement to the Corinthians, is an historical document indirectly attesting the fact that the Judaistic movements in their Church cannot have taken deep root, but that, on the contrary, the two epistles of the apostle must have had a powerful effect, since at the time when Clement wrote (the last decade of the first century) the Church was also disturbed by the Passover controversy, but in a totally different sphere from that of the apostolic time and without any trace of a Judaistic spirit.   Judaism, however, had not yet been overcome in the entire young Church of Christ, for it still appeared under manifold aspects in other Churches, with an animus personally hostile to Paul and full of party spirit.

The party cannot have made its appearance in the Church at Rome, at least before the composition of Paul's epistle, for the epistle itself does not contain a single testimony in favour of that supposition.   What the apostle says of the weak (chap. xiv., etc.) is of such a nature as to exclude the idea of a fundamentally legal and anti-Pauline tendency, of an *erroneous doctrine* (against Lutterbeck, ii. 90, 96), for in this case the apostle would not have recommended a loving and patient forbearance, but, on the contrary, would have fought against such tendency.   From xv. 8, etc., we may indeed draw the probable inference

that the weak in faith were Jewish Christians; but
their abstinence from flesh and wine (xiv. 2, 21) was
not founded on the Mosaic law, but went beyond it
in voluntary asceticism. And we may certainly conjecture that the warning against errorists who cause
divisions and offences (xvi. 17, etc.) is intended for
the Judaizing party, although its brevity and incidental character show that the apostle knows nothing
of such revolutionary movements as had formerly
disturbed the Roman Church, but is desirous only of
anticipating and preventing what might possibly
occur. Such was the state of things when Paul some
years later wrote to the Philippians from his prison
in Rome, at which time several people, without doubt
Jewish Christians, were preaching the word of God
from impure motives ($οὐχ$ $ἁγνῶς$), especially prompted
by envy and party interest ($διὰ$ $φθόνον$ $καὶ$ $ἔριν$ . . .
$ἐξ$ $ἐριθείας$), supposing to add affliction to the bonds
of the Gentile apostle (Phil. i. 15, etc.). Notwithstanding the brief character of these indications, they
lead to the inevitable conclusion that in Rome also
Judaizing, anti-Pauline teachers were then at work
seeking to form a party. But since Paul ultimately
rejoices that only Christ is preached, we must assume
that where the substance of their doctrine was concerned, the men in question did not actually oppose
the truth of Christ, the Son of God, and salvation by
grace. This appears the more probable if we compare with the above utterances of the apostle the
tone of passionate anger in which in the same epistle
(iii. 2, etc.) he warns the Christians at Philippi against
Judaistic errorists; neither this passage, however, nor
the whole tenor of the epistle giving rise to the idea
that such errorists had already gained a footing in

Philippi. The apostle points by way of precaution, as in Rom. xvi. 17, to the possible danger of such influences. But there can be no doubt, in the face of κατατομὴ . . . περιτομή (iii. 2 f.), of πεποιθέναι ἐν σαρκί (ver. 3 f.), of κακοὶ ἐργάται, comp. δόλιοι ἐργ. (2 Cor. xi. 13), and Paul's own testimony (vers. 4–6), that he has to do with *Judaizing* errorists who sought to overthrow his fundamental principles. Paul describes them as persons whose boast of circumcision was a perverted one (κατατομή), whose whole method and conduct were objectionable. On the contrary, it is more than doubtful whether those enemies of the cross of Christ, whose immoral course of life is branded (iii. 18, etc.), are the same as the above errorists. The latter is the view of Scharling (*ante*, 136, etc.). But it must be observed that in iii. 2, etc., it is *merely doctrine* that is touched upon, while, on the contrary, in ver. 18, etc., it is *merely conduct*, and we have no right whatever to unite the two after the apostle himself has referred to them separately.

Moreover, the emphatic denunciation contained in Phil. iii. 2, etc., is the last which the apostle hurls against pure Judaism. From this time he has to contend with mixed forms of error, in which indeed a tendency to legality still exists, but already in association with extraneous elements, and passing into distinct heretical developments. His parting address in Miletus to the elders of Ephesus, with respect to those errorists—some of whom like wolves fall upon the sheep from without, while others arise from the midst of the Church itself, speaking perverse things, to draw away disciples after them (Acts xx. 29, etc.)—is different from what we should have

expected if the apostle had had Judaistic errorists
alone in view ; and shows that by virtue of his
knowledge of the actual state of things and his intelligent glance into the future, he foresaw the appearance
of errorists of a different kind.

A phenomenon of this nature occurs, in fact, in
the errorists whom Paul opposed in his Epistle to the
Colossians. These were doubtless Jewish Christians,
inasmuch as they observed the laws respecting food,
feasts, new moons, and Sabbaths (Col. ii. 16, 21), and
it may be inferred from chap. ii. 11 that they also
attached value to circumcision. But, on the other
hand, they could not have pressed the Mosaic law as
the Galatian errorists did, for Paul does not find it
necessary to maintain against them evangelical freedom
and righteousness by faith. On the contrary, these
errorists united to their ascetic practices and external
dogmas (ii. 20, δογματίζεσθαι) a sort of philosophy
(ii. 8) consisting in theosophic views of the spirit-
world and a worship of angels recommending itself
by the show of exceptional humility, through which
the only and exclusive dignity of Christ as Redeemer
and Mediator was injured (ii. 8, 18–23). Thus we
have in the Colossian errorists the transition to
another kind of heresy, the first germs of a Gnostic,
ascetic aberration, still upon the basis and soil of
Jewish Christianity. The errorists of the *pastoral
epistles* present a farther-developed stage in the same
line. For it is clear from Titus i. 10 : ματαιολόγοι
. . . μάλιστα οἱ ἐκ περιτομῆς; 14 : ἰουδαϊκοὶ μῦθοι
καὶ ἐντολαὶ ἀνθρώπων, etc. ; ii. 9 : μάχαι νομικαὶ
(1 Tim. 1. 7 ff.) νομοδιδάσκαλοι, etc., that these
also must be looked for on the ground of Judaizing
Christianity. This is so plain that even Baur, who

considers them elsewhere as antinomians, cannot avoid admitting that " the heretics of the pastoral epistles are described in part as Judaists " (*Paulus*, 1 Aufl. p. 495). But the view that they embraced antinomianism has only an apparent foundation, for in the context the apostle shows by the phrase καλὸς ὁ νόμος that he clearly enunciates the truth to which error adheres; and, on the other hand, he directly contests the error of his opponents by the phrase ἐάν τις αὐτῷ νομίμως χρῆσται, and points out the way in which they abuse the law. To take the title "*teachers of the law*," which Paul gives to his opponents, as if it meant "opponents of the law," does such violence to all usage and all logic that ample refutation is superfluous. On the other hand, the whole attitude of the three pastoral epistles manifestly proves that the errorists in question adhered as little as the Colossians to the purely legal standpoint which was in fundamental opposition to free grace in Christ. In some respects their asceticism went beyond the Levitical, Mosaic observances, extending to all kinds of human enactments, for example, the prohibition to marry, etc. (1 Tim. iv. 3; Tit. i. 14), while they abandoned themselves to speculations (ψευδώνυμος γνῶσις, 1 Tim. vi. 20) respecting the origin of the higher spirit-world and the divine powers (1 Tim. i. 4, γενεαλογίαι ἀπέραντοι), all of which was a departure from a simple, sound faith, and led to legendary babbling and endless differences of opinion (μῦθοι βέβηλοι καὶ γραώδεις, 1 Tim. iv. 7, vi. 3 ff., 20; 2 Tim. ii. 16, 23, iv. 4; Tit. iii. 9). When Paul in 2 Tim. ii. 18 quotes an assertion of Hymeneus and Philetus to the effect that the resurrection was already past, the reference is to a perverted spiritualism and idealism; just as, on the other hand, the prohibition of marriage presupposes a dualistic aspect of the world, while the description of the mind and conduct of those men (1 Tim. iv. 1, etc., vi. 3, etc.; 2 Tim. iii. 2–9 ; Tit. i. 10, etc.) leads to the assumption that such theoretical aberrations were fundamentally connected with practical immorality. There can scarcely be a doubt of the fact that the errorists of the pastoral epistles represent a transition from the Judaistic to the Gnostic direction, and involve the fundamental lines of heretical Gnosticism, but in an entirely elementary form ; so that we have no right to identify these doctrinal errors with any developed Gnostic system of the second century which is historically known. .

After having thus followed the Jewish tendency during the lifetime of the Apostle Paul through its different stages and forms, we now turn back to take a view of

(B.) *The apostles themselves and the germ of the primitive Church in their position with respect to the Gentile Christians.*

It was the newly-founded Christian Church in the metropolis of Syria, that is, Antioch, consisting for the most part of converted heathen, that particularly occupied the attention of the Palestinian Jewish Christians for a considerable time. To this Church were directed those steps taken by the early apostles and the mother-Church at Jerusalem, in opposition to the Gentile Christians. The following are the individual facts which we learn partly from the Acts, and partly from the Epistle to the Galatians :—

First, the sending of Barnabas to Antioch. This happened (Acts xi. 22) as soon as the tidings came to the ears of the Church in Jerusalem that a considerable number of the inhabitants of Antioch, especially heathen, had become believers. In this case the appointment of delegates is not attributed to the apostles, as in the sending to Samaria (viii. 14), but, to judge from the context, to the *Church* in Jerusalem ; a circumstance from which we may reasonably infer that the interest taken in the Church of Antioch, which was certainly in many respects a new and surprising phenomenon, by the Christians of Jerusalem, was of a wide-spread and lively nature. Concerning the object of the sending, nothing more definite is here said than formerly with respect to the sending of Peter and John to the new converts of Samaria. But if from the proceedings of Barnabas in Antioch we may draw a conclusion as to the object of those who sent him there, their principal aim was to greet the new community as a sister-Church, to strengthen the new converts in fidelity to the Redeemer, and in general to forward the young Church in its life and conduct, without implying that there was something to rectify and alter.[1] But the greatest service rendered by Barnabas to the

---

[1] It is possible that there may have been some hesitation in Jerusalem, in face of the numerous Gentile Christians in the Churches at Antioch. But when Renan (*Les Apôtres*, 1867, 186 f.) speaks of "discontent and deplorable jealousy" prevailing in Jerusalem in consequence of the news from Antioch, and states that it was Barnabas who was able to prevent strict measures being taken, and that he had important influence in this respect, this is all a creation of fancy.

young Church, and that which had the most important consequences, was that he went to the neighbouring Tarsus, sought out Paul and brought him to Antioch (xi. 25). By this means the right man was put in the right place, the Gentile apostle was placed in connection with the future metropolis of Gentile Christianity, and, indeed, through the delegate, with the mother-Church of Jewish Christianity. The first contact between the Jewish and Gentile Christian circles was not only friendly and brotherly in the extreme, but was also particularly helpful and beneficial to the Christians from among the heathen.

Second, Another fact is mentioned in the Acts immediately after (xi. 27, etc.), viz. that " in these days came prophets from Jerusalem unto Antioch. And there stood up one of them named Agabus, and signified by the Spirit that there should be great dearth." The contribution collected in Antioch for Jerusalem we may here pass over, in order to touch upon it afterwards, but remark that in this passage the circumstance is noteworthy that " prophets " came to *Antioch* from Jerusalem, apparently without any special commission, and solely of their own accord, moved by the Holy Ghost. This presupposes a disposition toward the Church at Antioch, in conformity with which the latter was regarded as a true Church of God. If, moreover, we take into account the circumstance that one of these prophets stood up (ἀναστὰς . . . ἐσήμανε), which could have taken place perhaps only in a meeting of the Church, we arrive at the conviction that the Christians of Jerusalem put themselves into a relation of brotherly equality and friendly feeling with the Church of Antioch. The two facts just mentioned correspond, both testifying to an appreciative, loving spirit on the part of the primitive Church, in relation to a Church which consisted for the most part of Gentile Christians. The only difference between the two events is that the former bears a certain official character, inasmuch as the sending of Barnabas proceeded from the *Church* at Jerusalem; while the latter is rather a private affair, inasmuch as these " prophets " went to Antioch at the instigation of the Spirit, without having received a commission from others, and remained there for some time, appearing in the assemblies of Christians.

But we must not therefore imagine that no prejudices at all existed among the Jewish against the Gentile Christians. They certainly existed, as later events show, but were still dormant. They awoke as soon as believers from among the Gentiles became more numerous, and formed themselves into a group of Churches, a result brought about during Paul's first missionary journey with Barnabas. But when the strict party among the Jewish Christians roused themselves and took steps to persuade believers from among the heathen to receive circumcision and to put themselves under the Mosaic law, it was necessary for the apostles as well as the primitive Church itself, to come to an understanding respecting their relation to the Gentile Christians, and to take up a definite position with regard to the most important question of apostolic times.

This was done, *thirdly*, at the *apostolic convention* at Jerusalem,—a convention due to Judaistic machinations, which, beginning at Jerusalem, had spread alarm and perplexity throughout the Church of Antioch.

This matter requires the more thorough investigation, since, in accordance with the present state of scientific inquiry, it forms the central point of the apostolic period, from which, according as it is understood, the most decisive consequences follow, not only with respect to the relation between the early Church at Jerusalem and the Gentile Christians collectively, but also with respect to the relation between the early apostles and the Gentile Apostle Paul.

The modern school sees in the above occurrence, to use the words of the master, Dr. Baur, "a conflict of Pauline with Jewish Christianity; and the elder apostles are so far from being outside the conflict that, on the contrary, we find them still placed on a standpoint from which they had never looked beyond Judaism. On this occasion even the elder apostles appeared as Paul's opponents, by pressing upon the Gentile Christians circumcision, and with it the observance of the whole Jewish law—entire Judaism; so that the heathen could only become Christians by first becoming Jews. To this the Apostle Paul made the strongest opposition, and brought the matter to such a length that the Jewish apostles gave way to his predominant personality, recognizing him, together with Barnabas, as equally privileged associates in evangelical work, and agreed at least to tolerate a Gentile Christianity independent of Jewish Christianity. Thus far they were in accord, yet without a complete reconciliation between their respective views and principles" (*Paulus*, 1 Aufl. p. 120, etc., 124, etc.; 2 Aufl. i. 127, etc.).

According to the view most generally accepted, the narrative of Paul in Gal. ii. 1, etc., coincides with the account of the apostolic convention given in Acts xv. We likewise declare in favour of the coincidence of the two events as to time and subject, even if both accounts should not fully agree in substance. The reasons *against* the identity of Gal. ii. and Acts xv. may be reduced to two,—one chronological, the other matter of fact. The chronological reason which some have advanced in favour of the identity of Gal. ii. 1–10 and Acts xi. 30, consists in the fact that Paul could not have omitted the journey mentioned in the latter place, since he enumerated his journeys to Jerusalem in Gal. i. and ii. fully, and in regular sequence. But that is an erroneous supposition. Paul did not intend to give here a chronological and complete list of his journeys to Jerusalem.[1] It was rather his purpose to give prominence to those facts from which the independence of his preaching and apostolic office as well as his independent and yet friendly position with respect to the pillar-apostles could most clearly be seen. When Wieseler supposes a coincidence of the journey in Gal. ii. with Acts xviii. 21, etc., merely from chronological reasons, he gives excessive prominence to matters of fact in their bearing against the identity of Gal. ii. and Acts xv. The essence of his arguments lies in the circumstance that the progression in these accounts is too different to admit of both being referred to one and the same event. The testing of the latter objection rests on examination of the matter itself. We may, however, say in advance that we are unable to discover any discrepancy of such a nature as absolutely to prevent

---

[1] Zeller, indeed, maintains this view (*Apostelgesch.* 218 ff.), but bases it on an interpretation of the connection of Gal. i. 15, ii. 10, which mistakes the actual purport.

their being referred to one and the same event. If the same occurrence lies at the basis of both passages, the variation between them certainly appears the more striking, so that Baur ("Krit. Beitr. zur ältesten Kirchengeschichte," *Theol. Jahrb.* 1845, p. 262) exclaims: "With what dull eyes must a critic have read the Epistle to the Galatians, to suppose that the explanation here so clearly and accurately given by the apostle himself of his whole relation to the elder apostles, could be identified with such an account as is contained in Acts xv.!" Overbeck (*ante*, 217) finds a fundamental contradiction between the two parallel passages. Baur in his *Paulus* even declares that "the account of the Acts can only be regarded as an *intentional* departure from historical truth in the interest of that particular tendency by which the book is characterized. All attempts to harmonize the respective accounts are labour in vain."

Before putting implicit faith in these authoritative decisions, we shall first examine the arguments on which they are based, and that, too, with as great impartiality as possible. There are three principal points in which a difference appears between the parallel accounts: first, the method of the proceedings; second, the parties opposed to one another; third, the result of the proceedings. In our examination we shall consider these points separately, only taking them in connection when it becomes necessary.

First, The method of the proceedings.—According to Acts xv. 6–22, the apostles and elders assembled at Jerusalem, on account of the question which had arisen with respect to the Gentile Christians. As the Church was present at the proceedings, they were of a public character, and took the regular form of consultation and final determination in a church assembly. But Paul plainly speaks, in Gal. ii. 2, etc., of a private conversation with the most distinguished heads, from which circumstance Baur (*Paulus*, p. 116, 2 Aufl. i. 132, etc.) draws forthwith the conclusion that, according to Gal. ii., a public transaction cannot have taken place. Hence, in his view, the two accounts are completely at variance on this point, and there is an irreconcilable opposition between them. In order to harmonize the discrepancies, Neander (*Pflanzung*, i. 146) assumed that private meetings preceded the public council, to which Baur replied that such a thing might certainly be supposed if only something had been said about so great a meeting in the Epistle to the Galatians. But as nothing of the kind is there mentioned, this attempt at reconciliation is only a proof of uncritical arbitrariness. The objection is not entirely unfounded, since Neander (*ante*, note 1) had previously admitted that Paul makes no mention of a public transaction.

The words of the apostle have not been quite accurately examined on either side. Paul himself distinguishes between the private conversation and another transaction. He relates in Gal. ii. 1, etc.: ἀνέβην εἰς Ἱεροσόλυμα μετὰ Βαρνάβα . . . καὶ ἀνεθέμην αὐτοῖς τὸ εὐαγγέλιον ὃ κηρύσσω ἐν τοῖς ἔθνεσιν· κατ' ἰδίαν δὲ τοῖς δοκοῦσι. Now Baur, and with him Neander, assert that the words ἀνεθέμην αὐτοῖς do not point to any transaction in particular, but are only the indefinite expression for which a more definite one is immediately substituted: κατ' ἰδίαν δὲ τοῖς δοκοῦσι. But that is a mere assertion, without a shadow of proof, since the words themselves, both separately and in connection with the preceding and following context, show that reference is made to something really different,—a twofold occurrence, not merely one and the same thing first mentioned indefinitely and afterwards more plainly expressed. Paul says: "I went up *to Jerusalem*," and then continues, "and communicated unto them that gospel which I preach among the Gentiles." Here the pronoun αὐτοῖς, in consequence of the expression *to Jerusalem* which precedes in ver. 1, can signify nothing else than the believers in Jerusalem, the Church itself. We have therefore to suppose a statement before a number of Church members. When it is added: κατ᾽ ἰδίαν δὲ (ἀνεθέμην) τοῖς δοκοῦσι, the δοκοῦντες can only have been a *part* of the αὐτοί. The words are so taken by de Wette (*Kurze Erklärung*), Schrader (*Paulus*, ii. 304), Niedner (*Gesch. der Christl. Kirche*, 1846, p. 103, note 1), Hilgenfeld (*Gal.* 55 ff., 130), Koch (*ante*, 124), Elwert (*Annot. in Gal.* ii. 1–10, 1852, 8), Wieseler (*Chronol.* 186 ; *Comment.* p. 98, etc.), Ritschl (*Entst. der Altkath. Kirche*, 150), Keim (*Aus dem Urchristenthum*, p. 95, etc.). Baur himself has afterwards admitted the possibility of this interpretation of αὐτοῖς, which even Zeller (*ante*, 226, note 2) is forced to concede. Holsten (*Zum Evang. des Paulus und Petrus*, 1868, p. 272 ; *das Ev. des Paulus*, i. 1880, p. 71, etc.) acknowledges without reserve that Paul in ii. 2 narrates a twofold announcement of his gospel,—one to the whole Church, another to those of reputation. Overbeck also declares the view that makes Paul in Gal. ii. 2 speak solely of a private transaction, to be unfounded (*ante*, 218). Keim (*Aus dem Urchristenthum*, 1878, p. 765) remarks: "It was in particular the energetic opposition of Lechler (*Ap. Zeitalter*, 2 Aufl. 397, etc.) which brought about the full recognition of public negotiations."

In accordance with Gal. ii. 2, therefore, we cannot avoid distinguishing two different conversations in Jerusalem in which Paul was concerned: once he addressed himself to the Church (αὐτοῖς explained by Ἱεροσόλυμα, ver. 1); the other time he had to do only with a part of the Church, viz. with its most distinguished heads (οἱ δοκοῦντες). The other difference, to which the "δέ" draws attention, is connected with this; the second time, Paul describes the communication as secret and confidential (κατ᾽ ἰδίαν), while the first time the transaction is silently assumed to be public. The view which Baur takes of the κατ᾽ ἰδίαν δὲ τοῖς δοκοῦσι as only an addition explaining what went before, in the sense " especially those in authority," is absolutely disallowed by the constant usage of the New Testament.[1] We are ready to concede that Paul in the following sentences gives a detailed account only of the confidential conversation, leaving the public one quite out of consideration. But it would be very hasty to conclude at once from this circumstance, that according to Gal. ii. a public transaction did not take place. On the contrary, it agrees entirely with the nature of the case that the historian (Acts xv.) should confine himself to the public act, the knowledge of which

---

[1] The expression κατ᾽ ἰδίαν appears sixteen times in the New Testament, besides in this passage (three times in Luke, in his Gospel in ix. 10, x. 23 ; and in Acts xxiii. 19); but in every case, as required by the context, in the sense of *privatim*, in secret, in confidence. Why, then, should the fixed, undoubted usage be departed from in this case—not only without necessity, but when the usual sense, on the contrary, is quite good?

he might easily have got; while Paul, who had a personal interest in the matter, and took part in it, speaks of those discussions in particular that had taken place in a confidential conference between himself and some of the heads. The only remarkable circumstance is that the apostle passes over in silence, without a single indication, the public transaction in which he took so active a part, and which appears from the Acts to have been so significant and weighty. For the purpose of strengthening this suspicion, Schwegler reminds us that the apostolic convention forms the turning-point of the entire book of Acts, that it is its peculiar, practical, fundamental idea, the innermost motive of its composition, and the link between the history of the Pauline-Gentile mission and that of the primitive Church (Schwegler, *ante*, i. 116). Others maintain that Paul, in case the public transaction took place as described in the Acts, could not have passed it over in silence, since it was the main thing, but must have mentioned it in accordance with the occasion and purport of his letter, for he could not have brought forward a more decisive refutation of the Judaizing Galatians than by pointing them to that solemn act which gave the law to the whole Church. Accordingly it is inferred from the silence of the apostle respecting the public transaction, that it could not have taken place as the Acts narrate (Baur, p. 117, etc.; Schwegler, i. 122, etc.).

We cannot recognize this *argumentum e silentio* as conclusive, when we remember the polemic design of the Epistle to the Galatians. The Judaistic opponents of the apostle regarded the early apostles exclusively as genuine and legitimate,—as shown by the epistle, and confirmed by Baur, Schwegler, and especially

Holsten,[1]—and in their opposition to Paul, relied on the authority with which some of these were endowed. On account of the high dignity attributed to them by the Judaizing party, Paul gives them the title, οἱ δοκοῦντες (Gal. ii. 2, 6), or οἱ δοκοῦντες στύλοι εἶναι (ver. 9). Under these circumstances, the most powerful refutation that Paul could offer to his opponents was an appeal to the fact that *these very men*, so highly esteemed by the opposite party, had personally declared themselves in agreement with him. There is not a single passage to prove that his Galatian opponents wished to strike him down with the argument of numbers. It was not necessary, therefore, to be able to appeal to the weight of a great assembly, to the whole Church at Jerusalem itself. But because his opponents relied on a few prominent personalities, it was decisive on Paul's part to show that these very " pillars " were in his favour. Moreover, the Epistle to the Galatians gives probability to the view that the errorists of that place were in the habit of representing Paul as called in the beginning by the primitive apostles, and as having been in constant dependence on them ; the apostolic convention itself seems to have been interpreted in this sense, and turned to the detriment of the apostle. How natural that Paul should have given special prominence to that which set his independence over against the primitive apostles in a clear light ! and such was manifestly the case in the apostolic confer- ence far more than in the meeting of the Church. Hence the immediate object of the apostle was completely served by an account of that confidential

---

[1] Baur, *Paulus*, 1 Aufl. p. 109 ; Schwegler, i. 122 f., ii. 247 ; Holsten, *Zum Ev. des Paulus u. Petrus*, 250 ff., esp. 266-272.

conversation with the apostles which preceded the Church-meeting, apparently as a preliminary consultation, whilst he had no necessity to say more about the public transactions (which the Acts describe from the standpoint of the community and the Church in general) than is implied in the short hint ἀνεθέμην αὐτοῖς. Thus both accounts (Gal. ii., Acts xv.) are perfectly reconcilable with regard to the method of the proceedings.

The *second* question to which our examination extends is this: Who are *the parties opposed to one another* in the matter? That Paul and Barnabas stood on one side in the name of the Gentile Christians is undisputed; consequently our second question comes more exactly to this issue, What standpoint did the other apostles and the nucleus of the primitive Church take?

Dr. Baur asserts that, according to the statements of the Apostle Paul in the Galatian Epistle, the elder apostles did not by any means stand outside the conflict, but that Paul had the apostles themselves as opponents: that these apostles had not yet advanced a step beyond Jewish particularism, and had demanded circumcision as absolutely necessary, so that Paul could only save the Christian freedom of the Gentile Christians by the most energetic opposition to the primitive apostles (*Paulus*, 1 Aufl. p. 120, etc., 2 Aufl. i. 137, etc., 144; *Das Christenthum der drei ersten Jahrh.* 2 Aufl. 49, etc.). According to the Acts, the case stands quite differently. There it was only individual Christians who came from Judæa (τινες ἀπὸ τῆς Ἰουδαίας, xv. 1) to Antioch, and taught the Christians in that place, " Except ye be circumcised after the manner of Moses, ye cannot be saved."

Paul and Barnabas opposed these teachers, on which the Church determined that the former, together with certain others of them, should go up to Jerusalem unto the apostles and elders about this question. Thus far the apostles and the elders of Jerusalem stand outside the conflict. They appear not as a party, but as those from whom an impartial, judicial determination of the point in dispute might be expected. In Jerusalem there now rose up members of the Church who had formerly belonged to the sect of the Pharisees, with the demand that circumcision and the observance of the Mosaic law should be imposed on the Gentile Christians. In the assembly called together on this account, Peter reminds those present that some time previously, by the command of God, the gospel had been preached to the Gentiles by himself, and received with faith; and that God, by the gift of His Holy Spirit, had revealed Himself unto them, even as to the Israelites, purifying their hearts by faith. From these facts he proceeds to draw the practical conclusion that it is a tempting of God (that is, a culpable challenging of His own attestation) to impose the law on the disciples, and thus to burden them with a yoke which the Israelites themselves could not have borne; for it was only through the grace of Christ that either could hope to be saved. Paul and Barnabas themselves then gave an account of the signs and wonders that God had wrought through them among the Gentiles. Finally, James takes up the word, and appeals to the promise, according to which the rebuilding of the tabernacle of David includes also the conversion of the heathen to the Lord. In conclusion, James makes the conciliatory proposal that nothing more should be required of the Gentile Christians than their observance of certain enactments with respect to morals and conduct, a proposal which is unanimously raised to a decree.[1]

With regard to these two representations Baur assures us that the parties concerned with the dispute were not at all the same in both passages; that the Acts puts the other apostles outside the controversy, or rather on the side of Paul; whereas, according to the testimony of Paul himself (Gal. ii.), they had been his opponents on this question.

But we cannot see why the narrative of the Galatian Epistle, quite independently of Acts xv., should lead to this view. Baur remarks that the great earnestness with which Paul here defends his gospel is rightly understood only if he had to do not merely with the "false brethren brought in," but with the apostles themselves. He would not have repaired to Jerusalem to treat with the apostles themselves so urgently if he had not had good reason for supposing that they were not far removed from that imputation

---

[1] Zeller (*Ap. Gesch.* 230 ff.) tries to prove that neither Peter nor Paul nor James could have spoken as the Acts (xv. 7–21) narrate; in Paul's case, because it is improbable that he would have appealed merely to his miracles, instead (Gal. ii. 7, etc.) of to his teaching and his missionary success, as if σημεῖα καὶ τέρατα (ver. 12, comp. ver. 43, xiv. 27, xxi. 19, etc.) excluded and not much rather included the conversion of the heathen. James and Peter cannot, it is stated, have spoken thus, because it is inconceivable that the party insisting on the circumcision of the Gentile Christians should have appealed to these two men as their authority if they did not share the same principles,—a view which overlooks only the small circumstance that, according to the account of the apostle himself (Gal. ii. 16, etc.), Peter and James assented to his doctrine, and recognized the evangelical freedom of the Gentile Christians in a positive way, which fully corresponds with the opinions expressed by both according to Acts xv. 7, etc., 13, etc.

of the false brethren. But the great earnestness of
Paul is sufficiently explained by the nature of the
thing itself, independently of what is personal. The
matter at stake was nothing less than the rich
blessing of Christian freedom, the completeness of
Christianity, and the gospel's independence of the
Mosaic law.

Let us look at the words of the Galatian Epistle
more closely. Paul says (chap. ii. 2-10): "And I
went up by revelation, and communicated unto them
that gospel which I preach among the Gentiles, but
privately to them which were of reputation, lest by
any means I should run, or had run, in vain. But
neither Titus, who was with me, being a Greek, was
compelled to be circumcised: And that because of
false brethren unawares brought in, who came in
privily to spy out our liberty which we have in Christ
Jesus, that they might bring us into bondage: To
whom we gave place by subjection, no, not for an
hour; that the truth of the gospel might continue
with you. But of those who seemed to be somewhat
(whatsoever they were, it maketh no matter to me:
God accepteth no man's person): for they who seemed
to be somewhat in conference added nothing to me:
but contrariwise, when they saw that the gospel of
the uncircumcision was committed unto me, as the
gospel of the circumcision was unto Peter (for he
that wrought effectually in Peter to the apostleship
of the circumcision, the same was mighty in me
toward the Gentiles); and when James, Cephas, and
John, who seemed to be pillars, perceived the grace
that was given unto me, they gave to me and Barnabas
the right hands of fellowship; that we should go unto
the heathen, and they unto the circumcision. Only

they would that we should remember the poor; the same which I also was forward to do."

In this section some secondary points are certainly obscure on account of the abrupt manner of speaking and the insertions; but the leading points are fortunately not so. In one important particular we are quite in agreement with Baur, viz. that the clause, " Titus, however, was circumcised," can never be supplemented by the words (ver. 4), " for the sake of the false brethren."[1] On the contrary (in vv. 4 and 5), the occasion that gave rise to the transactions in question, which had not hitherto been mentioned, is appended by way of explanation, so that the connection is, " But because of brethren unawares brought in," serious negotiations arose.

We call attention to this circumstance in particular, that Paul, on whose side Barnabas and Titus stood, distinguishes three persons. By the αὐτοί (ver. 2) are doubtless to be understood the believers in Jerusalem, the Church there without distinction. Among this collective body the apostle gives special prominence,

---

[1] This explanation originated with Rückert (*Comm.* 1833, S. 73 ff.), while Elwert subsequently sought to establish it in detail (*Annotatio in Gal.* ii., 1852, p. 10–14). It has recently been adopted by Renan (*St. Paul,* 1869, p. 87 ff.). However acute the discussion of Elwert, yet it is not convincing. He finds it necessary to read between the lines the alleged motive from which Paul gave way, and consented to the circumcision of Titus, viz. consideration for the " weak " (S. 12 f.). Moreover, it has not been sufficiently considered that a mode of dealing so suspicious under the circumstances on the part of the apostle,—especially towards the Galatians, with their momentary inclination to Mosaism and circumcision,—would have been directly contrary to the aim of the epistle. Finally, we leave it a matter for consideration whether, to judge from the narrative of the Acts, chap. xv., which even Elwert acknowledges as essentially agreeing with Gal. ii., there is the slightest probability that Paul consented to the circumcision of Titus !

in the second place, to the δοκοῦντες, δοκοῦντες στύλοι εἶναι. Thirdly, he mentions also the παρείσακτοι ψευδάδελφοι (ver. 4). The latter are clearly not recognised by Paul as genuine Christians, as Church members, but are rather considered as to their faith and conduct. The apostle expresses himself quite differently regarding the δοκοῦντες. Of these heads of the Church, he says (ver. 6, etc.) not a word of the kind applied to the ψευδάδελφοι. On the contrary, his words are (ver. 6): ἐμοὶ οὐδὲν προσανέθεντο. The last word corresponds, according to the context, with ἀνεθέμην τὸ εὐαγγέλιον (ver. 2), except that a more exact designation or limitation is added in the πρός. The former signifies, " I explained the gospel to them ;" consequently the latter must mean, " They explained to me nothing in addition," that is, they gave me nothing new in relation to my gospel by way of supplement or rectification. When, therefore, Baur (p. 123) explains the words in question to mean, " They advanced nothing against me in which I could have acknowledged they were right, or which I could have adopted as a rectifying addition," he puts the chief thing into the text, viz. that the apostles might have actually attempted to urge upon Paul rectifying additions to his gospel, but that he could not conscientiously adopt them (comp. Wieseler, *Comment.* p. 132). While Paul says expressly, with reference to the false brethren, οἷς οὐδὲ πρὸς ὥραν εἴξαμεν τῇ ὑποταγῇ (ver. 5), we cannot, on the other hand, discover a single syllable in which any contradiction or opposition that he thought it necessary to make against the δοκοῦντες is indicated.[1] We must also

---

[1] Comp. Keim, *Aus dem Urchristentum*, p. 73: "Paul draws the line in the most definite way, and finds the focus of opposition only

subordinate the chief thing to the intermediate clause : ὁποῖοί ποτε ἦσαν, οὐδέν μοι διαφέρει· πρόσωπον θεὸς ἀνθρώπου οὐ λαμβάνει (ver. 6), and read between the lines if we would find that the apostles appeared in opposition to Paul as the δοκοῦντες εἶναί τι, claiming only submissive recognition of their authority on his part (Baur, p. 123). These words should rather be taken as alluding to the extraordinary reputation which the opponents of Paul in Galatia attributed to those pillar-apostles on account of their having been at one time immediate disciples of Jesus. There is no trace that would lead to the belief that the apostles themselves claimed an overweening importance in relation to Paul. He asserts positively, " The δοκοῦντες recognized my apostolic activity as equally valid with their own, because they had convinced themselves of the fact that God Himself had given me grace for that end, and that He had worked mightily in me toward the Gentiles " (vv. 8, 9), therefore they solemnly gave me the right hand of fellowship. After all this we cannot understand how the words of our section are found to be " full of suppressed resentment, inward excitement, ironical side glances, and ill-concealed depreciation with respect to the elder apostles " (Schwegler, i. 157, etc., ii. 109), unless we import excited feelings into the narrative. The expression in ver. 6, which is certainly very strong : ὁποῖοί ποτε ἦσαν, οὐδέν μοι διαφέρει· πρόσωπον θεὸς ἀνθρώπου οὐ λαμβάνει, that is, whatever they may have been before, it is

in the false brethren." As to the cognate passage, 2 Cor. xi. 1, etc., Holsten himself, who, in his work *Das Ev. des Paulus u. Petrus*, p. 27, note, thought that the original apostles were behind the Corinthian opponents, now affirms that to refer the ὑπερλίαν ἀπόστολοι, ver. 5, to the original apostles is positively arbitrary (*vid. Das Ev. des Paulus*, i. 221).

quite indifferent to me, probably means: Even if certain people have so high an opinion of the other apostles as to regard them as the only true, great, chief apostles, this has no importance for me; I have my calling direct from God; whether men recognize it or not, whether those who do recognize it are apostles or not, the fact remains unaltered (*vid.* Hofmann, *Schriftbcweis*, ii. 2, 42, etc.). This way of speaking betrays no irony, but only emphatic earnestness, not, indeed, directed against the apostles themselves, but against too high an estimate of their importance, against the abuse of their authority on the part of Judaistic partisans. That Paul had courage to oppose the apostles themselves when necessary is proved by Gal. ii. 11, etc., a passage to be discussed later on; but this very utterance bears indirect testimony to the fact that he had no occasion to appear against the apostles themselves in Jerusalem (Gal. ii. 1, etc.; Acts xv., for ver. 11, etc., form an unmistakeable climax to what goes before: Not only did I oppose the false brethren with effect, in agreement with the apostles, but afterwards I offered an open and energetic resistance even to the Apostle Peter himself, as it was necessary to do). When Baur (*Theolog. Jahrb.* 1849, 568) concludes from ver. 7—τὸ εὐαγγέλιον τῆς ἀκροβυστίας . . . τῆς περιτομῆς—that there was a difference of principle between the older apostles and Paul, he overlooks the circumstance that εὐαγγέλιον τῆς περιτομῆς is identical with ἀποστολὴ τῆς περιτομῆς (ver. 8), and with ἰέναι εἰς τὴν περιτομήν (ver. 9), according to the context, so that the words do not authorize us to suppose a peculiar gospel of the uncircumcision, and a peculiar one of the circumcision, as if the Pauline and Judaistic views of the law were different systems. The words can only denote a different circle of missionary activity, as is seen from the connection. By this means we get rid of everything else that some wish to derive from those words.

We have seen from the account of Gal. ii. the unmistakeable presence of a decided opposition, consisting in Judaistic demands on the one hand, and on the other hand, in energetic resistance for the maintenance of Christian freedom, but only between Paul and the " false brethren." Between Paul and the apostles of repute, viz. Peter, James, and John, on the contrary, we find here no opposition, inasmuch as the latter had no desire to urge anything new or rectifying upon Paul with regard to his apostolic preaching, nor was Paul on his side constrained to make any objection or resistance. The other apostles do not by any means appear as a party in opposition to Paul, but of their own accord tender him a solemn recognition of his activity as the apostle of the Gentiles. The parties engaged in the strife are therefore, in fact, the same as in the Acts. Here also we see no essential difference in the two accounts, and cannot at all admit the existence of an intentional departure on the part of the Acts from historical truth (Baur, *Paulus*, 105, 2 Aufl. i. 132, etc.[1]).

With regard to the *Church* at Jerusalem itself,—that is, the nucleus of the Church, as distinguished on the one hand from the apostles as the heads of it,

---

[1] It is perceived by modern scholars that Paul, in opposition to his Judaizing opponents, felt himself to be in essential agreement with the apostles, with respect to Gal. ii. 1 ff., for example, Bleek, *Beiträge*, 253 f.; Wieseler, *ante*, 189 ff.; Ritschl, *Altkatholische Kirche*, 115, 132, 134; Reuss, *Hist.* ii. 597 ff.; Koch, *de Petri*

and on the other from the "false brethren," that is, from those members having a Judaistic tendency, —there is nothing whatever in Paul's indication in Gal. ii. to favour the idea that they stood on the side of those who were in fundamental opposition to the evangelically free Pauline mission to the Gentiles. On the contrary, Gal. ii. 3 proves that the Church, as well as the other apostles, was far from wishing to impose circumcision on the Gentile Christians; for the party from whose side not a single protest was made in favour of the circumcision of Titus (vers. 3), —not to mention the whole body of Gentile Christians,—can, from ver. 2, be no other than the δοκοῦντες, that is, the apostles on the one hand, and on the other the αὐτοί, that is, the Church of Jerusalem as a whole.

Thirdly, the last subject of our historical and critical investigation is *the result of the apostolic transactions*. According to the Acts, the conciliatory proposal of James was accepted and raised to a decree. No decision was arrived at with respect to the Jewish Christians, while the Gentile Christians, in perfect conformity with Pauline principles, were not expressly exempted from circumcision and the Mosaic law (which the Judaists wished to make binding on them), but were only enjoined to abstain from flesh offered to idols, from fornication, and from things strangled, and from blood. This decree was at once transmitted to the Churches at Antioch, in Syria and Cilicia by means of a writing sent by two delegates

Theol. 103 ff.; Meyer, *Gal.*; Hofmann, *Schriftbeweis*, ii. 2. 42 ff.; but with especial clearness and candour by Holsten, *das Ev. des Paulus*, i. 1880, 1, 71 ff., 229 ff. But Weizsäcker seeks to prove (*Jahrb. für deutsche Theol.* 1873, S. 199 ff., 209) that the primitive apostles on this occasion had *not* the *Church* behind them.

from the Church of Jerusalem, who accompanied Paul
and Barnabas. In the Epistle to the Galatians, on
the other hand, we find no word of this decree, but
instead, a mutual recognition as brethren, and an
agreement made by the distinguished apostles with
Paul to the effect that Paul and Barnabas should
work among the Gentiles and they themselves
among the Jews (ἵνα ἡμεῖς εἰς τὰ ἔθνη, αὐτοὶ δὲ εἰς
τὴν περιτομήν),—the former being only enjoined to
remember the poor (μόνον τῶν πτωχῶν ἵνα μνημονεύωμεν, ver. 10), that is, that they should assist the
poor Churches in Judæa by contributions from the
Gentile Christian Churches.

Baur, Schwegler, and Zeller are of opinion that an
accommodation is out of the question here, and that
according to the Epistle to the Galatians, a decree
such as the Acts record had no existence; for if
such a decree had been actually made, Paul *could*
not have been silent about it in this place, without
derogating from the truth of his cause and his personal
rights over against his opponents. Besides, Paul
declares in the First Epistle to the Corinthians
that the eating of flesh offered to idols is in itself
allowable, a thing indifferent; and merely requires
abstinence from it for the sake of the weak. This he
could not have done if the decree in Acts xv. had
actually existed. Lastly, the appearance of the τινὲς
ἀπὸ Ἰακώβου in Antioch (Gal. ii. 12) makes it
probable that the statutes against which these people
acted had never been put forth.

To enter into the latter point, it is not entirely
clear what is meant by it. Paul does not announce
what these strangers from Jerusalem in Antioch
had properly to do. The context only leads us to

conjecture that they avoided intercourse with Gentile Christians. But did they in so doing act contrary to the position laid down in Acts xv., which referred solely and entirely to the Gentile Christians, and imposed upon them certain restrictions? If we assume, but not grant, that the conduct of these people was a violation of that Jerusalem decree, does it follow that the decree never existed? Is it inconceivable that individuals should act contrary to a certain decree even if brought about in a lawful way, which did not agree with their personal inclination and conviction? Is it inconceivable that the hotheads of a party should go farther than they ought to go by right? We cannot, therefore, perceive anything cogent in this objection.

The second argument rests on 1 Cor. viii. It is true that Paul here declares the eating of flesh offered to idols to be morally allowable in itself, and makes it a duty to abstain from it merely out of consideration for the conscience of others. But it is very doubtful if we should infer from this circumstance that the decree of Acts xv. had no existence whatever. Let us consider first, that this decree was mainly negative in character, a refusal of the Judaistic demand to make circumcision and Mosaic legality binding on the heathen, while the abstinence in question is certainly demanded as necessary ($\dot{\epsilon}\pi\acute{a}\nu a\gamma\kappa\epsilon\varsigma$, ver. 28), but without the positive motive being made prominent. When Paul now enjoins abstinence from meat offered to idols solely out of regard for the conscience of those who might take offence at it, this agrees in the main with the former decree, which also has its fundamental basis in consideration for others (Gentile Christians) enjoined on the Gentile Christians as a duty.[1] Paul certainly departs from this decree in *form*, and recommends abstinence not on account of the letter of the statute, but from an inner motive of evangelical freedom and love.[2]

That the decrees of Acts xv. 20 and 29 were actually valid in certain parts of Christendom for centuries, is proved by the following fact: When the persecution of the Christians in the year 345 broke out in Persia, Shahpur II. desired in an edict that the Christians should " worship the sun . . . *and drink the blood of animals* " (*Acta ss. martyrum orient.*, Rom. 1748, etc., 119, comp. 122, 129, 188, 204).

The latter command presupposes unconditionally that the Persian Christians abstained from blood for conscience sake; and this abstinence rested without doubt on the authority of those apostolic decrees which, according to Acts xv. 23, had been communicated to the

---

[1] Baur, in his *Christenthum u. christl. Kirche der drei ersten Jahrhunderte*, S. 112, 2 Aufl. S. 126, even understands the decree as " setting the Gentile Christians free from the law, only making it obligatory on them to abstain from those practices most offensive to the Jewish Christians, and most in the way of a mutual reconciliation."

[2] Ritschl, *Altkath. Kirche*, 1 Aufl. S. 120 f., thinks he has discovered an internal discrepancy between the decree itself and the preceding utterances, so that either the former, or more probably the latter, must be unhistorical. But he has overlooked the fact that only James, not Peter, makes the positive, formulated proposal ; while the views expressed by Peter might certainly lead to further concessions. Lutterbeck, *Neutestamentl. Lehrbegriffe*, ii. 84 ff., follows in the footsteps of Wieseler, who maintains that Gal. ii. 1, etc., refers to a later transaction than that narrated in Acts xv., and conjectures that the decree of the year 50 (Acts xv. 28, etc.) was, at a later council in the year 54 (Gal. ii.), by a new agreement so altered as—(1) to free the *Gentile Christians* from every Jewish law relating to food, and (2) to make it allowable, and even to some extent a duty, for the *Jewish Christians* not to observe the Mosaic law. A visionary, unhistorical hypothesis !

Syrian and Cilician Churches, and which they regarded as binding. For it is a well-known fact that Persian and Syrian Christianity were very closely connected.

This fact in the Oriental Church is supported by the testimony of a western Gallican Church. In Lyons, a female martyr called Biblias, in the persecution of A.D. 177, accused of "Thyestian feasts," repels the accusation with the question, "How could people eat children who were not even permitted to eat the blood of irrational beasts?" (οἶς μηδὲ ἀλόγων ζώων αἷμα φαγεῖν ἐξόν; Euseb. *K. G. V.* i. § 26).

We are reminded, in conclusion (*vid.* Zeller, *Apostel-gesch.* 236, etc.), that Paul could not possibly have left unmentioned in his Epistle to the Galatians the decree of Acts xv., in case it had been really enacted as described. This *argumentum e silentio* is not very cogent. We have already remarked that the persons who appeared in the Galatian Churches against Paul, disputed the independence of his apostolic authority. Accordingly the apostle, in Gal. ii., took up the whole matter mainly in its personal aspect. He proves that those very apostles on whom the opponents fondly relied, and whose authority they set above his own, expressly recognized his apostolic calling as on a par with their own, and his ministry as equally valid with their own. From the same point of view he mentions only that which concerned his personal rights and duties as an apostle ; and nothing further was imposed upon him as a duty, except care for the poor in Jerusalem. The enactment of Acts xv. was in fact, from its essentially negative character, nothing but a recognition of Pauline principles, an approval of the Pauline missionary-method, a charter for the Gentile Christians against the Judaistic propaganda. We recognize it as such from the joy of the Church at Antioch concerning the apostolic epistle (Acts xv. 30, etc.). In its positive aspect, however, the decree contains neither an admonition to Paul, nor anything essentially new and different where his former teaching and method of ordering the heathen Churches were concerned; for Paul had certainly inculcated the duty of giving no offence to the weaker from the beginning, wherever there was occasion. In neither respect did the enactment form an actual corrective of his gospel. The injunction concerning abstinence was not in itself doctrinal, but only formed a part of the moral and social Church-discipline.[1]

In the foregoing remarks we set out with the accounts of the result given in the Acts, and inquired what position Paul took with respect to it in his statements. If we now enter more closely into the utterances of Paul himself (Gal. ii. 6, 9, 10) concerning the result of his conference with the other apostles, we find that according to them it had a twofold character,—a negative and a positive. The negative was: ἐμοὶ οἱ δοκοῦντες οὐδὲν προσανέθεντο (ver. 6). If the false brethren had carried their

---

[1] Overbeck, de Wette's *Ap. Gesch.* 1870, S. 217, characterizes the decree recorded in Acts xv. 28, etc., as "a doctrinal one," but does not even attempt to prove that it entrenches upon faith, doctrine, dogma. Ritschl, *ante*, 150, comp. 133 ff., had already very clearly shown that the abstinence required of the Gentile Christians was "neither a supplement nor an abbreviation" of the Pauline gospel, and that the decree in question imposed "no condition of a *religious* nature" on the Gentile Christians (comp. Lekebusch, *Compos. der Apostelgesch.* 308 f. ; Baumgarten, *Apostelgesch.* ii. 1. 159 ff. ; Schneckenburger, *Stud. u. Krit.* 1855, p. 556 ff.; Hofmann, *Schriftbeweis,* ii. 2. 46 f.; Örtel, *Paulus in der Ap. Gesch.* 1868, S. 244 ff.; Trip, *Paulus nach der Ap. Gesch.* S. 95 ff.).

point, something new and essentially different from his former mode of procedure would doubtless have been imposed upon Paul with respect to his preaching of the gospel and his mode of planting and training Christian Churches among the Gentiles.[1] The latter, as distinctly false and defective, must have been rectified, inasmuch as circumcision and legal righteousness would have been declared to be necessary. But the distinguished heads, the "pillars of the Church," were not so minded. They imposed nothing on Paul that would have been a rectifying addition to his preaching of the gospel and his apostolic work.

Its *positive* aspect consisted in the fact that James, Cephas, and John, who were regarded as pillars, δεξιὰς ἔδωκαν ἐμοὶ καὶ Βαρνάβᾳ κοινωνίας, ἵνα ἡμεῖς εἰς τὰ ἔθνη, αὐτοὶ δὲ εἰς τὴν περιτομήν· μόνον τῶν πτωχῶν ἵνα μνημονεύωμεν (ver. 9, etc.), that is, they attested their mutual fellowship by the solemn joining of hands. They recognised this fellowship as already existing, and confirmed it for the future. Nor did they acknowledge Paul and Barnabas merely as brethren, but as apostles of the Lord. Thus, therefore, the full authority and ministry of Paul were formally acknowledged as equally justified and on a par with their own proper apostolic authority and ministry. According to Baur and his school (Baur, *Paulus*, 125, 2 Aufl. i. 141, etc., *Christentum*, 51, etc.; Schwegler, i. 120, etc.; Zeller, *Apostelgesch.* 237; Overbeck, 220; Holsten, *zum Ev. des Paulus u. Petrus*, 273), the result (Gal. ii. 19, etc.) consists in a purely external accommodation, in a complete separa-

---

[1] By this means the gospel of the Apostle Paul himself would have been a ἕτερον εὐαγγέλιον, "another gospel," as the apostle puts it in Gal. i. 6.

tion of the two parties, so that the Jewish and the Gentile missions do not cross, but each continues its own way independently, and undisturbed by the other ; that Jewish and Gentile apostles should leave each other quite unmolested, and that a double gospel should be preached, a gospel of circumcision and a gospel of uncircumcision. Does the κοινωνία then mean so little ? With what " dull eyes " (to use the words of Baur) must a critic have read the words of Paul if he sees here nothing more than an " unmeaning compact ! " Consider the moral reason that impelled the apostolic men to the step in question ! This was nothing less than the conviction that grace was given to Paul, the perception that " He that wrought effectually in Peter to the apostleship of the circumcision, the same was mighty in Paul toward the Gentiles." A clasp of the hand in fellowship, given because of this perception and from such a motive, is certainly not a mere sign of toleration and indifference, but a positive recognition and approval of the Pauline Gentile mission on the part of the Jewish apostles, and of the Jewish mission on the part of the Gentile apostle, a declaration of actual union in spirit and of true brotherly fellowship.[1] But the true and genuine character of the Christianity of the heathen whom Paul had converted, and their full citizenship in the kingdom of God, were thus indirectly acknowledged. We get some idea of the significance of such joining of hands, from the

---

[1] Hieronymus, *in Ep. ad Gal.*, *Opp.* ed. Vallarsi, vii. 1. 403 : " Propterea *dexteras* datas Paulo et Barnabæ *societatis* a Petro, Jacobo et Johanne, ne observatione varia diversum Christi evangelium putaretur, sed et circumcisorum et habentium præputium esset *una communio.*"

solemn scene that took place on the 4th October 1529, at the Castle at Marburg, when the Landgrave Philip of Hesse commanded the German and Swiss reformers to acknowledge each other as brethren, upon which Zwingli, with tears in his eyes, stepped forward and offered his right hand to Luther, who repelled the offered hand with the words, " You are of another spirit ! " How great the difference when the apostles Paul and Barnabas on one side, Peter, John and James on the other, actually joined their right hands in fellowship ! That was the real attestation of mutual recognition and of perfect union of spirit. How can it for a moment be supposed that a Paul would have given his hand to the Jewish apostles to seal the bond of fellowship, if it had involved the recognition of an essentially legal gospel of the circumcision (a Judaistic confession, as it were, in opposition to *his own* confession of free grace in Christ),— the same Paul who in Gal. i. 8, etc., pronounces an anathema upon every one that preaches another gospel than that which he proclaimed ?

The result of the conference, according to Gal. ii., was, first, *negative*—rejection of the pretensions of Judaistic partisans who wished to urge upon the Gentile Christians circumcision and the law as necessary to salvation, and to compel Paul to supplement the alleged deficiency of his preaching by yielding in this matter. Secondly, *positive*—a recognition of Paul's ministry as a genuine apostolic one, and a declaration of cordial communion with him ; and at the same time, also, an indirect recognition of the true and genuine character of the Christianity of the converted heathen, though free from the law ; together with a division of labour in the missionary sphere (to retain Wieseler's excellent expression). This division could not have been intended as exclusively and strictly national, but only as geographical: in other words, the meaning cannot have been, that if in heathen lands Paul were to meet with Israelites in the Diaspora, he was not to preach the gospel to them, or that Peter and the other apostles were not to preach Christ to such heathen as they might perchance encounter at the feasts in Jerusalem ; but the only thing defined on this occasion was the province of the Gentile world and of the people of Israel as a whole. The very circumstance that Peter was found in Antioch not long after (Gal. ii. 11, etc.), next that he addressed a letter to the Churches of Asia Minor (1 Peter), still farther, that John took up his abode in Ephesus and chose the Churches of Asia Minor for the circle of his activity, sufficiently proves that the separation agreed upon in the years 50 or 51 cannot have been either exclusive or valid for all time. It was not an egoistic "Go thou to the right, let me go to the left," but a separating and organizing of that which was recognized and treated as actual unity, having a wise regard to the already existing distinctions in men, and in accordance with the will of God and the clearly perceived calling of the Lord. It is manifest that not only was expression given to the independence of the Jewish and Gentile missions, of the Gentile and Jewish Church, but their connection as members of *one* whole, of the Church of Christ, was also recognised and held fast in the bond of peace. For the stipulation that the Gentile missionaries should "remember the poor" (Gal. ii. 10)—that is, that they should help the numerous poor in the Christian Churches of the Holy Land—did not refer solely to money-contributions as such, but the new Gentile Churches, by assisting the mother-Church at Jerusalem, were to bear testimony to their common faith and their gratitude towards it, and were to hold fast the unity of the spirit in the bond of peace (comp. Neander, i. 208 ; Baumgarten, ii. 1. 167, etc.).

If now we again look critically at the narrative of the Acts (taking into consideration the difference in point of view, inasmuch as Paul considers the matter more in a personal aspect, but the Acts from the standpoint of the Church), we find a remarkable agreement in the most essential points. Firstly, regarding the *negative* side, the decree of the council (Acts xv.) goes to prove that the conduct of the partisans, who by insisting on circumcision and the observance of the law had unsettled the Gentile Christians, was censured and condemned (ver. 24) as arbitrary and officious (οἷς οὐ διεστειλάμεθα); the observance of the Mosaic law is nowhere made binding on the Gentile Christians themselves, but only the observance of the so-called " Noachian commands " is required of them, as of " proselytes of the gate." The very expression : μηδὲν πλέον ἐπιτίθεσθαι ὑμῖν βάρος (ver. 28), agrees almost literally with what Paul says (Gal. ii. 6) respecting his own person : ἐμοὶ οὐδὲν προσανέθεντο.

Secondly, with regard to the *positive* side, in Acts xv. 23, etc., the apostolic dignity, fidelity, and trustworthiness of Paul and Barnabas are just as openly and distinctly recognised as in the narrative of Paul himself. The "apostles, elders, and brethren " designate Barnabas and Paul as their beloved brethren, as " men that have hazarded their lives for the name of our Lord Jesus Christ " (ver. 25, etc.). It is manifest that this honourable and appreciative testimony was meant to be a satisfaction and vindication on their behalf in opposition to the Jewish Christians who had attacked the calling and reputation of both. This declaration fully corresponds to the κοινωνία between Paul and the other apostles that had been solemnly confirmed, according to Gal. ii. 9.

That which appears only indirectly, but yet with certainty, from the Pauline passage, is expressed in the Acts of the Apostles directly, that is, the recognition of the Gentile Christians as fully authorized members of the Church of Christ; for this is plainly implied in the brotherly greeting at the beginning of the letter (ver. 25): ἀδελφοῖς τοῖς ἐξ ἐθνῶν χαίρειν.

There is still one point to be brought forward which has hitherto been but lightly touched upon, viz. that the transactions referred exclusively to *Gentile Christians*, according to both sources. They had their origin in disturbances that had arisen in Antioch from the fact that certain Judaistically-disposed strangers had tried to convince the Gentile Christians of that city that circumcision was necessary to salvation (Acts xv. 1), or, as Paul expresses himself, " false brethren unawares brought in" attacked the Christian liberty of the believers (Gal. ii. 4). The conferences themselves are limited to the question whether the converted heathen might be free from the law or not (Acts xv. 5–21, especially 5, 10, 11, 19, comp. xxi. 25); in other words, whether the gospel as formerly preached by Paul to the Gentiles could be recognised as complete and right (Gal. ii. 2, 5). The result, according to Acts xv., was a decree respecting the Gentile Christians, incorporated in a writing to the " brethren which are of the Gentiles."

According to Gal. ii. 6, 7, 9, the other apostles acknowledged Paul as the apostle of the Gentiles, and imposed nothing new upon him for this his proper sphere. All this shows that the Jewish Christians remained entirely out of account. The question whether the latter were to be further bound to the Mosaic law or not was left entirely out of consideration, because there was no occasion to discuss it. It appears to have been taken as a matter of course (at least on one side) that the ἀδελφοὶ ἐκ περιτομῆς had to observe the Mosaic law afterwards as before.[1] At this point we certainly meet with a difference between Paul and the Jewish apostles. Paul had doubtless assented to the decree that was made, which he was able to do inasmuch as the main thing in it, both in its negative and positive parts, was a confirmation of his own conviction and his previous conduct in relation to the proclamation of the gospel and Christian freedom. On the other hand, the deviation of Paul from the other apostles cannot be mistaken with respect to that which was not discussed at this time, but was apparently taken quietly for granted by the latter. They presupposed with regard to Jewish Christians the further observance of the Mosaic law as a permanent custom and religious duty. That such was the case is plain from a later occurrence (Acts xxi. 20, etc.), inasmuch as James and the elders assert that the Jewish Christians were all ζηλωταὶ τοῦ νόμου, and take offence at the circumstance that

---

[1] Comp. Hess, *Geschichte der Apostel*, vi. S. 386 ff. : "Whether the Jewish Christian should be raised above the ceremonial law, was a point that did not enter into the question. If he wished to observe his national law in all its parts as before, the apostolic precept did not hinder him ; it only prohibited him from extending this obligation to those strangers who embraced Christianity."

Paul seduced the Jews in the Diaspora, as they were told, to apostasy from Moses, and to the renunciation of the circumcision of their children and of the customs of their fathers. On the contrary, Paul, as we apprehend him from his epistles, was of another mind on this point. It is true that he observed the law in his own person (στοιχεῖ καὶ αὐτὸς τὸν νόμον φυλάσσων, Acts xxi. 24) inasmuch as he remained true to the Jewish feasts: once, in spite of all requests, refusing to stay in Ephesus because he wished to pass the impending festival-time in Jerusalem (Acts xviii. 20, etc.), for he was constrained to go up to Jerusalem to pray there and offer sacrifice. He even allowed Timothy, a disciple whom he wished to take with him as a missionary helper, and who belonged, on his mother's side, to the people of Israel, though his father was a heathen, to be circumcised (Acts xvi. 3).[1] In Jerusalem Paul yielded to the

---

[1] The statement that the same Paul who in Jerusalem, out of consideration for the Jews and Jewish Christians, had just refused with all his might to allow Titus to be circumcised, is said not long afterwards, from the same consideration, himself to have circumcised Timothy, is set down by Baur to the absolute incredibility of the Acts, because it would have been an act of characterless inconsistency (*Paulus*, 1 Aufl. 129 ff., 2 Aufl. i. 147 ff., note ; comp. Zeller, *Apostelgesch.* 239 ff.; Overbeck, 248 ff.). But when in Jerusalem it was demanded that Titus should be circumcised, it was required in the sense, as Baur (S. 253) excellently puts it, that it was "absolutely impossible to be saved by Christianity without professing Judaism, and submitting to all that the law prescribes as a necessary condition of salvation:" that is, it had to do with the fundamental question, whether the Mosaic law is necessary to salvation, or whether the grace of God in Jesus Christ is alone sufficient. In this case Paul would not have yielded πρὸς ὥραν, ἵνα ἡ ἀλήθεια τοῦ εὐαγγελίου διαμείνῃ. It was quite different in the case of Timothy, where this fundamental question did not come into consideration at all (comp. Gloag, *Comm. on the Acts*, 1870, ii. 103 f.). The Acts themselves declare Paul's motive for taking this step, in the words : "Paul

desire of James, and joined himself to the four men
who had taken a vow, in order that by this proof of
his fidelity to the law, the Judaists might be turned
from their unfavourable opinion of him (Acts xxi. 23,
etc.).[1]   While Schrader (*Ap. Paulus*, v. 561) is
inclined to treat the narrative as a calumniation of
Paul on the part of the historian, and Baur (*Paulus*,
198, etc.; 2 Aufl. i. 223, etc.), followed by Zeller

would have Timothy to go forth with him, and took and circumcised
him *because of the Jews which were in those quarters*,"—that is, in
order that the Jews might not reject the gospel because it was
preached to them by one who was uncircumcised.   This is plainly a
motive based on expediency and consideration for human nature, but
not on the divine necessity for salvation.   Zeller, indeed (*ante*, 240),
in order to let the impossibility of Paul's acting in this way appear
in the strongest light, maintains that Paul declares the adoption of
circumcision to be *under all circumstances* an absolute hindrance to
the saving of the soul ; and in support of this appeals to the passage
Gal. v. 2, etc., apart from its connection, which, however, can only
be rightly estimated if we reflect that the Galatian errorists demanded
circumcision as an indispensably necessary condition of salvation, and
that the Galatians, who were about to submit to circumcision, placed
their hope of salvation in it.   So far, and *only* so far, does the apostle
declare that circumcision is irreconcilable with grace and salvation
in Christ.   But apart from this and in themselves, circumcision
and uncircumcision appeared perfectly unimportant, that is, as
moral ἀδιάφορα (Gal. v. 6 ; 1 Cor. vii. 19).   Paul is as far removed
from the negative error of which he is here accused (fanatical opposition to the external ceremony as absolutely irreconcilable with salvation) as from the positive one to which the Judaists adhered (comp.
Schaff, *ante*, 265, note 1 ; Hofmann, *ante*, ii. 2. 45).   Thus the
refusal of Paul to allow Titus to be circumcised, and the circumcision
of Timothy on the other hand, are quite reconcilable without the
necessity of asserting a characterless inconsistency, a reprehensible
hypocrisy on the part of Paul, or of looking at it in an historical and
critical light as an absolutely incredible statement of the Acts (comp.
my discussion on this point in the *Stud. der evang. Geistlichkeit,*
Würtemburg, published by Stirm, 1847, ii. S. 130 ff.).

[1] Wieseler has fully shown that Paul did not himself take the
Nazarite vow (*Chronol.* 105 ff., *Comm. zu Gal.* 588 f.).   The remarks
of Baur in opposition to this view (*Theolog. Jahrb.* 1849, p. 480 f.)

(*Apostelgesch.* 277, etc.) and Overbeck (i. 273, etc.), regards the historical character of the act, which under the circumstances alleged would have been a " reprehensible ὑπόκρισις " on the part of the apostle, as at least doubtful, we find no reason to question the historical truth of the narrative, if looked at in the right light. It was by no means the intention of Paul to give his sanction to the fundamental principle of Judaists, that a born Jew, even if he believe in Christ, is bound to observe the law and the Mosaic custom in order to be saved. In this case he would undoubtedly have contradicted himself. His object was rather to prove that neither was he himself an apostate from the law, nor did he lead others to become so. In practice, therefore, according to the Acts which do not contradict the epistles in this respect, Paul most certainly observed the law himself, but in the spirit of perfect freedom—ἐλεύθερος ὢν ἐκ πάντων, 1 Cor. ix. 19—(comp. 1 Cor. ix. 19, 20 : ἐγενόμην τοῖς Ἰουδαίοις ὡς Ἰουδαῖος, ἵνα Ἰουδαίους κερδήσω, τοῖς ὑπὸ νόμον ὡς ὑπὸ νόμον μὴ ὢν αὐτὸς ὑπὸ νόμον, ἵνα τοὺς ὑπὸ νόμον κερδήσω). In so far he approached the Jewish apostles in life and conduct, while departing from them in *doctrine*, as well as in the importance he attached to Christian freedom and to the independence of believers with regard to the law. He was, as Niedner (*Kirchen-*

rest partly on an arbitrary limitation of the meaning of ἁγνίζεσθαι, partly on the conjecture put forth on behalf of this passage, that such as undertook for others the costs of the remission of the vow were accustomed also to take the vow upon themselves for some days ; partly on a further hypothesis with respect to the mode of reckoning the seven days (ver. 27). Zeller, on the other hand (*Apostelgesch.* 275), and Gloag (*Comm. on the Acts*, ii. 276, etc.), agree with the deductions of Wieseler.

gesch. p. 141) in his concise way puts it, " farther removed from Judaism than from the Jews, and was likewise nearer to the heathen than to heathenism." But the Jewish apostles, although reserving to themselves the περιτομή as their apostolic sphere of activity (Gal. ii. 9), still approach him in doctrine by the twofold principle that the gospel is intended for the Gentiles also, and that Gentile Christians are free from the law.

Looking back at the course we have hitherto gone over, we have seen how the Church of Christ from its first planting as a community attained to important growth within and without. The original united stream of Christian life divided into two arms according as believers came out of Israel or out of the heathen world. Individual communities were formed of converted Israelites and Gentiles, so that there were Palestinian communities which numbered converted Gentiles among their members, together with Israelites who had become believers and constituted the fundamental stock. On the other hand, there were Syrian communities, with some belonging to Asia Minor, etc., the majority of which consisted of converted heathen, though they also counted among them many Jewish Christians. But the fact was of much greater significance that a whole circle of Gentile Christian communities had been already founded over against the collective body of the Jewish Christian ones. It was natural and agreeable to the course which the Church of Christ took, that life in the worship and arrangement of the Churches was much more developed among the Jewish Christians than among the very young communities of the Gentile Christians about the

middle of the first century after Christ. The rise
and progress of numerous Gentile Christian communities must have always excited a lively interest
among the believers of Israel; it led to a crisis in
the primitive Church itself.[1] Zealous men among
them, filled with the hope that in the Messianic time
Jerusalem's gates would receive the fulness of the
Gentiles, that all the nations of the world would attach
themselves to Israel, the people of God, thought that
the Gentiles could only obtain full citizenship in the
kingdom of God and His Anointed, Jesus Christ, by
incorporation with Israel through circumcision, and
by submitting to the law of Moses without reserva-
tion. In a word, the Gentile Christians must rise
completely into converted Israel.

It became a question of putting these thoughts
into practice when the Palestinian intruders appeared
in the prominently Gentile Christian Church of Antioch, and laid down the principle that the reception
of circumcision was the indispensable condition of
salvation for converted Gentiles (Acts xv. 1, comp.
Gal. ii. 4).

The Apostle Paul at once recognized the magnitude
of the danger, the great range of the question, the
acuteness of the crisis which had set in. He saw
clearly what great interests were at stake. Not only
was the Christian freedom threatened in which the
Gentile Christians and he himself rejoiced ($\tau\grave{\eta}\nu$ $\dot{\epsilon}\lambda\epsilon\upsilon$-
$\theta\epsilon\rho\acute{\iota}\alpha\nu$ $\dot{\eta}\mu\hat{\omega}\nu$, $\mathring{\eta}\nu$ $\check{\epsilon}\chi o\mu\epsilon\nu$, Gal. ii. 4),—instead of which
Mosaic legality was to be imposed on them as a yoke
of bondage ($\mathring{\iota}\nu\alpha$ $\dot{\eta}\mu\hat{\alpha}\varsigma$ $\kappa\alpha\tau\alpha\delta o\upsilon\lambda\acute{\omega}\sigma\omega\sigma\iota\nu$),—but the *truth*
of the grace of God in Christ also was involved,
and of justification by faith, not by the works of the

---

[1] Comp. Holsten, *Das Ev. des Apostel Paulus*, 1880, S. 229 f.

law (Gal. ii. 5 : $\H{\iota}\nu\alpha$ $\H{\eta}$ $\dot{\alpha}\lambda\H{\eta}\theta\epsilon\iota\alpha$ $\tau o\hat{\upsilon}$ $\epsilon\dot{\upsilon}\alpha\gamma\gamma\epsilon\lambda\acute{\iota}o\upsilon$ $\delta\iota\alpha\mu\epsilon\acute{\iota}\nu\eta$ $\pi\rho\grave{o}\varsigma$ $\dot{\upsilon}\mu\hat{\alpha}\varsigma$). In conclusion, the apostle was naturally anxious as to the recognition of his former work in planting and training the heathen-Christian Churches (ver. 2 : $\mu\H{\eta}$ $\pi\omega\varsigma$ $\epsilon\grave{\iota}\varsigma$ $\kappa\epsilon\nu\grave{o}\nu$ $\tau\rho\acute{\epsilon}\chi\omega$ $\H{\eta}$ $\H{\epsilon}\delta\rho\alpha\mu o\nu$). Hence he resolved to have the matter decided in Jerusalem itself, a prompting not solely of human origin, but resting on a revelation imparted to him as a divine command ($ante$, $\kappa\alpha\tau\grave{\alpha}$ $\dot{\alpha}\pi o\kappa\acute{\alpha}\lambda\upsilon\psi\iota\nu$).[1]

The Churches of the Gentile Christians, with the Gentile apostle at their head and in their name, fought for their freedom in Christ and for the truth of salvation by grace without the works of the law ; blessings from God's hand, in the defence of which they were assured of doing God's work. The Judaistic zealots, on the other side, believed that in demanding the circumcision of the Gentile Christians and their subjection to the Mosaic legislation they represented the saving counsel of God and His ways, the indisputable privilege of Israel in the Messianic kingdom. Were not these irreconcilable opposites ? On both sides were decision, emphasis, sharpness. How easily might matters come to a complete breach, to a division that could not be healed, by separating the Church of Christ into two halves, a process that must tend to its destruction ! By God's help the fearful danger was averted.[2] It was a guarantee for peace when the apostle of the Gentiles took the step of repairing to

---

[1] This resolution by no means excludes the fact that the Church at Antioch itself determined ($\H{\epsilon}\tau\alpha\xi\alpha\nu$ $\dot{\alpha}\nu\alpha\beta\alpha\acute{\iota}\nu\iota\nu$ $\Pi\alpha\hat{\upsilon}\lambda o\varsigma$, etc., Acts xv. 2). Rather is it conceivable that Paul took that resolution first of himself by divine command, and that after he had disclosed it the Church took the matter into its own hands, and resolved to send the apostle with Barnabas and others as their deputies to Jerusalem.

[2] Comp. Renan, *St. Paul*, 1869, p. 83, etc.

Jerusalem to seek an understanding in the centre of Christendom, instead of roughly repulsing the partisans of Judaism in Antioch, and arranging on his own authority the affairs of the Gentile Christian Churches, without any regard to Jerusalem and the heads of the Jewish Christian circle. The mutual transactions at the apostolic convention saved the unity of the whole Church. The agreement between the two parties was certainly not one of fundamental principles, but a compromise with concessions on both sides. The elder apostles and the mother-Church at Jerusalem expressly renounced the obligation proposed by the Judaistic zealots fully to incorporate the Gentile Christians into Israel by circumcision and subjection to the Mosaic law. On the other side, Paul acquiesced in the Mosaic legality which prevailed among the Jewish Christians afterwards as well as before, as facts prove, and which was silently taken for granted by the elder apostles. Neither party fully renounced its convictions, but they agreed so far that the bond of peace was adhered to, the union between Jewish and Gentile Christians maintained, and the work of the kingdom of God continued on both sides. Assured by this understanding, matters gradually advanced towards a more complete union.

Another step in advance was made in Antioch when the Apostle Paul came forward with a resolute declaration against Peter. This is the fourth fact which adds to our knowledge of the relation between the elder apostles, the early Church, and the Gentile Christian circle respectively.

Paul gives this account of it in Gal. ii. 11, etc.: "But when Peter was come to Antioch, I withstood him to the face, because he was to be blamed. For before that certain came from James, he did eat with the Gentiles: but when they were come, he withdrew and separated himself, fearing them which were of the circumcision. And the other Jews dissembled likewise with him; insomuch that Barnabas also was carried away with their dissimulation. But when I saw that they walked not uprightly according to the truth of the gospel, I said unto Peter before them all, If thou, being a Jew, livest after the manner of Gentiles, and not as do the Jews, why compellest thou the Gentiles to live as do the Jews?" etc.

We distinguish the separate particulars:

First. The *conduct of Peter* in the beginning of his visit to Antioch. Paul says in ver. 12: μετὰ τῶν ἐθνῶν συνήσθιεν. By the ἔθνη, from the context, we can only understand *Gentile Christians.* With these Peter lived in brotherly intercourse, without regarding them as unclean, viz. he ate with them, making no distinction between meats that were Levitically clean and unclean; a course of proceeding which Paul in his discourse characterizes as ἐθνικῶς καὶ οὐκ Ἰουδαϊκῶς ζῆν (ver. 14). The Church at Antioch, mainly composed of Gentile Christians, had plainly disregarded the Mosaic commands relating to food, by virtue of their Christian freedom, so that the Jewish Christians there also considered themselves no longer bound by these laws. Now when Peter made a visit to this place (probably soon after the conference in Jerusalem) he acted in the spirit of this Pauline Church, and held fellowship with its members at table, maintaining unrestrained intercourse with the Gentile Christians, just as the Jewish Christians did. By this means he not only fully recognized the freedom of the Gentile Christians from the Mosaic law, but, as facts prove, also assented to the fundamental abrogation of the Mosaic decrees respecting food which Paul had preached as supported by Christian freedom (Holsten, *Zum Ev. des Paulus u. des Petrus*, p. 357).

Second. The arrival of certain delegates from James, the brother of the Lord. The τινες ἀπὸ ᾿Ιακώβου, as we saw (p. 178), were without doubt expressly sent by James. With what object, the apostle does not say. Holsten, *ante*, 357, etc. (comp. *Das Ev. des Paulus*, p. 78, etc., 152), categorically asserts that it was reported in Jerusalem that Peter held unreserved intercourse at table with the Gentile Christians, on which account James sent other members of the Church at Jerusalem to Peter to admonish him and the Jewish Christians in Antioch to separate from the Gentile Christians. This is only a conjecture. It is just as conceivable to suppose that the intention was to test by deputies whether the Syrian Gentile Christians adhered to the arrangement that was agreed upon on their behalf. But when they arrived they made the discovery that Peter himself, the apostle of circumcision, by no means conducted himself like a Jew faithful to the law, in the midst of a Church consisting mainly of Gentile Christians. On this point they may have made lively representations to him.[1]

It is expressly stated by Paul—and this is the *third* point—that as a consequence of the arrival of the delegates from Jerusalem, Peter withdrew from brotherly communion with the Gentile Christians, " fearing them which were of the circumcision." The words of ver. 12 : ὑπέστελλε καὶ ἀφώριζεν ἑαυτόν, are

[1] This is Renan's view, *St. Paul*, p. 295, etc.

rightly explained, as appears to us, by Holsten, when he says of Peter (*Das Ev. des Paulus*, i. 1880, p. 78, etc.), " he did not break away openly and at once, like a decided and self-reliant character, but withdrew by degrees." At any rate, the matter came to this issue, that Peter kept himself exclusively to the Jewish Christians, punctually observed the Mosaic laws respecting food and cleanliness together with them, and avoided all intercourse with Gentile Christians. His motive was fear of the men of the circumcision, φοβούμενος τοὺς ἐκ περιτομῆς, that is, he was anxious lest his vocation and repute in Jerusalem, especially among the Jewish Christian Churches, should suffer. The conduct of Peter was not isolated; it set the example to other Jewish Christians in Antioch; even Barnabas himself, the friend and like-minded companion of Paul, was carried away by the precedent, so as likewise to avoid intercourse with Gentile Christians.

Fourth. The judgment and *public rebuke of Paul* on this occasion, who says of Peter: κατεγνωσμένος ἦν (ver. 11), that is, neither—he was blamed by others, nor—*reprehensione dignus, condemnandus erat ;* but, he was condemned, viz. by his own manner of acting, inasmuch as his later conduct had been already judged by his earlier. In fact, his mistake was a ὑπόκρισις, for the words in ver. 13—συνυπεκρίθησαν αὐτῷ καὶ οἱ λοιποὶ Ἰουδαῖοι· ὥστε καὶ Βαρνάβας συναπήχθη αὐτῶν τῇ ὑποκρίσει—cannot possibly be understood to mean that the reproach of ὑπόκρισις fell only on the Jewish Christians, in the sense that " the other Jews were cowardly and hypocritical enough to join in " (Schwegler, *ante,* i. 129). The conduct of the Antiochian Jewish Christians was certainly hypocritical, inasmuch as they had already lived for years on the spot on an equal footing with the Gentile Christians; but if the συνυπεκρίθησαν αὐτῷ has any meaning at all, it must class Peter with those who ὑπεκρίθησαν, even characterising him as the prime leader in hypocrisy. This reproach of dissimulation, of the renunciation of personal conviction and conduct, is justly applicable to Peter, inasmuch as he showed a want of uprightness, arising from want of courage openly to adhere to his conviction against others of a different opinion. This lies also in the words, οὐκ ὀρθοποδοῦσι πρὸς τὴν ἀλήθειαν τοῦ εὐαγγελίου, that is, it was not an upright firmness, it was at variance with evangelical truth, a knowledge of which Paul moreover, as the context shows, expressly attributes to Peter and the rest. Paul now calls Peter to account, upbraids him with his error, even " to the face " (ver. 11), with the greatest frankness, and in the presence of all (ver. 14). The rebuke was as public as the culpable act. " *Non enim utile erat,*" Augustine says (*Expos. ep. ad Gal.*), " *errorem, qui palam noceret, in secreto emendare.*" Paul asks Peter for what reason he τὰ ἔθνη ἀναγκάζει ἰουδαΐζειν (ver. 14)? How far did Peter *compel* the Gentile Christians to live after the manner of the Jews? According to the context, this compulsion was only *indirect,*—a moral constraint, exercised by precedent and example,—inasmuch as Peter's present separation from the Gentile Christians and his exclusive intercourse with Jewish Christians was a virtual declaration that the Gentile Christians, if they would lay claim to brotherly fellowship with himself and with Jewish Christians in general, must consent to adopt a legally Jewish manner of life.

That the *ιουδαΐζειν* here means nothing more than the observance of the decrees of the apostolic council (Acts xv.), as Wieseler conjectures (*ante*, p. 195), we can never believe.

From this passage Baur and Schwegler, following the precedent of Gfrörer, *Heilige Sage*, i. 415, draw the conclusion that such an occurrence shows the narrative of the council (Acts xv.) to be quite un-historical (*Paulus*, 2 Aufl. i. 155 ; *Nachapost. Zeit.* i. 115, etc., 128, etc., ii. 106, etc.). Just the reverse ! The occurrence at Antioch presupposes a precedent such as Acts xv., for the historical development is already advanced a step here (Gal. ii. 11, etc.); the question no longer being whether the Mosaic law should be imposed on the Gentile Christians, but now turning on the point whether even the Jewish Christians in their intercourse with Gentile Christians should be released from the fetters of the law by which they had been formerly bound with respect to Gentiles. The Church at Jerusalem had come to the very important determination not to impose the burden of the law upon Gentile Christians, from which decision the idea was not remote that the Jewish Christians might venture to dispense with the observance of the law. In this latter case, we have an unforeseen result of that measure.

What now is the relation between Paul and Peter in this contest ? Paul himself confesses *ἀντέστην αὐτῷ* (ver. 11). It would be idle to take this opposition as only apparent, as Jerome, for example, has done, who proceeds on the assumption that neither the self - withdrawal of Peter from the Gentile Christians, nor Paul's reproach, was seriously meant ; Paul had only for appearance sake publicly blamed Peter: ut ὑπόκρισις observandæ legis, quæ nocebat eis, qui ex gentibus crediderant, correptionis hypocrisi emendaretur. In a far truer, franker, and more evangelical way is the relation apprehended by Augustine, who, in his interpretation of the Epistle to the Galatians, admits an error on the part of Peter, and understands the representation of Paul as an earnest *objurgatio*.[1] In this case, therefore, there was a real antagonism between the two apostles. The question is only whether it was merely a momentary and passing, or a permanent one; and again, whether the antagonism had its foundation only in the *conduct*, or also in the *conviction* of Peter. Baur and his school understand it in the sense that Peter, when he allowed himself to associate with the Gentile Christians, repudiated his own innermost conviction and did not again act in harmony with his own real mode of thinking till he withdrew from them (Baur, *Theol. Jahrb.* 1849, 475, etc.; Schwegler, *Nachapost. Zeitalter*, i. 120, etc.; Zeller, *Apostelgesch.* 187, note; Holsten, *Ev. des Paulus und des Petrus*, 1868, pp. 89, 141). But this amounts to a conversion of the thing into its opposite.[2] A cause must be in a bad state if it needs such violent

---

[1] A correspondence arose between Jerome and Augustine respecting the incident of Gal. ii. 11, etc., that caused a breach between the two men, of which Möhler gives an interesting account in the treatise: Hieronymus und Augustinus im Streit über Gal. ii. 14 (*Gesammelte Schriften*, i. 1, etc.). Overbeck treats the subject from a far more comprehensive point of view, " Ueber die Auffassung des Streits des Paulus mit Petrus bei den Kirchenvätern," *Baseler Programm*, 1878. Learned, but with an object.

[2] Marcion in his time seems to have given the very same turn to this event, but has already been fitly answered by Tertullian (*Adv. Marcionem*, i. 20): " You wish to understand a rebuke which applied solely to conduct (*solius conversationis*), also of an offence against

measures for its defence. It is clear as day that Paul reproves Peter's very renunciation of the association he had hitherto maintained with the Gentile Christians as a censurable error, a denial of his better conviction and previous conduct. Every ground and reason for Paul's forcible accusation of Peter (14–17) would have been obviated if the case had been otherwise. Hence Hilgenfeld, *Gal.* p. 60, etc., admits that ver. 14—ἐθνικῶς ζῆς—" seems to be unfavourable to the modern critical apprehension." Paul speaks with greater power and severity, the more clearly he recognizes that Peter agrees with him in his heart. The whole encounter proves that theoretically and practically Peter shares the principles of Paul with regard to the law, and that the primitive apostles are at one with Paul as to the foundation of Christian faith. Thus Peter, as in the palace of the high priest, repudiated his better conviction, from the fear of man ; it is " the old nature of Peter, which, though conquered by the spirit of the gospel, was still active, and at times became paramount" (Neander, *ante*, i. 352). But the very character of Peter, tending to rashness, yet open to the truth and to self-knowledge, makes it the more probable that he acknowledged his error, humbly accepted the reprimand of Paul, and remained in the bond of apostolic fellowship (κοινωνία, Gal. ii. 9) with him afterwards as before.[1]

God with respect to preaching (doctrine, *prædicationis*). But with regard to unity in preaching, they had, as we read above (*supra, i.e.* Gal. ii. 9), joined hands and united in fellowship of the gospel by separation in office."

[1] F. Zimmer, *Hilgenfeld's Zeitschrift für wiss. Theologie*, 1882, p. 165, etc., fully concurs in this view ; while Holsten, in his acute, dialectic analysis of the Pauline narrative and rebuke (*Das Ev. des Paulus*, 1880, p. 77, etc.), gives no opinion as to the probable consequences of the occurrence.

In answering the other question, as to the form which the mutual relation assumed from the standpoint of the Gentile Christians, in what way they regarded it, and what position they actually took with respect to the Palestinian Jewish Christians, the Acts as well as the Pauline Epistles give some indications.

There is one feature in particular which first meets the eye and which runs through the entire life and work of Paul, like a red thread as it were—we mean the thankfulness manifested in repeated services and assistance, the love and brotherly communion on the part of the Gentile Christians towards the Churches of Judæa, especially the primitive Church of Jerusalem. The first fact in point is related in the Acts, xi. 29, etc. In consequence of the prophecy mentioned above, relating to a coming famine, and perhaps after its actual commencement in Judæa (in the year 45, according to Wieseler, p. 149, etc., 221), the disciples in Antioch, each according to his ability, made a contribution for the brethren in Judæa, which was forthwith sent to the elders by Barnabas and Paul. Since Schrader, *der Ap. Paulus*, v. 1836, p. 536, etc., a great number of German scholars,—for example, Gfrörer, *die Heilige Sage*, 1838, i. 419 ; Zeller, *Ap. Gesch.* p. 222 ; Overbeck, *Kurze Erklärung*, p. 178, etc.,—and others have declared this journey of the apostle to be unhistorical, if not a fiction with an object (Overbeck, pp. 175, 179). The chief argument against the historical character of this collection-journey is drawn from the silence of the Galatian Epistle (chap. i., etc.) respecting it. But the object of the apostle in this section is not to give an absolutely complete and continuous narrative of his journeys to Jerusalem, but only to prove his independence of the apostles before him, the entire independence of his apostolic activity. Even Baur was impartial enough to concede in his last discussions of this point (*Paulus*, 2 Aufl. p. 130) that it was a matter of indifference whether he met with the other apostles again in Jerusalem. This is confirmed the more closely we examine the apostle's line of thought in the first chapter of his Galatian Epistle, as does Holsten, for example (*Das Ev. des Paulus*, p. 68, etc.). Besides, the Acts, xi. 30, xii. 24, do not say a word of apostles in Jerusalem, but merely of presbyters, to whom Paul and Barnabas handed the produce of the collection. We therefore hold that journey, which belongs to the time of the first activity of Paul in Antioch, and precedes his first missionary journey, to be historically certain.

From our point of view there are two things to be considered in this occurrence : First, that the Christians in Judæa, beginning with the Church at Antioch, are recognised as " brethren " (ver. 29) ; which we are the less able to regard as a mere form of speech, since we recognise the force of Schwanbeck's observation (*Quellen*, etc., i. p. 8, etc.), that here, as well as in chaps. xiii. and v., the original documents on which the narrative is based, proceed from an Antiochian standpoint. The other point is, that the contributions were not intended exclusively for the Church at Jerusalem, but in general for " the brethren which dwelt in Judæa." Thus the question related not merely to the mother-Church, but to the believers from among the Hebrews in the whole land of Judæa. If the Gentile Christians wished to prove in truth and reality that they actually looked upon the disciples in Judæa as brethren and loved them as such, they could not do it better than by such assistance in their necessity. This collection, as Baumgarten (*ante*, ii. 1, 4) finely says, was "the hand which the Gentile world for the first time reaches out to Israel over the old breach."

It agrees with this in a remarkable way, that, as Paul says in Gal. ii. 10, the heads of the Church in Jerusalem imposed one obligation on him and Barnabas, viz. that they should remember the poor, to which he immediately adds, " that he was also forward to do the same thing." Whilst, according to Acts xi., the members of the Church at Antioch, out of their own prompting, show their brotherly love by laying up and sending off gifts for the benefit of believers in Judæa ; the pillar apostles here bring to the recollection of Paul and Barnabas the poor of the Church, a thing which, according to the words of the epistle, appears as a personal request to the two men, though in reality it concerned the Gentile Christian Churches; for personal contributions by Paul and Barnabas are not meant, since the former had to support himself by the work of his hands, or was commended to the support of the brethren, for example to the Church at Philippi. The intention, therefore, was that Paul and Barnabas were to exert their influence upon the mixed Churches, inducing them to support the poor Churches in Jerusalem and Judæa. It follows, farther, from the context that this charitable assistance on the part of the Pauline Churches, extended to the poor Christians in Palestine, was looked upon as a sign and bond of communion, as a proof of brotherly love and union on both sides.

Paul says he strove to do this. We find, in fact, in many of his epistles that the offering of love for the Palestinian Churches lay very near the heart of the apostle. It extended, so far as can be proved from early documents, over Asia Minor, Macedonia, and Greece. In 1 Cor. xvi. 1–5, Paul thus exhorts the Corinthians: "As I have given order to the Churches of Galatia, so do ye." On the first day of the week every one was to lay by him in store, as he was able, in order that there might be no gatherings when the apostle came. From this we see that the apostle had ordered a similar collection in Galatia. He now informs the Corinthians, who had already received general instructions in the matter, how it was to be carried out in detail. In ver. 3 he expressly names Jerusalem as the place to which it was to be sent. But we learn from Rom. xv. 25–28, that besides the Churches of Greece and Asia Minor, others were found willing to help: "It hath pleased them of Macedonia and Achaia to make a certain contribution for the poor saints which are at Jerusalem."

The true significance of this ministration is clearly explained by the apostle in Rom. xv. 27 and 2 Cor. ix. 12, etc. In the former passage he interprets it as a proof of gratitude. They (the Christians of Macedonia and Achaia) are debtors of the saints in Jerusalem: "For if the Gentiles have been made partakers of their spiritual things, their duty is also to minister unto them in carnal things." Hence there is mutual participation. The Jews, from whom salvation came, imparted spiritual blessings to the Gentiles, and these testified their gratitude by worldly gifts. We find this subject most fully

discussed in all its aspects in 2 Cor. ix. 12, etc.,
which is a supplement to the former passage: "For
the administration of this service not only supplieth
the want of the saints, but is abundant also by many
thanksgivings unto God; whiles by the experiment
of this ministration they glorify God for your
professed subjection unto the gospel of Christ, and
for your liberal distribution unto them, and unto all
men; and by their prayer for you, which long after you
for the exceeding grace of God in you." Certainly the
importance of this collection cannot be more beautifully expressed. The apostle considers the immediate
relief of bodily necessities only as the foundation,
and the main thing to be the impression which the
work of love would produce on the recipients. In
it these latter perceive both the true faith of the
Gentile Christians who in helping believers likewise
make a genuine confession of Jesus Christ, and
the brotherly communion of the Gentile Christians
with themselves. We see from this in how many
ways such help would prove a bond of communion;
how tender an expression of union between Jewish
and Gentile Christians it would be, and how effica-
cious a means of promoting it. We can understand
how important it is, when Paul gives the name
κοινωνία to such a contribution (Rom. xv. 26, comp.
2 Cor. viii. 4, ix. 13; comp. Gal. ii. 9, etc.). Looking
back from this point to the first beginnings of the early
Church itself, we get a clear idea of the union in
brotherly fellowship existing between its members,
especially from the fact prominently brought forward on
several occasions, that believers employed their means
for the relief of the needy among them, and practised
a far-reaching mutual support (Acts ii. 44, etc., iv. 32,

34, etc.). Just as this true service within the *one* Church was partly effect and expression and partly a means of promoting harmony,—the Christian κοινωνία, —so also the willing and zealous assistance rendered by the Gentile Christians in Syria and Asia Minor, Macedonia and Achaia, to the poorer believers in Jerusalem and Judæa, was partly a proof of their brotherly disposition towards them, and partly a means well adapted to strengthen and deepen the mutual connection between the different parts of the Church of Christ, viz. their union, κοινωνία. This result was the more probable since the help was not limited to the mere handing over to the Christians in Jerusalem of a certain sum of collected money as an offering of love ; but the opportunity always served to strengthen and renew personal intercourse, inasmuch as some members travelled from the Church in question to Jerusalem,—for example, Paul and Barnabas from Antioch (Acts xi. 30), some members from the Church at Corinth (1 Cor. xvi. 3, etc.).[1] We can easily conceive how welcome in Jerusalem would be a visit from the Gentile Churches for such an object, how this intercourse would contribute to dissipate many prejudices in Judæa against Gentile Christians, or at least to lessen them. It is but natural to suppose that the Palestinian Christians must have been impressed in this way with the consciousness that believers among the Gentiles were still connected with them in the true love of Christ,

---

[1] The narrative (Acts xx. 4) of the seven men who accompanied the apostle from Macedonia and Asia Minor, as representatives of the converted heathen world, and bearers of the offerings of love of the Gentile Church collectively (as Baumgarten, *Ap. Gesch.* ii. 2, 39, etc., explains), would be very beautiful, if it were only certain that they all accompanied Paul as far as Jerusalem.

that they were actually participating brethren, on whom they could rely, and to whom, as associates in faith and brethren for Christ's sake, they stood much nearer than to unbelievers among their own people. On the other hand, it was a great joy to the Churches in Galatia, Achaia, and Macedonia, and a strengthening of the consciousness of brotherly communion, when their deputies returning from Jerusalem could say that the offering of love transmitted through them not only supplied a present want, but also excited the Christians there to heartfelt thanksgiving to God; when they related how the believers in Jerusalem prayed for their brethren in the heathen world (comp. 2 Cor. ix. 12, etc.).[1]

The sending of Paul and Barnabas, together with certain others, from Antioch to the apostles and elders in Jerusalem, on behalf of the Christian freedom of believers from among the Gentiles, was a step of a different kind on the part of the Gentile Christians. With respect to this transaction, which we have already discussed, we shall here only draw attention to the fact that the decision of the Christians of Antioch to appeal to Jerusalem by means of deputies, is of importance in determining the relation in which the Churches of the Gentiles stood to the Christians of Palestine, especially the Church in Jerusalem. We cannot, indeed, find anything in the narrative of the Acts to support Schrader's assumption (v. 546, etc.) that Paul appears in subjection to the other apostles, and that the Pauline Church gave up its

---

[1] Many correct observations are to be found in Holsten (*Das Ev. des Paulus*, 1880, p. 228, etc., 443, etc.) respecting the gift of love, and especially the effect which the apostle intended it to have on the mother-Church in Jerusalem.

independence. But we do hold that the Antiochians were most anxious to come to an understanding with the apostles and elders in Jerusalem with respect to the important question that had been raised. They did not wish to surrender their Christian freedom, nor, on the other hand, to fall out with the apostles and the early Church, and would not even take their own way without first consulting them (*vid.* p. 228). They felt the importance of a mutual understanding and agreement, for it was not a question concerning them alone, but a transaction of the Church as a body; for which reason they sent their delegates to Jerusalem, to discuss the matter in common and bring it to a decision. This is the pragmatic connection which we must assume according to the Acts, and is quite consistent with what Paul himself writes (Gal. ii.) concerning the object of his journey; only that he represents the matter, as before remarked, from a personal point of view, while the Acts regard it from the standpoint of the community or Church. We may therefore say that the sending of Paul and his companions to Jerusalem, to confer respecting Gentile Christian matters, was an act of true brotherly feeling, having for its object an understanding and union between the Jewish Christian and Gentile Christian Churches. The result was in effect as favourable as was possible under the circumstances, the freedom of the Gentile Christians from the law being formally acknowledged, and the *κοινωνία* both between the apostles themselves and between the Jewish Christian and Gentile Christian Churches solemnly sanctioned and firmly upheld.

These are the facts attested by the New Testament Scriptures regarding the mutual relation between the

Churches of the Palestinian Jewish Christians and the Gentile Christians outside Palestine in the apostolic age. It is true they are but fragments which are not sufficient to give a complete picture of the actual inter-communion. But they suffice to establish the view that the relation was on the whole a peaceable and friendly one, since a mutual participation and ministration existed. Believers of the Hebrews imparted spiritual blessings to the Gentiles (Rom. xv. 27), salvation came from the Jews; and even if those who were of the circumcision, with a zeal not according to knowledge, wished to bring the law also to the heathen who had become believers, it was done, on the one hand, with a good intention, from a conviction that salvation could not be obtained without the law and circumcision; on the other hand, according to the evidence of the New Testament, it was only individual fanatics (Gal. v. 9), members of the Judaistic, legal party, who sought to impose their old leaven on the converted heathen. But the great majority of the Jewish Christians, even if " zealous for the law " where they themselves were concerned, were ready to acknowledge the freedom of the Gentile Christians as soon as it became necessary; and continued in brotherly fellowship with them. The Gentile Christians, on their side, willingly acknowledged their indebtedness to those Churches from which, by means of the gospel, spiritual blessings in Christ had flowed in upon them. They sought to testify their gratitude chiefly by material assistance and support, and were on all occasions anxious to come to an understanding with the Churches in Judæa, and to grow up with them more and more into one fellowship, one body of Christ.

SECOND SECTION.

JEWISH AND GENTILE CHRISTIANS DURING THE PERIOD BETWEEN THE DESTRUCTION OF JERUSALEM AND THE CLOSE OF THE APOSTOLIC ERA (A.D. 70–100).

Important epochs in history owe their prominence, as a rule, not merely to one solitary event, but to several, occurring contemporaneously. This holds good of that epoch by which the first and second halves of the apostolic era are separated. Its importance for us lies chiefly in the death of the Apostle Paul. But the Apostle Peter also suffered martyrdom about the same time (according to Wieseler, in the year 64). A few years later the Roman-Jewish war began, ending, in the year 70, in the destruction of Jerusalem and the temple. The latter event was of uncommon and far-reaching significance for the kingdom of God. Notwithstanding the fact that Neander as well as Baur and his school (*Theol. Jahrb.* 1844, p. 567 ; Schwegler, *Nachap. Zeitalter*, ii. 191) attach small value to its importance for the Church, we yet feel justified in adhering to the view re-asserted by Rothe, defended by Uhlhorn (*Homilien und Recogn. des Clemens rom.* 1854, p. 387, etc.), and assented to by Renan,[1] viz. that this event had the utmost importance. It is true we have no direct authentic testimony as to the effect produced on the Christians by the destruction of Jerusalem ; but its importance may be perceived indirectly from many circumstances.

---

[1] Renan, *St. Paul*, 1869, p. 495 : L'évènement—rendra au christianisme le plus grand service qu'il ait jamais reçu dans le cours de sa longue histoire. Comp. *L'Antechrist*, p. 545, etc.

Where there is a firm conviction that the standpoint of Christianity at that time was exclusively "Ebionitic," that is, Judaistic, as with Baur and his school, a higher estimate should, in consistency, be formed of the convulsion that must have been produced in the minds of the Christians by the destruction of the temple and the termination of the Levitical cult. If indeed we could believe that "the Jews and Jewish Christians who returned to the ruined city soon found the necessary means for the restoration of the Levitical cult" (Schwegler, *ante*, ii. 308, etc.), we should have no reason to regard the destruction of the city as so epoch-making an event. But this conjecture is quite untenable, and has been refuted by Friedmann and Grätz in a thorough and scholarly way, particularly by the help of Talmudic testimony ("Die angebliche Fortdauer des jüdischen Opfercultus nach der Zerstörung des zweiten Tempels," *Theol. Jahrb.* 1848, p. 338, etc.). It has here been convincingly shown that with the destruction of the temple under Titus the Jewish sacrificial system reached its complete end, and that the Levitical worship did not survive the overthrow of the temple and the downfall of the Jewish state.[1] If Judaism, as a religious and political power, as a nationality, received its death-blow from the destruction of the capital and of the temple, the recoil from it in the Christian Church must have been the more keenly felt the nearer a part of its members stood to Judaism in their religious consciousness.

What a visible punishment of God inflicted upon

---

[1] This is confirmed by J. Derenbourg, *Histoire de la Palestine*, Paris 1867, Appendix, note 14, "Le sacrifice après la destruction du temple," p. 486, etc.

the unbelieving and disobedient people must the
destruction of the holy city, "where the Lord was
crucified," have been in the eyes of all believing
Christians, when it made an impression so deep and
humiliating on the thoughtful and sensitive Jews!
A contemporary of the Jewish war, who was present
at the destruction of Jerusalem, Rabban *Jochanan
Ben Zakkaï,* on seeing a woman who had formerly
been rich and prosperous, gathering up barley-corns
under horses' feet for her miserable subsistence,
exclaimed in deep sorrow : " Unhappy people ! since
you would not serve your God, you must now serve
strange peoples; since you would not pay half a
shekel to the temple, you must now pay fifteen
shekels into the exchequer of your enemies !" [1]

CHAPTER I.

THE JEWISH CHRISTIANS.

The annihilation of the Israelitish state and the
destruction of the temple naturally exercised a very
direct influence on the Palestinian Jewish Christians.
It is well known that shortly before the siege and
destruction of Jerusalem, under the impression of a
divine revelation, the Christian Church of that city
fled to Pella beyond Jordan, moved to this step not
merely by the threatening danger of war, but also by

---

[1] Delitzsch, *talmudische Studien,* in *Zeitschrift für luth. Theol.*
1854, p. 646, etc. ; and Grätz, *Geschichte der Juden, vom Untergang
des jüdischen Staats bis zum Abschluss des Talmud,* Berlin 1853,
iv. 23, etc. On Jochanan Ben Zakkaï comp. Derenbourg, *ante,*
xix. p. 302, etc.

the increasing intolerance and fanaticism of the Jews, from which the Christians had to suffer.[1] Pella itself, belonging to the Decapolis, was situated on Hellenic soil.[2] Without doubt fugitive Jewish Christians there came into contact with Gentile Christians. A community soon reassembled in the desolate city, in which one of the few remaining buildings that had been spared was, we are told, the little Christian church on Mount Zion (Epiphanius, *de mensuris et ponderibus*, xiv.). But they could now live there in greater security and peace; for the moment they had nothing more to fear from the Jews. Several circumstances, however, indicate that from this time the relation between Jews and Christians in Palestine became strained, forcing the latter to withdraw themselves more and more from the former. The annihilation of the Jewish state, which had at least been able to keep up an appearance of life for several generations, had this result among others, that the Sanhedrim, to which the Palestinian Christians as well as the Jews themselves had been hitherto subject, transferred its seat from

[1] Eusebius, speaking of the Jewish war and the destruction of Jerusalem, *H. E.* iii. 5, § 3, after the death of James the Just, mentions the fact that the rest of the apostles, who were harassed by the Jews in innumerable ways with a view to destroy them, and driven from the land of Judæa, had gone forth to preach the gospel to all nations. He then continues: οὐ μὴν ἀλλὰ καὶ τοῦ λαοῦ τῆς ἐν Ἱεροσολύμοις ἐκκλησίας, κατά τινα χρησμὸν τοῖς αὐτόθι δοκίμοις δι' ἀποκαλύψεως δοθέντα, πρὸ τοῦ πολέμου μεταναστῆναι τῆς πόλεως, καί τινα τῆς Περαίας πόλιν οἰκεῖν κεκελευσμένου· Πέλλαν αὐτὴν ὀνομάζουσιν, ἐν ᾗ τῶν εἰς Χριστὸν πεπιστευκότων ἀπὸ τῆς Ἱερουσαλὴμ μετωκισμένων, ὡσὰν παντελῶς ἐπιλελοιπότων ἁγίων ἀνδρῶν αὐτήν τε τὴν Ἰουδαίων βασιλικὴν μητρόπολιν καὶ σύμπασαν τὴν Ἰουδαίαν γῆν, ἡ ἐκ θεοῦ δίκη λοιπὸν αὐτοὺς ἅτε τοσαῦτα εἴς τε τὸν Χριστὸν καὶ τοὺς ἀποστόλους αὐτοῦ παρηνομηκότας μετῄει.

[2] Comp. Schürer, *Lehrbuch der neutestamentlichen Zeitgeschichte*, 1874, p. 398; Renan, *L'Antechrist*, 1873, p. 298, etc., 540.

Jerusalem to Jabne (Jamnia) on the Philistine coast, having lost much of its importance and influence. Thus one bond which had hitherto joined the believing Jews to the whole people was loosed. Moreover the entire sacrificial service and Levitical cult, to which the Christians had hitherto attached themselves in some measure, had come to an end along with the temple. A separation of the Churches from the synagogue seems to have occurred at the same time, by which a second bond of a directly religious and sacred nature was loosed, the former having been a juridical and civil tie.

It is one of the most remarkable phenomena in history that the Jewish people gathered together again and formed a national centre of religion even after the destruction of the holy city and the temple which had been the nucleus of their real life. This is an evidence not only of the indestructible, tenacious life-power dwelling in them, but also of the divine origin of the revelation of the Old Testament that had been given to them, and not least of a divine plan with regard to Israel, who, as a people of the future, had still their promise. The work of preserving and reforming was accomplished in the first two centuries by a succession of Rabbins, who are called the Tanaïm. It was the above-named Jochanan Ben Zakkaï who opened a house of instruction in Jabne, and after the fall of Jerusalem founded a Sanhedrim there with full religious power and the functions of a supreme court of justice (בֵּית דִּין), thus providing not only for the living transmission of doctrine, but giving again a religious and national centre to the Jewish nation.[1] After him Rabban Gamaliel II.,

____
[1] Comp. Renan, *Les Évangiles*, 1877, p. 11, etc.

or Gamaliel of Jabne, continued the work. He became Nassi, that is, Patriarch, President of the Sanhedrim, and laboured with all his power and might to make the patriarchate the centre of the Jewish state and to maintain unity of doctrine. While the powerful impression of the destruction of Jerusalem, as a judgment on stiff-necked Judaism, threw many Jews into the arms of the Christian Church, the two men already mentioned still found means to maintain and carry on the stability of the Mosaic tradition, of the Levitical customs, and even of the Jewish state which had been shattered for the moment. Not only did they fill up in some measure the gap which had arisen through the fall of the temple, with doctrine, prayer, and works of benevolence, observing the Levitical laws of purification with extreme punctiliousness; but, in the hope that the temple would again be restored, possibly in the immediate future, as it had formerly been after the exile, they even retained certain religious customs which had their place and true significance only in the temple. But the greater the moral power by which the Jews again assembled and concentrated themselves as people of the law, the more sharply and decisively did they separate from the Christians internally and externally; most sharply from the Jewish Christians, as was natural, for the Gentile Christians stood farther from these in any case. The Rabbins who gave the tone, anxious for the preservation of genuine Judaism, feared nothing more than Christianity and the Christians, whom they called *Minnim* (מִינִים, not yet etymologically cleared up). Rabbi Tarphon said: " The gospels and all the writings of the Minnim deserve to be burnt, together with the sacred names of God which appear in them; for heathenism is less dangerous than the Christian sects, because the former from ignorance is unable to apprehend the truths of Judaism; the latter, on the contrary, deny them with a clear consciousness of what they are; it would be better therefore to flee for refuge into a heathen temple than into the meeting-houses of the Minnim." For such reasons a formal wall of separation between Jews and Jewish Christians was built up by means of different regulations recommended in letters from the Sanhedrim to all Israelite communities: flesh, bread, and wine were forbidden to Christians; all business intercourse with them was strictly prohibited; a sentence of condemnation was pronounced upon their sacred writings, which were compared to books of magic; a formula of cursing against the "*Minnim* and denounced" was inserted in the daily prayer, with the remark that whoever omits this in the public recitation of the synagogue shall be expelled. This imprecation on the heretics (בִּרְכַּת הַמִּינִים), the composition of which is ascribed to the Rabban Gamaliel II. (A.D. 80–118), runs thus, " To apostates let there be no hope, let all malevolents perish ! let the kingdom of arrogance be rooted out, broken, speedily humbled in our days " ! In this solemn curse the disposition of the Jews towards the Jewish Christians is expressed with such passion as to afford an insight into the excited fanatical spirit that animated the Jews of that time against the Christians as persons proscribed.[1] In Christianity

<hr>

[1] Comp. Renan, *Les Evangiles*, 1877, p. 71, etc. ; Derenbourg, *Histoire de la Palestine*, Paris, i. 344, etc., 354, etc. The curse against the Christians was known to them still later; Justinus M., *Dial.*

they saw a falling away from the law; in the Jewish
Christians, an apostate sect who denied the religion
of their fathers knowingly and willingly. Doubtless
their antipathy to the Christians had only been
increased by the catastrophe which had taken place;
as they attributed the terrible judgment of God not
to the guilt of their own people but solely to those
who had provoked the wrath of God by their so-
called apostasy from the law, that is, to the Christians
among their countrymen.

We cannot wonder that those against whom such
fanaticism was kindled, viz. the Palestinian Christians,
should feel themselves more and more strongly
repelled. The very fact that the demolition of the
temple and the consequent cessation of all sacrificial
service had roused the Christians to a conviction
that the Mosaic law and the Old Testament theocracy
had been abolished by God Himself; that the
destruction of Jerusalem and the house of God
had produced an impression of God having rejected
His people because they had rejected His Anointed,
His only-begotten Son,[1] severed the bond that had
formerly attached the believing Israelites to the

contra *Tryph.* xvi., describes the Jews as καταρώμενοι ἐν ταῖς συναγωγαῖς τοὺς πιστεύοντας ἐπὶ τὸν Χριστόν. And Epiphanius, *Adv. Hæres.*
i. 29. 9, says: Οὐ μόνον οἱ τῶν Ἰουδαίων παῖδες πρὸς τούτους (Ναζωραίους)
κέκτηνται μῖσος, ἀλλὰ ἀνιστάμενοι ἕωθεν καὶ μέσης ἡμέρας καὶ περὶ
τὴν ἑσπέραν, τρὶς τῆς ἡμέρας, ὅτε εὐχὰς ἐπιτελοῦσιν ἐν ταῖς αὐτῶν
συναγωγαῖς, ἐπαρῶνται αὐτοῖς καὶ ἀναθεματίζουσι φάσκοντες, ὅτι
ἐπικαταράσαι ὁ θεὸς τοὺς Ναζωραίους. Καὶ γὰρ τούτοις περισσότερον
ἐνέχουσι διὰ Ἰουδαίων αὐτοὺς ὄντας Ἰησοῦν κηρύσσειν εἶναι Χριστόν.

[1] Comp. Eusebius, *H. E.* iii. 5, § 3, and *Const. Apost.* vi. 5. 2 (ed.
Ueltzen): Ἀποβληθείσης τῆς συναγωγῆς τῆς πονηρᾶς ὑπὸ Κυρίου τοῦ Θεοῦ
καὶ τοῦ οἴκου ἀπορριφθέντος ὑπ᾽ αὐτοῦ—᾽ ἐγκαταλιπὼν οὖν τὸν λαὸν ὡς
σκηνὴν ἐν ἀμπελῶνι (Jes. i. 8)—περιελὼν δὲ ἀπ᾽ αὐτῶν καὶ τὸ πνεῦμα τὸ
ἅγιον καὶ τὸν προφητικὸν υἱόν, ἐπλήρωσε τὴν αὐτοῦ ἐκκλησίαν πνευματικῆς
χάριτος, καὶ ὑπερύψωσεν αὐτὴν ὡς οἶκον ἐπ᾽ ὄρους, etc.

old theocracy and to their own people, and took from Jewish Christianity the national soil on which it rested. We cannot doubt that the predominant zeal for the law, which characterized the Palestinian Christians about ten years before the destruction of Jerusalem (see the Epistle to the Hebrews, and Acts xxi. 20), considerably cooled during the years and decades immediately following the Jewish war—the Judaistic tendency being completely eradicated. If we add to this the circumstance that they were formally proscribed and systematically attacked by the Jews, it follows that the mutual repulsion between Christianity and Judaism, and the inner emancipation of the Jewish Christians from legality and narrowness, must have become more and more complete.[1]

This fully agrees with the fact that those books of our canon, written in the latter part of the first century, when opposing errors and errorists, do not deal with Judaistic aberrations, but rather with errors and vices of heathen origin.

CHAPTER II.

THE GENTILE CHRISTIANS.

It is well known that the second half of the apostolic age, of which we are here treating (A.D. 70–100), is one of the darkest periods in the history of Christian antiquity: primitive documents belonging to this time and beyond it being very rare.

[1] Comp. Grätz, *Gesch. der Juden*, iv. p. 11, etc., 112 d. ; Lutterbeck, *ante*, i. 204, etc. ; Lange, *ante*, ii. 432, etc. ; Schaff, *Gesch. der ap. Kirche*, 398, etc.

It is true that we have a writing in the group of the apostolic fathers, which was probably composed before the close of this period, viz. the First Epistle by the Roman Clement to the Corinthians, but it belongs in spirit so decidedly to the post-apostolic Church, that we can give but little consideration to it here. There remains, therefore, as a source of information in regard to this period, apart from the Talmudic documents respecting Judaism and Jewish Christians, nothing but the Johannine writings and the Epistle of Jude, together with the Second Epistle of Peter. But even these writings present but little historical material. Historical traces of the apostles themselves after Paul died a martyr's death, before the Jewish war, are so utterly lost that, with the exception of John, the very general account of Eusebius is the only existing one (*H. E.* iii. 5, see *ante*, p. 249, note 1): showing that the apostles were driven out of the land by innumerable and dangerous intrigues of the Jews, after the violent death of James, who presided over the Church at Jerusalem ; and that they travelled in various directions in order to preach the gospel to all nations. This account is perfectly credible. The fanaticism of the Jews increasing with accelerated force in the face of the approaching religious war, threatened not only the life of the apostles, but so effectually restrained all further efforts on behalf of their people that they must have clearly seen they could no longer abide there, but that, on the contrary, it was God's will that they should take their staff and wander into Christian lands to preach to the Gentiles the Redeemer whom their own people appeared to reject a second time and for ever.

This was the beginning of the time of the Gentiles. The centre of the Church of Christ changed; it was no longer in Jerusalem and with believing Israel, but with the Gentile Christians, particularly in Asia Minor, chiefly in Ephesus. The most powerful attacks against the Church, both from without and from within, no longer came from Judaism but from heathenism.

The only personality that meets us with unique historical clearness in this age, is that of the Apostle John, who had his dwelling-place at Ephesus. This fact is established by the Apocalypse, and also by a number of later testimonies.[1]

That the Apostle John had his last place of abode and field of labour in Asia Minor is a position so well attested by witnesses of the second century that it requires great boldness to contest it in face of this evidence. Irenæus, himself a native of Asia Minor, in his youth a personal pupil of Polycarp, speaks not only once, but no less than eight times, from very varying points of view, of the Apostle John as living in Asia Minor; and appeals not only to *one* authority

---

[1] The residence of the Apostle John in Asia Minor has indeed been frequently questioned, first by Erh. F. Vogel, *der Evangelist Joh. u. seine Ausleger vor dem jüngsten Gericht*, 1801, then by Lützelberger, *die kirchliche Tradition über den Ap. Johannes*, etc., 1840; Theod. Keim, *Gesch. Jesu von Nazara*, i. 1867; J. H. Scholten, *de Apostel Johannes in Klein Azië*, Leiden 1871. The three last, however, have only disputed the ecclesiastical tradition that John resided and worked in Ephesus for a considerable period, because they do not allow him to have been the author of the Fourth Gospel. This very motive leads to a well-founded mistrust of that hypercritical view which is rejected not merely by men who are reckoned among the apologists, but also by scholars that belong without doubt to the critical school, such as Schwegler, *Theol. Jahrb.* 1842; W. Grimm, Ersch. u. Gruber's Encyklopädie, *Joh. d. Ap.* Hilgenfeld, *Zeitschrift f. wiss. Theol.* 1868, p. 230, etc., and 1872, p. 372, etc.; Krenkel, *der Ap. Johannes*, 1871, p. 133, etc.

(Polycarp), but to several elders who had seen and
heard the apostle when he spoke about the Redeemer
(*Adv. Haer.* v. 33. 3). Where Irenæus speaks most
fully of Polycarp and of John himself, in the Epistle
to Florinus (in Euseb. *H. E.* v. 20, § 4, etc.), he
expresses himself so concisely and clearly, drawing
from true memories, that we are involuntarily led to
put faith in him. The evidence of this early testimony is so convincing that Scholten has no other
resource than the bold assumption that the Epistle
to Florinus is a tendency - writing, foisted into
Irenæus ; "a desperate assertion," as Hilgenfeld
rightly judges (*Zeitschrift*, 1872, p. 378). After
Irenæus, the witnesses for the abode of the Apostle
John in Ephesus are Polycrates, Bishop of Ephesus,
and Apollonius, an opponent of Montanism, in a
work composed specially against the new prophecy,
forty years after its first appearance. The former
mentions John's burial in Ephesus (*apud* Euseb.
H. E. v. 18, § 3) ; the latter that John raised a dead
man in Ephesus by the power of God (Euseb. *H. E.*
v. 18, § 14). In addition to these writers belonging
to Asia Minor, there is the Alexandrian Clement who
gives us that beautiful narrative, drawn from some
other source, in his small work Τίς ὁ σωζόμενος
πλούσιος; xlii., respecting the youth whom the
apostle brought back from his evil course. In the
narrator's view it is entirely a secondary thing that
the occurrence took place in the neighbourhood of
Ephesus. In short, the fact that the Apostle John
lived many years in Asia Minor is so well attested
by *more than one* witness belonging to the second
century, that we may look upon it as historically
certain.

It is a noteworthy circumstance that John should have chosen Ephesus, one of the most favoured but also most critical stations of the Pauline Gentile mission, for his post, and should have remained there to the end, with the exception of his abode in Patmos. The apocalyptic letters (ii. etc.), and the fact that the Apocalypse itself as a whole is a letter to the seven Churches (i. 4, 11), prove that the circle of the apostle's activity stretched from Ephesus to a number of communities in Asia Minor (comp. Lücke, *Versuch einer vollst. Einleitung in die Offenbarung*, 2nd ed. p. 420, etc.).   Several traditions, for example, the one just mentioned respecting the youth who had become an apostate, whom the apostle brought away from his robber band and led back to the Church and to Christ, as well as the story of the old man's touching words at his departure, testify in what blessed memory his work continued among the Christians of Asia Minor. This much, however, is certain, that when towards the close of the apostolic period he was leader of the Churches of Asia Minor, his work was not confined to planting and watering, building up and guiding, but also consisted in frequent struggles, in warding off and protecting; and it is at once evident that the powers against which the apostle needed weapons for protection and defence did not belong so much to Judaism as to heathenism.   In the Apocalypse (ii. 9, iii. 9) mention is made of blaspheming proceeding from persons professing to be Jews, but who are in reality a synagogue of Satan; this is the only case, however, in which attacks upon believers are insti-gated by Jews.   On the other hand, heathenism together with the heathen world-power appear so very prominently in the foreground of the Revelation as the chief enemy of the Church of Christ, that we feel the centre of antichristianism to be no longer in Judaism but in heathenism. Naturally so, for the former was already smitten and broken in the very centre of its life. This is consistent with the fact that the internal disturbances of Christian faith and life in the midst of the communities themselves, against which it was necessary to watch and struggle, did not grow out of the essence of Judaism but of heathenism. For the Nicolaitanes or Balaamites, who sinned by unchastity and participation in idolatrous feasts (Apoc. ii. 6, 14, etc., comp. 20) are described with sufficient plainness to show that there was an amalgamation of the Christian with the heathen element, not with the Jewish; it was obviously an after effect of heathen immorality, a process by which Christian freedom from the law degenerated into heathen licentiousness, which Paul with anxious glance had already detected in its first beginnings. Doubtless it was the same error which is described in the aspect of its doctrinal development (ii. 24) as a pretended $\gamma\nu\hat{\omega}\sigma\iota\varsigma$, but was in fact a sinking into the depths of Satanic wisdom ($o\emph{i}\tau\iota\nu\epsilon\varsigma$ $o\emph{v}\kappa$ $\emph{e}\gamma\nu\omega\sigma a\nu$ $\tau\grave{a}$ $\beta a\theta\acute{\epsilon}a$ $\tau o\hat{v}$ $\sigma a\tau a\nu\hat{a}$, $\emph{w}\varsigma$ $\lambda\acute{\epsilon}\gamma o\upsilon\sigma\iota\nu$). The latter circumstance reminds us forcibly of the warning against a $\psi\epsilon\upsilon\delta\acute{\omega}\nu\upsilon\mu o\varsigma$ $\gamma\nu\hat{\omega}\sigma\iota\varsigma$ (1 Tim. vi. 20), all the more because Timothy had his post in the same district of Asia Minor which John had now to superintend. If we inquire into tradition, we learn through the medium of Irenæus (*Adv. Haer.* iii. § 3. 4, and xi.) that Cerinthus was the man whose errors in particular John had to combat. It is now ascertained, both from sources already known and from Hippolytus vii. 33, x. 21, that this heretic, commencing with a

Judaizing low view of the person of Jesus, whom he considered as begotten, not in a supernatural but a natural way, passed over to a gnostic conception, ascribing the creation of the world to a power inferior to the highest God ; and, mistaking the union of the divine and human in the person of the Redeemer, asserted that Christ, proceeding from the highest Being,[1] came down upon Him at His baptism in the form of a dove, and departed from Him again before He suffered, so that Jesus alone, not Christ, suffered and rose again. We here have before us a form of transition from Judaistic to heathen-gnostic error. In the Johannine epistles, particularly the first, errorists are in like manner described who went out from the Christian Church, and having separated from it, fell away (ii. 19: ἐξ ἡμῶν ἐξῆλθον—εἰ γὰρ ἦσαν ἐξ ἡμῶν, μεμενήκεισαν ἂν μεθ᾽ ἡμῶν; comp. Düsterdieck, *Comm.* i. 332, etc.); but soon after attempted to seduce believers (ii. 26: οἱ πλανῶντες ὑμᾶς, comp. iii. 7). They are called ψευδοπροφῆται (iv. 1), after the manner of the Old Testament, and even ἀντίχριστοι (ii. 18), forerunners of the *one* Antichrist, inasmuch as the spirit of Antichrist is already in the world and speaks through them (iv. 3). But in what does their false doctrine, their lying (ii. 21, etc.) consist ? In denying that Jesus was the Christ : and he that denies the Son has not the Father, and is the adversary of Christ. The words taken simply by

---

[1] Baur, *Christenthum*, vol. ii. p. 190, designates the Christ of Cerinthus as "the Son of the most high God." This, however, is inaccurate, and agrees neither with the account of Irenæus, i. 26, § 1, nor with that of Hippolytus, from which it professes to be chiefly drawn, for "*Son* of God" is the very conception that has here (vii. 33) been purposely avoided (see 2nd ed. Duncker, p. 404, especially 525).

themselves might certainly mean Jewish unbelief:
unbelieving Judaism with its denial that Jesus of
Nazareth was the promised Messiah. But it is
perfectly clear from the context, ver. 18, etc. (ἐξ ἡμῶν
ἐξῆλθον, etc.), that erring Christians, not unbelieving
Jews, are combated; and what is here described in
an indefinite way, according to its most general
but unmistakably anti-Christian tendency, is more
exactly defined by the apostle in iv. 2, etc. In the
latter passage the negation μὴ ὁμολογεῖ τὸν Ἰησοῦν,
is to be explained by the affirmation in ver. 2,
ὁμολογεῖ Ἰησοῦν Χριστὸν ἐν σαρκὶ ἐληλυθότα,
that is, who is deceived by false doctrines, or denies
Jesus Christ who is come in the *flesh* (comp.
2 John 7). Although this description is wide enough
to exclude *everything* unchristian and anti-Christian,
as it embraces the divine and the human in the
Redeemer in like proportion, it has yet one distinguishing mark, viz. ἐν σαρκὶ ἐληλυθώς, which most
distinctly emphasizes the true humanity of the
Redeemer, and points to the circumstance that the
error inclined to *Docetism*. We do not mean to say
that John came forward against the developed view of
the Docetæ, but what Koestlin, *joh. Lehrbegr.* 220, etc.;
Erdmann, *primæ Joh. ep. arg.* 152, etc.; and Lünemann, *Comm.*, assume cannot be proved, viz. that
John has here in view none else than Cerinthus and
his heretical Christology. Yet it is certain that the
erroneous doctrine with which he has to contend is of
the gnostic Docetic kind: being an unsound mixture of
Christianity with heathen speculation. Besides, the
final warning (v. 21) against idols proves the direction in which the prevailing danger to the Churches
of that time lay, viz. in heathenism and the inclina-

tion to unite heathen elements with Christianity. Coming back to a point which we have already touched upon, we remark, in addition, that it appears to us doubtful (with Lücke, Lünemann, and others) whether we should suppose a formal *secessio*, a separation of the errorists (comp. Thiersch, *Apostol. Zeitalter*, 257, 265). It is much more likely that the words imply "an internal process of separation."

Even the heretics against whom the warnings in the Epistle of Jude and in Second Peter are directed assuredly belong not to a Judaizing, but to a heathen corruption of Christianity; moreover their unspiritual assumption of grace and freedom, which changed into positive godlessness and denial of the Redeemer and His reappearing (Jude 8, comp. 10 : κυριότητα ἀθετοῦσιν, δόξας δὲ βλασφημοῦσιν ; 16 : γογγυσταὶ μεμψίμοιροι, — λαλεῖ ὑπέρογκα ; 18 : ἐμπαῖκται ; Ver. 4 : ἀσεβεῖς, τὴν τοῦ θεοῦ ἡμῶν χάριτα μετατιθέντες εἰς ἀσέλγειαν, καὶ τὸν μόνον—κύριον ἡμῶν 'I. X. ἀρνούμενοι, comp. 2 Pet. i. 16, ii. 18, etc., especially ἐλευθερίαν ἐπαγγελ- λόμενοι, etc., 2 Pet. i. 10, iii. 4), points to the fact that they did not set out with legal ideas, but rather with Pauline conceptions of grace and Christian freedom, which they perverted in a heathen way into antinomian gnosis. With this agrees the terrifying description of their insolent viciousness and fundamental impurity, which cannot possibly have arisen from legal asceticism, but on the contrary from heathen insubordination alone.[1]

Putting together all that has been said, we get the impression that, in respect to the Gentile Christians in the second half of the apostolic age, heathenism was

---

[1] Comp. Neander, *Pflanzung*, ii. 622, etc.

the vastly predominant power that partly from without threatened the Church, and partly from within prepared the most hazardous disputes. It was an antichristian gnosis proceeding from heathen ideas; frequently also a moral error stained with heathen licentiousness, that became dangerous to souls. On the other hand, according to all the documents of the later apostolic time that we possess, Judaism, broken as a political power, was no longer a dangerous opponent of the Church of Christ as a spiritual power; the time in· which Judaizing errorists possessed a powerful influence over spirits was visibly passed.

SECOND PART.

THE APOSTOLIC DOCTRINES.

CONSCIOUSNESS, thought, and knowledge proceed from facts, from life. Our actual perception does not go beyond our own peculiar
experience. The entire religious perception of
Israel rested upon facts in the life of the nation, on
the acts of God. The great fact of deliverance from
bondage in Egypt is at the foundation of the consciousness of the people of Israel that they belonged
to God as His peculiar possession. At the head of
the ten words and of every moral requirement in the
Old Covenant, stands the following: "I am the Lord
thy God, which have brought thee out of the land
of Egypt, out of the house of bondage" (Ex. xx. 2).[1]
And the central point of the announcement of Jesus
was the joyful news that the kingdom of God, with
its salvation, was at hand, for He, the promised
Messiah, was come to save the lost.[2] Those acts of
God, forming part of the peculiar experience of the
apostles, were the steps on which they rose by
degrees to a higher and fuller insight into the truth,
or, to speak more correctly, were led by the Spirit of

[1] Comp. Hermann Schultz, *Alttestamentliche Theologie*, 1869, i.
131.

[2] Comp. Bernhard Weiss, *Lehrbuch der bibl. Theol. des N. T.*
§ 13.

God (comp. John xvi. 13: τὸ πνεῦμα τῆς ἀληθείας ὁδηγήσει ὑμᾶς εἰς τὴν ἀλήθειαν πᾶσαν). The progress, therefore, is gradual : this internal growth is not the effect of passive infusion, but the apostles themselves act and go forward independently, under divine guidance. Such guidance, however, makes use of various means and ways. Sometimes it employs direct manifestations of God's power (μεγαλεῖα τοῦ θεοῦ, Acts ii. 11), as in the raising of Christ from the dead, or immediate gifts of God, such as the outpouring of the Spirit, or again, revelations, such as the appearance of the risen Saviour, first to one and then to another disciple, finally to Paul (1 Cor. xv. 8); or, once more, successful issues imparted by God's grace to Paul, Peter, and others, in their apostolic calling. From all such experiences a new light continually streams forth, resulting in a wider insight into the truth, naturally, to some extent, the result of personal reflection on the ideas of God, and, as a matter of course, differing considerably according to the greater or less simplicity of mind, keenness of spirit, and power of logical thought—the individuality, in short, of the person concerned.

FIRST SECTION.

DOCTRINE IN THE EARLY APOSTOLIC TIME.

The Acts of the Apostles form the chief source of information as to the " apostles' doctrine " (Acts ii. 42) in the beginnings of Christianity, *i.e.*

during the first ten years, before Paul began his successful course as apostle of the Gentiles; and before the founding of Gentile Christian communities became a centre of development for life and doctrine. This book describes two missionary addresses to the people of Israel (ii. 14–40 and iii. 12–26), and one missionary discourse before heathens (x. 28–43), besides two discourses in defence against the Sanhedrim (iv. 8, etc., v. 29, etc.), finally, several utterances within the Church (v. 3, etc., vi. 2–4, viii. 20–23, xi. 5–17). In addition to these, we have a prayer of the Church (iv. 24–30). It is Peter, for the most part, who speaks on these occasions, and we are justified in recognizing him as the leader of the Twelve, the Church's speaker,[1] and in inferring from him the ideas which they and it entertained. While the above-mentioned utterances give a tolerably uniform view, the discourse of Stephen (vii. 2–53, comp. 56, 59, etc.) shows us that the Hellenistic element, which had become strong in the Church at that time, had brought with it a change of spirit in the disciples.

CHAPTER I.

THE SPEECHES IN THE ACTS.

We use the speeches contained in the first half of the Acts as sources for obtaining a knowledge of the primitive apostolic preaching, with this limitation however, that the historian recast, independently,

---

[1] Chrysostom, *Homil. in Ev. Joh.* 83, characterizes Peter as ἔκκριτος τῶν ἀποστόλων, καὶ στόμα τῶν μαθητῶν, καὶ κορυφὴ τοῦ χοροῦ.

the traditions that he employed, using them partly
as memoranda, yet with the conviction that he was
giving us in an essentially faithful form, solid
material of historical value.[1]

The *resurrection of Jesus* appears in primitive
Christian preaching as the fundamental fact, the
Alpha and Omega of apostolic announcement. Even
in the early time when the choice of a twelfth
apostle in place of Judas Iscariot is in question,
Peter says, "One must be witness with us of the
resurrection of Jesus" (μάρτυρα τῆς ἀναστάσεως
αὐτοῦ—σὺν ἡμῖν), i. 22. The point on which the
Pentecost address turns is the testimony: τοῦτον τὸν
Ἰησοῦν ἀνέστησεν ὁ θεός, ii. 32, xxiv. In like
manner, the resurrection of Jesus is the main theme

---

[1] The discourses of the first part of the Acts are regarded by
critics of Baur's school merely as the composition of the author, and
the ideas which are there expressed as the historian's own view.
Even the unmistakably original speech of Stephen is declared by
Baur (*N. T. Theologie*, p. 338) to be the composition of the author
of the Acts, who develops in it *his own peculiar view* of the relation
of the Jews to Christianity. Overbeck, *Ap. Gesch. Einleitung*, liii.,
etc., denies the genuineness of the discourses, finding evidence of the
author's skill in them. Even Wendt, Meyer's *Handbuch*, 5th ed.
p. 18, etc., sees in the discourses compositions of the writer in the
customary method of ancient historiographers. The latter view, viz.
that the intercalated discourses were freely invented, rests on prejudice. In modern times, thorough antiquarians, such as Prof.
Jebb of Glasgow (Abbot's *Hellenica*, 1880), and Reifferscheid of
Breslau (*Conjectanea in Thucydidem*), have carefully examined the
speeches of Thucydides with reference to their historical contents,
and both have come to a similar conclusion, viz. that the historian,
while elaborating the discourses, kept closely to what he had before
him. But Livy, *Hist.* iii. chap. 47, shows plainly that he consulted
his sources respecting the speeches, using them only after previous
examination. Philological scholars, *e.g.* Kohl, *Ueber Zweck und
Bedeutung der Livianischen Reden*, 1872, p. 21, have recognized
that the historian took the contents and succession of ideas in the
speeches from his sources. None of the recent critics (comp. Zeller,

in the following discourses, iii. 15, iv. 10, v. 30.
In conformity with this, the historian himself calls
the preaching of the apostles "the witness of the
resurrection of the Lord Jesus," iv. 33. The
resurrection of Jesus is the beginning of His exaltation and glorification. The *dogma* based upon this
fact is that *Jesus is the Messiah and the Lord* (ὅτι καὶ
κύριον αὐτὸν καὶ Χριστὸν ὁ θεὸς ἐποίησε, ii. 36,
comp. x. 36). Israel crucified Him, God exalted
Him to be King and Lord in the kingdom of God,
to be the Messiah.

Herein lie the fundamental truths, on the one
hand, of the *person* of Jesus and His *work*, on the
other hand, of the *salvation* offered in Him.

The *person* of Jesus is so described, that He appears
unmistakably as *a man*, for example (ii. 22), Ἰησοῦν
τὸν Ναζωραῖον, ἄνδρα, etc., an actual descendant of
David (ii. 30), but ἅγιος καὶ δίκαιος (iii. 14). The
latter words, from their connection, are mainly intended to give prominence to the *blamelessness* of

Ap. Gesch. 500, etc. ; Overbeck, *Einleitung*, lvii.) dispute the theory
that Luke used written sources in the first half of the Acts also. It
is even conceded, though with all reserve, that the spirit of Peter
and the primitive apostles is actually reflected in the Petrine discourses (Holsten, *Zum Ev. des Paulus und des Petrus*, p. 141 ;
comp. Overbeck, p. 55). This rests, however, upon personal im-
pressions, conjectures, and inferences. But we have a positive
testimony in favour of the primitive Christian preaching as it lies
before us in these discourses, in the assurance of the Apostle Paul
that the announcement of the atoning death of Christ, and of His
resurrection on the third day, according to the Scriptures of the Old
Testament, was common to him and the other apostles (1 Cor. xv. 11,
together with i., etc., comp. *ante*, p. 16, etc., and Holsten, *ante*,
p. 138). The investigations into the linguistic character of the
Petrine discourses made by Bernhard Weiss in the *Krit. Beiblatt zur
deutschen Zeitschrift für Christliche Wissenschaft*, 1854, No. 10, etc.;
and M. Kähler, *Theol. Studien u. Kritiken*, 1874, p. 492, etc.,
agree perfectly with what we have said.

Jesus as contrasted with that criminal for whom the people by their intercession had obtained life and freedom, while Jesus, misapprehended by His people, was obliged to suffer the punishment of death. But the apostle doubtless ascribes to his Lord, not merely in comparison with the gross criminal but absolutely and without parallel, perfect holiness (in relation to God, ἅγιος) and righteousness (in the sight of men, δίκαιος); in other words, unique holiness, to which the definite article appended points. Thus *a relation to God* is indicated, which is still more plainly referred to by Peter, when, applying Old Testament language, he calls Jesus the ὅσιος τοῦ θεοῦ (ii. 27), that is, Him on whom the good pleasure of God rests. But it is peculiar to these Petrine discourses that Jesus is called ὁ παῖς τοῦ θεοῦ (iii. 13, 26), a title which is repeated with the addition ὁ ἅγιος παῖς τοῦ θεοῦ in the prayer of the Church (iv. 27, 30). The older interpreters have explained this, "Son of God," a signification which it never has: the same predicate being attributed in iv. 25 to David, and in Luke's Gospel, i. 54, to the people of Israel. On the contrary, παῖς here means *servus, minister*, as Bengel formerly perceived, and as all late interpreters, German and English, assume, since the remark of Nitzsch's (*Studien u. Kritiken*, 1828, p. 331, etc.). The conception corresponds to the "servant of Jehovah" in Isaiah (comp. Matt. xii. 18); Jesus is therefore the servant of God in particular, the minister and executor of the divine ideas and counsels in a unique sense. We must remember, however, that divinity, pre-existence, and incarnation are nowhere attributed to Christ in these discourses, nor does the expression υἱὸς τοῦ θεοῦ, which is so frequent in the

New Testament, ever occur.[1] The strongest phrase which Peter uses is only this, ὁ θεὸς ἦν μετ' αὐτοῦ (x. 38), σημεῖα ἐποίησεν ὁ θεὸς δι' αὐτοῦ (ii. 22).

We find the *dignity* of Jesus depicted in such a way as to make Him κύριος καὶ Χριστός: God anointed Him with the Holy Ghost and with power (x. 38, comp. iv. 27, ὃν ἔχρισας), thus consecrating Him King of the kingdom of God, the Messiah, and enabling Him to perform acts and wonders of divine power. God made Him both Lord and Christ (ἐποίησεν, ii. 36, comp. x. 36 : πάντων κύριος), He is become the corner-stone, that is, the foundation of the building of God, its all-sustaining and pre-serving support (γενόμενος εἰς, iv. 11); God exalted Him to be a Prince and a Saviour (v. 31 : τοῦτον ὁ θεὸς ἀρχηγὸν καὶ σωτῆρα ὕψωσε; Bengel : exaltavit illum, ut sit princeps et salvator). All this con-cordant testimony points to the fact that Jesus did not originally possess His unique and exalted dignity as Lord in the kingdom of God, as the Anointed One, the Saviour, but only attained to it in the course of time, being chosen by the act and power of God. It is self-evident that the personality of Jesus must originally have been characterized by something

---

[1] Comp. Koch, *de Petri theologia per diversas vitæ, quam egit, apostolicæ periodos sensim explicata*, Leiden 1854, p. 57, etc.; Weiss, *der petrinische Lehrbegriff*, 1855, p. 241, etc. The conjecture of Weizsäcker, *Reuter Repert.* 1856, Febr., that the use of the two different expressions παῖς θεοῦ and υἱὸς θεοῦ might be attributed to Luke's having made use of various sources, does not in any way alter the position of the matter. If the conjecture were certainty, the assumption that the Petrine source with παῖς θεοῦ and the Pauline with υἱὸς θεοῦ have the genuine and original element, would come very near to arbitrariness. The predicate παῖς θεοῦ is still found in some primitive Christian prayers contained in the newly discovered Διδαχὴ τῶν δώδεκα ἀποστόλων, from ix. 2, x. 2, etc.

singular, a salvation-originating power, when such exclusive position and dignity as that of *κύριος, Χριστός*, etc., could be conferred upon Him by God; but it does not appear, from what is presented to us, that this idea was clearly and consciously apprehended; rather do these testimonies to the faith show that the apostles were originally imbued with an intuition of the *historical* reality of Jesus, mainly of His exaltation connected with the resurrection and ascension. Jesus is the prophet who, like Moses, was promised to His people (iii. 22, etc.); by Him God announced the glad tidings of peace (x. 36: *εὐαγγελιζόμενος εἰρήνην διὰ Ἰησοῦ Χρ.*) from Galilee and throughout all Judæa, not with words only, but also with deeds did He go about doing good, conferring benefits, and healing all those who were possessed (x. 38, comp. ii. 22).

Notwithstanding the fulness with which Jesus is thus extolled as a prophet in word and deed, we are struck, nevertheless, with the light in which His death was regarded by the apostles; frequently as Peter recurs to the crucifixion of Jesus in his discourses (for example, ii. 23 and 26, iii. 13, etc., iv. 10, 11, x. 39), he always refers to it in connection with the persons who brought it about: it is characterized as a crime on the part of the nation and their rulers, an unjustifiable sin, but not as a salvation-bringing act. The death of Jesus is mentioned as a well-known fact still fresh in the memory of all, but the offence to which it necessarily gave rise is removed by the notification that it was willed and pre-ordained by God, and had been foretold by the prophets (ii. 23, iii. 18, iv. 28, v. 32, etc.).[1] On the other

---

[1] This discussion of primitive Christian testimony respecting Jesus' death on the cross has met with much opposition. Weiss,

hand, the apostles preach the resurrection of Jesus as something new, laying stress on it as the most important fact, an act of purely divine agency. The statement in ii. 24 is a remarkable one: οὐκ ἦν δυνατὸν κρατεῖσθαι αὐτὸν ὑπ' αὐτοῦ (τοῦ θανάτου), comp. ver. 31 : ὅτι οὐκ ἐγκατελείφθη εἰς "Αδου. We have here, on the one hand, a presumption of the entrance of Jesus into the kingdom of the dead, and, on the other hand, a declaration of the impossibility that death should hold Him. How is this to be explained ? It is obvious from the connection that the ground of this impossibility lies in the promise

N. T. Theol. § 38, says : "If the death of the Messiah took place on the ground of a divine decree, it must also have its significance in relation to the Messianic activity of Jesus." Certainly we cannot shut out this perception, the question is only whether Peter and the apostles were at that time conscious of this connection. Weiss appeals to iii. 18, etc., to make the latter view probable, but the only meaning of these words is that the sin of Israel, committed in the crucifying of Jesus, *can* be forgiven because the decree of God that the Messiah should suffer, was fulfilled in the death of Jesus. Ed. Reuss, *Histoire de la théologie chrétienne au siècle apostolique,* 1852, ii. 601, has excellently formulated it as follows : Sa mort était un *fait providentiel,* prédit par l'écriture et rentrant dans les decrêts de Dieu, mais on n'apprend pas *pourquoi* Jesus dût mourir. Hofmann remarks with justice : " It will not appear strange to us when we hear the apostles speak of the sufferings and death of Jesus in a manner that gives prominence to the historical appearance, not to the internal significance of the fact, for we find it so in all the apostolic addresses to the Jews contained in the Acts. That His ignominious death was the work of the Jewish people, but also that it befell Him in accordance with the decree of God, this and nothing else does Peter say," etc. (*Schriftbeweis,* ii. 1, 1853, p. 213, etc.). Holsten, *Zum Ev. des Paulus und des Petrus,* p. 148, etc., distinguishes a twofold view of the death of Jesus on the cross in the apostolic time, a dogmatic-religious one (a saving act of God, an atoning death), and a historical-religious one (a divine decree). Peter at first held both views together, but without inferring the religious consequences, and transforming thereby his Jewish consciousness of salvation. This opinion is in harmony with our conception of the matter.

which had been given to David and must be fulfilled
to his posterity (ver. 25); see Bengel, comp. Koch,
ante, 63, etc. This does not, however, exclude the
fact that the victorious might and fulness of life,
prophetically predicted of God's Anointed, was the
internal ground of the promise as well as of its fulfilment. Connected with the resurrection of Jesus,
the apostles emphasize His ascension, exaltation to
the right hand of God, and reception of the Holy
Ghost (in order that He may impart it in full
measure to whom He will), as the facts by which His
dignity is consummated (ii. 32, etc.); consummated not
so much by the divine power originally inherent in
Himself, as by God's own might, who did not suffer His
Holy One to see corruption, who raised Him up ('Ιησοῦν
ἀνέστησεν ὁ θεός, ii. 32, iii. 26; ὁ θεὸς ἤγειρεν ἐκ νεκρῶν,
iii. 15, iv. 15, x. 40; once, x. 41, " He is risen "), who
showed Him openly to chosen witnesses (x. 40), who
exalted Him by His right hand,[1] who made Him
Lord and Christ, a corner-stone, imparted to Him the
Spirit (namely, for free bestowal on believers), and

[1] The words, ii. 33, τῇ δεξιᾷ τοῦ θεοῦ ὑψωθείς, v. 31, τοῦτον ὁ θεὸς—
ὕψωσιν τῇ δεξιῷ αὐτοῦ, are taken erroneously to mean exaltation *to
the right* hand of God, by Bleek, *Studien u. Kritiken*, 1836, p. 1038 ;
Lekebusch, *ante*, 405 ; Koch, p. 64, etc.; Weiss, *N. T. Theologie*,
§ 39. 6. For ver. 34, κάθου ἐκ δεξιῶν μου, does not necessitate such
translation, and grammar is entirely opposed to the taking of the
dative as equivalent to πρὸς τὴν δεξιάν (though Koch, p. 66, labours to
make the grammar fit in). The sense that this exaltation to the
right hand of God was effected only by the glorious power of God
suits the connection very well. So Meyer, Zeller (*Ap. Gesch.* p.
502, etc., note 2), Overbeck. Since Peter, in ver. 34, applies the
words of Psalm cx. 1, it is evident that the idea might readily occur
to him that Jesus was exalted by God's omnipotent act to His right
hand, that is, to divine power and glory. This is expressed in
Bengel's sentence : "Christus *dextra Dei* exaltatus est *ad dextram*
Dei."

who will finally send Him again at the restitution of all things (iii. 20, x. 42).

Jesus, who was raised up after His crucifixion and exalted by God (iii. 13), is He in whom alone salvation is to be found: οὐκ ἔστιν ἐν ἄλλῳ οὐδενὶ ἡ σωτηρία· οὔτε γὰρ ὄνομά ἐστιν ἕτερον ὑπὸ τὸν οὐρανὸν, τὸ δεδομένον ἐν ἀνθρώποις, ἐν ᾧ δεῖ σωθῆναι ἡμᾶς (iv. 12). He is the σωτήρ (v. 31). The impressiveness with which Peter emphasizes exclusive salvation in Jesus is noteworthy and significant, as is also the impressiveness with which he refuses the power of deliverance and help to every other man, to every other name in the world, in which one might wish to seek salvation. Peter not only confesses Jesus as a Saviour in a general way, but as *the* Saviour, the only Saviour; he expresses himself in true evangelical language, bearing testimony to Jesus as the only foundation which is laid (iv. 11: κεφαλὴ γωνίας). This salvation in Christ (σωτηρία), the full and complete Messianic salvation of body and soul,[1] is, in the first place, negative: rescue from impending judgment and ruin, by means of moral separation from an untoward generation (σώθητε ἀπὸ τῆς γενεᾶς τῆς σκολιᾶς ταύτης, ii. 40). On the other hand, it contains a certain positive element, since it is actually said of Jesus, referring to the promise given to Abraham: ὁ θεὸς — ἀπέστειλεν αὐτὸν, εὐλογοῦντα ὑμᾶς, whence a positive benefit was to be bestowed upon the nation, the fulness of

---

[1] For the immediate occasion of this apologetic discourse is the healing of the lame man in the name of Jesus. We have no right to exclude, with Meyer, everything corporeal, *e.g.* the healing of bodily diseases, from the conception of the Messianic salvation, and to take it as entirely abstract and spiritual.

the long-promised blessing, through Jesus as the
servant of God. Bodily healing is doubtless to be
added to this salvation in Jesus, this blessing, since
the healing of the lame man was expressly effected
ἐν τῷ ὀνόματι Ἰησοῦ Χριστοῦ τοῦ Ναζωραίου (iii. 6,
16, iv. 10). Jesus is ἀρχηγὸς τῆς ζωῆς (iii. 15),
the herald and giver of all true life. Peter, however,
lays special emphasis on the *forgiveness of sins* and
the gift of the Holy Spirit, as the greatest blessings
that salvation could bestow on man, and those to
which, through Jesus, he should actually attain: ἄφεσιν
ἁμαρτιῶν λαβεῖν διὰ τοῦ ὀνόματος αὐτοῦ (x. 43, comp.
ii. 38 ; iii. 19 : εἰς τὸ ἐξαλειφθῆναι τὰς ἁμαρτίας,
ver. 31, together with x. 36 : εἰρήνη). The *gift of
the Holy Ghost* is the positive supplement to the
forgiveness of sins. The outpouring of the Spirit at
Pentecost was indeed, as Peter explains (ii. 16,
etc., 33), the fulfilment of the most important promises; hence this costly gift (δωρεὰ τοῦ ἁγ. πν., ii.
38, viii. 20, xi. 17, comp. 15) was bestowed upon
every one who fulfilled the conditions imposed by
God; the Holy Spirit at once empowering those who
had received it to become competent witnesses of
Christ (v. 31).

A change of heart and faith in Jesus are demanded
as the condition of participating in this salvation
offered in Jesus of Nazareth. When Peter's hearers
on the day of Pentecost, after a discourse whose
words went to their hearts, asked, What shall we do?
the apostle replied: μετανοήσατε καὶ βαπτισθήτω
ἕκαστος ὑμῶν ἐπὶ τῷ ὀνόματι Ἰησοῦ Χριστοῦ, εἰς
ἄφεσιν ἁμαρτιῶν, etc. The latter, viz. the reception of baptism, is manifestly connected with a
confession of *faith* in Jesus, and therefore a change

of mind, or repentance and faith together are named as conditions of forgiveness; whilst in other passages (for example, iii. 26, v. 31), only μετάνοια or ἀποστρέφειν ἀπὸ τῶν πονηριῶν is made the condition of repentance and blessing. The repentance which the apostle demands consists not merely in such a change as would lead to the avoidance of particular individual sins, but in a complete abandonment of the former state, which was a wicked and evil one (iii. 26, ἀπὸ τῶν πονηριῶν αὐτῶν, where we remark that πονηρία may denote moral wickedness as well as the evil which is its fruit and punishment); besides, in this passage the impulse and power of turning, according to New Testament idiom and the context[1] (εὐλογοῦντα ὑμᾶς ἐν τῷ ἀποστρέφειν ἕκαστον ἀπὸ τῶν πον. αὐτ.), is traced back to Jesus Christ Himself, who leads souls to give up their πονηρίαι. Hence the change of mind in v. 31 and xi. 19 (δοῦναι μετάνοιαν) is regarded as a gift, consequently as a thing wrought by the exalted Christ and God Himself, whilst in ii. 38, iii. 19, viii. 22, it appears as the resolve and act of man. Thus we find repentance regarded not only as the individual act of man, but also at the same time as the effect of divine grace and the gift of Christ; both, however, move side by

---

[1] Ἀποστρέφειν (act.) is never employed in the New Testament in an intransitive sense, but always with a transitive meaning. It is therefore not to the point to appeal with Meyer to classical Greek, even if the transitive meaning did not at all suit the text; but this is so far from being the case, that the transitive meaning is rather supported by the fact that ἀποστρέφειν appears to be taken in the more comprehensive sense of εὐλογεῖν, which in any case implies an operation of Christ; and ver. 19, on which Meyer relies, agrees with this sense very well. Overbeck supposes that the transitive sense leads to an idea that is without analogy—as if δοῦναι μετάνοιαν, v. 31, were not completely analogous!

side without apparent mediation. On the other hand, great importance is attached to *faith* in the Lord Jesus, particularly in those passages in which salvation in its positive aspect is set forth, where, for example, it is narrated of the lame man who was healed: καὶ ἐπὶ τῇ πίστει τοῦ ὀνόματος αὐτοῦ τοῦτον — ἐστερέωσεν, καὶ τὸ ὄνομα αὐτοῦ, καὶ ἡ πίστις ἡ δι' αὐτοῦ, ἔδωκεν αὐτῷ τὴν ὁλοκληρίαν ταύτην (iii. 16), that is, by reason of faith in Jesus as the Messiah, by virtue of faith in His name, God has made this man strong, and faith (in His name) working through him, that is, through Jesus Himself, has made the lame man whole, *vid.* Meyer and Koch, *ante*, 84, etc., Bengel: Christo Petrus fidem ipsam acceptam refert. And again, xi. 17, where Peter says of Cornelius and his house: τὴν ἴσην δωρεὰν (the Holy Ghost) ἔδωκεν αὐτοῖς ὁ θεός, ὡς καὶ ἡμῖν πιστεύσασιν ἐπὶ τὸν κύριον Ἰησοῦν Χριστόν (comp. xv. 9). But this faith, in its inner essence, is not conceived as a mere acknowledgment of the truth, but as an act of obedience, when, in v. 32, the gift of the Holy Ghost is attached to πειθαρχεῖν τῷ κυρίῳ; it is even a moral *force*, when faith works miracles (iii. 16) and conditions the forgiveness of sins (x. 43).

These two things, repentance and faith, are said to be attested and verified by baptism, particularly faith, for it is a βαπτισθῆναι ἐπὶ τῷ ὀνόματι Ἰησοῦ Χρ., on the basis of the name of Jesus, that is, on the basis of the recognition of Jesus as the Christ. Moreover, baptism is not merely a confessional act on the part of man, but also an act of God by which He effects and imparts forgiveness of sin (ii. 38), and with which the gift of the Spirit is connected. In the latter case the distinction must be observed that the gift of the Holy Spirit may *follow* baptism as an effect (ii. 38), or *go before* it as a foundation (x. 47, comp. ver. 44, etc.).

But *for whom* is this salvation in Jesus ordained? How far does the design of God to heal and to deliver by His Anointed One, Jesus, reach? The apostles turn to the people of Israel, in which respect they follow the command that the Lord Himself gave them (x. 42 : παρήγγειλεν ἡμῖν κηρύξαι τῷ λαῷ; ver. 36 : τὸν λόγον ἀπέστειλε τοῖς υἱοῖς Ἰσραήλ). They consider Jesus especially as the deliverer of His people, comp. v. 31 : τοῦτον ὁ θεὸς σωτῆρα ὕφωσε — δοῦναι μετάνοιαν τῷ Ἰσραὴλ καὶ ἄφεσιν ἁμαρτιῶν. But there is already a widening of the horizon, where Peter, after the healing of the lame man, when the people ran together to him and John in Solomon's porch, thus addresses the Israelites: "Ye are the children of the prophets, and of the covenant which God made with our fathers, saying unto Abraham, And in thy seed shall all the kindreds of the earth be blessed. Unto you *first* God, having raised up His Son Jesus, sent Him to bless you, in turning away every one of you from his iniquities" (iii. 25, 26). It is noteworthy here that blessing and salvation, though promised first to the Israelites, are not to be given to them *alone;* consequently that salvation is not given to the Israelites absolutely and unconditionally, but only in so far as they repent.[1] That which

---

[1] Schneckenburger, *Stud. und Krit.* 1855, p. 519, takes the πρῶτον as the *first* sending of Jesus, in opposition to His return, in which case it certainly contains no allusion to the heathen. This is wrong, for according to the position of the words it is not possible to connect πρῶτον with ἀπέστιλεν, rather is it necessary to join it to ὑμῖν, so

is only indirectly implied in the latter passage, viz.
that salvation is also for the heathen world, is directly
and unequivocally stated in the discourse of Peter at
Pentecost, when he says: "For the promise is unto
you, and to your children, and *to all that are afar off*,
even as many as the Lord our God shall call " (ii. 39).
This statement may be divided into three distinct
propositions—first, the promise, or the communica-
tion of the promised blessing concerns you ($\dot{\nu}\mu\hat{\iota}\nu$),
the Israelites; second, it is not limited to the present
time and generation, but is lasting and permanent,
and will extend to the future families of Israel ($\tau o\hat{\iota}\varsigma$
$\tau\acute{\epsilon}\kappa\nu o\iota\varsigma\ \dot{\nu}\mu\hat{\omega}\nu$); but it has, thirdly, a still more comprehensive destination: it is intended for $\pi\hat{\alpha}\sigma\iota\ \tau o\hat{\iota}\varsigma$
$\epsilon\grave{\iota}\varsigma\ \mu\alpha\kappa\rho\acute{\alpha}\nu$, that is, for all the nations that are afar
off, viz. the heathen. The natural objection, as to
how these can participate in it when they know
nothing of it, and are, moreover, afar off, is immediately answered by the subsequent clause: God will
call them that are afar off, to be near.[1] This truth,

that Israel is emphasized in natural opposition to the heathen, which
is rendered probable, moreover, by the appended promise, ver. 25,
comp. Gen. xx. 18. See Meyer, Weiss, *N. T. Theol.* § 43 a : Bengel :
prævium indicium de vocatione gentium. Peter seems to take it for
granted,—as Baumgarten, *Apostelgesch.* i. 82, etc., and Weiss, maintain,—that Israel must first be converted before the blessing is transferred to the heathen peoples.

[1] By $\pi\acute{\alpha}\nu\tau\epsilon\varsigma$ $o\acute{\iota}$ $\epsilon\grave{\iota}\varsigma$ $\mu\alpha\kappa\rho\acute{\alpha}\nu$, Beza and others understand late descen-
dants, which would obviously be a repetition of $\tau\acute{\epsilon}\kappa\nu\alpha$ $\dot{\nu}\mu\hat{\omega}\nu$. On the
other hand, Meyer-Wendt and Baumgarten, *ante*, i. 65, etc., under-
stand the expression to mean the *Israelites* scattered in distant lands,
because, as they think, the context does not lead Peter to speak of
the heathen. But the latter view is incorrect, since the promise in
Joel iii. 5, comp. Acts ii. 21, is so comprehensive, that Peter applies
it to all without exception. Besides, all Israel, as far as it is still in
existence, is the meaning of $\dot{\nu}\mu\hat{\iota}\nu$, and all Israel of the future is the
meaning of $\tau\acute{\epsilon}\kappa\nu\alpha$ $\dot{\nu}\mu\hat{\omega}\nu$. The apostle evidently considers his hearers as

which Peter here emphasizes in the comprehensive promise, he did not clearly apprehend till afterwards by means of the peculiar revelation of God vouchsafed him in the affair of Cornelius, so that he exclaims, in consequence of the experiences he there gained (x. 34, 35): "Of a truth I perceive that God is no respecter of persons, but in every nation he that feareth Him, and worketh righteousness, is accepted with Him." The clause οὐκ ἔστι προσωπολήπτης ὁ θεός denies all partial preference of the Jewish nation as such; the clause ἐν παντὶ ἔθνει — δεκτὸς αὐτῷ extends salvation to all nations, so that every one, irrespective of external conditions, viz. distinction of

representatives of the entire nation, not merely of the Palestinian Jews; moreover, the majority of the hearers, ii. 5, etc., consisted of Jews of the dispersion. The Israelites settled in heathen lands needed no peculiar call, as this is implied in οὓς ἂν προσκαλέσηται, but they belonged originally to the people of promise, as well as those present. The manner in which the προσκαλεῖσθαι is effected is left indefinite. Possibly a miraculous calling of the heathen nations to the theocracy, through no human mediating agency, is meant, comp. Weiss, *Petrin. Lehrbegriff*, p. 148. We abide by the interpretation of the words οἱ εἰς μακράν which has been adopted by most of the older expositors, and in modern times by De Wette, Lange, van Hengel, Koch (*ante*, 72, etc.), Hackett, Gloag, Overbeck, and others,—an interpretation which refers the words to the heathen, who are thus described not only as locally distant, but also as alienated from the theocracy. Overbeck takes the words πᾶσι τοῖς εἰς μακράν, etc., ii. 39 and iii. 25, etc., in the right sense, but sees in them only the ideas of the historian, not of Peter; maintaining that the latter cannot possibly go beyond historically attested Judaism (p. 58). And yet it is historically attested that the Messianic hope, which had passed into the living consciousness of the people of the time of Jesus (comp. Schürer, *N. T. Zeitgeschichte*, pp. 565, 575; Schnedermann, *Das Judenthum und die christliche Verkündigung in den Evangelien*, 1884, p. 246, etc.), included in itself the prophetic view that salvation should also become the possession of the world, that the heathen would finally serve the true God and His Anointed (Hermann Schultz, *N. T. Theolog.* ii. 231, etc.).

race, birth, or descent, may be accepted of God, being brought into His kingdom by the word of salvation, through faith and repentance; that is, every one who fears God and follows after righteousness according to the measure of his religious apprehension. Expositors differing most widely are agreed as to their interpretation of the latter words, viz. that δεκτός means, qualified to be received by God, viz. into His kingdom, or: acceptabilis, cui gratia possit contingere. The meaning, therefore, as Bengel, in opposition to the frequent misunderstanding and misemployment of these apostolic words, well and justly says, is: non indifferentismus religionum, sed indifferentia nationum asseritur.[1] Afterwards, in the transactions at Jerusalem, Peter appeals to his experience with respect to Cornelius (xv. 7–9); while James (on the same occasion, ver. 15, etc.) refers to those prophecies of the Old Testament that treat of an extension of the kingdom of God to the heathen.

The *return of Jesus* as the judge of living and dead, is an important article of faith with the apostles, according to the Acts. In the presence of Cornelius, Peter says that they, the apostles, are commanded to testify, ὅτι αὐτός ἐστιν ὁ ὡρισμένος ὑπὸ τοῦ θεοῦ κριτὴς ζώντων καὶ νεκρῶν (x. 42). But, at the same time, the return of Jesus is fraught with joyful meaning for believers and those who are converted, as appears from the important passage iii. 19–21. Here Peter thus exhorts his hearers: "Repent ye

---

[1] The interpretation given by Weiss,—*Petr. Lehrbegriff*, 151, note, viz., " Every one who fears God and doeth righteousness,—by him the gospel (ὁ λόγος), which God has sent to His people, may be accepted," —is very forced. It is scarcely necessary to prove its impossibility in detail.

therefore, and be converted, that your sins may be blotted out, when the times of refreshing ($\kappa\alpha\iota\rho\grave{o}\iota$ $\dot{\alpha}\nu\alpha\psi\acute{v}\xi\epsilon\omega\varsigma$) shall come from the presence of the Lord; and He shall send Jesus Christ, which before was preached unto you: whom the heavens must receive [1] until the times of restitution ($\chi\rho\acute{o}\nu\omega\iota$ $\dot{\alpha}\pi o\kappa\alpha\tau\alpha\sigma\tau\acute{\alpha}\sigma\epsilon\omega\varsigma$) of all things, which God hath spoken by the mouth of all His holy prophets since the world began." These words afford a glance into the view of things which, according to the apostles, lies at the foundation: the historical appearance of Jesus as the Saviour, and His resurrection from the dead are already a fulfilment of divine prophecy. But there still remain many great promises of God, given through the prophets, which have not been fulfilled during the life of Jesus now ended, and yet must be fulfilled.[2] The time of the fulfilment and full realization of these promises can only begin when Jesus returns from heaven; which is not to happen until all Israel shall be converted. This, therefore, is the time of the judgment of the world (x. 42), for believers a

---

[1] The explanation of Bengel, at first adopted by Meyer, $\ddot{o}\nu$ $\delta\epsilon\tilde{\iota}$ $o\dot{v}\rho\alpha\nu\grave{o}\nu$ $\delta\acute{\epsilon}\xi\alpha\sigma\theta\alpha\iota$, who must occupy the heavens (*occupare*), was abandoned by this expositor in the second edition on account of the usage of $\delta\acute{\epsilon}\chi\epsilon\sigma\theta\alpha\iota$, which was absolutely opposed to it, and he returned to the usual view. Baumgarten, however, i. 81, appears again to adopt it.

[2] Most interpreters understand $\dot{\alpha}\pi o\kappa\alpha\tau\acute{\alpha}\sigma\tau\alpha\sigma\iota\varsigma$ $\pi\acute{\alpha}\nu\tau\omega\nu$ $\dot{\omega}\nu$ $\dot{\epsilon}\lambda\acute{\alpha}\lambda\eta\sigma\epsilon\nu$ $\dot{o}$ $\theta\epsilon\acute{o}\varsigma$ as a restoration to the former condition, particularly of the theocracy, of the Davidic kingdom (Baumgarten, i. 78, etc., alluding to Acts i. 6), of the whole world (Bengel: rerum ex turbis in priorem ordinem restitutio). We must admit that $\dot{\alpha}\pi o\kappa\alpha\tau\acute{\alpha}\sigma\tau\alpha\sigma\iota\varsigma$ expresses restitution in the first place, according to the constant usage of language. But we must not make this word the sole criterion. The words connected with it, $\pi\acute{\alpha}\nu\tau\omega\nu$ $\dot{\omega}\nu$ $\dot{\epsilon}\lambda\acute{\alpha}\lambda\eta\sigma\epsilon\nu$ $\dot{o}$ $\theta\epsilon\acute{o}\varsigma$, do not justify us in laying special emphasis on the moment of restitution, but point merely to the realization of that which was foretold, the fulfilment

time of comfort and refreshing from the presence of the Lord, but in itself the period of the fulfilment of all things. In conformity with this view, the present time is provisional and preparatory, as it were, a state of transition. That which is decisive and final will first be ushered in with the return of Jesus from heaven, when all that has formerly been foretold by the prophets will be fulfilled, becoming fact and reality. An impression is here forced upon us of the great prominence given in these primitive apostolic testimonies to the expectation of Christ's return and the last things. In iii. 20, in the words $\dot{a}\pi o\sigma\tau\epsilon\dot{\iota}\lambda\eta$ —'$I\eta\sigma o\hat{\nu}\nu$, the second coming of Jesus appears as His true and proper coming; whereas the appearing which had already taken place, recedes into the background. We remark, at the same time, that this doctrine of last things is by no means sensuously depicted, but has a simple and moral bearing. The centre of Christian consciousness is in the future, in which all the prophecies of Scripture are to be perfectly fulfilled, although the Crucified One occupies an exalted place by virtue of His resurrection and ascension. The fact that Scripture had been already fulfilled in Jesus, in His sufferings and death (iii. 18), as well as in His resurrection and ascension, and in

of that which was promised. Meyer's reference of $\check{\omega}\nu$ to $\chi\rho\acute{o}\nu\omega\nu$, which has also been adopted by Hofmann, *Schriftbeweis*, ii. 2. 594, etc., and Overbeck, is disproved by its being placed immediately after $\pi\acute{a}\nu\tau\omega\nu$. But the further context, v. 22–25, which is plainly a continuation of ver. 21, since reference is made to the prediction of Moses, as well as to the prediction of the prophets from the time of Samuel, and finally to the promise given to Abraham, by no means points to a *restitutio in integrum*, but rather to a future that, leaving the past behind, would gloriously fulfil all the hope of Israel and of humanity. Baumgarten was the first to draw attention to the distinction between $\kappa\alpha\iota\rho o\acute{\iota}$ and $\chi\rho\acute{o}\nu o\iota$ here, as in i. 7.

His gift of the Spirit, together with the conviction of what the apostles had personally seen and heard, constitutes the religious substance of their preaching with respect to all that was and is. The climax of the primitive Christian faith and confession is the fact that Christ should come again as judge of the world, that all Scripture should then first be fulfilled, that all the words of God should become facts and deeds, and that all His promises should be realized. It is the genuine gold of noble Christian faith and hope, but put in a genuine, Israelite - psychological form. As Israel was the people of the future in a religious respect, the same peculiarity is mirrored in the Christianity of the primitive apostles: it is a Christianity of *hope*, a religion of the future; inasmuch as it was a form of Christianity susceptible of the highest development, and having a strong power of development within itself.

If we look back at the question in the light of the historical credibility of the Acts, we must confess that the speeches of the apostles are actually narrated in a way that bears all the features of internal truth in itself, and is a guarantee of their historical genuineness. Not only the entire colouring, not only the standpoint as a whole, not only the Old Testament background, and the method of Scripture proof employed in the speeches, not only the longing of the spirit after the Messianic future, but also individual traits and favourite expressions, for example, respecting the person of Jesus, are of such a nature as to present an internal testimony for their truth, so that a free composition, or more correctly, fiction, from a later standpoint, could not possibly have produced these discourses.

Weiss, *N. T. Theol.* § 35, shows that the discourses
in the Acts have seldom been duly estimated in
Biblical theology. Lechler was the first (*Apost. Zeitalter*, 2nd ed. pp. 15–30) who gave an independent
representation of the original preaching of the apostles
contained in the book.

A peculiar form of the primitive Christian mind
comes before us in the address of the Hellenist
Stephen, one of the Seven, which is not a missionary
discourse (Acts vii.), but a defence before the Sanhedrim and a Jewish crowd. It passes from the
position of an accused party to one of attack and
incisive severity. The matter of the discourse is
borrowed from Old Testament history exclusively;
but the formal treatment and spirit decidedly belong
to the New Covenant. One feels that while Stephen
appears to lose himself in the past, the present is
constantly in view, Christ and His rejection by the
Israelite people being kept steadily in sight. It was
Baur[1] who first directed attention to this point,
setting it forth as the leading idea of the discourse.
The more splendid had been the benefits bestowed
by God upon Israel, the more rebellious had always
been the conduct of the people, reaching its highest
point in the rejection of Jesus. But we are compelled
to doubt, with Baumgarten, i. 128, etc., and Meyer,
whether the entire purport of the speech consists in
that circumstance,—all the more so as the first part
(vv. 2–16), with the exception of ver. 9, makes no
mention at all of sinful opposition. On the contrary,
we do not think that either the exhibition of a regular

____

[1] *Tüb. Weihnachtsprogramm*, 1829 : " De orationis habitæ a Stephano Act. vii. consilio," etc.

and gradual advance in the history of revelation connected with the Old Testament (Baumgarten, i. 31, etc.,
142, etc.), or the subordinate position of the law in
respect to the promise (Luger, *Zweck, Inhalt und Eigentümlichkeit der Rede des Steph.*, Lübeck, 1838), is the
essential idea at the basis of the discourse, but rather
on *God's part* His δόξα, ver. 2, that is, the *infinite
glory* and absolute independence in virtue of which
He reveals Himself from the beginning as He wills
and where He wills, ordering and disposing the time,
place, form, and manner of His revelation entirely
without limit, so that the exclusive seat of His
presence is not the temple, nor is Canaan the only
land in which He reveals Himself;[1] and again, on
Israel's part, as we have already said, the constant
sinful opposition of unbelief directed against God's
Spirit and the men of God.   From these fundamental
ideas of the discourse arises something peculiar, the
proper doctrines of Christian belief being but lightly
touched.   Stephen invokes Jesus by name only when
he prays Him to receive his spirit (vii. 59 : κύριε
'Ιησοῦ) ; he calls Him Lord (ver. 60), the Just One
(ver. 52 : ἡ ἔλευσις τοῦ δικαίου, οὗ νῦν ὑμεῖς προδόται
καὶ φονεῖς ἐγένεσθε).   But it is remarkable that he

---

[1] Baumgarten, *ante*, 131, 134, etc., following Bengel's exposition of
this view, rightly regards the conception of the δόξα θεοῦ as a peculiar
fundamental idea of the discourse. So also Lange, *Ap. Zeitalter*,
1853, ii. p. 84, and Luger, with special reference to the temple,
consider it one of the three fundamental ideas. But how plainly the
look of Stephen was directed to the *land* in particular, in order to
show that the grace of God was by no means limited to Canaan,
appears at once when we observe, from ver. 2 and onward, the geographical element, especially the oft-repeated, intentional mention of
Egypt, then of the wilderness, Mesopotamia, etc. With respect to
the latter, Alph. Witz, *Jahrbücher für deutsche Theologie*, 1875, p.
588, etc., has made some correct observations.

says, in ver. 56, he sees τὸν υἱὸν τοῦ ἀνθρώπου ἐκ δεξιῶν ἑστῶτα τοῦ θεοῦ. Here he uses the name which Jesus was accustomed to give Himself, which none other applied to Him, according to the Gospels, a name that never appears in any of the twenty-one apostolic epistles.[1] The prayer: μὴ στήσῃς αὐτοῖς ταύτην τὴν ἁμαρτίαν, ver. 60, implies the idea that the exalted Christ, the Just One, can lay sin to the charge (ἱστάναι) or blot out and forgive. But when Baur (*Paulus*, 41, etc., 2nd ed. i. 66, etc., especially 69) and Zeller (*Apostelgesch.* 146) ascribe to Stephen a breach between his religious consciousness and the Mosaic law, attacks upon the permanent validity of the law, the discourse does not favour that view, for Stephen acknowledges the commandments of Moses to be divine living words (λόγια ζῶντα); he does not reproach the Jews with making too much of the law, but with making too little of it (ver. 52),[2] and that they are uncircumcised in heart and ears, circumcision itself being undoubtedly a thing belonging to the divine covenant (ver. 51, comp. 8). It is true Stephen declares that the Israelites received the law εἰς διαταγὰς ἀγγέλων, ver. 53, *i.e.* by the arrangement of angels; Moses received the commandments in order to make them known to the people, conversed with the angel of the Lord (ver. 38), and saw the angel of the Lord at Horeb in the burning bush (ver. 30). But he nowhere attaches a value to this theological

---

[1] Bengel, *Gnomon on Matt.* xvi. 13. It is not without reason that Schaff, *Geschichte der Apost. Kirche*, 2nd ed. 1854, p. 217, note 1, takes this unusual expression as a testimony in favour of the fidelity and originality of the narrative.

[2] See Schneckenburger, *Stud. u. Krit.* 1855, p. 529, etc. Baur's assertion is also disputed by Holsten, *Zum Evangelium des Paulus und des Petrus*, 1868, p. 255.

tradition in opposition to the law. In like manner he has but little polemic (as Baur, *ante*, 46, etc., 2nd ed. i. 55, etc., and Zeller, *ante*, 147, assume) against the temple building as defiling the free worship of God, ver. 47, etc.; he merely rejects the delusion that the presence of God and His revelation were bound up with the temple.[1] Stephen did not by any means set law and gospel in opposition, as Paul did afterwards; rather does he seem to have looked at the gospel in union with the law. Just as little was he polemical against the temple itself; but he was zealous on behalf of the spiritual and moral fulfilment of the law against the customary carnal and external apprehension of it and the fulfilment awaiting it,—a distinction which the prophets of the Old Testament had already made (ver. 48, etc.), and which Jesus Himself emphasized with energetic spirit. It is manifest that Stephen, after some years of the Church of Christ had elapsed, and the missionary preaching of the apostles had on the whole fallen upon uncircumcised ears and hearts, the Holy Ghost being resisted, had the presentiment of Israel's being a people opposed to the preaching of Christ, and so incurring His condemnation. On the other hand, Stephen's speech does not betray a trace of his having foreseen the transference then imminent of the gospel to the heathen; though such presage may lie in its fundamental ideas.

[1] Meyer on vii. 48, etc.; Baumgarten, i. 141, etc.; Thiersch, *Die Kirche im ap. Zeitalter*, 1852, p. 88.

CHAPTER II.

JAMES.

In bringing forward James as a speaker of the early apostolic Church we proceed on two preliminary assumptions,—first, that the Epistle of James is authentic, *i.e.* really composed by James, "the Lord's brother," who was not an apostle; not Zebedee's son, who had been beheaded under Herod Agrippa, A.D. 44; nor the son of Alpheus, James the less; but one of the brothers of Jesus, who was at the head of the elders at Jerusalem, president of the Church in that city, designated as bishop after the second and third centuries. Comp. Kern, *Der Brief Jakobi*, Tüb. 1838; Woldemar Schmidt, *Lehrgehalt des Jakobusbriefes*, 1869, p. 139, etc.; Bleek, *Einleitung in das N. T.*, 3rd ed. 1875, p. 623, etc. Objections have been made to the authenticity of the work, some external, others internal. The former include the argument that the testimonies for the epistle being a part of Holy Scripture are late, after the end of the second century, for example, Clement of Alexandria; on the contrary, it is already used by Clement of Rome, First Epistle, chap. x. ver. 17 (Abraham " $\phi i \lambda o s \ \tau o \hat{v} \ \theta \epsilon o \hat{v}$," comp. Jas. ii. 22), consequently about A.D. 95. The epistle having been sent to Jewish Christians, there is nothing strange in the fact that the Church of the second century, which mainly consisted of Gentile Christians, did not become acquainted with it till a late period; whereas the Syrian Church, founded by persons from Palestine, probably one of the first recipients of the

letter, took it into the Syriac version called the
l'eschito, in the beginning of the third century at
the latest (W. Schmidt, *ante*, 150). Internal arguments lay chief weight upon the ideas of the epistle,
which, it is alleged, are not sufficiently Ebionite
(Schwegler, *Nachapost. Zeitalter*, i. 413, etc.). But
this argument lays down a self-made picture of pre-
sumably Christian Ebionism as a rule to measure by.
Other points will be mentioned immediately.

Our second assumption is, that the date of the
epistle belongs to the beginnings of the apostolic
Church. Though we once thought that the influence
of the Pauline doctrine might be perceived in it, we
have come to retract that opinion in consequence of
continued converse with the work. Not only does
the letter belong to those writings of the New Testament about whose character, date, and author very
different views may be taken (as Willib. Grimm
rightly says, in *Zeitschrift f. wiss. Theol.* 1870, p. 377);
but also to those regarding which the opinion of one
and the same man may readily change.[1] Such is
the nature of James's small letter that, take it as we
will, it presents under all circumstances certain
riddles. Nothing is more incumbent than the duty
of making an honest attempt to look at it from the
point of view which itself presents.

The author turns in his composition to the " twelve
tribes scattered abroad " (i. 1). The readers dwell in

---

[1] Whereas Kern in 1835 (*Tüb. Zeitschrift*, ii. 1, etc.) disputed the
authenticity of the epistle, he endeavoured to prove it in 1838, *Der
Brief Jakobi untersucht und erklärt.* In like manner De Wette,
in the earlier editions of his *Einleitung in das N. T.*, rather opposed
the authenticity, his doubts being strengthened in the 4th edition,
1842 ; but in the 5th edition, 1848, the tongue of his balance inclined
to the side of the authenticity.

lands outside Palestine.[1] This circle presupposes Palestine indirectly, especially Jerusalem itself as its centre, and so points to Jerusalem as the writer's abode, and in respect of time, to a date before the destruction of Jerusalem, with which event the city ceased to be the nation's centre. But as the writer calls himself a servant of God and of the Lord Jesus Christ, the assumption is natural that the readers whom he has in view are the Israelites who believe in Jesus as the Messiah and Saviour. Hence the epistle cannot have been written before the gospel among the Jews of the dispersion had begun its successful course, *i.e.* in no case before the persecution in which Stephen died a martyr's death, and in consequence of which the believers were driven out of Jerusalem as far as Phenice, Cyprus, Antioch (Acts viii. 1, 4, etc., 11, 19), and Damascus (ix. 10, 14, etc.). This circumstance leads us to a *terminus a quo*. Another observation, viz. that there is no trace of Gentile Christians in the epistle, but that we have to represent the Churches for which it was intended as consisting of Jewish Christians solely, gives a *terminus ad quem*, so that the epistle appears to have been written before Paul's mission to the Gentiles had met with its first great success, *i.e.* the end of forty years at the latest, when the question respecting the obligatory power of the Mosaic law over Gentile Christians became a burning one. The whole colouring of the epistle agrees with this ; and, appropriating Mangold's words (Bleek, *Einleitung in das N. T.*, 3rd ed. 1875, p. 637, note), we may say, "The simplest

---

[1] The constant use of language does not allow us to explain the διασπορά of strangers, in opposition to the heavenly home, and to extend it to Palestinian readers (Hofmann, *H. Schrift*, vii. 3, p. 9).

expression of Christian consciousness still untouched by complex dogmatic reflections, as it must have developed with original freshness in the circle of Jews that believed in the Messiah."

The case indeed would stand otherwise if the view we formerly took were well founded, viz. that the discussion of faith and works, ii. 14–26, presupposes the writer's acquaintance, as well as that of his readers, with the Pauline form of the subject (comp. W. Schmidt, *Lehrgehalt*, 180 ; Reuss, *Geschich. der h. Schriften N. T.* 5th ed. § 145). This state of the matter is not free from doubt. Exact and impartial expositors like Theile, *Comm. in ep. Jacobi*, 1833, p. 162, etc., have been led by their interpretation to the result that James wrote the discussion in question without respect to Paul's doctrine. Even Wold. Schmidt, though compelled to assume allusion to the Pauline teaching, has yet admitted through cautious inquiry that James's acquaintance with Paul's Epistles, particularly with those to the Romans and Galatians, can only be considered possible, not at all certain (*Lehrgehalt*, pp. 172, 174). And since, too, the alleged use of the Epistle to the Hebrews and the Apocalypse is merely asserted, not proved, we believe we may venture to accept the Epistle of James, with Schneckenburger, *Annotatio*, 1832, as a monument of pre-Pauline preaching ; Theile, *Comm.* 1833 ; Weiss, *Jakobus und Paulus, deutsche Zeitschrift*, 1854, No. 51, etc., p. 407, etc. ; *Bibl. Theol. des N. T.* 4th ed. 1884, p. 120, etc. ; Ritschl, *Entstehung der altkath. Kirche*, 1857, pp. 109, 112, etc. ; Beyschlag, *Theol. Stud. und Krit.* 1874, p. 105, etc.

If we seek the fundamental current of thought running through the epistle, it is at once evident that an ethical tendency in the direction of practical Christianity prevails in it. The peculiar, ever-recurring, leading idea which it applies, as a rule, to everything is this: Christianity, the actual life of the Christian, must be one whole, and come forth out of the fulness within; the same must be something complete (τέλειον), not a thing which is half, divided, hollow (δίψυχος, i. 8, iv. 8; κενός, μάταιος, ii. 20, i. 26). The Christian himself should be τέλειος (iii. 2, especially i. 4). As God's gift, as the law of liberty is perfect (τέλειος, i. 17, 25), so the faith of the Christian must be completed (τελειοῦσθαι), which is effected by works (ii. 22). But work itself (ἔργον) should likewise be τέλειον (i. 4, comp. ii. 8, τελεῖν νόμον βασ.); therefore one part of the law must not remain behind (ii. 11). Neither hearing without doing, nor speaking without doing, nor faith without works, is sufficient (i. 22, ii. 12–22).[1]

In accordance with his usual practical tendency, James apprehends Christianity as *law*, but as νόμος τέλειος ὁ τῆς ἐλευθερίας, i. 25, ii. 12. That the Mosaic law is not to be understood by this designation is raised above all doubt. James does indeed assert the validity of the command, " Thou shalt love thy neighbour as thyself," which he terms the royal law (comp. Matt. xxii. 38), and of other commands of the Decalogue (ii. 8, 11); but it is obvious that he distinguishes the Mosaic law (ὁ νόμος, ver. 9, etc.)

---

[1] We were led in an independent way, by careful reading of the epistle, to perceive this fundamental idea of totality and completion, and were afterwards rejoiced to find that Baur (*Paulus*, 692, 2nd ed. ii. 340) had anticipated us by a very short observation to the same effect.

from the νόμος τῆς ἐλευθερίας, and passes over the ceremonial law in silence. Hence when he characterizes Christianity as νόμος, that is, as the rule of life and conduct, he considers it chiefly under the aspect of its union with the Old Testament, whose fundamental character is TORAH. There is, however, no lack of insight into the distinguishing and peculiar characteristics of the New Testament, viz., first, νόμος τέλειος, i. 25, by which expression the law of the Old Testament is indirectly judged imperfect; but Christianity is hereby apprehended not as a (relatively) perfected law, but as being absolutely perfect. In the context, where that deep and high conception comes to light, the fulfilling of the law is the leading idea intended (i. 22–27, ii. 8–13). The other distinguishing mark is, secondly, νόμος ἐλευθερίας, a law which does not burden with a yoke and enslave with enactments, but by virtue of regeneration and renewal (i. 18–25) is fulfilled spontaneously in a condition of internal liberty, through the union of the human with the divine will, in grace and love (comp. ii. 8). This is obviously not a Jewish legal, but a Christian evangelical characteristic.[1]

The object of James in his epistle is not to

---

[1] Comp. Reuss, *Hist. de la théologie chrétienne*, etc. i. 380: la partie purement rituelle (de la loi) est passée sous silence, et rien ne nous autorise à préjuger la valeur reservée par l'apôtre à cette dernière. But when Reuss asserts with reference to the words expressing opposition between the friendship of the world and the friendship of God (which he regards as the predominating fundamental idea): il n'y a pas un mot qui dépasse le niveau de l'Ancien Testament, p. 374, he appears to mistake the spirit of the discourse. It is quite different with E. Bonifas, *L'Unité de l'enseignement Apostolique*, 1866, p. 36, etc.

plant faith in the first instance, his aim being rather to lead the believing Israelites of the dispersion to moral perfection, and to supply the lack of Christian *life* in his readers. Nevertheless we find incidental evidences of faith, which are sufficiently clear. James calls himself θεοῦ καὶ κυρίου Ἰησοῦ Χριστοῦ δοῦλος (i. 1); he confesses Jesus as κύριος ἡμῶν Ἰησοῦς Χριστός (ii. 1, v. 7, 8), and in common with his readers acknowledges Him as the Messiah and Saviour.

These words refer to the person of Jesus, to the real history of His life and work. But they are, at the same time, evidences of faith in Christ, as Him in whom the promises of God respecting His people, the Messianic predictions, are fulfilled. James calls the preaching of Jesus the word of truth (i. 18)— he nowhere calls it the gospel. The significance of this word of truth, that it is not a mere word, but rather a vital power, creative and life-giving, appears from the effects which James ascribes to it (ἀπεκύησεν ἡμᾶς—ἀπαρχήν τινα τῶν—κτισμάτων). Hence the word of truth is here designated λόγος ἔμφυτος (i. 21), a word which has been implanted in the heart, thus becoming an inward possession. This, however, does not imply that the word of truth, the law of freedom, ceases to stand above man, or to stand over against him. James is so very practical, and so much a man of real life, that in the same connection he says the Christian must always receive the word anew (δέχεσθαι, i. 21), and, by laying aside all uncleanness, prepare himself for active obedience, and give himself up to it perseveringly (i. 25, παρακύψας—παραμείνας).[1]

---

[1] Comp. Weiss, *N. T. Theologie*, 4th ed. p. 177.

Jesus Christ, who proclaims the word of truth, to whom we owe the law of liberty, is only once expressly named in this epistle (ii. 1), if we except the author's designation of himself as "the servant of God and of the Lord Jesus Christ." But in the passage just referred to, Jesus Christ is named with full emphasis, being called not only ὁ κύριος —τῆς δόξης, but being also described as the chief object of faith: τὴν πίστιν τοῦ κυρίου—τῆς δόξης. From this direct testimony, as well as on the ground of indirect intimations, a definite picture of Christ floating before the mind of James may always be traced. He belongs to those who do not make frequent use of the Redeemer's name, but follow Him with entire fidelity, and do the will of God (Matt. vii. 20). Christ thus stands before his mind chiefly as Lord and Master, as He who has fully revealed the holy will of God for our salvation: in Old Testament language, as the *prophet* who had been promised. To him, therefore, the Spirit of Christ is a rule for the apprehension and application of the Mosaic law; *for which reason* he considers the law a complete whole (ὅλος ὁ νόμος—πάντων ἔνοχος, ii. 10), whose fundamental command is love to one's neighbour (ii. 8, comp. Matt. xxii. 36, etc.),[1] especially love that showeth mercy (i. 27, ii. 13, comp. Matt. xxiii. 23). And if James lays stress solely on the moral commands of the Torah, leaving the ceremonial laws untouched, he is in perfect harmony here also, both with the example and precept of Christ. Jesus, too, in word and deed withstood the prevailing tendency towards trifles, the inclination of

---

[1] Comp. my treatise, "Das A. T. in den Reden Jesu," *Stud. u. Krit.* 1854, p. 803.

Pharisaism to externalize everything making a sharp distinction between moral intention and external performance (Matt. xxiii. 23 : $\mu\grave{\eta}$ $\dot{a}\phi\epsilon\hat{\iota}\nu\alpha\iota$—$\pi o\iota\hat{\eta}\sigma\alpha\iota$, a valuation which manifestly makes a distinction in principle).[1] How very prominent James makes the prophetic trait in Christ's character, appears from the fact that precepts from the Sermon on the Mount in particular constantly occur, though without express mention of Jesus.[2]

When the assertion is made that in James's epistle Jesus is nothing more than the upright teacher of the law (Sam. Lutz, *Biblische Dogmatik*, 1847, p. 381), the expressions referring to the *royal* dignity and activity of Christ are overlooked. So, especially, when Jesus Christ (ii. 1) is designated as $\dot{o}$ $\kappa\acute{\upsilon}\rho\iota o\varsigma$ $\tau\hat{\eta}\varsigma$ $\delta\acute{o}\xi\eta\varsigma$, as the Lord full of divine majesty, exaltation, and might. By this language not merely a higher dignity (Baur, *N. T. Theologie*, p. 285), but the absolutely highest dignity, true Deity, is attributed to Christ (Ritschl, *Altkatholische Kirche*, p. 113 ; Schmidt, *Lehrgehalt*, p. 70), yet without a word of the pre-existence of Christ and His original equality with the Father. When James opens out

---

[1] Weiss, *Theol. des N. T.* 4th ed. p. 177, note, in the last sentence confirms what is said in *Ap. u. nachap. Zeitalter*, 2nd ed. 1857, p. 165, viz. that James in his exhortations never mentions the ceremonial obligations of Mosaism, while his first sentence draws, from what I have said, a conclusion for which he himself is solely responsible. We agree with Ritschl, *Altkath. Kirche*, 2nd ed. 1857, p. 110, in his remark: "This (silence respecting the Mosaic ceremonial law) does not hinder us from believing that the writer as well as the readers of the epistle considered themselves bound by its enactments ; although it does follow from this fact that James cannot have regarded the ceremonies as the element of the Christian law."

[2] Comp. W. Schmidt, *Lehrgehalt*, p. 73.

the definite view before believing Christians, that if they resist the devil, he will flee from them (iv. 7), we justly ask, Whence does the writer draw this confidence? Undoubtedly from his belief that Jesus had overcome Satan (comp. Luke x. 17, etc.). Another important fact is that James applies κύριος = Jehovah, the Old Testament name of God, to Christ as well as to God, for it requires no proof that παρουσία τοῦ κυρίου (v. 7–14) is said not of the Father, but of Christ; while in i. 7, iv. 10, etc., κύριος must be taken as referring to God.

Although unmistakable expressions in the epistle point to the " prophetic and kingly office " of Christ, it must be unconditionally admitted that nowhere is express mention made of expiation by suffering and the death of the cross. For it appears plain from the concluding clause, which gives the motive, a clause which would not be appropriate in any other case,[1] that τέλος κυρίου, v. 11, cannot be referred to Jesus' death, but to the end of the trials of Job which God appointed. The preaching of the apostles in the primitive time of Christianity, as we see from the Acts of the Apostles, agrees with the fact that James does not speak of the atoning death of Christ. It is true that the apostles there mention the crucifixion of Jesus, but they do not speak of it as an act of the Saviour, effecting reconciliation and salvation (see above, p. 271).

It is quite in harmony with the prevailing moral and practical character of the epistle that James treats so often and so emphatically of sin in a tone of· admonition and warning. He pursues it in all its manifestations: in lust (i. 14, iv. 2), in word

---

[1] Contrary to Schmidt, *Lehrgehalt*, p. 76, etc.

(iii. 2, 6–9, v. 12) and work (ii. 9, 11), in doing and not doing (iv. 17). But he rises also to the ultimate origin of sin within the personal life and consciousness, repudiating the error that would attribute to *God* the authorship of evil. James does this by setting forth the history of sin in every man, that is, in its three stages of development, viz. ἐπιθυμία, ἁμαρτία, θάνατος, i. 13–15. The first is the lust that draws away and entices to evil, ἡ ἰδία ἐπιθυμία, dwelling within man himself and working from within outwards, and not inwards from without; this, when it has conceived (through the action of the will), brings forth sin (ἁμαρτία); and sin, when it is finished, brings forth death, viz. corporeal death, as the climax of evil. Intimately connected with this exposition of sin, resting equally on careful, delicate self-observation and on a profound knowledge of human nature, is what James says, ii. 6–8, of sins of the tongue. He perceives that they are so manifold, and have so great an influence on the conduct, character, and destiny of man, that he calls the tongue a whole world of iniquity (ὁ κόσμος τῆς ἀδικίας), ascribes to it an importance in respect to the entire man equal to that of the rudder by means of which a great ship is guided (iii. 4, etc.), or to a little fire which may kindle a whole forest (ver. 5, etc.). He asserts that the tongue may defile the whole body with sin, the impelling power of human nature, the wheel of life, (τροχὸς τῆς γενέσεως, iii. 6), and set it on fire of hell (σπιλοῦσα—φλογίζουσα). Hence he describes it as ungovernable, an unruly evil, full of deadly poison (ver. 8: μεστὴ ἰοῦ θανατηφόρου). It is not expressly said that ἐπιθυμία itself is sin (ver. 14, etc.), but sin is directly involved in its tempting allurements. The universality of sin is very strongly attested by James, iii. 2 : πολλὰ πταίομεν ἄπαντες, however fully he recognizes the original created likeness to God, iii. 9 : καθ' ὁμοίωσιν θεοῦ γεγονότες.

James does not, however, by any means treat of sin and death merely with respect to the individual man,[1] but in connection with humanity and with a power of evil in the invisible world. The exhortation to his readers to confess their faults one to another, v. 16, presupposes that even the converted are never free from sin ; how much more completely must the rest of humanity lie under its ban ! This is attested by the statement : ἡ φιλία τοῦ κόσμου ἐχθρὰ τοῦ θεοῦ ἐστιν, iv. 4. By κόσμος we cannot here understand the whole creation, with Weiss, *N. T. Theol.* p. 188, and Schmidt, *Lehrgehalt,* 89 ; for φιλία and βουληθῇ φίλος εἶναι τοῦ κόσμου, which are to be distinguished from ἐπιθυμία, presuppose an antithesis : amicum mundi esse velle aperte est a mundo amari velle (Theile) ; hence κόσμος can only mean here the world of mankind, which James regards as alienated from God, fallen into sin (Schmidt, *Biblische Theologie,* 1859, p. 392). In the visible world, as James believes and confesses, sin is connected with a kingdom of darkness in the invisible world. The tongue may be set on fire of hell (iii. 6 : φλογιζομένη ὑπὸ τῆς γεέννης), and then kindles the whole body. Ungodly wisdom is not only earthly and sensual, but also devilish (δαιμονιώδης, iii. 15) ; the opposition to σοφία ἄνωθεν implies that it comes from below, the abyss. He that will be a friend of God must withstand the *devil,* iv. 7, which the Christian *can* do, and with such

---

[1] In opposition to Baur, *N. T. Theologie,* p. 287.

success that the devil must flee. Yet the δαιμόνια tremble, ii. 19 (for fear of the judgment, which is not concealed from them any more than the existence of God).

In Jas. i. 18, with the doctrine of sin is connected the equally weighty and genuine Christian doctrine of *regeneration:* " Of His own will begat He us with the word of truth, that we should be a kind of first-fruits of His creatures." Hence conversion is nothing less than a new birth, the implantation of an essentially new life, a second creation of God. The medium of it is the word of truth, that is, the gospel of Christ, which is thus a life-producing, creative word. The object of this new birth is that we should be the first-fruits of His creatures, that is, the first-fruits dedicated to God, the sanctified peculiar people of God. The original ground of it is the free, good, gracious will of God (βουληθείς), so that regeneration is solely God's gift and boon (δώρημα, i. 17). In reality, Christianity is to James " the communication of a new, divine principle of life,"—see Neander, *Pflanzung und Leit.* ii. 867.

That which believers are, they do not owe to themselves, but to God alone, who has chosen them (ἐξελέξατο, ii. 5). But the idea of choice has not here the character of a prehistorical decree, but only that of its historical accomplishment in salvation. As God chose the people of Israel, singling them out from the nations of the world, so has He chosen those whom He has ordained to be rich in faith and heirs of His kingdom. The idea of Israel is suggested by the Old Testament κληρονόμους.

If the word of God be implanted in the soul as a new life (ἔμφυτος), it has power to save souls, i. 21, by virtue of the moral life which is born of God through the word, and comes from faith.

Entering more closely into the conception of Christian life, we come to faith in relation to works. Here the polemic discussion, ii. 14, etc., is often considered by itself, apart from other passages. This explains how it can be said that in James " faith is deprived of all that is practical, no indication being given that it is the principle of the ἔργα, of moral action " (Baur, *Paulus*, p. 680, 682, 2nd ed. ii. 326, etc.). This is quite incorrect, for it may be clearly seen from i. 3, 6, ii. 1, 5, v. 15, how high James puts faith, particularly that he views πίστις in internal union with ὑπομονή and ἔργον, as well as with prayer, and that faith is to him something great and glorious, elevating man and enriching him inwardly (πλούσιοι ἐν πίστει, ii. 5).[1] But because James, in accordance with his fundamental tendency, rejects all that is incomplete and one-sided, demanding something whole and perfect, he emphatically insists that the πίστις shall be τελεία, and only the πίστις τελειουμένη ἐκ τῶν ἔργων, ii. 22, is to him a πίστις τελεία. But it is sufficiently plain, from the tenor of the whole epistle, that these ἔργα

---

[1] Baur himself cannot help seeing the weight of these expressions, and honestly confesses (*N. T. Theologie*, 283, etc.) that James attributes a saving power to the prayer of faith, v. 15, and speaks of Christians as rich in faith. Hence he finds it incomprehensible that James should place so small a value on faith as compared with the δικαιοῦσθα. Instead of making a fresh examination into the correctness of this alleged depreciation, it has been concluded, from ii. 19, that James makes the monotheistic confession the only or most important object of faith. But this conclusion is quite unauthorized; James only adduces faith in *one* God *by way of example*. This is acknowledged, not only by Weiss, *N. T. Theol.* p. 179, and R. Kübel, *Verhältniss von Glauben und Werken bei Jakobus*, Tüb. 1880, p. 59, but also by Weiffenbach, *Exeg. theol. Studie*, 1871, p. 20.

are not Jewish works of the law, but acts prompted
by Christian feeling, by love to God and one's neighbour. Nor is it to be overlooked that this much-
discussed passage, attacking a faith that is unreal
and dead, is by no means in itself a principal part of
the epistle, since Baur himself expressly acknowledges
that this antithetic portion is not the main subject,
but only a part of the contents of the epistle, which
is in general practical throughout, consisting of
exhortation and instruction (*Paulus*, pp. 689, 691,
etc., 2nd ed. ii. 339).[1]

In ii. 14, etc., James repudiates the faith that with
many is only a pretence, and proves that the genuine
faith by which Christians are saved and justified is
active, while a professed faith, that is without works,
is dead, null and void. That this discussion is polemic
cannot reasonably be doubted. But it is quite another
question whether James was in conscious opposition
to the fundamental ideas of Paul.[2] This can only
be answered by an examination of the section itself.
James warns his readers against the practice of
partiality, against the disparagement of the poor as
compared with the rich, which is absolutely irreconcilable with faith in the exalted Saviour (ii. 1, etc.),
is in fact sin (ver. 9); judgment without mercy shall

[1] E. Pfeifer, *Studien und Krit.* 1850, i. p. 163, etc., has thrown
new light on the internal connection of the epistle, with the object
of showing that it is continuous and methodical, and seeks to
prove that the section ii. 14, etc., by virtue of its connection with
the exhortations and warnings in i. 21, as well as with ii. 1, etc.,
has no polemical reference to strange doctrine. This attempt does
not seem to have been very successful, inasmuch as it lays too much
stress on the connection, while the section itself bears clear enough
evidence *in favour of* a polemical allusion.

[2] This is maintained by Weiffenbach, *Exeg. theolog. Studie über
Jakobus,* ii. 14 16, 1871, p. 104.

befall him who has showed no mercy in his dealings
(τῷ μὴ ποιήσαντι ἔλεος, ver. 13). Here, and in what
follows, it is moral errors that the writer exposes—a
disposition to faith and confession without corresponding virtue in conduct, without active love to
one's neighbour, without meekness and a peaceable
disposition (iii. 13, etc.), an eagerness for useless
teaching (iii. 1, etc.). It is these errors in matters of
practice, not errors of doctrine, or theoretical views,
that James attacks. So, for example, ii. 14–26,
where, as in i. 25, etc., he warns his readers against
self-deception that endangers the soul. He shows
that a faith without works is of no avail or profit
either to the believer himself or to others (ii. 14 : τί
ὄφελος ; μὴ δύναται σῶσαι αὐτόν ;); faith without
works is vain, without effect (20, ἀργή), without true
life, without vital power (17 and 26, νεκρά), like a
body without a spirit (the same verse). The latter
figure is not quite appropriate;[1] it cannot be pressed,
for the statement that the life-power, the Spirit, can be
absent from πίστις as from σῶμα, in itself considered,
is not logically consistent with other utterances of
James, for example i. 3, 6, v. 15. Ver. 26 can
only mean that faith, if it have no works, like the
body without the spirit, is dead.[2] The position which
Jame sestablishes in the presence of an existing
inclination to Christian faith without exemplification
in upright, virtuous conduct, is this : faith without
works is of no effect, without fruit or profit, like a
piety that limits itself to fine words, without corresponding act or charitable gift (vv. 15, 16). Such
faith cannot save man and make him happy (σῶσαι,

---

[1] Contrary to Weiffenbach, p. 54, see Weiss, *N. T. Theol.* p. 181.
[2] See Hofmann, *Brief Jakobi*, 1876, p. 84, etc.

ver. 14); it is like that belief in the existence of God which the devils have, who notwithstanding tremble and shudder for fear of the judgment which they expect. A fruitless faith can bring no peace, no rest of soul even to him who has it.

It is certain that faith without works cannot be shown or demonstrated to have actual existence: faith can only be proved by works that may be seen (ver. 17). That this digression is intended for a reply is shown by the use of the formula: ἀλλ' ἐρεῖ τις. The speaker introduced cannot, however, be a direct opponent, as may be seen from the substance of his words compared with vv. 14–16. That he is a "mediator," wishing to mediate between James and his opponents,[1] we doubt, for the reason that there has been no previous mention of an opponent (James first addresses such a one in ver. 19 as σύ, and in ver. 20 with the harsh expression ἄνθρωπε κενέ); how should this refer to a "mediator"? That James himself replies by κἀγώ is "the most impossible thing of all."[2] James takes from Scripture (vv. 20–25) the most striking proof of his position that faith without works is of no effect, even lifeless; and here, first, while proceeding to Scripture proof, led by the testimony concerning Abraham, he arrives at the idea of justification and the principle of justification by works, not by faith alone: ἐξ ἔργων δικαιοῦται ἄνθρωπος, καὶ οὐκ ἐκ πίστεως μόνον (ver. 24). The meaning of δικαιοῦν (vv. 21, 24, etc.), according to the connection and in conformity with the usage of הִצְדִּיק,—for example, in Exod. xxiii. 7,—and δικαιοῦν in the Septuagint is,

---

[1] In accordance with the view of Weiffenbach, p. 15, etc.

[2] *Vid.* Hofmann, *Jakobus*, p. 67.

to justify in a court of justice, the justification of
God, His pardon of a sinner, the announcement of
His good pleasure in a man.[1] The σώζειν (ver. 14)
is a more comprehensive idea, which includes that
of the δικαιοῦν; both presuppose a state of imminent
destruction, but imply a transference into the sphere of
salvation. But the φίλος θεοῦ ἐκλήθη (ver. 23), which
is used in a passive sense : quem sua Deus amicitia
dignatur, shows that δικαιοῦν denotes a divine *judgment*. From the history of Abraham James tries to
give Scripture proof that faith without works is vain
(ἀργή, 20). The patriarch is not declared by God
to be just until he has laid his son upon the altar,
has proved his obedience by his act (ver. 21); for
the promise which had been given long before was
then fulfilled, "Abraham believed God, and it was
imputed unto him for righteousness" (23, comp.
Gen. xv. 6); what had formerly been only promised
has now been fulfilled, and Abraham receives the
honourable title "friend of God," favourite of God.
So also Rahab, when she had hospitably received
the messengers, the spies of Israel, and had helped
them in their flight from the city, thus saving
their lives, was said to be justified in consequence
of *what she had done*. In gratitude for this her life
was spared, and that of her kindred (Josh. vi.
23, 25).

Thus it is proved that James (ii. 20–25) makes
justification, that is the divine judgment by means of
which God justifies sinful man, forgives sin, and

---

[1] Comp. Huther's explanation on ii. 21 ; Wold. Schmidt's *Lehrgehalt*, 107, etc. On the other hand, the attempt of v. Hofmann,
Jakobus, p. 71, etc., to help out his interpretation of δικαιοῦν, so as
to render it equivalent to making righteous, is not at all convincing.

grants him His favour, not dependent on faith alone, but also on works. If we proceed to inquire in what relation faith and works stand to one another according to James, we meet with many answers to this question. In one passage he says of Abraham's faith that it wrought with his works ($\dot{\eta}$ $\pi\acute{\iota}\sigma\tau\iota\varsigma$ $\sigma\upsilon\nu\acute{\eta}\rho\gamma\epsilon\iota$ $\tau o\hat{\iota}\varsigma$ $\check{\epsilon}\rho\gamma o\iota\varsigma$, ver. 22). It is very clear that a power is here ascribed to faith, which works together with conduct, and is indispensable to works in order that they may serve as a justification before God.[1] Consequently, in the same verse (22[b]), James testifies that the faith of Abraham is made perfect by works, $\dot{\epsilon}\tau\epsilon\lambda\epsilon\iota\acute{\omega}\theta\eta$, that is, it has attained to its full maturity and power. Hence we have a double statement; faith co-operates in the performance of works; without it no action pleasing to God can be accomplished; but even faith fails to attain its fulfilment, its full fruition, without works. This corresponds to the truth contained in i. 3, etc., according to which faith when it is tried works patience ($\kappa\alpha\tau\epsilon\rho\gamma\acute{\alpha}\zeta\epsilon\tau\alpha\iota$); but this latter must have its perfect work, that we ourselves may become *perfect* Christians ($\tau\acute{\epsilon}\lambda\epsilon\iota o\iota$, etc.). The thought clearly lying at the foundation of all this is, that faith, to quote the words of Luther, is " a living, powerful,

[1] Weiffenbach believes he gives a correct rendering of James's view, in maintaining that according to him $\pi\acute{\iota}\sigma\tau\iota\varsigma$ and $\check{\epsilon}\rho\gamma\alpha$ are two principles working side by side : $\check{\epsilon}\rho\gamma\alpha$ being undoubtedly the higher principle, complete and living in itself ; while $\pi\acute{\iota}\sigma\tau\iota\varsigma$ is imperfect and insufficient (*ante*, 57, etc.). But in order to reduce faith to this level, he must, in the new interpretation of the words 22[a] (p. 35, etc.) which he had propounded, read the main thing continually between the lines, "*only* auxiliary," "the *mere* auxiliary," "the *weaker* auxiliary," *only* $\sigma\upsilon\nu\epsilon\rho\gamma o\hat{\upsilon}\sigma\alpha$ with the mistress ($\check{\epsilon}\rho\gamma\alpha$), etc. (p. 32, etc.). Comp. Ritschl, *Chr. Lehre von der Rechtfertigung und Versöhnung*, ii. 357, etc.

active thing," but that its attestation in obedience, in active love to God and one's neighbour, is indispensable to its growth and full maturity. Hence the two principles do not stand *side by side*, but are connected in a living, organic way; so that works grow out of faith, and in their turn react on faith, which only thus attains its completion.[1]

James, with all the moral earnestness he has for the present, firmly and steadfastly fixes the eye of faith on the future. Jesus Christ, the Saviour exalted to glory (ii. 1), will come again; His παρουσία indeed is at hand (v. 8, comp. 7). He comes as judge (v. 9). Not only does judgment threaten ungodly men of the world (v. 1, etc.), but also believers, if they are only hearers and not doers of the word (i. 25), if they know to do good and do it not (iv. 17), if their worship of God is internally empty and hypocritical (i. 26), if they set themselves up as teachers without being called (iii. 1), if they do not practise merciful love (ii. 13); but rather commit wrong against their neighbour with words of reproach and censure (iv. 11, etc.), in which case a judgment all the more severe awaits them (ii. 13, κρίσις ἀνίλεως; iv. 12, ὁ δυνάμενος ἀπολέσαι). But those who love God (i. 12, ii. 5: τοῖς ἀγαπῶσιν αὐτόν), walk in humility and seek God (iv. 6, etc.), practise merciful love, and keep themselves unspotted from the world (i. 27), sow a seed of peace in their walk (iii. 18), and are not only rich in faith already, blessed in their deed (ii. 5, i. 25), but shall in that day be heirs of the glorious kingdom which Christ has promised, and

---

[1] Comp. Schmidt, 102, etc., who does not hold that faith, according to James, "only receives vitality through works" (*vid.* Weiss, *N. T. Theol.* 181, note), but expressly rejects this view, p. 104.

shall receive the crown of a blessed life (ii. 5, comp. i. 12 ; Matt. v. 3).

The same tendency which the Epistle of James has in its most complete and purest form, and which we may call the Jewish Christian tendency, also belongs to the Gospel of Matthew. This Gospel, like the Epistle of James, was written exclusively for believers in Israel ; its object is to convince them of the Messianic dignity of Jesus, using as a means to this end proof of the fulfilment of the prophecies of the Old Covenant in Jesus. But although, according to the Gospel of Matthew, Jesus has come not to destroy the Mosaic law but to fulfil it (v. 17, etc.), and speaks not against the law, but only against the Pharisaic misunderstanding and abuse of it (v. 21, etc., xxiii. 1, etc.), yet an idea reaching far beyond the standpoint of the law itself lies in the fact that according to this Gospel "the Son of Man," that is, Jesus the Messiah, demands faith in *His person* as the Son of God (xviii. 6, xvi. 15, etc.) ; belief that He will not only come again at a future time as king and judge of the world (xix. 28, xxiv. 30, xxv. 31, etc., xxvi. 64), but that He has even now power to forgive sins (ix. 6, xxviii. 18), which only God can do ; and more especially that eternal salvation or condemnation will depend on the attitude assumed towards *His person*, on confession or denial of Him, on following after or departing from Him (x. 32, etc., xix. 29, xxv. 34, etc., comp. xii. 49, etc.). We have also an indication of a higher view than the usual legal one in the alleged maxim of Jesus, frequently repeated in Matthew, that regeneration is the indispensable condition of the righteousness of the kingdom of God : for example, in the far-reaching, profound expression, πᾶσα φυτεία, ἣν οὐκ ἐφύτευσεν ὁ πατήρ μου—ἐκριζωθήσεται (xv. 13, comp. xviii. 3), that has so frequently been overlooked and misapprehended; and again, when Jesus goes back beyond the Mosaic legislation even to the original arrangement of God in creation. The same characteristic is implied in the fact, that although Jesus " was only sent to the lost sheep of the house of Israel " (xv. 24), although He sent His disciples at first to them only, and forbade them to enter heathen boundaries, or even Samaritan cities (x. 5, etc.), yet He announces to unbelieving Israel that the kingdom of God should be taken from them and given to the Gentiles (xxi. 43, comp. viii. 11, etc., xxiii. 38, xxiv. 1, etc.); and finally, before His ascension to heaven, expressly commissions His apostles to make disciples of and baptize *all nations* (xxviii. 19, etc.). It is worthy of remark that the precedence of Peter over the other apostles appears in none of the evangelists so prominently as in Matthew (comp. Lutterbeck, *ante*, ii. 165). In this Gospel Peter is called before all the other apostles (iv. 18, etc.); he is designated "the first" (x. 2), which is not the case in the parallel passages. In xvi. 18, etc., he receives the weighty promise, which is absent both from Luke and Mark. These circumstances, the prominence given to the precedence of Peter in connection with the book's unmistakable design for Churches formed out of Israel, and the fact that the eye of the author is specially directed to the Old Covenant and the union of Christianity with the Old Testament, place the Gospel of Matthew in the rank of Jewish Christian Scriptures belonging to the Canon, while the presence of many passages respecting the divine dignity of the person of Jesus, the founding of the New Covenant by His atoning death (xxvi. 26), the necessity of regeneration to righteousness in the kingdom of God, and hints of the world - embracing destination of Christ's Church, must prevent us from ascribing a narrow, low, legal standpoint to the first Gospel.

SECOND SECTION.

THE DOCTRINAL SYSTEM OF THE APOSTLE PAUL.

The Apostle Paul is the most prominent factor in the doctrine as well as in the life of early Christianity. In the sphere of missions, the founding and organizing of Churches, and the advancement of the Church as a whole in opposition to the aims of the religion of the world, and in the spirit of evangelical freedom, he leads the way.   He also took a foremost place in an entirely different manner from Peter who preceded him.   But not the less was he a leader in *doctrine*— a pioneer.   How clearly he recognized the new nature of Christianity; Christ as the end of the law; the gospel as a power of God for the salvation of *all* who believe it, Jews as well as Gentiles; justification through faith without the works of the law; the freedom of the Christian; with what penetration of spirit has he investigated and defended these truths, bringing them to a triumphant recognition!   His life-work and his Christian thought were closely interwoven.   We may say of both what he himself acknowledges to have been his personal experience, " Christ lived in him " (Gal. ii. 20); he only revealed what had been given in Jesus Christ, His teaching,

His person, and His work, but had till that time lain concealed and unknown.[1] That the Apostle Paul was able to effect so much in life and doctrine was due, as he openly confesses, to his own personal experience, to the guidance of God and the revelation of Jesus Christ (Gal. i. 1, 12, 16). Not only the power of God in his conversion, but also events in the course of his career as an apostle, led him to a deeper insight into the mind of God and the things concerning Christ's kingdom; but without doubt it was the revelation of Jesus Christ in his conversion that laid the foundation for the character, work, and teaching of Paul in its later development.

In beginning our investigation of the apostle's doctrine with the fact of his conversion, we are in harmony with his own personal confession. If we could lay the three accounts of this occurrence given in the Acts at the basis of our discussion (ix. 3, etc., xxii. 6, etc., xxvi. 12, etc.), we should be met with the objection that they contradict one another, and prove themselves to be unhistorical.[2] Without stopping to make a critical examination of these accounts, we turn to the statements of the apostle himself in his epistles, hitherto so often applied as irrefragable testimonies against the narrative of the Acts. But what do we see? Just as little value is attached to the utterances of the apostle himself, on this point, as to the narrative of the Acts. Paul is a safe witness only of that which he *believes* he saw; the thing attested is a *vision* of Christ, but his-

[1] Comp. my treatise, "Das A. T. in den Reden Jesu," *Stud. und Krit.* 1854, p. 848, etc.

[2] Comp., for example, Zeller, *Apostelgeschichte*, p. 191, etc., especially 194, etc. On the other hand, Zimmer, in Hilgenfeld's *Zeitschrift*, 1882, p. 465, etc., has tried to show by a critical examination of sources that Luke used older sources here.

torical criticism must try to apprehend this vision as a subjective act of the spirit itself; as a determining resolve which clothes itself in the form of an objective revelation, —a resolve which ripened in consequence of a dialectic process in his religious thinking.[1] The first question is, What conclusions are we to draw from the utterances of the apostle himself respecting his conversion ?

First, that it was not his own act, but in truth an act of *God*. This he states in Gal. i. 15, etc.; having previously described his manner of thought and action before that time, viz. a Pharisaic, fanatical spirit, and an ardent zeal for persecuting the Christian Church (ver. 13, etc.). He then testifies : " It pleased God (εὐδόκησεν, of His free divine *purpose*, by virtue of a decree of His unconditioned favour), who separated me from my mother's womb (chose me for a holy calling), and called me by His (undeserved) grace, to reveal His Son in me, that I might preach Him among the heathen." Paul here declares as strongly as possible that his conversion was an act of God, resting on God's determination and gracious choice, not on *his own* consideration and determination ; that it was an act of compassionate grace and undeserved favour.

Secondly, we learn from the utterances of Paul in what God's influence upon him at the time of that event consisted, viz. in the *revelation of Jesus Christ*, the *Son of God*. *This*, and not the call to be an apostle to the Gentiles, was the substance of the ἀποκάλυψις, the call was the *object* of the revelation ;[2] but the latter

---

[1] Baur, *Paulus*, i. 74, etc. ; Holsten, *zum Ev. des Paulus und des Petrus*, p. 65, etc. ; Otto Pfleiderer, *der Paulinismus*, 1873, pp. 3–16 ; Schenkel, *das Christusbild der Apostel*, 1879, pp. 53–56.

[2] It is at least open to misunderstanding, when Holsten, *Ev. des Paulus*, 1880, i. 142, says that the object-clause, ἵνα, etc., with the τὸν υἱὸν αὐτοῦ, explains the substance of the formula ἀποκαλύψαι.

itself consisted in the fact that Paul, by divine illumination of his soul, was convinced that Jesus was the Son of God,—convinced not merely of His Messiahship, but also of His divine majesty. This agrees admirably with the circumstance that the revelation, which here appears as the act of God the Father, is described in ver. 12 as the act of Jesus Christ, His revelation of Himself, for we hold firmly with Meyer, Wieseler, Holsten (*ante*, 140), that Ἰησοῦ Χριστοῦ is not intended as genitive of the object but of the subject, while in opposition to Meyer (note on i. 12) we refer both, the ἀποκάλυψις Ἰησοῦ Χριστοῦ (i. 12) and ἀποκαλύψαι τὸν υἱὸν αὐτοῦ, to one and the same fact, viz. the vision before Damascus. So, too, in Eph. iii. 3, Paul bears witness that the mystery (the redemption of the world, designed for the Gentiles as well as for Israel) was made known to him by revelation, κατὰ ἀποκάλυψιν.

Thirdly, the Apostle Paul declares that in that incident, which he characterizes in Gal. i. as the revelation of the Son by the Father, and as the self-revelation of Jesus Christ, Christ who had risen appeared to him in visible form (1 Cor. xv. 8, ὤφθη κἀμοί). The fact that Paul here refers to the incident of his conversion is placed beyond doubt by the circumstance that he mentions his persecution of the Church and his call to be an apostle in immediate connection with the appearance of the risen Saviour (ver. 9), and testifies " by the grace of God I am what I am " (ver. 10).[1]   With this utterance we

---

[1] That the apostle, in ver. 8, speaks of that appearance of Christ which led to his inner change, is admitted without reserve by Heinrici, 1 *Korinther*, 1880, p. 480, and Holsten, *Ev. des Paulus*, p. 412.

connect the question put forward in the same epistle (ix. 1), οὐχὶ Ἰησοῦν τὸν κύριον ἡμῶν ἑώρακα. Paul does not here refer to a possible seeing of Jesus in His earthly life, as is shown by his calling Him ὁ κύριος: he has in view the Risen One, the exalted Saviour.[1] Moreover, the mention of his apostolic dignity in the foregoing question seems to place his seeing of Jesus and his call to the apostleship in intimate connection.

If, with Holsten, we try to apprehend the conversion of Paul as "the immanent act" of his human spirit,[2] we are at variance with the repeated and unequivocal testimony of the said apostle, and give the lie to his declaration that his gospel is not κατ' ἄνθρωπον, Gal. i. 11 ; maintaining, in defiance of the apostle, that his gospel was the creation of his own mind. To make such an assertion with respect to a man who was so successful in the apostleship to which he was consciously called only by this event, involves great courage, especially since, according to his declaration in Gal. i. 15, the words are applicable to him which are addressed to Peter by Jesus in Matt. xvi. 17: "Blessed art thou: for flesh and blood hath not revealed it unto thee, but My Father which is in heaven."

The nature of the process which effected the conversion of Paul serves also as a confirmation of the account in Acts ix. 22, 26. It consists in the following particulars :—

[1] This is the view of Heinrici, *ante*, 238, note 2, and Holsten, *ante*, 314, note 2, while Meyer, though he understands it as directly referring to the vision at Damascus, connects it with later visionary appearances of Christ, a view which is precluded by the question that goes before it.

[2] "Paul's vision of Christ," in *Zum Ev. des Paulus u. des Petrus*, 1868, 68, pp. 65–114.

1. Jesus, who had risen from the dead and was exalted to heaven, did *actually reveal* Himself to Paul, as the Living and Glorified One, in divine majesty and splendour. Saul persecuted the disciples under the delusion that Jesus, who was crucified as a malefactor, had remained subject to death, and could by no means be the Messiah. But now Jesus reveals Himself to him, he sees Him bodily ($\dot{\epsilon}\dot{\omega}\rho\alpha\kappa\alpha$, 1 Cor. ix. 1), in majesty and glory ($\tau\dot{o}\nu$ $\kappa\dot{\nu}\rho\iota o\nu$ $\dot{\eta}\mu\hat{\omega}\nu$), so that he is as certain as of his own existence that Jesus lives although He was dead ; He is risen again (1 Cor. xv. 4, $\dot{\epsilon}\gamma\dot{\eta}\gamma\epsilon\rho\tau\alpha\iota$; ver. 8, $\ddot{\omega}\phi\theta\eta$ $\kappa\dot{\alpha}\mu o\acute{\iota}$), He lives and is the Anointed of God, the Messiah and Lord. This self-revelation of Jesus was coincident with the revelation actually imparted to Paul by God, that Jesus is the Son of God.

2. This vision was directly connected with the *call to be an apostle*. In all three passages, Gal. i. 16, 1 Cor. xv. 8, and 1 Cor. ix. 1, both are inseparably joined together in thought and word, while the calling to his Gentile apostleship occurs only in the passage in Galatians, where, however, it is the more expressly emphasized as the object of the revelation.

3. But in the fact that the self-revelation of the risen and glorified Son of God was vouchsafed to him at the moment when he was persecuting the Church of God, that is, while he misapprehended and persecuted the Redeemer in His believers, above measure ($\kappa\alpha\theta$’ $\dot{\nu}\pi\epsilon\rho\beta o\lambda\dot{\eta}\nu$, Gal. i. 13), he must have perceived unmerited grace, compassionate, redeeming love for the blinded and mistaken sinner. This feeling is intimated in Gal. i. 15, in the words $\kappa\alpha\lambda\dot{\epsilon}\sigma\alpha\iota$ $\delta\iota\dot{\alpha}$ $\tau\hat{\eta}\varsigma$ $\chi\dot{\alpha}\rho\iota\tau o\varsigma$ $\alpha\dot{\nu}\tau o\hat{\nu}$, but is much more strongly and

forcibly expressed in 1 Cor. xv. 8–10, where it is uttered with the deepest humility and emotion, so that his confession comprehends the sum of all: "By the grace of God I am what I am."

This omnipotent divine act, this merciful revelation of Jesus Christ, was so great and of such intrinsic importance, it took such a sudden and violent hold of the ground on which the disciple of the Pharisees and Zealot had planted himself, overthrowing his position from its very foundation and penetrating into his innermost life, that the fruit which was to spring from the seed needed much time. If the pious old French proverb—

"En peu d'heure
Dieu laboure,"

be applicable to that divine act, the German proverb—

"Gut Ding will Weile haben,"

may be applied to the labour of man expended in the appropriation of the thoughts of God, and in the external manifestation of that which has been bestowed by God.

What Christ, by His revelation and calling, effected in Paul remained permanent in his soul, impressed its seal on all his thoughts and actions, and in particular gave to his apostolic preaching and teaching its unique character. The apostle, however, did not at once attain to this peculiar conception in all its purity and fulness, but step by step, and under the influence of experiences made in the pursuit of his calling, he penetrated more and more into its depths, and built up his doctrinal system in growing fulness and independence. In this course we have to follow him.

CHAPTER I.

THE ORIGINAL PREACHING OF THE APOSTLE PAUL.

As source for the preaching of the gospel by Paul in the first decade of his apostolic work, we employ partly the Pauline discourses in the Acts of the Apostles, and partly the two Thessalonian epistles.[1]

(A.) *According to his discourses in the Acts.*

The Acts give a mere summary indication of the first utterances after conversion, in the synagogues at Damascus (ix. 20, 22), next a short reproof addressed to Elymas the sorcerer in Cyprus (xiii. 10, etc.), proceeding to record two missionary discourses— a longer one delivered in the synagogue of Antioch in Pisidia (xiii. 16–41, 46, etc.), and a shorter one addressed to the Gentile inhabitants of Lystra (xiv. 15–17). Then follow brief notices of discourses to the new converts of Asia Minor (xiv. 22), of the missionary report in Antioch (xiv. 27), of the address of Paul and Barnabas at the apostolic convention (xv. 12), and of the dialogue with the jailor at

---

[1] B. Weiss shows just discernment in treating the preaching of Paul in its beginning as a particular stage in the development of his Christian views, in regarding his system of doctrine not as a whole, completed at one casting, but as the result of progressive insight on the part of the apostle. We assent to this view, but in drawing from the discourses of Paul in the Acts, do not limit ourselves with Weiss to those delivered before the heathen, but have regard also to those addressed to Jewish hearers, for we have to do with the whole Paul, who was always the same, whether he became a Jew to the Jews, or a heathen to the heathen (comp. 1 Cor. ix. 20).

Philippi (xvi. 31), succeeded by the sermon on Areopagus in Athens (xvii. 22–31, comp. ver. 18). The farewell discourse to the elders of the Church at Ephesus, delivered at Miletus (xx. 18–35), is unique of its kind. When a prisoner, Paul made several speeches in self-defence: in Jerusalem partly before the people (xxii. 1–21), partly before the Sanhedrim (xxiii. 1–6); in Cæsarea before Felix (xxiv. 10–21, comp. ver. 24, etc.); lastly, before Festus and Agrippa. The discourses to the Jews at Rome (xxviii. 17–20 and 23–29) form the conclusion of the book. Of these speeches five are given more fully: two missionary addresses to the Jews (xiii.) and to the Gentiles (xvii.); two are delivered in self-defence (xxii., before the Jewish people; xxvi., before persons in authority); and one discourse forms a pastoral address to the elders of a Church which he founded (xx.). Those Pauline discourses, given at length, consequently form a complete circle, every important kind being represented by one example at least. This bears testimony to a certain systematic design on the part of the historian, but without authorizing the assumption of a " free composition " of the discourses themselves throughout.

The gospel which Paul preaches, in conformity with this evidence, is the gospel of *Jesus* as the *Lord* and *Saviour*. Immediately after his conversion he preaches in the synagogues at Damascus " that Jesus is the Son of God " (ix. 20). Meyer, Overbeck, and others understand *ὁ υἱὸς τοῦ θεοῦ* in an ethical sense = the Messiah. But it neither has been nor can be proved that the terms Son of God and Messiah in the New Testament are synonymous, nor that the former does not express a peculiar relation to God (comp.

Weiss, *N. T. Theologie*, 4th ed. p. 56, etc.). How fully this account of Luke harmonizes in letter and spirit with the testimony of the apostle himself (Gal. i. 16), that God revealed to him at his conversion τὸν υἱὸν αὐτοῦ! The theme is varied in ver. 22: ὅτι οὗτός ἐστιν ὁ Χριστός. This mode of treatment agrees with the verb συμβιβάζων there employed, which presupposes a proof out of the Old Testament Scriptures, a verification of the consistency of Messianic promise with its actual fulfilment. In this way Paul could only establish the position that Jesus of Nazareth is the Messiah, but not that He is the Son of God, the latter being set forth by the confession of his innermost conviction, by appeal to his own experience (ἐκήρυσσεν, ver. 20). From this time forward Jesus constantly appears in the character of Redeemer and glorified Lord, as the centre of Paul's preaching, whether he speaks in the synagogue of Antioch in Pisidia (xiii. 23, comp. 32), or points out the way of salvation to the jailor at Philippi (xvi. 31, πίστευσον ἐπὶ τὸν κύριον Ἰησοῦν, καὶ σωθήσῃ, etc.). In Thessalonica the Jews, distorting his doctrine into high treason, represent as its leading feature the fundamental principle: βασιλέα ἕτερον εἶναι Ἰησοῦν (xvii. 7). In Athens he does not indeed expressly name Jesus, but it is self-evident that Jesus is meant by the Man ordained by God, accredited by His resurrection from the dead, by whom God will judge the world in righteousness (xvii. 31). The apostle reminds the elders of Ephesus that he has always preached among them πίστιν εἰς τὸν κύριον ἡμῶν Ἰησοῦν Χριστόν (xx. 21). Before the people in Jerusalem, as well as before Festus and Agrippa, he openly confesses Jesus as the Lord (xxii.

28, xxvi. 15, etc.). Finally, in treating with the Jews in Rome he bears witness of the kingdom of God, and seeks to persuade them concerning Jesus out of the law and the prophets (xxviii. 23).

Jesus is a descendant of David conformably to the promise; a fact which Paul emphasizes when addressing the Jews (xiii. 22, etc.); but in the same discourse he declares Jesus to be also the Son of God (ver. 33, comp. ix. 20), in whom the promise (Ps. ii. 7, etc.) of the theocratic ruler, whom God appointed His Son, is fulfilled. In proof of his confession that Jesus is the Messiah, the Son of God, he appeals to the fact of His *resurrection*. To the Athenians he says, God has placed faith in Him within the reach of all, made it possible ($\pi i \sigma \tau \iota \nu \ \pi a \rho a \sigma \chi \acute{\omega} \nu$, xvii. 31), consequently accredited Him by His resurrection from the dead. In the synagogue also he takes his stand on the resurrection of Jesus (xiii. 30, etc.), which was attested by the Galilean disciples, who were eye-witnesses of His appearances. Hand in hand with this divine ratification, Paul appeals to the fulfilment of the prophecies of the Old Covenant. Such process of proof is shown in the Pisidian discourse[1] (chap. xiii.), where first, the Davidic descent (ver. 23),

---

[1] Weiss, *N. T. Theol.* p. 199, note, considers the historical part of the discourse a copy of the discourse of Stephen and of the Petrine discourse of the first part of the Acts (comp. Baur, *Paulus*, 101, etc., 2nd ed. i. 115, etc. ; Zeller, *Ap. Geschichte*, 301), while Schrader, *Paulus*, v. 540, describes it as a lifeless collection of Jewish narratives. But the facts in the history of Israel, of which Paul here treats, are made subservient to a fundamental idea different from that which is embodied in the discourse of Stephen ; namely, Paul, xiii. 17-22, sets forth the *free grace of God*, and His unmerited choice, by which Israel had become the people of God, and David the servant of God and king of Israel ἐξιλίξατο, ver. 17, ἤγειρεν τὸν Δαουίδ — εἰς βασιλία); the contrast to this consists in the removal of what is

second, the death on the cross (27–29), third, His resurrection (30–34), are set forth as the fulfilment of God's promise. This certainly corresponds to the primitive Christian preaching, Paul himself in 1 Cor. xv. 3, etc., giving prominence to the redemptive death of Christ, His burial, resurrection on the third day, with the appearances of the Risen One, as facts in the history of salvation, which he announces in common with the other apostles.

Next to the resurrection, the crucifixion of Jesus appears as the principal fact in these discourses, not only as being quite unmerited (xiii. 28, $\mu\eta\delta\epsilon\mu\ell a\nu$ $a\ell\tau\ell a\nu$ $\theta a\nu\acute{a}\tau o\nu$ $\epsilon\dot{\nu}\rho\acute{o}\nu\tau\epsilon\varsigma$), but also as foretold by the prophets (vv. 27, 29), and even as Christ's title to souls (xx. 28, $\dot{\eta}$ $\dot{\epsilon}\kappa\kappa\lambda\eta\sigma\ell a$ $\tau o\hat{\upsilon}$ $\kappa\upsilon\rho\ell o\upsilon$, $\dot{\eta}\nu$ $\pi\epsilon\rho\iota\epsilon$-$\pi o\iota\acute{\eta}\sigma a\tau o$ $\delta\iota\grave{a}$ $\tau o\hat{\upsilon}$ $a\ddot{\iota}\mu a\tau o\varsigma$ $\tau o\hat{\upsilon}$ $\dot{\iota}\delta\ell o\upsilon$). The blood of Jesus shed in His death on the cross, by which souls that without His sufferings and death could not have been His, have been made His own, His peculiar people,—the sacrificial blood of Christ has redemptive power, and has laid the foundation of the Church of the Lord. This profound thought finds expression in the only discourse addressed to believing Christians, and to elders and rulers of a Church, to impress on them the duty of spiritual pastorship.

Jesus of Nazareth, the descendant of David and Son of God, the manifested Messiah, is raised

adverse (ver. 22, $\mu\epsilon\tau a\sigma\tau\acute{\eta}\sigma a\iota$ $\tau\grave{o}\nu$ $\Sigma a o\acute{\upsilon}\lambda$). But the pervading thought with Stephen is the absolute majesty of God as regards His revelation. Weiss himself concedes that there is much that is peculiar in the Pisidian discourse (vv. 29, 31, 33, etc.). What is said of Jesus is peculiar in so far as everything is brought into connection with David: the historical survey of the Old Covenant is carried down to David; Jesus is the offspring of David; King David is the type full of promise, whose fulfilment has taken place in Christ.

from death, and leads a life for ever incorruptible (xiii. 34). He it is to whom we owe *salvation*, the soul's deliverance. He is σωτήρ, but in the first place only for Israel (xiii. 23); the preaching of Jesus is ὁ λόγος τῆς σωτηρίας (xiii. 26). Σωθήσῃ σὺ καὶ ὁ οἶκός σου (xvi. 31), Paul promises the jailor, on the condition of faith in Jesus Christ. The gospel is τὸ εὐαγγέλιον τῆς χάριτος τοῦ θεοῦ (xx. 24), ὁ λόγος τῆς χάριτος αὐτοῦ (ver. 32). The grace of God coming through Jesus Christ consists above all in the forgiveness of sins: διὰ τούτου ὑμῖν ἄφεσις ἁμαρτιῶν καταγγέλλεται· ἀπὸ πάντων, ὧν οὐκ ἠδυνήθητε ἐν τῷ νόμῳ Μωϋσέως δικαιωθῆναι, ἐν τούτῳ πᾶς ὁ πιστεύων δικαιοῦται (xiii. 38). This declaration asserts literally that every believer is fully justified (that is, from all guilt and punishment), " from which ye could not be justified " (delivered) in the law of Moses. What does this mean ? Is the sense (Schwegler, *Nachapost. Zeit.*, ii. 96, etc.) only that through Christ one can obtain forgiveness even for those sins for which there was no justification in the law ? by which interpretation the righteousness of faith is not substituted for righteousness by the law, but has only a relative superiority, as supplementing it and being fuller. On this assumption we must read all together as *one* sentence ; but even if we do not, with Lachmann and Tischendorf, reject the καί before ἀπό (ver. 39) as spurious, yet it follows from the πάντων, in place of which, by virtue of its close connection, πασῶν must stand, that a new sentence in fact begins with ver. 39, and that a colon and not a comma must be put at the end of ver. 38. Hence καί (assuming its authenticity) is not to be taken as equivalent to " also," but in the sense of " and that."

The passage must therefore be understood as containing two positions, first, negatively: no actual forgiveness of sins and justification is given in the law; second, positively: forgiveness and justification on behalf of all sins are proclaimed and offered to believers through Christ. In this statement judgment is indirectly pronounced against the Mosaic law as unable to give justification, but at the same time it is implied that forgiveness may be obtained by Jesus. Hence an absolute, essential distinction between the law and the gospel is set forth. The repetition of the specifically Pauline conception δικαιωθῆναι after ἄφεσις ἁμαρτιῶν is at the same time worthy of note. The latter is a negative conception; but δικαιωθῆναι includes in itself, besides the negative (ἀπὸ πάντων), a positive element. The less the law in essence was able to lead to forgiveness and justification (οὐκ ἠδυνήθητε), so much the more decidedly is Christ set forth as the only mediator of justification, and that for every believer (πᾶς ὁ πιστεύων).[1]

The means of participation in the salvation of Christ is *repentance* (xxvi. 20 : μετανοεῖν καὶ ἐπιστρέφειν ἐπὶ τὸν θεόν, ʹ ἄξια τῆς μετανοίας ἔργα πράσσοντας; comp. xvii. 30, xiii. 24, xiv. 15) and *faith* (xx. 21 : διαμαρτυρόμενος ᾿Ιουδαίοις τε καὶ ῞Ελλησι τὴν εἰς τὸν θεὸν μετάνοιαν, καὶ πίστιν τὴν εἰς τὸν

---

[1] Therefore Schwegler, *ante*, has no foundation for saying that the passage (ver. 38, etc.) is decidedly un-Pauline in its treatment of justification by faith. Zeller is more cautious, and only maintains the *possibility* of interpreting the words to mean forgiveness for those sins for which the law affords none, *Apostelgesch.* 299. But not only does the connection give no support for such a division of sins, but the foregoing clause, διὰ τούτου ὑμῖν ἄφισις ἁμαρτιῶν καταγγίλλιται, rather excludes it. Wendt defends the true exegesis, especially against Overbeck, in Meyer's *Comm.*, 5th ed. 1880, p. 295, etc.

κύριον ἡμῶν Ἰησοῦν Χριστόν; xvi. 31: πίστευσον ἐπὶ τὸν κύριον Ἰησοῦν Χριστὸν, καὶ σωθήσῃ; xiii. 39: πᾶς ὁ πιστεύων δικαιοῦται; comp. xvii. 31, xxvi. 17). The antithesis to appropriation by faith is ἀπωθεῖσθαι τὸν λόγον τοῦ θεοῦ καὶ οὐκ ἄξιον κρίνειν ἑαυτὸν τῆς αἰωνίου ζωῆς, xiii. 46. It is God alone, since the whole gospel has its foundation in His decree (xx. 27), who is able to build up (ἐποικοδομῆσαι, xx. 32), and to give the inheritance (δοῦναι κληρονομίαν). Believers, gathered from Jews and Gentiles, xx. 21, xxvi. 23, comp. xxviii. 28, form one flock, a united community (ἐκκλησία τοῦ θεοῦ), in which overseers are placed by the Holy Ghost to feed the Church (xx. 28).

The declarations respecting the heathen contained in Acts xiv. and xvii. are remarkable. They consist in the following propositions : first, the living God who made and sustains the world (xiv. 15, xvii. 24, 28), who has distributed man on the face of the earth according to His will (xvii. 26), who has revealed Himself to all, even the heathen, and by fruitful seasons and a natural feeling after God has borne witness of Himself (xvii. 23, 27, etc.). Second, He will have men to worship Him in a becoming way ; He does not desire that men, who are the offspring of God, should think that the Godhead is like unto images made by themselves (xvii. 27, 29, comp. ver. 22). Third, God formerly allowed the times of ignorance to pass unpunished (xiv. 16, xvii. 30). Fourth, He now requires all men to turn aside from the vain worship of idols, to serve Him, the living God (xiv. 15, xvii. 30).

The two discourses from which we here draw, the Lycaonian one, of which we have a summary in xiv.

15, etc., and the Athenian one, which is given some-what more copiously, are distinguished by containing peculiarly Pauline ideas, particularly of Christ as the turning-point of the world's history; in other words, they contain a view of human history as divided by the appearance of Christ into a pre-Christian period, and a period of Christian revelation. The Athenian discourse in particular, linked to an inscription which the apostle read in that city, and which he makes the foundation of his speech, his text as it were, is disposed with such wisdom, that men employed in missionary work to this day consider it the invaluable type of a missionary discourse. Stanley, *Sermons and Essays*, p. 168, calls the mission speeches of the Apostle Paul " invaluable models of missionary preaching."

In looking closely at the ideas and tendency which lie at the foundation of the discourses, we observe that the glance of the apostle is directed chiefly to the next world, the *kingdom of God* which is to come, and to the approaching judgment of the world; the day of judgment is already appointed, the judge is ordained and accredited (xvii. 31). When Paul and Barnabas admonish the new converts, reminding them " that we must through much tribulation enter into the kingdom of God " (xiv. 22), the $\beta a\sigma\iota\lambda\epsilon\acute{\iota}a$ $\tau o\hat{v}$ $\theta\epsilon o\hat{v}$ is conceived as lying beyond all $\theta\lambda\acute{\iota}\psi\epsilon\iota\varsigma$, a kingdom of blessedness and splendour on which all Christian hope is concentrated. Even the designation of Christ by the hostile Jews of Thessalonica as $\H{\epsilon}\tau\epsilon\rho o\varsigma$ $\beta a\sigma\iota\lambda\epsilon\acute{v}\varsigma$ (xvii. 7), though based on a mis-apprehension, presupposes that the missionaries were in the habit of speaking a great deal of the kingdom of God. This is confirmed by the view of the judg-

ment with which the discourse at Athens concludes
(xvii. 31), which is intended to lead the minds of
the hearers to repentance.   Brief as these indications
are, they yet prove that the missionary preaching of
the apostle has an eschatological background throughout, a fact which becomes clearer still if we listen
to the declarations of this same Paul in his own
Epistles.

(B.) *The original preaching of the Apostle Paul,
according to the Thessalonian Epistles.*

We draw from this source without scruple, convinced that *both* Epistles to the Thessalonians are
genuine productions of the Apostle Paul, and the
earliest of his Epistles which have come down
to us.[1]

Something like a tone of first love is heard in these
Epistles which are addressed by the apostle to one of
the first Churches that he founded on European soil.
So full is his heart of gratitude and holy joy by

---

[1] The *first* Epistle was universally acknowledged to be the genuine
work of the apostle until the year 1845.   D. Baur was the first who
denied both to the apostle (*Paulus*, 1845, p. 480, etc., 2nd ed.
ii. 94, etc., 341, etc.).   Here he remained alone ; not one, even of
his own school, agreed with him in this view, except the Dutchman
van der Vies (not van Vries, as Hilgenfeld, *Einl. N. T.* p. 239, has
it) : *De beide brieven aan de Thess.*, Leiden 1865.   Its genuineness
has, however, found many advocates, among whom even W. Grimm,
R. A. Lipsius (*Stud. und Krit.* 1850, p. 753, etc. ; 1854, p. 905, etc.),
and Hilgenfeld, *Einl. N. T.* 1875, p. 239, etc., may be named.   Most
recently Herm. v. Soden, in a treatise contained in *Studien und
Kritiken*, 1885, pp. 263–310, has thoroughly vindicated the Pauline
origin of the First Epistle of Thessalonians on every side.   With
the *second* Epistle the case is different.   J. E. C. Schmidt, *Bibliothek
f. Kritik u. Exeg.* etc. ii. 380, etc., in 1801 first questioned the
genuineness only of ii. 1-12 ; but afterwards in 1804, *Einl. ins*

reason of their Christian state (1 Thess. i. 2, ii. 13 ; 2 Thess. i. 3, etc., ii. 13), so firm his confidence in them (2 Thess. iii. 4, etc.). But from this same fatherly, pastor-like heart proceed also all those exhortations and warnings, all those counsels contained in these Epistles, which enable us to form an idea of the Christian insight which the apostle had at that time.

The Christian state of the Thessalonians consists in their faith, their love and hope (1 Thess. i. 3). It is clear from the designation of all Christians as οἱ πιστεύοντες (1 Thess i. 7, ii. 10, 13, or οἱ πιστεύσαντες, 1 Thess. i. 10 ; 2 Thess. i. 10), and of non-Christians as μὴ πιστεύσαντες τῇ ἀληθείᾳ (2 Thess. ii. 12), that the fundamental thing in this trilogy is *faith*. Faith is the life - element of Christians, and therefore also their distinguishing characteristic (1 Thess. iii. 2, 5, etc. ; 2 Thess. i. 3) ; inner advancement takes place only when the life of faith is strengthened and its deficiencies supplied (καταρτίσαι τὰ ὑστερήματα τῆς πίστεως ὑμῶν). But what is faith in itself ? It has its origin in assent to the

---

N. T., that of the whole Epistle. He was followed by Kern, *Tüb. Zeitschrift*, 1839, ii. 145, etc. ; Baur, *Paulus* (see above) ; Hilgenfeld, *Einl.* p. 642, etc. ; van Manen, *Onderzoek naar de echtheid van Paulus tweeden brief aan de Thessalonicensen*, Utrecht 1865. Its defence was undertaken by Reiche, *Prog.* 1829 ; Pelt, *Mitarbeiten*, 1841, ii. 74, etc. ; Grimm, *vid. ante ;* Reuss, *Gesch. der h. Schriften N. T.*, 5th ed. 1874, p. 72, etc. ; Bleek-Mangold, *Einl.*, 3rd ed. 1875, p. 451, etc. The most thorough and exhaustive examination, also resulting in a verdict of genuineness, has been undertaken by T. Fr. Westrik, in his work, *De echtheid van den tweeden brief aan de Thess. op nieuw onderzocht*, Utrecht 1879. We affirm with Riggenbach (*Einl. zu 1 Thess.*, *in Lange's Bibelwerk*, § 3) that the best vindication of the authenticity of the Epistles lies in a full comprehension of their meaning.

revealed word of truth (ἐδέξασθε — λόγον θεοῦ, 1 Thess. i. 6, ii. 13 ; πίστις ἀληθείας, 2 Thess. ii. 13) ; it is not merely an assent of the understanding, but also a determination of the will in favour of the living God and His salvation (ἐπεστρέψατε πρὸς τὸν θεὸν ἀπὸ τῶν εἰδώλων, 1 Thess. i. 9 ; comp. δουλεύειν θεῷ ζῶντι καὶ ἀληθινῷ, and ver. 8, πίστις πρὸς τὸν θεόν). Faith is obedience to the gospel, 2 Thess. i. 8. Hence the apostle speaks of a " work of faith," 1 Thess. i. 3, 2 Thess. i. 10, as a continuous process comprehending in itself stedfastness and fidelity, 1 Thess. iii. 7 ; 2 Thess. i. 4. Nevertheless faith is not the product solely of human reflection and determination, but also of a powerful operation of God in the soul (θεὸς — ἐνεργεῖται ἐν ὑμῖν τοῖς πιστεύουσιν, 1 Thess. ii. 13 ; comp. 2 Thess. i. 11, πληρώσῃ — ἔργον πίστεως ἐν δυνάμει, and 1 Thess. i. 5, ἐν δυνάμει καὶ ἐν πνεύματι ἁγίῳ).

The life of faith turns our attention back to *the acts of God*, the manifestation of His love and His revelation in Jesus Christ. The one God, the true and living God (1 Thess. i. 9), has revealed Himself in His Son Jesus Christ our Lord (ὁ κύριος ἡμῶν, often repeated from the salutation of the Epistle, 1 Thess. i. 1, etc., because the idea of His dominion and kingdom fills the soul of the apostle). Jesus died for us (ὑπὲρ ἡμῶν, 1 Thess. iv. 14, v. 10) ; the Jews indeed put Him to death (1 Thess. ii. 15), but the Father raised Him from the dead (1 Thess. i. 10, iv. 14); He is now in heaven, whence we look for Him (*ibid.* ἀναμένειν τὸν υἱὸν αὐτοῦ ἐκ τῶν οὐρανῶν). God has done all this in order to deliver us by Jesus from deserved wrath impending over the world of sinners (ὀργὴ — σωτηρία placed in direct opposition to one another, 1 Thess. v. 9, comp. i. 10, ἡ ὀργὴ ἡ ἐρχομένη ; ii. 16, ἔφθάκεν ἐπ᾽ αὐτοὺς ἡ ὀργή ; v. 3, αἰφνίδιος ὄλεθρος ; comp. 2 Thess. i. 5, δικαία κρίσις ; ver. 9, δίκη ὀλέθριος ; ii. 12, ἵνα κριθῶσιν — οἱ μὴ πιστεύσαντες). The transference to a state of faith and deliverance from future judgment are due to the *election* of God from the beginning (ἐκλογή, 1 Thess. i. 4 ; 2 Thess. ii. 13, εἵλατο ὑμᾶς ἀπ᾽ ἀρχῆς, according to the reading supported by overwhelming testimony, including also the Sinaitic MS., while ἀπαρχήν, preferred by Weiss, p. 211, seems to demand a more exact definition in the genitive). The souls which He has chosen, He has also *called* to His blessed kingdom and to future glory (1 Thess. ii. 12 ; 2 Thess. i. 11, κλῆσις ; comp. 1 Thess. v. 24) ; thus God called the readers of these Epistles (ἐκάλεσεν, 2 Thess. ii. 14), when the gospel of Christ was preached to them ; but the calling is generally spoken of as a present and continuous act of God (ὁ καλῶν ὑμᾶς). The gospel of Christ (εὐαγγέλιον τοῦ Χριστοῦ, 1 Thess. iii. 2 ; 2 Thess. i. 8 ; εὐαγγέλιον τοῦ θεοῦ, 1 Thess. ii. 8 ; τὸ εὐαγγέλιον ἡμῶν, 1 Thess. i. 5 ; 2 Thess. ii. 14) is a *joyful* gospel, because it bears witness of the love of God (ἠγαπημένοι τοῦ θεοῦ, 1 Thess. i. 4 ; comp. 2 Thess. ii. 16, ἠγαπημένοι ὑπὸ κυρίου). Hence *joy* is the keynote of the Christian. The reception of the word is already, in spite of all persecution, associated with a joy that is the gift of the Holy Ghost (1 Thess. i. 6). But this rejoicing is to be constant (1 Thess. v. 16, 18). The apostle himself is filled with holy joy and gratitude for the faith of the Thessalonians (1 Thess. ii. 13, 19, 20, iii. 9) ; for this is the unmerited *grace* of God and of our Lord Jesus Christ

(2 Thess. i. 12, ii. 16); the word of man could not have brought them to their present state; it has been accomplished by the word and power of God alone (1 Thess. ii. 13, λόγος θεοῦ, ὃς καὶ ἐνεργεῖται ἐν ὑμῖν; comp. i. 5, οὐκ ἐν λόγῳ μόνον ἀλλὰ καὶ ἐν δυνάμει καὶ ἐν πνεύματι ἁγίῳ; comp. θεοδίδακτοι, iv. 9); and His Holy Spirit which He implants in the heart (διδόντα, 1 Thess. iv. 8) works continually to the same end.

This faith, which is the work of God, must prove itself in *love* to God, in active brotherly love and in a holy walk. *Sanctification* is the will of God; to this end the exhortations of the apostle were directed from the beginning (1 Thess. iii. 2, etc., 13, iv. 11, etc.; 2 Thess. iii. 10); both his Epistles have this object in view (1 Thess. iv, 1, etc., v. 4, etc., 12, etc.; 2 Thess. iii. 5–15). In particular he enforces strict avoidance of heathen immorality, excess and unchastity (πορνεία, 1 Thess. iv. 3, v. 6, etc.), enjoining, on the contrary (ver. 6), complete disinterestedness and uprightness, besides regular, honest work and honourable conduct (1 Thess. iv. 11, etc.; 2 Thess. iii. 10–12). With peculiar pleasure Paul commends the Church for their labour of love; they are taught by God to cultivate love among themselves, and they already show brotherly love to all believers in Macedonia (1 Thess. i. 3, iv. 9, etc.; 2 Thess. i. 3). Yet the apostle urges them to increase more and more in brotherly love till they become perfect (1 Thess. iv. 10, περισσεύειν μᾶλλον); beseeching them with all earnestness to employ brotherly exhortation and correction among themselves, and not to act coldly towards such as have gone astray as if they were enemies, but to appeal to their conscience, admonishing them as brethren (1 Thess. v. 14, etc. ; 2 Thess. iii. 14, etc.).

The third characteristic which, together with the work of faith and labour of love, marks the state of the Christian as one of righteousness, is the "patience of hope in our Lord Jesus Christ" (1 Thess. i. 3), that is, stedfast hope in the revelation of Him as the exalted Lord and Judge of all the world.   The great and decided prominence of hope in the second coming of Christ and the consummation of His kingdom, is characteristic of the Thessalonian Epistles, that is, of the doctrine and preaching of Paul in the beginning of his apostolic work.   His whole Christian consciousness at this stage has an eschatological direction. Next to the monotheistic feature of conversion to God, the turning aside from false gods to serve the living God, the specific Christian feeling in the heart of the believer is in 1 Thess. i. 10 (comp. ver. 9) made to consist in " waiting for the Son of God from heaven, whom He raised from the dead, even Jesus, which delivers ($\dot{\rho}\nu\acute{o}\mu\epsilon\nu o\nu$) us from the wrath to come."   Accordingly, the substance of the redemption accomplished for us and applied to us by Christ, lies in deliverance from the approaching judgment of wrath on the world of sinners, not to be realized until a future time.   According to 1 Thess. ii. 12, the calling of God, which is not a thing already finished but continuous ($\theta\epsilon o\hat{v}$ $\tau o\hat{v}$ $\kappa a\lambda o\hat{v}\nu\tau o\varsigma$ $\dot{v}\mu\hat{a}\varsigma$), culminates in the $\beta a\sigma\iota\lambda\epsilon\acute{\iota}a$ $\kappa a\grave{\iota}$ $\delta\acute{o}\xi a$ $a\dot{v}\tau o\hat{v}$, that is, in future participation in the glorious, blessed kingdom of God and in the divine glory which He will give His elect to enjoy ($\beta a\sigma\iota\lambda\epsilon\acute{\iota}a$ and $\delta\acute{o}\xi a$ do not form a hendiadys, but are two distinct though cognate conceptions.   Lünemann in Meyer's *Comm.*, 2nd ed.

p. 58).   According to v. 8, etc., Christian hope has for its object future happiness, its appropriation and personal attainment (comp. 2 Thess. i. 5).   Hence the intercessions and wishes of the apostle, as well as his present strivings for the confirmation of the faithful, are directed to the end " that their hearts may be stablished unblameable in holiness before God, at the coming of our Lord Jesus Christ with all His saints " ($\dot{\epsilon}\nu$ $\tau\hat{\eta}$ $\pi\alpha\rho\upsilon\sigma\dot{\iota}\alpha$ — $'I\eta\sigma o\hat{\upsilon}$, etc., 1 Thess. iii. 13 ; $\ddot{\alpha}\gamma\iota o\iota$ are here probably angels).   Comp. the similar wish, v. 23, whose aim also is the complete moral blamelessness of the faithful, in spirit, soul, and body, at the coming of Jesus Christ.[1]   The joy which the apostle now experiences together with his fellow-workers, on account of the Christian state of the Church in Thessalonica, the crown of praise with which in spirit he sees himself already adorned, rests on the hope that the Church will stand with honour before the Saviour at His appearance.   Hence the believers won from among them are even now His joy and crown of rejoicing (1 Thess. ii. 19, etc.).

When is the $\pi\alpha\rho\upsilon\sigma\dot{\iota}\alpha$ to begin ?   That is a question with which these Epistles are occupied more than once, especially the second.   In the first the apostle says, v. 1, etc., that the brethren in Thessalonica need no special information as to the times and seasons ($\chi\rho\dot{o}\nu\omega\nu$ — $\kappa\alpha\iota\rho\hat{\omega}\nu$) ; they know perfectly that the day of the Lord ($\dot{\eta}\mu\dot{\epsilon}\rho\alpha$ $\kappa\upsilon\rho\dot{\iota}o\upsilon$, ver. 2) comes unexpected, as a thief in the night.   But ye are the

---

[1] Weiss, p. 214, note, in opposition to Usteri, p. 415, etc., and others, contends on insufficient grounds that the threefold distinction here made in the nature of man, though popularly expressed, is not trichotomous.   One point we concede, viz. that this passage does not represent Pauline anthropology in its final development, but only the anthropological ideas of Paul in their first stage.

children of light, therefore watch, be sober, and in faith and hope always ready (vv. 4–11). It is worthy of observation that this very idea which prevails throughout the first Epistle is unmistakeably connected with a maxim of Jesus, even with an image employed by Him (comp. Matt. xxiv. 43, etc.; Luke xii. 39, including ver. 35, etc.; and Rev. iii. 3, xvi. 15). Moreover, it is the image, *together with its application.* For in the passage in Matthew the breaking in of a thief plainly refers to the worldly man walking in ungodliness; to the faithful servant the Son of man does not come as an enemy who robs him; hence the admonition to the disciples, Watch, let your loins be girt about, and your lamps burning (Luke xii. 35, etc.). We find the same application of the figure in both apocalyptic words. And we observe the very same relation in 1 Thess. v., as appears most clearly from ver. 4. The moral application of the idea that the day of the Lord comes unexpectedly, has in both cases respect to internal preparation in soberness of conduct and steady watchfulness.

In the *second Epistle* the eschatological idea takes a much wider range and has a more prominent significance than in the first. In mentioning the attacks to which believers are exposed (chap. i. 4, etc.), the apostle is led to speak of the fearful everlasting judgment which, when Jesus is revealed from heaven, shall come on those who persisted in disobedience to the joyful news of salvation. The ἀποκάλυψις of the Lord Jesus with the angels of His power in flaming fire (i. 7, etc.), is described so vividly in its terrible aspect, as the accomplishment of a judicial sentence, that the brightness and revelation of the glory of the Redeemer in His angels and in believers (ver. 10, comp. 5) is only mentioned incidentally.

The second Epistle enters more closely into the question which had already been touched upon in the first, viz. the point of time when the second advent of Christ would appear, giving the most copious information respecting it to be found throughout the two Epistles. The apostle refers to an idea which had found acceptance with many Christians in Thessalonica and had given rise to uneasiness (ii. 2); an idea which had been fostered by prophets in the Church (διὰ πνεύματος, *ibid.*), and even by alleged words of Paul himself (*ibid.*), viz. that the day of the Lord was close at hand (ὡς ὅτι ἐνέστηκεν, etc.). Paul combats this idea. He maintains that the Lord will not come until there first come a falling away (from God), and the adversary, who opposes all that is lawful and exalts himself to a god, be fully revealed; but then He will appear and destroy the antagonist of God, ii. 3–12, " For the mystery of iniquity doth already work " (ver. 7: τὸ μυστήριον ἤδη ἐνεργεῖται τῆς ἀνομίας; comp. 12: ἐνέργεια πλάνης). But it is not yet openly revealed; it is withheld by a definite obstacle (ver. 6, etc.: τὸ κατέχον, ὁ κατέχων). Only when the latter is set aside will the adversary reveal himself by Satanic working (ver. 8: ἀποκαλυφθήσεται). That too is a coming (ver. 9: παρουσία), but a Satanic one, with all power and signs and lying wonders, to the deceiving of many (vv. 9–11). The mysterious adversary is unmistakeably a *human personality* (ὁ ἄνθροπος τῆς ἁμαρτίας, ὁ υἱὸς τῆς ἀπωλείας, ver. 3; ὁ ἄνομος, ver. 8). In him sin and enmity to God reach their highest point. His appearance is a direct work of Satan. This " man of sin " is the direct counterpart of Christ, the Antichrist pure and simple, only that the name of " Antichrist " is as foreign to these as to the other Pauline epistles. It is peculiar to the Johannine Epistles alone in the New Testament.

The different stages of progress are as follows :—

First, The present period of time shows a state of confusion; the mystery of iniquity is already active and at work; powerful errors, powers of lying are in the arena, and sent by God; sin is punished with sin (ver. 11); but the full revelation of the wicked one is still withheld by the κατέχον, the κατέχων.

Second, There follows a period in which the κατέχων is removed, when the adversary will reveal himself in his character of God's opponent, even in the deification of himself, with Satanic powers of seduction, so that the end is apostasy (ἀποστασία, vv. 3, etc., 9, etc.).

Third, Jesus Christ appears in His glory, and by His advent annihilates that of the pseudo-Christ (ver. 8, etc.).[1]

[1] The obscurity in which this section is involved has its essential foundation partly in the fact that the apostle takes for granted an acquaintance with his previous verbal instruction (ver. 5, etc.), while *we* have no knowledge of it. We have neither call nor title to clear up this obscurity in an arbitrary way, and prefer to content ourselves with an honest *non liquet*. This is not the place to make a critical examination of the endlessly diverse explanations which have been given of the words of the apostle, from the Fathers down to the present day. We allude only to two of these attempts at explanation : Kern, on 2 Thess. ii. 1–12, *Tübingen Zeitschrift für Theologie*, 1839, p. 145, etc., explains the passage as referring to contemporaneous historical, especially political relations and events; the expected reappearance of Nero (= the man of sin), Vespasian (= ὁ κατέχων). This interpretation, which has been adopted by Baur, *Theol. Jahrb.* 1850, p. 150, etc., does not rest upon exposition, but

Thus between that time and the second coming of Jesus important events were still to be looked for, presupposing a considerable lapse of time. But we must not therefore at once conclude that the apostle held it to be impossible that he himself should live to see the coming of Jesus. He may perhaps have anticipated a rapid development of events. For we have in the first Epistle an utterance in which he assumes that he will be among those who live to see the advent of Christ.

Christ comes down from heaven ($\kappa\alpha\tau\alpha\beta\acute{\eta}\sigma\epsilon\tau\alpha\iota$ $\dot{\alpha}\pi'$ $o\dot{\upsilon}\rho\alpha\nu o\hat{\upsilon}$, 1 Thess. iv. 16 ; comp. i. 10). He appears *visibly* in all His glory (2 Thess. i. 7, ii. 8), accompanied by angels, through whom He exercises His power with a commanding shout ($\kappa\acute{\epsilon}\lambda\epsilon\upsilon\sigma\mu\alpha$), as Lord of the heavenly hosts, with the voice of an archangel

upon facts taken from other sources. When Weiss, *N. T. Theol.* p. 217, sees the apostasy in unbelieving Christ-opposing Judaism, the pseudo-Messias in "the man of sin," the hero of the Jewish revolution, and in the κατέχων, the Roman emperor, we cannot agree with him. It can only be conceded that the fanatical Jews, as the first opponents of Christ and His gospel, are indicated in the Thessalonian Epistles. But the Gentiles follow them in this respect (1 Thess. ii. 14). That the enmity of the Jews to Christ, carried to its highest pitch, should be called an ἀνομία (ὁ ἄνομος, 2 Thess. ii. 8), does not agree with the historical character of fanatical Judaism, which was rather a zeal for the law. The opponent κατ' ἐξοχήν was not thought of by Paul as a pseudo-Messiah, much less as "hero of the Jewish revolution" (Weiss, 220*d*); not a trace of this can be shown. Paul conceives of the ἄνομος, in fact, as an ἀντίθεος (Chrysostom), not merely a pseudo-Messiah. Jesus also does not speak of "*the* pseudo-Messiah," but of *many* false prophets, and *many* that say "I am the Messiah," Matt. xxiv. 5, 11. Moreover, ver. 4: ὑπεραιρόμενος ἐπὶ πάντα λεγόμενον θεὸν ἢ σέβασμα, alluding to Dan. xi. 36, etc., can in no case be supposed to refer to a person out of Israel. It is at least possible to find in the expression τὸ κατέχον an allusion to the Roman power and its judicial administration, but it can hardly be established that the ὁ κατέχων was meant for a Roman Cæsar in the Pauline consciousness.

and the sound of the trump of God (1 Thess. iv. 16 ;
comp. iii. 13 ; 2 Thess. i. 7), with flames of fire
(2 Thess. i. 8). Those who sleep in Christ shall
then arise ; believers who are still alive at that time
shall then be caught up in the clouds, together with
those who have been raised from the dead, to meet
the Lord in the air (to be received with honour);
and so shall they be ever with the Lord (1 Thess.
iv. 16, etc. ; comp. ver. 14 and 2 Thess. ii. 1). This
whole account, from its connection with 1 Thess.
iv. 13, is intended to allay the uneasiness which had
arisen from the idea that those Christians who were
already asleep were deprived of the happiness which
the advent of Christ brings with it, and are at a
disadvantage compared with those who live to see it.
In opposition to this anxiety he appeals to " the word of
the Lord,"[1] and tells his hearers that believers of both
kinds, those who are alive and remain and those who are
already asleep, shall be united at the coming of Christ,
and shall together partake of the same blessedness.

It is also clear from the words : $\dot{\eta}\mu\epsilon\hat{\imath}\varsigma$ $o\dot{\imath}$ $\zeta\hat{\omega}\nu\tau\epsilon\varsigma$ $o\dot{\imath}$
$\pi\epsilon\rho\iota\lambda\epsilon\iota\pi\acute{o}\mu\epsilon\nu o\iota$ $\epsilon\grave{\iota}\varsigma$ $\tau\grave{\eta}\nu$ $\pi\alpha\rho o\upsilon\sigma\acute{\iota}\alpha\nu$ $\tau o\hat{\upsilon}$ $\kappa\upsilon\rho\acute{\iota}o\upsilon$, iv. 15,
17, that the apostle reckons himself and his believing
contemporaries among those who hope still to be alive
at the second coming, and may possibly live to see it.
This thought, by no means expressed categorically as
doctrine, is quite consistent with the admission made

---

[1] The " word of the Lord " (ver. 15) cannot be understood as a
direct revelation imparted to the apostle (with Gess, *Person Christi*,
1856, p. 56 ; Alford, Lünemann), for the reason that the apostle never
employs the phrase $\lambda\acute{o}\gamma o\varsigma$ $\kappa\upsilon\rho\acute{\iota}o\upsilon$ of personal revelations. Paul more
probably refers to a positive saying of Jesus Christ which he had
received by tradition. The fact that we are unable to point this out
clearly in the canonical Gospels (Matt. xxiv. 31 comes nearest to it)
does not prove that the apostle meant something else by $\lambda\acute{o}\gamma o\varsigma$ $\kappa\upsilon\rho\acute{\iota}o\upsilon$.

by the apostle that he knows neither the times nor
the seasons, and with the assurance that the day of
the Lord will come unawares (1 Thess. v. 1, etc.).[1]

The παρουσία will bring to believers deliverance
from all persecution and trouble (ἄνεσις, refreshing
rest, 2 Thess. i. 7), and blissful enjoyment in the
possession of the completed salvation of the βασιλεία
καὶ δόξα θεοῦ (1 Thess. ii. 12).   The punishment of
the persistently obdurate is but briefly notified in the
statement that it will be a righteous judgment of
retribution (δικαία κρίσις, δίκαιον, ἐκδίκησις, 2 Thess.
i. 5, 8, 12), consisting in perdition and ruin (ἀπολ-
λύμενοι, 2 Thess. i. 9), executed in all severity by
the agency of the justice of the holy God (ὀργή,
1 Thess. i. 12, v. 9), whose love when despised is as
firm to reject as His compassionate love is strong to
save those who lay hold of it in the obedience of
faith.   But him in whom a disposition against God
is concentrated and reaches its climax, will Christ at
His coming consume with the breath of His mouth
(2 Thess. ii. 8 ; comp. Isa. xi. 4, " with the breath of
His lips ").

CHAPTER II.

THE DOCTRINE OF THE APOSTLE PAUL IN ITS MATURE
FORM.

We find this doctrine most definitely expressed in
the four Epistles to the Galatians, the Corinthians, and
the Romans, all written during the third missionary
journey of the apostle, and also in the four Epistles

---

[1] Comp. Hölemann's exposition, *Neue Bibelstudien*, 1866, p. 261,
etc.

of the Roman captivity, to the Ephesians and Philippians, to the Colossians and to Philemon;[1] while the three pastoral Epistles form a group by themselves.

In attempting to present the doctrinal system of the Gentile apostle in its coherence in such a way as to do justice to its peculiar nature, the first question that arises is, What is the kernel, the life-centre of his *Christian* feeling and doctrine? The answers are very different.[2] Even those who look for this

---

[1] To make a division here, taking the first four Epistles as the foundation of a separate presentation of Pauline doctrine (with Weiss, *N. T. Theologie*), seems to us both needless and unwarranted, since the peculiar fundamental ideas contained in these Epistles clearly appear in the Epistles of the captivity also, though less emphatically asserted and developed; while those points of view which are specially and emphatically prominent in the four later Epistles are also to be found in the four earlier. We may here fitly abstain from bringing evidence to prove that the Epistles of the captivity were written in Rome, and not in Cæsarea (Reuss and others). With respect to *authenticity*, that of the Philippian Epistle is fully recognised even by critics like Hilgenfeld (*Einl.* p. 347, etc.); while the opposition to the Epistle to Philemon on the part of Dr. Baur has met with no assent on any side. Concerning the Epistles to the Ephesians and Colossians, the question of authenticity is still far from settled; but the reasons for doubting their genuineness rest partly on a very questionable interpretation and judgment of their range of thought, partly on actual observation of facts of whose elucidation there is no reason to doubt. We nevertheless hold firmly to the genuineness of the four Epistles in question.

[2] The able Roman Catholic scholar Hug, *Einl. in das N. T.*, 2nd ed. 1821, ii. p. 300, holds the peculiarity of Paul, "that which gives the keynote to his whole activity," to consist in "the impression that had been made on him by the *idea* of a *universal* religion. D. Kuhn, *Jahrb. für Christliche Theologie u. Philosophie*, 1835, v. 1, p. 4, is right in observing that this is too abstract and modern a conception of the principle of Pauline Christianity. Schwegler, *Gesch. des nach-apost. Zeitalters*, i. 152, declares the original principle of Paul's doctrinal system to be the thought that Christianity is not merely fulfilled Judaism, but a thing historically new, a καινὴ κτίσις. But this thought, though genuinely Pauline, was certainly not the original, psychologic fundamental idea of Paul, from which the other

central point in connection with Paul's conversion have not always hit upon the right answer.[1]

We have already seen, p. 312, that the impression of the revelation of the risen Saviour which led to the conversion of Paul, consisted in the manifestation, equally humiliating and elevating, of *God's grace in Christ towards the guilt-laden sinner.* The sense of his own personal guilt and of the saving grace of God in Christ towards himself, remained the keynote of

truths were evolved. Zeller, *Theol. Jahrb.* 1845, p. 88, finds "the centre of Paul's dogmatic, the leading historical thought in the genesis of his doctrinal system, in the doctrine of *justification by faith,* without the merit of works." He has here hit the centre of Pauline dogmatic ; but we doubt his correctness as to the original first principle, because the thought is too doctrinal, and is not taken from the standpoint of direct religious consciousness. Neander, *Pflanzung u. Leitung,* 4th ed. 1847, ii. 645, etc., takes the twofold conception νόμος and δικαιοσύνη as the centre of Pauline doctrine, embracing the unity as well as the contrariety of the earlier and later standpoint. He is followed by Schmid, *Bibl. Theol. d. N. T.,* 2nd ed. 1859, p. 488, etc.; Messner, *Lehr. der App.* 1850, p. 197, etc.; Schaff, *Gesch. der Apost. Kirche,* 2nd ed. 1854, p. 629 ; and Bonifas, *Unité de l'enseignement ap.* 1866, p. 71, etc. The first makes the δικαιοσύνη the fundamental conception of Pauline doctrine, so that the whole system thus falls into two parts : the want of righteousness and its restoration.

[1] Baur, *Paulus,* 512, etc., 2nd ed. ii. 133, etc., in order to apprehend the principle of Paul's Christian consciousness in its peculiar nature, has kept to the characteristic fact of his conversion. He represents the kernel of this fact to be (according to Gal. i. 15, etc.) that God revealed to him the person of Jesus as the Son of God. Usteri, *Entwicklung des Paulinischen Lehrbegriffs,* 1832, p. 9, had already fixed upon the same starting-point, but both failed to keep to this alleged Ariadne thread, and struck into another way of the development of Pauline doctrinal ideas. Thus Baur has not, as we might have expected, discussed the doctrine of the person of Christ. His Godhead and humanity as a leading fact, but only in the last chapter of the doctrinal ideas, among " subordinate questions of dogma " (*Paulus,* 2nd ed. ii. 262, etc.). I chose the same point of departure in the first two editions of this book, but followed it consistently, dividing the doctrine of the apostle into two principal parts :

his Christian feeling. This keynote runs more or less through all the varied melody of his thoughts and the rich harmony of his doctrine. When called to be the apostle of the Gentiles, and throughout the course of his life-work, his struggles and sorrows, he recognised and preached that which had become personal certainty by means of his own experience, with ever-increasing fulness and depth, as a divine truth of universal importance.

Accordingly the doctrinal system of the apostle falls into two divisions: first, sin; then grace and salvation, each of these being subdivided into various sections.

FIRST DOCTRINAL PART.

SIN.

This lies in the self-consciousness of the apostle: I was an enemy to God, persecuting the Church of God and the disciples of Jesus. But he makes this confession in the name of many, when in Rom. v. 10

1. Christ the Son of God; 2. Sin and grace. I have, however, come to the conclusion that this way does not do justice to Pauline doctrine, and feel myself bound here to take another path. The point of departure has some resemblance to that indicated by Kuhn. He declares the permanent impression made on Paul by the vision of Christ before Damascus to be "that the righteousness of the law does not effect the salvation of man, but the grace of God in Christ is necessary to this end;" *Genetische Entwicklung des paulin. Lehrtypus, Jahrb. f. christol. Theol. u. Philosophie*, v. i. p. 4. We must remember, however, that this doctrinal proposition was first developed and defended by the apostle in contending with Judaistic errorists, while the original impression, though deeper, was far more simple.

(comp. ver. 8) he says : "We were enemies, we were sinners." He even asserts it as a fact predicable of all humanity : πάντες — ἥμαρτον καὶ ὑστεροῦνται τῆς δόξης τοῦ θεοῦ, Rom. iii. 23 ; comp. 2 Cor. v. 19 : θεὸς — κόσμον καταλλάσσων ἑαυτῷ.

FIRST PART.

SIN AND DEATH AS REGARDS INDIVIDUAL MAN.

The two confessions : "We were sinners and enemies" (Rom. v. 8, 10), and "We were the children of *wrath*, and were *dead* in our trespasses and sins" (Eph. ii. 1, 3), indicate the different truths of which we here treat.

I. SIN AND ITS ORIGIN.

That sin in its essence is *enmity against God*, is the pervading conviction of the Apostle Paul. As soon as he attained to self-knowledge by experience he became conscious that in persecuting the disciples he had manifested hostility to Jesus Himself, the Son of God; that he had been an enemy of God (1 Cor. xv. 9: ἐδίωξα τὴν ἐκκλησίαν τοῦ θεοῦ; comp. Gal. i. 13). This was the fundamental position which led him to see clearly that sin, whatever form it might assume, whatever deeds it might bring forth, was always in opposition to God, was, in fact, enmity against God (Rom. viii. 7 : φρόνημα τῆς σαρκὸς ἔχθρα εἰς θεόν; Col. i. 21 : ἐχθροὺς τῇ διανοίᾳ). On the other hand, sin leads to weakness of will (Rom. v. 6 : ὄντων ἡμῶν ἀσθενῶν), incapacity for obedience to God and for the performance of that which is good (Rom.

viii. 7 : οὐχ ὑποτάσσεται, οὐδὲ γὰρ δύναται ; comp. vii. 19).

The depth of Paul's sense of sin proves itself by the fact that he makes sin to consist not merely in *action* (ἁμαρτίαι, ἁμαρτήματα, etc.), but describes it as a mysterious power dwelling in man (ἡ οἰκοῦσα ἐν ἐμοὶ ἁμαρτία, Rom. vii. 17, 20). The way in which sins of action arise, he discovers through self-examination. The holy will of God is declared in this law with its separate commands and prohibitions (ὁ νόμος — ἐντολή), and is made binding on the conscience. Ἁμαρτία is present as a power, but slumbers, without activity or sign of life ; it does not yet appear in its true character (ἁμαρτία νεκρά, Rom. vii. 8). Only when occasion arises does it stir and come to life (ver. 9 : ἀνέζησεν). This occasion is given by the law : a command is addressed to man in such a way as to make him conscious of its application to himself (vii. 9 : ἐλθούσης τῆς ἐντολῆς). By this means the indwelling power of sin in man is stimulated to all possible desires (ver. 8), and to his deception (by the false appearance of good that is nevertheless unattainable), ver. 11 : ἐξηπάτησε ; comp. 1 Cor. xv. 56 : ἡ δύναμις τῆς ἁμαρτίας ὁ νόμος. A dualism is now awakened in the soul : the inner man related to God (the ἔσω ἄνθρωπος, Rom. vii. 22 ; comp. νοῦς, 23) has its delight in the law of God and wills the good, does not, however, attain to the thing desired, but only to the practice of evil (ver. 18, etc.).

It is not enough for the apostle, however, to show that sin is an indwelling power in man, but he goes on to answer the cognate question, What is the actual *seat* of sin in man ? where does the *source* of sin lie in each individual ?

The answer runs thus: the source of sin lies in the
σάρξ, Rom. vii. 18 : "I know that in me (that is, in
my flesh) dwelleth no good thing," comp. Gal. v. 24,
according to which the παθήματα and the ἐπιθυμίαι
belong to the flesh. What then does Paul understand
by σάρξ? This is, in fact, not easy to determine, and
is therefore liable to various interpretations. True,
there is neither doubt nor dispute as to the fact that
σάρξ, according to general usage, denotes in the first
place the flesh as a component part of the body, and
in the second place the sensuous corporeity of man.
The apostle himself, in his doctrine of sin, takes this
idea as his starting-point. Hence many expositors,
for example Hofmann, *Schriftbeweis*, i. 470, etc.;
Hahn, *Theol. d. N. T.* i. 424, etc.; O. Lorenz, *das
Lehrsystem im Römerbrief*, 1884, pp. 12, etc., 34, etc.,
have maintained that, according to the doctrine of
the Apostle Paul, σάρξ is neither more nor less
than the corporeal nature of man, or sensuousness.
Holsten,[1] in his attempt to prove that, according to
Paul's doctrine, σάρξ is the living, material substance
of the σῶμα, and πνεῦμα, on the other hand, its
immaterial substance, has shown the most acuteness,
decision, and consistency. The dualism of these
substances, a dualism of spirit and matter, by which
the Jewish - Hellenistic world - view was already
dominated, forms the animating soul of Pauline
theology (p. 446, etc.). In Paul's view, σάρξ is an
expression of the idea of the finite (p. 393). Σάρξ,
as the sensuousness of the living, material substance

---

[1] *Die Bedeutung des Wortes σάρξ im Lehrbegriffe des Paulus*,
1855. This treatise has been enlarged and reprinted in his book,
Zum Ev. des Paulus und des Petrus, 1868, pp. 365, etc. We quote
from the last edition.

in man, is at the same time the evil; and all evil has in his view its principle only in the σάρξ (p. 396, comp. p. 405). Hence Holsten does not hesitate to assert that, in Paul's opinion, sin is *necessary*, man " determines to sin " (p. 403, etc.) ; yet there is in human nature, according to the apostle's doctrine, nothing like and allied to the essence of God (to the πνεῦμα) (p. 392). According to this view, the Pauline doctrine of sin is formed in a dualistic way, just as the error of a Marcion or of Manichæism implies a physical necessity of sinning, and misapprehends man's affinity and likeness to God. It is no wonder that Holsten's representation has met with opposition even from Baur and Pfleiderer (*Paulinismus*, p. 62, etc.), not to speak of interpreters of a different school. The question is, whether that representation does justice to the utterances of the apostle himself. This we decidedly deny._ Paul cannot possibly understand σάρξ as something *merely* material and corporeal, for among the works of the flesh (Gal. v. 19, etc.), together with those sins which certainly spring from sensuousness, viz. unchastity, excess, etc., he enumerates such also as do not by any means arise exclusively from sensuous impulses, *e.g.* ἔχθραι, ἔρις, ζῆλος, διχοστασίαι, αἱρέσεις. This passage gains more light from 1 Cor. iii. 3, where the apostle thus reproaches the Corinthian Christians: " ye are yet carnal (σάρκινοι) ! for whereas there is among you envying and strife and divisions, are ye not carnal, and walk as men (κατὰ ἄνθρωπον)?" He denounces the party spirit of the Corinthians (ver. 5) though it had not arisen from sensuous motives, but rather belonged to a moral, intellectual department, and nevertheless reproaches them, " ye are yet σάρκινοι!" And this although believers, as such, are πνευματικοί!¹ The kindred thought contained in Col. ii. 18, comp. ver. 23, is decisive. Paul here utters a warning against people who, after a form of piety peculiar to themselves, have attained to a striving after spirituality, an ascetic severity, in which they ruthlessly neglect the body (ἀφειδία σώματος, ver. 23); and yet the apostle attributes their error to a self-exaltation produced by the fleshly mind (ver. 18 : φυσιούμενος ὑπὸ τοῦ νοὸς τῆς σαρκὸς αὐτοῦ). Here the characteristic mark of sensuousness, of the living, material substance, is clearly subordinate in the idea of the σάρξ; while the mark of selfishness is put prominently forward. Add to this that in Rom. viii. 6 a φρόνημα is ascribed to the σάρξ, a mode of thinking and moral direction, therefore something spiritual, from which it follows that σάρξ is a selfish, ungodly manner of thought and aim which gives the reins to sensuousness, and allows the members of the body to become a means of enticement to sin, instruments of the flesh (Rom. vi. 19 : μέλη — δοῦλα τῇ ἀκαθαρσίᾳ, etc.), but does not by any means call into activity all that is contained in the living, material substance. And again, when the apostle in an exhortation to holiness (2 Cor. vii. 1) insists on the duty of " cleansing ourselves from all filthiness of the flesh and spirit," the flesh is here spoken of as exposed to possible pollution, and consequently is not regarded as absolutely sinful in itself.²

¹ Holsten's remark, *Evangelium des Paulus*, 1880, i. 270**, " Actuality and dogmatic postulate do not here agree," is an indirect confession that this passage does not consist with his theory of the Pauline conception of σάρξ.

² Weiss forcibly reminds us, *N. T. Theologie*, p. 243, note 2, that this utterance of Paul is opposed to Holsten's view of the σάρξ, since

II. Sin and Death.

The fruit of a life of sin, its end, is death (Rom. vi. 21, vii. 5, viii. 13). The apostle puts it concisely thus: τὰ ὀψώνια τῆς ἁμαρτίας θάνατος. Death is the well-earned, legitimate wages of sin. The thought here starts from sin and goes on to death. In 1 Cor. xv. 56, on the other hand, Paul starts from death and comes back to sin, τὸ κέντρον τοῦ θανάτου ἡ ἁμαρτία, that is, the property of sin which actually wounds and destroys (the deadly sting of the scorpion, as it were) is sin; this it is which leads to fear of death in the face of well-deserved punishment, of divine wrath. Reference is here made in the first place to corporeal death. But this cannot be exclusively meant, as is proved by the avowal in Rom. vii. 9: "Sin revived (by the commandment) and I died." Consequently Paul understands death as including also other evils of the body and soul, espe-

he takes Holsten's attack on the integrity of the passage (*Zum Ev. des Paulus und Petrus*, p. 387) as an involuntary admission of the fact. Lorenz indeed acknowledges that flesh and sinfulness are not synonymous (*ante*, p. 13), that a necessity of sinning does not exist, p. 12; yet in pp. 19 and 32 he imputes to the apostle the view that "the material substance in man is already *by nature* the seat of sin." But according to the teaching of the apostle this is the case not by virtue of the nature implanted in man at his creation, but rather as the result of human conduct and guilt. According to Rom. v. 12, sin entered into the world by *one* man. Moreover, if the apostle held the material substance of man to be by nature the seat of sin, he would have given a very different explanation of the power of sin in the Gentile world from that contained in Rom. i. 18, 21, etc.; where he traces it to the fact that men, although possessing a certain knowledge of God, did not render Him due honour and gratitude. This guilty omission God justly punished, by abandoning the heathen to their unclean desires. Hence these fleshly lusts were not the *Prius*, and godlessness the *Posterius*.

cially the oppressive sense of guilt, having fallen
under the judgment of God (Rom. iii. 19 : ὑπόδικος τῷ
θεῷ), the consciousness of God's wrath, that is, of His
disfavour and right to punish, the strife of accusing
and excusing thoughts (Rom. ii. 15), together with
abandonment to sin as a despotic power (Rom. vii. 14:
πεπραμένος ὑπὸ τὴν ἁμαρτίαν; comp. ver. 23 :
αἰχμαλωτίζοντά με τῷ νόμῳ τῆς ἁμαρτίας; vi. 20 :
δοῦλοι τῆς ἁμαρτίας; viii. 15 : πνεῦμα δουλείας εἰς
φόβον). In the conception of death, the physical
mark of corporeal death and misery must always
stand side by side with its intellectual and moral sign ;
for a life of sin leads to such a state of misery and
death, that the groan breaks forth from the oppressed
heart: "O wretched man that I am ! who shall deliver
me from the body of this death?" (Rom. vii. 24).
The climax of the misery consists in the fact that the
body has become a σῶμα τοῦ θανάτου, a prey to
death, has fallen a victim to its power even before
actual dissolution. It is characteristic of the apostle
that he perceives the unity of life complete in itself,
and points out the union of the spiritual and corporeal
by an expression that corresponds to the actual, a
thorough grasp, as it were. Of this nature is the
circumstance that Paul fixes his eye upon sensuousness as a main starting-point and chief instrument of
sin, consequently sets forth the dominion of sin where
still unbroken as active in the body, sin reigning in
the body, βασιλεύει ἐν τῷ σώματι, Rom. vi. 12, viz.
as queen, whose members are subject to it (τὰ μέλη
ὑμῶν ὅπλα ἀδικίας τῇ ἁμαρτίᾳ). The apostle can
find unity even where, on the first view, there is wide
diversity. A guilty neglect of the honour of God in
the end brings its own punishment, even in the body,

through the shameful dishonouring by men of their own bodies, an offence which springs in the first instance from the disgraceful lusts of the heart (Rom. i. 24). Like sin, death also in the Pauline view must be conceived of as both mental and corporeal. Hence the cry of misery, "Who shall deliver me from the body of this death?" uttered in the deepest anguish of soul.

Thus the life of sin in the individual ends with an utter sense of misery, a longing for deliverance, an asking: $\tau i \varsigma \mu \epsilon \rho \dot{\upsilon} \sigma \epsilon \tau a \iota$; This seeking and longing is not consciously and immediately directed to God, but is rather a groping in the dark, a yearning inquiry if perchance a saviour may be found?

SECOND PART.

SIN AND DEATH IN GENERAL, AND THE REVELATION OF GOD IN THE PRE-CHRISTIAN WORLD.

I. SIN AND DEATH IN THE WORLD.

With his comprehensive glance and large heart the apostle looks at humanity as a whole, and perceives it to be a world characterized by sin, and therefore fallen under the sentence of God; Rom. iii. 19: $\pi \hat{a} \varsigma \ \dot{o} \ \kappa \acute{o} \sigma \mu o \varsigma \ \dot{\upsilon} \pi \acute{o} \delta \iota \kappa o \varsigma \ \tau \hat{\omega} \ \theta \epsilon \hat{\omega}$. Every individual has sinned (Rom. v. 12: $\pi \acute{a} \nu \tau \epsilon \varsigma \ \ddot{\eta} \mu a \rho \tau o \nu$; comp. iii. 23), all have sinned and come short of the glory which God possesses and can bestow ($\dot{\upsilon} \sigma \tau \epsilon \rho o \hat{\upsilon} \nu \tau a \iota \ \tau \hat{\eta} \varsigma \ \delta \acute{o} \xi \eta \varsigma \ \tau o \hat{\upsilon} \ \theta \epsilon o \hat{\upsilon}$), according to van Hengel, *Interpretatio*, ep. 1854, p. 321, etc. Not only have all committed acts of sin, but all are likewise subject to the *power* of sin, as slaves to their masters, πάντες ὑφ' ἁμαρτίαν εἶναι (Rom. iii. 9). These, according to the apostle, are facts of experience. But he also finds them revealed and confirmed by the word of God, in proof of which in Rom. iii. 10–18 he appeals to a number of Old Testament sayings in the Psalms and prophets, ver. 10, καθὼς γέγραπται, etc. According to ver. 10, all these divine utterances go to prove that no man, no not one, is *righteous*. In Gal. iii. 22 he puts it thus: "The Scripture hath concluded all" (τὰ πάντα), that is, humanity with the exception of Christ, under sin (συνέκλεισε). Elsewhere the apostle treats this fact of experience, which is attested by the Scripture, in the light of a divine decree whose final aim is mercy and salvation for all (Rom. xi. 32: συνέκλεισεν ὁ θεὸς τοὺς πάντας εἰς ἀπείθειαν, ἵνα τοὺς πάντας ἐλεήσῃ).

The call to be an apostle of the Gentiles, and on the other side the self-righteousness of the Pharisees by which he himself had formerly been characterized, and again the composition of the Churches founded by him, consisting of Jewish and Gentile Christians, led the apostle to establish universal sinfulness with reference both to Jews and Gentiles. He did this by laying down the truth, οὔκ ἐστι διαστολή (Rom. iii. 22), *i.e.* there is no essential difference between Jews and Gentiles in respect to sinfulness.

That the Gentiles are sinners appeared to the Israelites as a self-evident truth. This axiom is presupposed by Paul when he expresses himself, addressing Peter in Gal. ii. 15: "We who are Jews by nature (birth) and not sinners of the Gentiles."

He here speaks from his Israelitish consciousness, but without the false self-confidence of a Jew. He constantly appropriates to himself the verdict, the heathen are certainly sinners, not only as being aliens from the commonwealth of Israel, but also strangers from the covenant *of God* which contained the promise, and ἄθεοι ἐν τῷ κόσμῳ, without God, without knowledge of the only true God or fellowship with Him (Eph. ii. 12).

Not only the heathen, however, but the *Jews* also are sinners. The Jew has doubtless the revelation of God, His covenants and His law. But he has transgressed the law, and by his transgressions has incurred the righteous punishment of God (Rom. ii. 5). That the Jews also are sinners, all without exception, the apostle proves from their own law, on which they pride themselves (Rom. iii. 10–18, 19).

Here there seems to be a point of dissimilarity, inasmuch as the Jew has fallen under the sentence of God because he has transgressed the law which he had and knew, while the Gentile was ignorant of the law. But in Rom. i. 20, Paul has already declared that the heathen are without excuse (ἀναπολόγητοι), inasmuch as they have not been entirely deprived of the most necessary knowledge of God and of His holy will. He ascribes to them a knowledge of the δικαίωμα τοῦ θεοῦ (i. 32), of the divine decree, *i.e.* a consciousness of the moral government of the world and of God's punitive justice. Thus the difference between Israel, possessed of the revelation and law of God, and the Gentile world having neither, is so far adjusted regarding moral responsibility and guilt as to justify the conclusion, οὔκ ἐστι διαστολή (Rom. iii. 22; comp. ii. 12). We therefore find the apostle having two maxims, according to which Jew and Gentile stand on the same moral basis.

(*a*) Jews and Gentiles are alike sinners.

(*b*) Gentiles as well as Jews have fallen under the divine judgment.

But the apostle does not stop with this experimental fact which he proves by Old Testament Scripture. Taking humanity as a living, abstract unity, he derives the actual sinfulness of all, together with its consequence and punishment, universal mortality, from *one* beginning, and appealing to the revelation of the Old Testament, goes back to the first sin of the first man, to Adam's fall. True, there is only one passage (Rom. v. 12, etc.) in which this argument is fully set forth, but 1 Cor. xv. 21, etc., and 2 Cor. xi. 3, also refer with unmistakeable clearness, though briefly, to the sin of Adam, as the starting-point of the death (and sin) of all mankind (comp. Holsten, *Ev. des Paulus*, p. 418, note ***). Hence we are the more justified in regarding the proof of this connection an essential part of the Pauline doctrine as a whole, and are not authorized to treat it as a position accidentally borrowed from the Old Testament, having subordinate significance for Paul. On the contrary, its elaboration in the development of doctrine in the Epistle to the Romans is so instructive and so weighty, that we must attribute very great importance to it.

The leading thought of the whole section (Rom. v. 12–21) is this, the δικαιοσύνη θεοῦ destined for all mankind, together with its fruit, eternal life, is due to the one man Jesus Christ and His obedience, His grace; just as sin, which reigns in all men, and its effect death, entered the world by one man, Adam (ver. 14), and was transmitted to all.

We here limit ourselves to the latter, viz. the teaching of the apostle respecting sin and death, their origin and progress in humanity. The context points clearly to (1) the connection between *sin* and *death*: sin the cause, death the effect (ver. 12: διὰ τῆς ἁμαρτίας ὁ θάνατος, etc.; ver. 15: τῷ παραπτώματι —ἀπέθανον; comp. vv. 17, 21: ἐβασίλευσεν ἡ ἁμαρτία ἐν τῷ θανάτῳ). But this is not the main thing with the apostle. The emphasis lies (2) on the *connection* between the *one* and *all* (the many, ver. 15: οἱ πολλοί), as regards *sin* and *death*. This connection consists not merely in the distinction of time, Adam being the first sinner, and the first who became subject to death, while the rest of mankind sinned and died afterward. But the point is, that the sin of that one became the *cause* and *source* of the sin and death of all (ver. 19: διὰ τῆς παρακοῆς τοῦ ἑνὸς ἀνθρώπου ἁμαρτωλοὶ κατεστάθησαν οἱ πολλοί; comp. ver. 15), *i.e.* they were made sinners by the disobedience of Adam, so that they stand as sinners before the eye of God.

The further question follows, wherein consists the dependence of the sinfulness and death of all on the sin of one?

The apostle answers:

First, in the fact that by one man sin and death first entered the world;

And again, in the fact that sin and death were transmitted from one to all.

With respect to the former, the following questions present themselves:—(*a*) Was *the first man*, in Paul's opinion, *without sin before the fall* or not? On the basis of Schleiermacher's hypothesis, Usteri, *paulin. Lehrbegriff*, 4th ed. p. 27, in Rom. v. 12, etc., finds that "the sinfulness of human nature appeared in the sinfulness of Adam, which was first revealed as actual, conscious sin, in the transgression of God's command." So, too, Baur, *Paulus*, 2nd ed. ii. 268; *N. T. Theologie*, 191, comp. 138; and Holsten, *Zum Ev. des Paulus und Petrus*, p. 418, comp. p. 413, taking the pantheistic standpoint of Hegel, maintain that the apostle knows nothing of a fall as the first cause of original sin, but that in his view it was the unholiness inherent in human nature, the unconscious tendency to sin, "the principle of sin" (Baur) that entered the visible world as a reality. According to this explanation, the chief thing, namely, the alleged unholiness and sinful tendency of Adam, already present as an unconscious predisposition, must be put into the words of the apostle and read between the lines. In fact, the conception is absolutely excluded by the letter and spirit of what Paul says, as we maintain with Weiss, *N. T. Theol.* p. 237, and Rich. Schmidt, *paulin. Christologie*, p. 43. As ἁμαρτία in v. 12 does not denote a single act of sin, but sin as a power, as a principle (which we take it to be, with Pfleiderer, *Paulinismus*, p. 38), εἰσέρχεσθαι εἰς τὸν κόσμον can mean nothing else than the first entrance into the world of a power which did not exist unconsciously and merely in germ, but had no existence at all. Again, the Old Testament basis of the Pauline doctrine of creation and fall, upon which the section in question rests, and to which other passages refer, *e.g.* 1 Cor. xv. 21, 2 Cor. xi. 3, excludes the idea that an original sinfulness of man lies at the foundation of the first act of sin. In Eph. iv. 24 the apostle speaks of the new man, ὁ κατὰ θεὸν κτισθεὶς ἐν δικαιοσύνῃ καὶ ὁσιότητι τῆς ἀληθείας, which obviously implies that a look is thrown back from the new creation to the first, *i.e.* it is presupposed that the first man also was created sinless after the image of God.

(*b*) Does the *nature* of man experience a *moral change* by the entrance of sin? Yes, inasmuch as man was formerly without sin, and is now infected with it. Therefore the condition of man has become different in a moral aspect. No, inasmuch as the *nature* of man remains morally the same, being personal, and endowed with freedom of will afterwards as before. This is not at variance with the argument contained in 1 Cor. xv. 45–49, as Reuss asserts (*Hist. de la théol. chrét. au siècle ap.* ii. 119). For the apostle there treats not of sin and sinlessness, but solely of corporeity; he contrasts Jesus Christ, who is πνεῦμα ζωοποιοῦν, πνευματικός, ἐπουράνιος, as the "last Adam," with the first man, who is χοϊκός, ψυχικός, ψυχῇ ζῶσα (comp. Gen. ii. 7: עָפָר, נֶפֶשׁ חַיָּה). The sinful nature is not identical with the body formed from the dust of the earth or the psychical body, and is not associated with them.

(*c*) Was the first man before the fall *immortal* or not? No, inasmuch as Paul does not expressly ascribe immortality to the first man as a positive conception, an essentially moral possession which is not a purely natural quality. Yes, inasmuch as death in its present actual form would not have entered without sin, for it is the fruit and wages of sin (Rom. vi. 23; διὰ τῆς ἁμαρτίας ὁ θάνατος, v. 12); sin is the deadly sting, by virtue of which death is what it is (κέντρον, 1 Cor. xv. 56).

The *second* question is this: What is meant in the section by the *transmission* of sin and death *from one to all?* It must be conceded that the apostle gives no definite account of the *manner* of this operation; for to him it is a question of religious truth for heart and conscience, not of the satisfaction of a scientific need, the solution of a problem of research. It is, however, clear from the progress of the section that the apostle affirms an historical and causal connection between the first sin of the first man on the one hand, and the sin and death of all mankind on the other. The context, by its association of the whole human race and its tendency to sin with the *one* progenitor and originator of it, certainly proves that nothing but affinity by nature and transmission by generation as the ladder for sin and death, can be meant (Weiss, *N. T. Theologie*, p. 239, etc.; Beck, *Römerbrief*, 1884, p. 412, etc.).

We have no indication, much less any statement to justify the position that Paul intended by the connection to convey the meaning that in Adam all have sinned (Meyer and Philippi, *Comm.*), always assuming that the Catholic exposition resting on the Vulgate (ἐφ' ᾧ, *in quo*, v. 12) cannot be received. Besides, the Scriptures clearly say (as Beck, *ante*, p. 414, proves), by one came sin; and in 1 Cor. xv. 22 in Adam all *died*, but never, in him all *have sinned*. Yet Pfleiderer's exposition (*Paulinismus*, p. 39, etc.) of the (impersonal) sin of humanity as a whole, which was bound up in the sin of one, leads to the latter hypothesis.—The much-disputed ἐφ' ᾧ πάντες ἥμαρτον, ver. 12, cannot with Hofmann be explained on the assumption that ᾧ as a simple relative refers to θάνατος, which word, however, does not immediately precede it; nor even with Beck, iv. 15, as having reference to the *clause* which goes before = on which (alleged) ground all have sinned, but it is to be taken as in 2 Cor. v. 4 = ἐπὶ τούτῳ ὅτι, for this reason, that all have sinned. The apostle considers this sinning of all, in the spirit of the whole discussion, v. 12–21, not as a thing absolutely autonomous, independent of the sin of the one, but as something induced by the entrance of sin as a power into the world; comp. Weiss, p. 238, note. It is by no means the evil example of the ancestor *alone* (Lorenz, *Lehrsystem*, pp. 45, etc., 51), by which the apostle explains the sin of posterity.

The apostle, however, not only looks at the sin of the individual in connection with the sinful tendency of the human race, but also at the collective sin of humanity in connection with the invisible *kingdom of darkness*. This kingdom of wickedness (πονηρίας, Eph. vi. 12) is peopled by δαιμόνια, 1 Cor. x. 20, and is variously divided into ἀρχαί, ἐξουσίαι, Eph. vi. 12; its ruler is Satan (2 Cor. ii. 11; comp. xii. 7), ὁ διάβολος (Eph. vi. 11), ὁ πονηρός (ver. 16), βελίαλ (2 Cor. vi. 15). Where Paul is incidentally led to speak of Satan and his pernicious power, he declares that as the god of this world he blinds the mind, that unbelievers are subject to his dominion, and are shut out from the light of the truth in Christ (2 Cor. iv. 4; comp. Eph. vi. 12: οἱ κοσμοκράτορες τοῦ σκότους τούτου). But he leads even believers into temptation, going to work with much cunning and disguise in order to ensnare souls (μεθοδεῖαι τοῦ διαβόλου, Eph. vi. 11; μετασχηματίζεται εἰς ἄγγελον φωτός, 2 Cor. xi. 14, etc.). It is true that Christ has overcome and disarmed these unholy powers by His

atoning death (Col. ii. 13); yet there is need of a
constant struggle against them (Eph. vi. 12).

Notwithstanding his keen insight into the heart and
the world, with their deep night-side, Paul is still far
from teaching that mankind and the world are evil
through and through, and absolutely corrupt. Powerful as sin and death are in the world, not only
has the grace that appeared in Christ become much
more powerful (Rom. v. 20), but even in the period
of the first Adam the living God approached mankind, seeking them with His revelation, and paving
the way for salvation.

II. The Revelation of God in the pre-Christian Age, in the Gentile World and in Israel.

The apostle looks at everything with a glance that
is all-comprehensive ; he does not care to examine an
isolated phenomenon, but goes from the present back to
the past, looking also to the future, and always with
a mind opened by a never-to-be-forgotten heart-
experience to the influence of the supreme God,
whose purpose it is to accomplish salvation by His
dear Son Jesus Christ. Paul, the apostle of the
Gentiles, looks on the vast world of nations outside
Israel not simply as a mass fallen under the power
of sin and death, but also as God's creatures, endowed
with reason and subject to God's holy guidance.
Seeing the Gentiles, as sinners, overtaken by the
wrath of God, he asks himself, how is this possible ?
How can this punitive justice be reconciled with the
fact that the Gentiles have not the revelation possessed by Israel—are without the law ? His answer
is : the Gentiles are not without a certain knowledge

of the truth, a form of divine revelation. Paul treats of this in Rom. i. 18–31, ii. 15, etc.

He even recognizes a double revelation of God to the heathen, never characterizing it as an *ἀποκαλύπτειν* however, but only as a *φανεροῦν* (Rom. i. 19). The universal revelation, imparted even to the Gentiles, lies partly in the visible creation and partly in the conscience. God Himself has revealed to man that which can be apprehended of His nature (ver. 19 : *τὸ γνωστὸν τοῦ θεοῦ*), namely, His eternal power and Godhead (*θειότης*, so that the heathen have an intuition, though vague and dark, of the Godhead). This knowledge reaches them by means of the visible creation, since by the aid of reflection (*νοούμενα καθορᾶται*) they may perceive the invisible presence and power of God in His works (*ποιήματα*), His creatures, His providential rule, and particularly in His benefits (comp. Acts xiv. 15–17). Hence a certain knowledge of God is not lacking even to the heathen ; from which it follows that they are able, yea, bound by duty, to reverence God and to serve Him with gratitude and obedience (ver. 21). But in this they failed, which failure was sin, and brought its own punishment in the fact that their minds became more and more involved in vain imaginings and in a darkening of the truth (*ἐματαιώθησαν, ἐσκοτίσθη—ἡ καρδία*, ver. 21). Hence not only the foolish worship of pictures and images, but also the deeper sinking of the heathen world into godlessness and iniquity, into a shameful life of sin and vice, conformably to the divine decree according to which sin is punished by sin (Rom. i. 21–31). The terrible description of the pool of moral corruption here given by Paul is only confirmed by the testimony of Roman authors, whether philosophic thinkers like Seneca, or satirists like Juvenal.

With respect to heathen polytheism, Paul is only looking at the matter from a different point of view when he states that idolatry is in fact the worship of evil spirits (1 Cor. x. 20, etc.), and belongs to the kingdom of Satan.

In short, the heathen are responsible for their error, and may justly expect punishment, the more so since God reveals Himself and His holy will to the Gentiles not only in creation and nature, but also in their *conscience.*

The apostle testifies this in the weighty statement contained in Rom. ii. 14–16 : the Gentiles have not indeed a positive law, the Mosaic νόμος, but are nevertheless not quite without a divine law : they are a law to themselves ; it is written in their hearts, that they may do what the law commands, for their moral consciousness (συνείδησις) bears them witness, whether they do right or wrong, their own thoughts as it were either accusing or else excusing one another.[1] Without doubt they are cognizant of the righteous law of God, that those who commit sin are worthy of death (i. 32).

---

[1] Lorenz, *Lehrsystem,* p. 24, etc., thinks that the ἴθη here are Gentile *Christians,* as Ambrosiaster had already done. He supposes that the apostle would have completely contradicted himself had he asserted that there were pre-Christian heathen who fulfilled the law and would have attained to that legal righteousness which he refuses to all, Gentiles and Jews. But the apostle does not by any means say that a Gentile ever fulfilled *the* law and procured righteousness by it ; he merely says that there are heathen who did (in some respects) that which God's will ("the law") requires. There is not a word to intimate that the apostle speaks of heathen converted to Christ, which is, to use van Hengel's words, *ab hac omni disputatione alienissimum.*

But the people of Israel, according to Paul, stand in a very different relation to God, and God to them ; for to them the *law* (properly speaking) is given ($\dot{\eta}$ $\nu o\mu o\theta\epsilon\sigma i a$, besides a covenant of God with the nation, Rom. ix. 4). The law contains the revelation of God ($\tau\grave{a}$ $\lambda\acute{o}\gamma\iota a$ $\tau o\hat{v}$ $\theta\epsilon o\hat{v}$, Rom. iii. 2 ; $\acute{o}$ $\nu\acute{o}\mu o\varsigma$ $\tau o\hat{v}$ $\theta\epsilon o\hat{v}$, Rom. vii. 22, comp. ver. 25), made known by Moses as mediator between God and the people, $\acute{\epsilon}\nu$ $\chi\epsilon\iota\rho\grave{\iota}$ $\mu\epsilon\sigma i\tau o\upsilon$, Gal. iii. 19, comp. 2 Cor. iii. 7, 13, 15, engraved in writing on tables of stone ; it expresses the holy will of God and emanates from His Spirit ($\mathring{a}\gamma\iota o\varsigma,\acute{\epsilon}\nu\tau o\lambda\grave{\eta}$ $\mathring{a}\gamma i a$, Rom. vii. 12; $\pi\nu\epsilon\upsilon\mu a\tau\iota\kappa\acute{o}\varsigma$, ver. 14). The law is ordained to give life, true life ($\dot{\eta}$ $\acute{\epsilon}\nu\tau o\lambda\grave{\eta}$ $\dot{\eta}$ $\epsilon\grave{\iota}\varsigma$ $\zeta\omega\acute{\eta}\nu$, Rom. vii. 10). But whether it actually begets and secures life and blessed peace is quite another question. The apostle denies this most emphatically, declaring that the possession of the law, viz. to hear, know, and follow it, gives no advantage, no honour in the sight of God, unless honestly and steadily exemplified in moral behaviour (Rom. ii. 13, 17, etc. ; comp. ver. 3).

But where is this to be found ? Jews as well as Greeks (Gentiles) are subject to the dominion of sin, according to the Scripture and even the law itself (Rom. iii. 9–19), for the utterances contained in the Psalms and the prophets are simply regarded as God's word in the law. But the apostle here refers not merely to persons who are morally corrupt and vicious. He lays down the axiom unconditionally, that no man can be justified before God by the works of the law ; $\acute{\epsilon}\xi$ $\acute{\epsilon}\rho\gamma\omega\nu$ $\nu\acute{o}\mu o\upsilon$ $o\grave{\upsilon}$ $\delta\iota\kappa a\iota\omega\theta\acute{\eta}\sigma\epsilon\tau a\iota$ $\pi\hat{a}\sigma a$ $\sigma\acute{a}\rho\xi$, Rom. iii. 20; comp. Gal. ii. 16, iii. 11 ; Eph. ii. 9. His glance is fixed chiefly on the Mosaic law and its fulfilment. His conception of $\nu\acute{o}\mu o\varsigma$ is, however, so far-reaching that it comprehends also the will of God revealing itself in the conscience.

The reason why righteousness is unattainable by the works of the law does not lie in the law itself, which is the revelation of the holy God who is spirit (see *ante*: νόμος ἅγιος, πνευματικός, ὁ νόμος τοῦ θεοῦ). The ground of the impossibility of a δικαιοσύνη ἐξ ἔργων νόμου lies rather in the σάρξ alone, Rom. viii. 3 : ὁ νόμος ἠσθένει διὰ τῆς σαρκός, *i.e.* because the sinfulness, the selfish, ungodly tendency of mind and purpose (which makes sensuousness and the members of the body its instruments) dwells in man, hinders good and produces evil, so that the law cannot effect the purpose for which it was designed. It cannot give life, Gal. iii. 21 : ὁ νόμος οὐ δύναται ζωοποιῆσαι. Instead of giving life, the law on the contrary serves to bring about a curse, condemnation, and death. When the law comes to man, it awakens sin which slumbered in him, and imparts to it for the first time life, force, and activity (Rom. vii. 7–11 ; comp. iii. 20 : διὰ νόμου ἐπίγνωσις ἁμαρτίας; iv. 15 ; 1 Cor. xv. 56 : ἡ δύναμις τῆς ἁμαρτίας ὁ νόμος). Hence those who are of the works of the law are under the curse (Gal. iii. 10). The letter (of the law) killeth (2 Cor. iii. 6). The service of Moses is a διακονία θανάτου, κατακρίσεως, vv. 7, 9. If we ask how it can be reconciled with the wisdom of God that the law which was given for life serves on the contrary as an incitement to sin and leads to death, the apostle answers, the law was only intended as a schoolmaster to lead us to Christ, παιδαγωγὸς εἰς Χριστόν, Gal. iii. 24. The contrast between Paul's view of the Mosaic law before and after his conversion is remarkable. As

Saul, the law was to him the absolutely highest, eternally valid revelation of God, the only way to δικαιοσύνη before God, to life and blessedness. After his conversion, in consequence of many experiences made in his apostolic calling in addition to mature reflection on the ways of God, his salvation and purposes, though still regarding the law as God's revelation, he assigns to it a *subordinate* place in the plan of salvation, no longer looks upon it as an object in itself, but as the means to a higher object (Christ and His redemption); he no longer attributes to the Mosaic law an eternal significance, but only an importance that is transient and temporary (Gal. iii. 19: ὁ νόμος ... προσετέθη ἄχρις οὗ ἔλθῃ τὸ σπέρμα, etc.; Rom. v. 20: νόμος — παρεισῆλθε); in Gal. iv. 3, 9, etc., he even places the law in the same rank with the στοιχεῖα τοῦ κόσμου, viz. the elements and elementary powers of the visible creation, which in ver. 9 are called " weak and beggarly," because they cannot give man what he seeks.[1]　The law was later than the promise that was given to Abraham, and was a means for the fulfilment of that promise.　Hence it forms only an episode in the course of revelation, an intermediate

---

[1] We take στοιχεῖα in an objective, physical sense, with Bengel, Schneckenburger, Holsten, *Ev. des Paulus und Petrus*, p. 323, *Ev. des Paulus*, p. 168, etc., and not with Calvin, de Wette, Wieseler, Weiss, *N. T. Theol.* p. 266, in a subjective, psychological sense, *rudimenta institutionis, rudim. cultus divini*, elementary wisdom or elementary beginnings of religion.　In this consideration we are influenced by ver. 10: ἡμέρας, μῆνας, — ἐνιαυτούς.　The heathen worshipped the powers of nature and even the heavenly bodies as gods; Israel took the heavenly bodies, the sun and moon, at least as a sign by which to regulate their celebration of sabbaths, new moons, and jubilee-years, and in so far were slavishly subject to them (the στρατηρεῖσθαι, ver. 10; a πάλιν δουλεύειν, ver. 9).　Κόσμος especially

step in the history of salvation, having its proximate
aim in sin, its final aim in grace. The law therefore
serves in the first place to the ripening, growth, and
consummation of sin, Gal. iii. 19 : τῶν παραβάσεων
χάριν προσετέθη, i.e. that by its means the sin already
present should become conscious, its guilt be felt, and
its power enhanced; but only in order that sin might
finally be overcome by grace (comp. Rom. v. 20: νόμος
παρεισῆλθεν, ἵνα πλεονάσῃ τὸ παράπτωμα).[1] But
sin shows its complete antagonism to God and its
enormity in the very fact that it turns even the
commandment which is holy and good to evil (Rom.
vii. 13 : ἵνα γένηται καθ' ὑπερβολὴν ἁμαρτωλὸς
ἡ ἁμαρτία διὰ τῆς ἐντολῆς). So much the more
urgent and imperative does the longing for redemption, salvation, and grace become (Rom. vii. 24).
On the other hand, the law has its object in Christ,
inasmuch as it exercises a strict discipline by its
statutes, and enslaves men during their minority (Gal.
iii. 23, etc. : ὑπὸ νόμον ἐφρουρούμεθα συγκλειόμενοι ;
iv. 3 : δεδουλωμένοι ; comp. ver. 1, etc.). But even
in this respect the law has only a passing, provisional
power, and is throughout of a limited, subordinate
significance. As soon as the time is fulfilled, and

must be taken in an objective sense, and not with Meyer in a moral-
religious sense, as if it denoted non-Christian humanity. But when
Hilgenfeld, *Galaterbrief*, p. 67, finds that in iv. 3 the religion of law
is " identified " with the heathen religion, he goes beyond the range
of the apostolic utterance, which simply includes νόμος and heathen
religions in one and the same category, and is far from asserting their
identity.

[1] So with Luther, 1519 : *ut transgressiones abundarent* ; Ritschl,
Entstehung der altkath. Kirche, p. 74, etc. ; Weiss, p. 264 ; Pfleiderer,
Paulinismus, p. 80. The explanation of τῶν παραβάσεων χάριν, *ad
coërcendas transgressiones*, which many of the Church Fathers and
modern writers give, is absolutely against the use of language.

redeeming grace which was promised from the beginning and decreed from eternity enters, the law loses its force and significance, it is done away (2 Cor. iii. 11 : *καταργούμενον*).[1]

The whole sum of the product of pre-Christian time is a painfully unsatisfactory one: no righteousness before God; all are sinners together: no salvation or life, but rather judgment, condemnation, and death upon all, for there is no distinction, there is no respect of persons with God. At best there is a longing and sighing after deliverance and redemption, arising out of an internal struggle. It was this that the divine teaching intended; it was an education of the human race leading on to Christ.

---

[1] The apostle's reverting to the more and most original elements in the course of God's revelation, reminds us of the grand doctrinal view of the Redeemer Himself. Comp. my essay, "Das alte Testament in den Reden Jesu," *Theol. Studien und Kritiken,* 1854, p. 807, etc., 848, etc.

END OF VOLUME I.

MORRISON AND GIBB, EDINBURGH,
PRINTERS TO HER MAJESTY'S STATIONERY OFFICE